The Human Animal

TESS R. MARTIN

ISBN: 0990629503
ISBN-13: 978-0990629504

DEDICATION

For Stella, my favorite dreamer. And for William, for dreaming with me, at least for a little while.

CONTENTS

ONE

I move through the empty streets like a shadow. For this, I pride my dark hair. The towheaded boys following me don't have the luxury of vanishing as easily into darkness. I like to move up on a target until I can touch him on the shoulder. I never touch them, but I like to sneak in close. The surprise is the goal. And the capture.

I'm doing this now. Tracking. The boys behind me are silent. I put my right hand up and we cross to the other side of the street in a tight, orderly knot. I can hear anxious breathing. Loud footsteps. A gasp.

We're close.

The AA has two divisions, Intelligence and Enforcement. The former moves first—mostly concerning itself with investigatory procedures—and the latter second—the boot heel that crushes any and all resistance. I'm in Enforcement.

We travel in packs, groups of six, maybe seven, that patrol the streets of the Capitol City all hours of the night and day. Our duties are numerous, but Intelligence hands down the most exciting assignments. A pack must deal with these tasks swiftly, violently, and without mercy.

Tonight we have such a matter.

Eight years since the end of Reconstruction and still the conversion from carnivorous to herbivorous habits isn't progressing as smoothly as officials initially hoped. The response to this matter comes from the highest ranks of the Liberationist government: the Party Chairman himself, Chairman Goldstein. The answer isn't diplomacy but, rather, brutality. Thus, the matter falls into the capable hands of the AA.

Of the ten packs selected for the action tonight, mine is one of them. I've dealt with this particular issue for the past few years but it continues to be a problem. Speakeasies. It makes me sick.

These are the underground clubs where meat's still available. If we destroy one, another sprouts up in a different location within a few months. At this moment, more than eleven clubs are suspected of operating in the Capitol City alone. They're mobile, only staying in one location for a few days before shifting to another in order to stay one step ahead of the authorities. It's a dangerous business. But it isn't my job to find them. I only torch them when Intelligence gives me a location.

Tonight, we received five locations, each pack taking one with another pack going along as back-up. My pack already found the club in question and began the process of incinerating it. Now all that remains is to round up any stragglers and bring them back to the speakeasy location for processing and execution.

I fall into step behind the straggler we're pursuing on silent feet. The night air's thick with smoke and alive with gunfire—the sights and sounds of a successful raid. Screaming too. Punishments are left to pack discretion: firing squad, burning, bludgeoning, or a hearty mix of all three.

I suppress a laugh as I follow this man, drawing ever closer without his noticing. All suspects seem very much the same. From time to time, he stops and cocks his head, no doubt trying to evaluate the distance between himself and a rabid pack of AA agents. His every movement advertises his guilt. The quick way he scurries along the empty street. How he jumps when screams give way to gunfire which gives way to more screams. He doesn't look behind him. Perhaps he's frightened of what he might find there. His fear is as thick as the smoke in the air. Around him, the streets are barren. It isn't illegal to be out this time of night—no official mandatory curfew exists, though there is a voluntary one—but a wise citizen finds it best not to roam the city streets after a certain hour. The AA can't melt into shadows during the day, but the night belongs to us and we move through it like phantoms.

The straggler stops again, this time in front of a rather large poster of the Party Chairman. He cocks his head at the distant screaming, which has started again with renewed vigor. He sniffs at the air, keeping eyes on the stern, angular face of Chairman Goldstein and trembling quite visibly.

I slide in right behind him and hold up a closed fist to my comrades—*silent, careful, do not move a muscle.* My stomach tightens with

3

the certainty of this man's guilt. I can't see his face or smell his breath, but I know.

"What are you doing?" I ask loudly. I want to startle him.

The man jumps and spins around, eyes widening as he takes in the six of us, our black clothes and armbands. His gaze lingers on the gun at my hip for a long time.

"I heard screaming," he whispers, tone sickeningly reverent, though he's my senior by twenty years or more. "I was curious." When his eyes finally meet mine, the desperation in them reads plainly enough, even in the dim light. His luck has run out and he knows it.

I give him a dark sneer. "That killed the cat, you know." The boys behind me snicker and I don't stop them.

He nods obediently. "Yes."

I rest my left hand on the butt of my gun, in absolutely no hurry. He's begun to sweat, though the air's cool. A sure sign of guilt, but I like to be certain.

"Where are you coming from, if I may ask?" I say, raising an inquisitive eyebrow. I like to be polite. At first.

"I'm taking a walk. I live right over on Hyatt and Twenty-Second." He points in the general direction.

My smile expands, flashing him a glimpse of straight teeth. Such blatant lies, and always so transparent. Giving too much information or not enough. A narrowing of the eyes or a twitching of the mouth. Shifting from foot to foot or standing stock-still.

Sweating. Swallowing. Stuttering. Smooth talking that lacks the pauses of natural speech. Dead giveaway after dead giveaway.

"You're awfully far from home, aren't you?" I ask, and the boys behind me grunt in agreement. I have no doubt their smiles are as vicious as my own. "And after voluntary curfew?"

He swallows audibly and attempts a smile. "I enjoy long walks." He pauses. "And quiet streets."

"Do you often walk on this particular street?"

He gives a shrug as forced as his smile. "I take various routes."

The boys laugh and even I give a low chuckle this time. "I'm finding it quite difficult to believe you, comrade."

He says and does nothing—besides looking as though he's slowly sinking to the bottom of a very deep pit—as I close the gap between us and lean into his face, so close his hair tickles my forehead when the wind blows. I inhale. Here it is. *Meat.* Easy as that. I picture him ordering a steak and eating it bite by dripping bite. I now have full authority to take him back with the others. My suspicion alone is actually sufficient to provide this authority—so is my whim, to be honest—but I prefer to have actual proof when I take people into custody, as it won't end well for them.

I step away from the man and don't attempt to mask my disgust. "You have meat on your breath, traitor." At these words, two packmates seize him by the arms.

"*Meat,*" I repeat, drawing it out so the damning syllables hang in the air. "Explain it."

"I can't," he says, which is too bad. I often find the excuses given afterwards more amusing than the lies given beforehand.

I punch him hard in the stomach. Grunting, he starts to double over, but my boys keep him upright.

"Explain it," I say, calmer this time.

"I can't."

My disgust crests with my anger. No good excuse exists for what he's done, so it's fortunate he hasn't attempted to offer one. But this creates a kind of paradox, in that the very act of not troubling himself to offer justification for his abhorrent actions enrages me.

I punch the straggler again, this time in the face. The hands on his arms withdraw unceremoniously and he falls to the sidewalk. The smell of meat won't leave my nostrils. I want to administer a vicious beating for his blatant disregard of the law. I have my club and can use it. I prefer my hands, but don't have the time for such things now. I dismiss him with a disgusted flick of my hand.

"Take this traitor back where he belongs." I watch with little interest as my packmates force him to his feet. My blood's up from the hunt but that fades fast and, with it, my attentiveness. This diminishing focus is a somewhat recent development. I still have my passion, but it wanes much faster than it waxes.

My packmates busy themselves with showing no mercy. I allow it, though it's technically my job as pack leader to administer punishments. They beat the man until he spits blood and teeth. I already broke his nose—of that, I'm absolutely certain.

"Boys," I say.

They get their final hits and kicks in before dragging him to his feet. He falls immediately to the pavement. The boys shake their blonde heads, sneering and cackling. We watch him writhe on the ground for a few moments, moaning but not trying to get up. I kick at him half-heartedly and wait until he finishes groaning to speak.

"Get up."

He stands slowly, holding his nose and mouth, blood dripping through his fingers to catch the light. A packmate slides in and puts a gun to the back of the straggler's head.

"Walk," I say, and he complies. I keep pace with his slow shuffling. I like to do this—accompany them as they move towards the inevitable. Occasionally, I ask them questions. I want to know their motivations, the whys and the hows. Nowadays, dissent isn't simply illogical, it's suicidal, so talking to those that take the risk interests me. The foundational principle of the regime is so self-evident—*all animals are equal in importance and right to life, human and nonhuman*—I find I must seek to understand a person who doesn't accept it, innate as it seems to all others.

I don't ask the straggler any questions. The mood of the boys is boiling at an especially volatile level. Now isn't the time for conversation. I'm angry too but, as pack leader, must channel this irritation into endeavors more useful than simply beating this man senseless. I want to see the man bloody for his crimes same as the boys do, but I also want to understand why he'd risk so much just to have the fleeting pleasure of a meal. This understanding will lead to the complete eradication of speakeasies and all other black market pedaling of meat. It will end whatever remains of the dwindling resistance for good. Knowing your enemy makes it much more difficult for him to hide from you.

But tonight I have neither the time nor the inclination for conversation. My head began to throb at the start of the raid and has only gotten worse. I think about the quiet comfort of my flat where I can attend to my headache in peace and want this mess over with quickly. Leaving now is out of the question. Of the two packs assigned to this particular speakeasy, I'm the most senior agent. All will be waiting for me at the site. I have to give the orders.

"We're going to do to you what you've done to those animals!" a packmate cries. I say nothing to discourage the outburst. Passion's important, but I openly frown upon these types of utterances, as their awkward delivery lacks any discernible sense of authority. This one's particularly bad, implying we mean to kill and then consume the straggler. Too much passion often cancels out logic completely.

Everyone laughs like hyenas.

I don't laugh. I sigh and the wind conceals it.

The straggler gives me a number of quick sideways glances as we walk. It's really too bad about the boys. He looks like he wants to talk. It's hard to tell. He could merely be fishing for a sympathetic ear, though this is unlikely. Much like the regime itself, the AA doesn't come across as sympathetic. It seems to me that the straggler has something of import to express. I find most people, once caught, feel an intense need to explain what they've done. The new laws are incredibly strict and, oftentimes, the perpetrator's relieved to have such a burden removed from his shoulders, regardless of the severity of the consequences.

The closer we get to the speakeasy, the more the air stinks of smoke and cooking flesh. This would be the illegal meat. Though I hate the smell, it means victory. Another speakeasy found and burned it to the ground. Besides the black market meat and the building itself, nothing else—no *one* else—can be touched until the senior agent gives the order. In most cases, including tonight, that agent is me.

We step around the corner—a straggler surrounded by a pack of giggling hyenas—and can see the crackling flames. I give a small, dangerous smile as I look upon the group of wailing traitors huddled in the street, held at gunpoint by a number of AA brethren. Intelligence gave us a rough estimate of thirty speakeasy patrons, which is about right.

I point to the cluster of criminals and the packmate brandishing his weapon forces our straggler to join them. I prefer hand signals and subtle nods or shakes of the head to speaking aloud. I stride to the front of the group as the rest of the pack disperses into the crowd of black clad agents, strengthening the AA presence around the traitors. Those who haven't already done so unholster their weapons and begin systematically firing into the air to keep the captive in line.

I stand very still, watching as a member of the other pack strikes a man in the face with the butt of his assault rifle when he stands to protest. Such things are foolish, but someone invariably tries to be the hero at times like these, as though it will make a difference to the outcome. The man goes to the ground holding his mouth and nose. I eye our straggler huddled in close to a young woman, a brunette with trembling hands and enormous eyes. Perhaps they will give each other whatever comfort the situation allows.

I rest my hand on the butt of my gun and wait. Behind me, the flames are growing stronger, the heat making the throbbing in my skull worse. The thick stench of roasting flesh hangs over all of us, stoking our anger as it turns our stomachs. I want to get on with this but have to confer with the other pack leader before giving the final order. He's just opposite me, across the pool of captives, striking a man for some transgression. He sees me watching him and signals that he'll be with me directly. I nod but don't move otherwise. He approaches me quickly, a muscular agent with a shock of orange hair that stands out against his black uniform. He has soot smeared on his cheeks and forehead. His pack was in charge of setting the fire.

"Our half of the job's done, comrade," he says, smiling with vicious glee.

That much is more than obvious. I nod but don't return his smile. "Yes."

"Only thing left is to deal with them." He hooks a thumb at the captives.

"Have they been processed?" Processing involves little more than checking identification cards and running fingerprints. We aren't authorized to conduct interrogations.

He's nodding before I even finish. "Of course."

"The meat?"

He nods, although it's more correct to say he never stopped nodding from before. "We inventoried and burned it before lighting up the speakeasy."

The main objective fulfilled, all that remains is dealing with the captives.

I step away from him to stand front and center.

"Attention," I say, voice just below a shout despite my escalating headache. "Each of you is guilty of committing a crime punishable by death." I wait for the waves of gasps, moans, whimpers, and pleas for mercy moving through the crowd to subside. Criminals always act like these are an unknown consequences only recently put in place by some last minute vote by the Tribunal. One man's actually blubbering uncontrollably into his hands while others captives look on with contempt. A shame to have one's final moments tarnished by this pathetic display. I feel little emotion. The excitement that fueled my actions earlier in the evening has completely abandoned me.

I continue as though no one made a single sound. "We're here to collect your confessions and administer the correct punishment according to the law." I pause as yet another collective wail rises skyward but don't wait for it to abate. I merely raise my voice. "The delivery of your punishment is entirely up to you. If you cooperate, the punishment will be swift, which is quite a bit more than you deserve. But if you refuse to cooperate, quite frankly, you will wish you had."

I pause again, for dramatic emphasis, and no one makes a sound. Even the pathetic young man ceases his incessant sniveling. I stand motionless, watching them watch me. In their stares, I see no hatred, no fury, only fear for the yawning inevitable.

"Who owns this abomination?" I ask in a booming voice. The captives cower like children. Even my packmates flinch. I don't often shout.

A man stands slowly from the middle of the group, very well dressed and well kept, with an open, broad face that appears quite serene despite his obvious fear. The bravery it takes to be the first to admit wrongdoing earns a bit of my respect, though, given the way he's dressed, he couldn't have hidden among the others for long.

"I do," the man says in a tone I judge commendable considering the circumstances. "If you punish anyone, please punish me."

I smile. "Is that your confession of guilt?"

"I suppose so."

I free my gun, take a step, and shoot the man pointblank in the neck. Hot blood sprays back onto my face. I don't so much as flinch. The man's legs fold and he tumbles onto those around him, one of them the straggler. Several people begin screaming as they shift the lifeless, bleeding body around. I watch our straggler shove the body away from himself and the wide-eyed, shrieking woman next to him, then frantically wipe the man's blood onto his pants. He and the woman embrace, she burying her pretty face into his neck and he struggling with something I guess to be nausea by the look of it.

I return my gun to its holster and wait for the shouting to die down. To expedite this, the sneering, circling boys fire their weapons into the air. The screaming ceases as though the boys flipped a switch on a sign reading *scream* rather than *applause*. Many captives continue to cry softly, which is tolerable.

I shrug and let a grin stretch over my face in a gruesome impression of pleasant, good-natured humor. "Do you see?" I ask. "Nothing to it." I rest my left hand on the butt of my gun. "Who's next?"

A man jumps to his feet, this one nowhere near as distinguished as the last. He is, however, gigantic. The speakeasy's bouncer, most likely.

"Won't you have mercy on us?" he cries, sweaty face twisted, desperate. We're so close, I can see the veins popping out of his thick, muscular neck. Under different circumstances, this man could easily break me in half. "What crime warrants this kind of torture?"

"I'll take that as your confession," I say, and shoot him in the face. Fresh blood sprays my cheeks and forehead.

The falling bouncer falls directly onto the woman next to the straggler. She shrieks hysterically and a fair number of others join her in that endeavor.

Heroic as always, the straggler pushes the carcass off the young lady and pulls her into a crushing embrace so he can whisper in her ear. She actually calms and I wonder what he came up with that somehow gave her the semblance of consolation.

"Next," I say.

Silence. Even the whimpering has tapered off, as though I'd decide to take sobbing as a confession of guilt as well.

"No one wishes to confess?" I wait as long as my headache allows, and then shrug. The smoke's too much. The smell. This business is making my body ache. "Very well. As I said before, you will wish you had." I address my AA comrades. "Cook them."

The night detonates with sound—boys howling at the smoky sky, weapons firing, captives shouting for mercy. We always have gasoline on hand. Half the boys retrieve it from the jeeps while the other half guard the crying, shrieking, begging traitors. They weep so passionately at the loss of their own lives but never shed a tear for the animal slaughtered for their amusement.

The pleading escalates to fierce screams as the black clad boys begin soaking the captives with gasoline. One man springs to his feet and runs off shrieking. A woman follows his example, only she bolts in the opposite direction, hobbling on an injured leg. They're both shot, dragged back to the group, and doused in more gasoline. This seems to serve as a deterrent, as no further runners opt for an impromptu fifty-yard dash.

I watch the boys drench the captives, feeling tired all over. It's disconcerting. My passion for these sorts of things once ran so hot I could ride that energy through three or four such raids. But now? The constant headaches are only part of the problem. I'm perpetually plagued with exhaustion a good night's sleep doesn't alleviate.

The boys' eyes are on me now, waiting for the order.

The straggler's clutching onto the pretty woman, whose tears are inconsolable. Will he still be able to hold her when the burning starts? His dark eyes suddenly meet mine. I take in a deep breath, lungs filling with acrid, gasoline filled air.

"Let's cook them like they cooked those nonhuman animals!" I shout, heart scarcely into it.

The boys cheer as they shoot their guns into the sky.

A towheaded packmate slides past me, cheerfully discharging his weapon. I take him lightly by the arm. The noise is building and I want to whisper this. He drifts closer, a strange look on his face. I'm pulling him away from the excitement just when it's getting good. I can tell this annoys him, but he doesn't have the authority to refuse me. He needn't worry. The captives, though dripping wet with gasoline, won't burn until I give the final order.

This boy's in my pack. I wouldn't have stopped him if not. I have authority to give orders to any man on the street tonight in uniform, but I trust my own packmates absolutely. This one never struck me as particularly clever, but his passion for the job compensates for any lack of intelligence. Releasing his arm, I lean in to whisper.

"Take our straggler to the jeep."

He pulls back. "Do you mean—?"

I meet his baffled expression with a severe one, which halts any further discussion. Turning away, he goes to our nearest packmate, leans in, and speaks quickly. The boys then pull the straggler out of the mad crush of traitors with no explanation. The woman sitting beside him watches in horror. Her momentary consolation has ended while his has just begun. For now, at least.

My packmates drag the straggler across the street and toss him into one of four black jeeps parked a safe distance away from the blazing speakeasy. Once he's secured, all wandering eyes return to me. I wait for my packmates to reenter to the circle, then signal the boys to light matches and hold them above their heads. I raise a hand high and let it fall to my side.

The boys release their matches.

Flames devour the captives in an instant. More screaming, so high-pitched and urgent, it stings the ears. One AA agent suddenly catches fire as well, a consequence of his carelessness when pouring the gasoline. He howls and another comrade has the presence of mind to spray him with an extinguisher. I notice with some satisfaction that this man isn't in my pack, though he is on my floor, so I'm annoyed at the same time. I commit his agent number to memory. Tomorrow he may find himself on a different floor entirely or, at the very least, on mandatory physical training.

The mingled sounds of cheering and bloodcurdling screams fill the air, underscored by gunfire. The heat's magnificent, the greedy flames blinding as they consume everything. Very soon, the traitors' shrieks die away, leaving only the chanting of my AA comrades.

Their words rise higher and higher, like smoke from the smoldering speakeasy—*meat is murder!* in an endless, deafening rhythm.

TWO

My veganism started well before the prohibition. After the government fell, the AA enacted a minimum six month vegan requirement for all potential recruits. Anything over six months let a person move up in the organization. I had three years at the time of the Overthrow. So I moved up.

The early stages of the organization didn't involve me. I only came in after, but with no less fervor. An AA agent moves on a single principle: exploiting nonhuman animals is wrong, no exceptions. Training teaches a series of absolutes—meat is murder; dairy is rape; fur is sacrilegious—mirroring the regime, which operates in black and white, with no gray to confuse or subvert matters. When the Overthrow and subsequent Reconstruction came to an end after many tumultuous, blood-soaked years, and meat was officially illegal, I was the highest ranking agent in the AA for my age bracket.

After the Overthrow, only Animal Liberationists existed. The goal in the beginning was for this party to hold all political posts— city, state, federal. We named the takeover successful when a

Liberationist stepped into the White House with absolutely no intention of only serving two terms. This pillar of the Liberationist Party was Chairman Goldstein, who runs the regime to this day.

Reconstruction followed the Overthrow and lasted several grisly, ensanguined years. During this time, the AA truly began to take mature form. The Party thought it prudent to change the agency's name from the inflammatory Animal Anarchists to a more reassuring Animal Alliance after the old government crumbled, but our brutal means remained the same, as did our purpose. The Animal Liberationist Party sanctioned all we did from the date of inception, though not always overtly. At least, not at first.

Long before the Overthrow, the AA ushered in change. At the start, the organization was scarcely more than a loosely bound nonhuman animal rights group with an abundance of passion but little long-term direction. This young band of vegans believed in the abolition of animal exploitation by any means necessary. Eventually, these means extended to increasingly radical methods.

The revolution, as it came to be known, didn't begin as such a violent affair, or at least it didn't seem so. It was a very strange, dreamlike process in that it happened almost too quickly to halt the rapid shift in the political climate. The general public, painstakingly groomed for these changes over the course of several years with careful but constant proliferation of information via internet, television, and radio, could do little more than watch the changes occur, as though it was happening to someone else, someplace else.

One day, the AA was an unknown, underground collection of disgruntled but harmless vegans whose convenient joblessness provided the abundance of time necessary to stage mostly unnoticed protest rallies and upload angry rants to various websites. The next, as if by magic, the AA achieved nationwide recognition and touted thousands of committed, wild-eyed members from all rungs of the socioeconomic ladder. Even then, it seemed a grassroots organization—a collection of tireless, white clad good guys battling it out with a government cloaked in black, all in the name of a higher principle. In actuality, the man behind the seemingly benign, friendly machine known simply as *revolution du jour* orchestrated the finest symphony since the Revolutionary War. This man never invited us to look behind the curtain, however, and we never thought to do so, not until it became too late to do anything but fall into step and take orders.

I recall sitting rapt in the living room of my parents' modest home just outside the Capitol City, watching events unfold. I identified with the vibrant picture the papers and nightly news journals presented me: a ragtag group of do-gooders leading protests, marching outside government buildings with signs and catchy slogans shouted into bullhorns, encouraging boycotts, and rallying for support and donations on various websites. I remained in awe of them, even as their methods grew extreme and the average member became less ragtag and more militant. I agreed with their central goal—zero nonhuman animal exploitation—and so also quietly supported their escapades as they grew in severity. From marching peaceably to splashing wealthy women in fur coats with bleach and red paint. From gathering signatures on petitions to breaking shop windows of businesses that dealt in animal products with Molotov cocktails. From simple, straightforward websites clearly put together by well-meaning novices to hacking into government sites or freezing the accounts of corporations earning money on the backs of exploited nonhuman animals. From unobtrusive requests for support to shouting obscenities and assaulting anyone seen eating meat or dairy, frequenting a business that sold animal products, or wearing fur and leather. Overnight, the AA went from motley to hyper-organized, from quiet entreaties, to cold, unflinching demands. No longer the simpering group of unemployed, seemingly pacifistic vegans begging for financial and moral support, the bare bones of an agency flush with financial resources and willing members emerged onto the world's stage. The method to their sudden madness began to reveal itself as well, playing out in the news for a rapt, bewildered nation.

My tender age at the beginning of the Overthrow kept me from joining the AA the moment I first learned of them. Favorable mention of the escalating revolution playing out in the newspapers, evening television news, internet, and, eventually, the streets earned me a stern lecture and day's grounding in my room. Suffice to say, I couldn't be with the AA in body, but I attended in spirit as they began threatening and blackmailing members of Congress, placing bombs in supermarkets and restaurants, and viciously beating any individual seen exploiting an animal in any way, whether by eating, wearing, or being cruel to said animal. Computer hacking began on a large scale, bringing both commerce and the squeaky, ill-fitting wheels of government to a grinding halt. Money disappeared from the accounts of many influential individuals, leading to the popularization of the AA as the embodiment of the modern day Robin Hood, only the money never reappeared in the hands of the poor.

Very soon, whispered talk began about a possible link between the AA and the new, alarmingly popular Animal Liberationist Party led by a charismatic man named Goldstein. No one could prove this link existed, not that it mattered. The growing number of people enamored with the Liberationist Party didn't believe a man as innocuous and well-groomed as this Goldstein would involve himself in such excessive, needless violence. Though his message appeared to be similar—better treatment for nonhuman animals and humans alike—he didn't advocate violence. Instead, he suggested replacing those in government with politicians who would do the work necessary to get the job done. A tired, disillusioned populace turned to him like flowers in a darkened room turn towards the nourishing rays of the sun.

The newspapers and evening news journals were very diligent when it came to reporting the recent upsurge of aggressive animal rights activity in the years before the Overthrow. I watched these reports nightly, scoured the internet for every bit of information on the subject, and clipped articles to hang on my bedroom walls. The shifting political climate fascinated me. I couldn't read enough, couldn't buy too many magazines or spend too much time on the computer getting drunk on the day's events. I liked the pictures of the butcher shops burning and the screwed up, angry faces of the woman wearing bleach soaked fur or suede, their indignant hands in the air. I even liked the increasingly darker stories—men found hanging upside down on their own kill floors, throats slashed from ear to ear so they could bleed dry; people found skinned alive and draped with a leather or fur coat. My overactive imagination furnished the pictures that these kinds of stories lacked.

Even my parents consumed the news as it came, in a rush and a flood so one could only gulp, not partake piecemeal. The process was extremely hypnotic, even if one didn't agree. A magic show played out for us from morning until night and we all waited, eyes wide, hands clasped and ready to applause, for magician's secrets that never came. I spent the last handful of months before the Overthrow in perpetual disbelief, unable to comprehend how far the movement had traveled in such a short period of time. Looking at the articles taped to my walls, I traced the revolution's progress with my fingers, feeling the power of it, the overwhelming sense of camaraderie, though I had yet to take part in anything at all. I felt I belonged there, in the thick of it, battling a faceless, heartless government and pulling down the bricks of hypocrisy one by one. The good guys didn't dress in white after all, but in black. I began to do the same, much to the chagrin of my parents. I spent long evenings in my room, locked in a holding pattern, unable to actually join the revolution by a rather stern parental mandate. Silently complicit to the dismantling of the current government, I waded through the rushing deluge of information, sharpening my arguments, readying myself for the violence I felt sure would come.

Near the middle of the Overthrow, the media launched no more pointed attacks against the radical group of organized, black clad vegans who moved like phantoms in the night to accomplish their ends. The public already knew these men and women—these modern day Robin Hoods who stole rights and privileges from the rich to give to the most innocent and helpless among us: the nonhuman animal—possessed a frightening willingness to go as far as possible to achieve their goals. During the last vicious months of the Overthrow, the media issued nothing but an alarming, bewildering silence. But news stories proved unnecessary, because the news was out on the streets. One couldn't travel anywhere without seeing and hearing *the news*. Neighborhoods transformed into battlegrounds, schoolyards into barren wastelands. Public offices, left open in the dizzying blur of violent upheaval, passed from hand to hand like a hot potato. That rapid and violent shift in the political climate suddenly took on a life of its own and without the media's constant chatter, no one was present to tell the nation's citizens how to feel about such a shift. In silence, the better part of the nation held its collective breath, waiting, watching, and kept the doors to their homes securely locked.

This silence was faux silence. A trick of the clever man behind the curtain in order to confuse and prepare those who couldn't formulate a thought without first being told what that thought should be. This manufactured silence lasted for months as a bloody, valiant struggle played out in the streets. Then more information flooded the radio, television, printed press, and internet than one mind could bear.

To satiate my curiosity, I went to an AA rally as the Overthrow was nearing its end. I agreed with the organization's basic principles and didn't see the harm in poking my nose around a little, though my parents forbade me to do so. The atmosphere, the like-minded individuals, the vehement arguments—it pulled me in by the pressed collar of my shirt. The quiet months spent safely sequestered in my room, poring over literature and conducting internet research as a battle raged beyond my clean, streak-free window had all been for this moment. My diligence paid off, as did my passion. I took up an argument, easily besting a much older opponent, and proved myself an unwavering supporter of increased rights for nonhuman animals as well as tougher consequences for human offenders. I spoke at length with a number of distinguished members of the organization's local division. At the end of the night, the branch leader approached me. My life within the AA began at that moment. I was nearly fifteen.

I officially joined the AA in the nascent stages of Reconstruction. During this volatile period, ambiguity did not pay. One had to make one's allegiances clear. To this end, a person had very few options. One could actively join up with the Animal Liberationist Party—each citizen of the new regime became a mandatory, card carrying member, though only some took active roles in the Party. This branch of the new government was proactive, being mostly a combination of the old executive and legislative branches, minus the stickiness of checks and balances. If this didn't suit, one could join the Animal Anarchists, now known as the Animal Alliance, which was sharply reactive, being mostly judicial and punitive all in one neat, deadly little package. One could also dissent and many did, but this had consequences.

After the Liberationists overthrew the preceding government, they passed severe laws demanding protection for all nonhuman animals and serious punishments for citizens breaking these laws. The foundational tenant of this new government—*equality for all animals, human and nonhuman*—rang from sea to shining sea. The Bill of Rights disappeared. Congress ceased to exist. Due process floated away on the breeze. Crowds cheered as these things dissolved. A small tribunal directly beneath the Party Chairman now decided the laws and the citizens of the new regime had no choice but to conform to them. At this point, the justice system also ceased to have any real value. Jails crumbled beneath wrecking balls. Incarceration became wholly unnecessary, much like the justice system itself. Justice became a thing that could be administered without the hindrances of judges, juries, or delays of any kind. People cheered this without really understanding what would come.

The AA was given the task of upholding these fresh laws as well as administering swift and exacting justice. A person seen or even suspected of breaking the law was beaten and tortured until he confessed his crimes. After confession came execution in a manner

tides began to turn outside our home and my commitment to the AA underground ignited. I chuckled at the rich and violent tapestry the news reports wove for me each evening. The burning buildings. The scientists led from their sterile white laboratories at gunpoint and executed on the street. The panic when the legislative branch ground to a screeching halt, when the President fell from an assassin's bullet, when a series of fantastic explosions leveled the Supreme Court with all nine justices inside. The terror on the faces of the correspondents as they pointed to some ominous but exhilarating new poster with a black background and bold red letters—*The AA is Watching* or *We Protect Nonhuman Animals, but Who Will Protect You?*

I was a man without a country and then, as if by magic, one appeared. The revolution gave my bored, disenchanted generation a cause for which to fight and a purpose for our directionless lives. No longer required to be spectators in the tiresome world of our parents and teachers, we now possessed the ability to become active participants. All the new government asked of us was unwavering obedience. When the call came for AA enlistment, I could not sign my name on the dotted line fast enough, despite the protests of my parents. My decision to be a vegan perplexed them. My obvious excitement at the relatively quick deterioration of the previous government annoyed them. My underground activity—the clandestine tasks and blood-soaked nights—concerned them. But my decision to officially join the AA truly upset them, as once a person pledges his allegiance to the agency, it can't be taken back again. It brought my mother to tears. She dropped to her knees and begged me not to go. My father pinned me against the wall and forbade it. But their distress couldn't keep me from what I considered my sole purpose in life.

AA training is intensive—seven days a week, eighteen hours a day, for the better part of five months. As new recruits, we sat through daily lectures—lovingly referred to as *indoctrination sessions*—underwent intense psychological evaluations, military exercises, pack mentality training, olfactory exercises, hand-to-hand combat and weapons training. We had to be psychologically sound. We had to be wholeheartedly committed to the credo of our new government—*Equality for all animals, human and nonhuman.* We had to be wholeheartedly committed to the credo of the AA—*honor when it is easier to do the opposite; integrity when those around us lack it entirely; loyalty to those unarmed innocents above all else.* I spent hours repeating these mottos until they played in my mind on an involuntary loop. We had to swear our allegiance to the will of the Party Chairman. We had to swear to die before dishonoring the regime or the AA. We had to cut ties with the families that birthed us in order to accept a new black clad brotherhood. We had to be able to shoot a moving target. We had to be able to shoot a static target at pointblank range, even when said target was begging for mercy. We had to be able to move and think as a pack. We had to be able to sustain as well as administer torture. We had to be able to detect the slightest scent of meat on a person's breath—even with variables such as freshly brushed teeth, breath mints, or chewing gum—therefore the instructors trained a recruit's sense of smell until it became a thing of beauty. No one involved was more than thirty years of age. We wore nondescript gray uniforms marked with our provisional agent numbers and shaved heads. The ones in charge were clad in black. We had to earn AA colors, they told us, not simply hold out our hands for them. Training would break us, they assured each fresh-faced recruit during that first formation. All we learned over the next handful of weeks would remake us. Boys going in. Men coming out.

In initial training, our days never deviated from a basic schedule. The day began at four. Physical training at four fifteen. Showers at five thirty. Breakfast at six as we heard our first lecture of the day. Session one classes and exercises from six thirty to twelve. Lunch in the field. Session two classes and exercises from twelve thirty to four. Combatives at four fifteen. Showers at five. Basic pack mentality training at five-thirty. Dinner at six. Repetition from six thirty to seven—repeating the AA credo in louder and louder voices. Session three classes from seven fifteen to nine. Thirty minutes personal time. Room inspection at nine forty-five. Lights out at ten.

The man who gave the morning lectures was always the same—the one with dark eyes and fair hair, the one who never spoke above a whisper after finishing the morning's oration. Rumors spread quickly about this taciturn young revolutionary. Other instructors verified that the man had been directly involved in the agency's establishment. He had our respect without question, not simply because he held the highest rank at the training compound, but because he'd seen and done the things we recruits merely dreamed about. He gave a memorable speech day I arrived for training.

"We are surrounded on all sides by traitors. We call them family and friends. We know them as respected members of the community. Some even call themselves *religious*." The way he spat the word made his contempt plain, though his blank expression didn't change. "These traitors preach the sanctity of life while eating a hamburger. They go on about benevolence and equality, about kindness and mercy, while shunning the most innocent and deserving among us. There's only one word to describe such behavior, brothers. *Hypocrisy*." He gave us a scathing, ugly glance. "What is meant by the sanctity of life if it is not the sanctity of all life? How can an individual preach about what is sacrosanct when he continues to rely upon and indulge in the mutilated carcasses of fellow sentient beings for sustenance?" He paused and no one said a word. "That community has been leveled, brothers. That duplicity has seen its end. *This* is your community now." He pointed to the band on his right arm—black with two red A's sewn onto it. "The tables have turned. We no longer treat as sacrosanct that which can reason and spout the most horrendous hypocrisies as though poetry. We no longer agree that importance is decided along the arbitrary line of species.

"We're moving forward. Speciesism is the new disease and it wears many masks. This is our duty: to seek out those masks and eradicate them. We have the cure, as well as the means to distribute it. The cure is equality among species, but we have to humble them first, brothers. Humble them before we can inoculate them. All those speciesists, all those elitist hypocrites. We have to make them remember that the line between ourselves and nonhuman animals is lightly dotted at most, not bold.

"This new status quo, this new ethos, *we* enforce it, brothers." He pointed to the double A's on his arm again. "As we were once the harbingers of change, we'll now be the sustaining force of this new order. We'll use their means to do it. Violence. Coercion. Convenient lies dressed up as truth. Appeals to a higher morality that always manage to sanction exactly what we're doing. There's no room for mercy here, for playing fair, for excuses. There's room for conformity and nothing more. And to what end, brothers?" he asked, pausing long enough to give a small, chilly smile. "We will join the human hand with the hoof, with the paw, with every nonhuman animal appendage, and therein enjoy a peace free of pretense, a peace we have ushered in with blood and with bullets. We'll lay down our guns then, brothers."

The cheering started, the dining hall reverberating with sound, as though we had the hooves and paws ourselves. We howled, stamped our feet against metal benches, and beat our hands together. We made wild sounds at first but, eventually, screamed the same things together.

Meat is murder! Dairy is rape! Fur is sacrilegious!

It became a deafening rhythm when the beating of our hands and the stomping of our feet fell into time. I screamed my throat raw and beat my hands into hunks of numbed flesh. It was with this frenzied, unabating fervor that I completed my training.

THREE

The AA is housed in the Complex, a fashionably dismal building in the center of the Capitol City. Today, all Third Shift agents are to report to an eight a.m. meeting, regardless of division. The AA has four shifts and to say one works First Shift or Third doesn't really mean what it appears to mean, as the hours don't correspond with a particular part of the day. It's more a way to divide up ranks and allow for maximum agency presence on the street at all times. If one shift has an off-day or a mandatory meeting, the other three must be working. Agency street presence is a necessary asset in reminding citizens to mind the straight and narrow.

It's my custom to report early on the morning after a raid. I foresee having a fair amount of explaining to do. Normally, traitors found during a speakeasy raid are processed and executed. I've never brought one back to the Complex. The practice isn't forbidden. On the contrary, it's encouraged if further questioning might garner useful information. I don't often question speakeasy offenders at length, but the straggler gave me a strange feeling. The more I thought about it last night, the stranger it became. The man has something to say and I mean to give him the opportunity to say it.

I walk up the steps to the Complex's entrance. The building's immense, shooting up a full one hundred twenty-five stories to caress the gloomy clouds. It's one of four buildings huddled together to form the Capitol City's central governmental district: the Complex for the AA, the Bureau of Propaganda for the offices of PETA, the Plaza for the Animal Liberationist Party and the offices of its officials—this building also houses the Party Tribunal—and the Loop for various mandatory social events and lectures for the general public. It also provides the necessary but unfortunate service of reeducation and reintegration for misguided citizens whose offenses aren't serious enough to warrant execution. This specific section of the Loop is called The Bureau of Thought Reform. Together, all four buildings are known as Headquarters. To keep things uniform and aesthetically balanced, each building stands one hundred twenty-five stories high, making them the tallest in the city.

I hesitate on the Complex steps, sipping my coffee and contemplating the ominous clouds in juxtaposition to the building's dark, mirrored facade. The raid didn't end until three in the morning. I drain my coffee in a few harsh swallows. I have to be sharp when I face my superiors, especially in light of the business with the straggler. I adjust the band on my upper right arm, ensuring the double A's are facing forward as I listen to the morning's recordings.

The loudspeakers peppering the city streets report important news of the day, remind citizens of upcoming meetings, tally off the

requirements for being a loyal Party member, and broadcast other
vital information. This morning the detached, maternal voice of the
regime is merely repeating Party slogans.

*Meat is murder, comrades. We do not eat anything with a face. All life
is sacrosanct. Speciesism is a disease of hubris. Fur is sacrilegious. We are truly a
free people when we no longer depend on the suffering of other sentient beings. Let
us be free from harm. Tomorrow is another day closer to perfection.*

I toss my paper coffee cup into the proper receptacle.
Recycling is no longer optional. The penalties for failing to sort one's
refuse range from substantial fines to thought reeducation at the
Loop. I step into the Complex and the door seals shut behind me. I
step to a second sealed door and press my thumb against a pad
located just below eye level. After a moment, the door opens. I step
into the lobby and walk past the security desk. The man seated there
gives me a slight nod of his head and a tired expression. I nod back.
A bulletproof chamber fully encases his work station.

The lobby is little more than the security desk and a line of
steel doors along the rear wall. To the right of each door, a small
silver keypad. I go to one and punch in my number. The machine
makes a short series of beeping sounds. A light goes from red to
green.

Access granted.

I walk into a short hallway. Each steel door leads to its own
elevator, which proves helpful during certain rush hour periods, as
only one agent can enter the door at a time, though several can share
an elevator. I look up at the video camera positioned on the wall

above my head. The control room's on floor four. These agents monitor the extensive system of video cameras and recorders throughout the Complex. An agent's watching me right now, summoned to do so the moment I entered my code into the keypad. Once cleared by security, it isn't necessary to use one's thumbprint or agent number to exit the building at the end of a shift.

The elevator comes quickly. I press the button for floor one ten. The cafeteria's on floor one nineteen. I consider stopping for another cup of coffee after checking in with my direct supervisor. But my head's questionable. Not aching, but it feels groggy despite the medication I took before going to bed for what remained of the night. Perhaps adding more caffeine isn't prudent.

I get out of the elevator on floor one ten. I don't have an office of my own, but each pack has a space. Floor one ten is made up of these Shift Three packrooms, housing ten elite packs and ten lower. I'm the senior pack leader on the floor. As the senior pack, our room's the largest.

The door to the packroom is locked. Most everyone else slides in around seven-fifty or so, which I consider a bit of a gamble. Small but annoying glitches in the security system can cause serious delays in reaching one's floor. There can also be a bit of a queue when a mandatory meeting's scheduled for first thing in the morning. No one on the floor arrives as early as I do, so I've never experienced such delays, but have heard the full gamut of excuses from agents reporting late to formation. Without a legitimate reason, missing one's call time results in at least two demerits as well as mandatory physical training on floor one nineteen.

I unlock the door and go in. The lights come on above my head. They're set on a motion sensor, which can be aggravating during a late night alone at my desk, poring over reports and maps. But this is the work I enjoy most—long hours spent thumbing through evidence, maps, reports, and case files. True fervor is solitary. It's fostered by sleepless nights, forfeited lunch breaks and off-days, and the willingness to sacrifice anything—youth, leisure time, family—for the cause. Not many of my AA comrades understand this. The younger they are, the harder it is for them to grasp. For many, the agency offers a position of power in a still shifting socio-political era, allowing for a species of unwarranted elitism. Many enjoy the ride as that absolute power corrupts them absolutely. They bask in the sunshine allotted to those at the top of the podium and become lazy. This leads to an unwillingness to work the late hours, to sacrifice. Many complain openly about the taxing work and limited pay. Such carelessness, if not held in check, can also lead to reeducation at the Loop. Or execution. Regardless of how high one climbs the AA ladder, collecting power with every rung ascended, one's true loyalty must be to the regime and its doctrine— *equality of all animals, human and nonhuman.*

I cross the room to stand in front of the packroom's large floor to ceiling window. This view is worth all the stress of being senior pack leader. It's most of the reason I don't mind working late or spending the night away from my government-issued flat.

The doorknob turning pulls me away from my much-coveted view of the city. My direct superior steps into the packroom. He's the supervisor for all the packs on floor one ten as well as the senior supervisor for Third Shift. There are whispers that the higher-ups are considering him for the position of supervisor for both Third and Fourth Shift, known as Blue Shift—First and Second Shift is Red Shift—but that has yet to be confirmed. There are also whispers that I, as senior pack leader on the floor, would take his current position if he receives that promotion. I'm not particularly excited about this. My place is on the street, in the thick of it. I'd be happy doing Enforcement grunt work for the duration of my AA career. Getting my hands dirty, working until exhaustion invades my bones, conducting raids—it's what attracted me to the agency to begin with. The farther one progresses up the ladder, the less these things happen, though I understand upward mobility should be the goal.

"I received an interesting report from Kill room Five this morning," Sup3 says. We call him this because he's the supervisor for the Third Shift branch of Enforcement. No one uses his real name here. I don't even know Sup3's name. I haven't heard my own spoken aloud in years. I'm no longer the person I was before enlisting. The AA issued me a number—687—and that's my identity now.

I've worked with and for this man since completing my training—nearly eleven years. I consider him a mentor, though he's only two or three years older than I am, perhaps thirty-two or thirty-three years old. I've never asked him outright. He wasn't at the raid the night before but when he does come along, it's always as an unofficial member of my pack, which I don't mind. He's my superior, but he never interferes with my authority. I consider him an asset to the pack, as he possesses even more advantages than I do. I have the dark hair necessary for melting into shadows, but he has that combined with deep coffee-colored skin and the agility of a cat, all three making him nearly invisible during a nighttime raid.

"I understand this man was found at the speakeasy site?" he asks, crossing his arms over his broad chest and lifting a dark eyebrow.

"Slightly west of that location." These words are the first I've uttered since leaving the raid much earlier this morning.

"He's a confirmed patron?"

"I smelled the meat on his breath myself."

"Why not eliminate him with the others?"

No confession is necessary to end the life of a person caught at an illegal club. An AA directive states that the public isn't to know of the speakeasy business. As far as the average citizen knows, meat's no longer available in this country. Agents must deal with those possessing knowledge of speakeasies or other facets of procuring meat from the black market swiftly, viciously, and above all, in secret.

"I believe he has information," I say.

Sup3 uncrosses his muscular arms. Floor one nineteen houses a rather impressive gym, which the agency encourages all operatives to use. Sup3 favors the weights. I favor the treadmill.

He rests his right hand on the butt of his weapon. This trick came to all of us in training—an intimidation technique, as it draws the eye directly to the point of immediate danger, thus ensuring compliance—but, after awhile, it simply becomes habit. I find myself trying to rest my left hand on an absent weapon on the rare occasion I'm dressed in street clothes.

"How valuable do you believe this information to be?" he asks.

"Hard to say."

He takes a moment to deliberate before speaking. "The success of the raid gives you some leniency, but this man's a speakeasy patron. Such leniency can't extend past today."

I nod to indicate my understanding. I smelled the meat on his breath. I want the straggler executed for his crimes as much as anyone. I don't take these questions as evidence of a lack of faith, instead recognizing the conversation for what it is: less reprimand and more Sup3 steering me clear of trouble from our shared superiors over this unsanctioned breech in procedure.

He looks at his watch. "Quarter to eight." He leaves without another word. Supervisors have to be at morning roll calls earlier than the rest of us grunts. I look at my desk and sigh. A successful raid means copious amounts of paperwork the following day. It's nothing compared to what Sup3 has to take care of, as he has many packs beneath him as opposed to my one. In addition to the routine paperwork, I'll also need to file extensive reports on the straggler. I suddenly regret detaining him for the simple fact that my paperwork will triple because if it. But the look in his eye was too curious to ignore. And if he has information? Then perhaps all will not be for naught.

My pack will have gone directly to the meeting room, on floor fifty. I leave the packroom without locking the door. A few agents are waiting by the elevators already, checking watches and straightening uniforms. None of these are from my pack. I do know all of them, at least in passing. They give me the obligatory greetings one gives a superior—*morning, comrade*—and I nod in lieu of a reply.

The elevator takes us down to floor fifty and I go directly to the enormous meeting room. It has enough seats to accommodate a full shift at a time. Blue Shift meets weekly on Mondays and Red Shift on Fridays. The times of these meetings, much like everything else in the AA, vary.

I go to my pack's table and sit next to Sup3 at the head. The highest-ranking AA operative—Chairman Anderson—sits at the front of the room with his officials.

If we've done well, these meetings are little more than weekly pep rallies. If we've done poorly, they're stern lectures. I see the need for such meetings, but the morning after a raid finds me growing weary of their repetitiveness and predictability. The Chairman first asks each supervisor to verify that all his agents are present and accounted for. If an agent isn't present, he'd better provide a good reason, such as death or serious injury. After this, the Chairman judges the previous week a success or failure. In the latter case, the Chairman proceeds to publically chastise each agent involved in the failure until he trembles from the viciousness of the lecture. If the matter's a serious one, the Chairman can even have agents removed from the building at gunpoint and taken to the Loop for an extended reeducation vacation. After this, the Chairman adjourns the meeting. Each agent has then to report to his floor for the brief division meeting covering the duties for the day.

The meeting room fills with silent, attentive agents. We're all the same—black clad, guns, clubs, and handcuffs hanging from our belts, black bands on our upper right arms, the bright red A's proclaiming our allegiances clearly.

The room hums with tense anticipation.

At exactly eight o'clock, the meeting begins.

*

The division meeting on floor one ten runs short that morning. I have a feeling Sup3 crafts it that way to give me an opportunity to take care of the man in Kill Room Five before the higher-ups start asking questions. The AA Chairman urged us to redouble our efforts to bring a swift end to the speakeasies and the black market meat coming into the regime from overseas as well as apprehend any citizen breaking the law in either thought or deed. It's always easy to order these matters taken care of quickly, but the real work is grueling and brutal. Our division meeting concerns the immediate methods by which we can achieve these goals, not simply the goals themselves. Those in charge typically tell us what they want done without any information as to how we're supposed to do it. Instead of allowing such challenges to annoy me, I use them to sharpen my cunning. I receive a vigorous pat on the back in both meetings. I was the senior agent on the street last night, which makes me responsible for the outcome, positive or negative. As always, the meetings end with a five minute session of repetition, with agents first murmuring, then shouting the AA credo until the room boils over with shared passion.

The Kill Rooms are on floor seventy. There are thirty such rooms in all, used for intelligence gathering, which is a pretty way of saying *interrogation and torture*. The agency doesn't simply call them *interrogation rooms* because execution always follows the questioning. Once a person lands in a Kill Room, the chance of ever seeing the light of day again reduces to zero.

I know how to extract confessions. I also know basic torture techniques. AA training taught them at length. No one chooses where he goes after the preliminary instruction, which is three months in duration. You can voice an opinion, but this means next to nothing to those in charge. I was chosen as an AA junior pack leader based solely on the merits I exhibited in training, and thus went to AA leadership training for the remaining two months of my initial instruction. The ones who work permanently on the Kill Floor are a special breed. Much desensitizing is involved in the training, as the work is incredibly trying. Though I'm well-known for my rabidity on the streets, I don't think I could stomach the work on floor seventy on a regular basis.

I'm not against beatings and the like to extract a confession, but think most of the torture administered on the Kill Floor moves us further from the goal instead of closer. A bit of finesse is required.

A person will admit to anything if beaten long enough or threatened in the correct manner. If a true admission of guilt is the objective, what good does it do to beat a person until he breaks? I want true confessions. Hence, finesse. An element of violence is necessary, but one must also engage the mind of the accused, not simply the instinct to protect himself from harm. This means talking to the criminal, pinpointing weaknesses, and exploiting those weaknesses to get the desired result. This also means fostering a certain amount of hope in the person—hope that he might make it out of the interrogation alive if only he speaks the truth. Alas, a man who thinks the way I do has no permanent place on the Kill Floor.

I ride the elevator to floor seventy and step into a small lobby. Another security desk sits here, though not protected by bulletproof glass. The agent manning the desk gives me a long look but says nothing. I go to the gleaming steel door along the far wall and punch a code into a shiny keypad. My code for entrance into the building and the one for admittance onto this floor are two different animals. I push past the door and enter the area known as the Kill Floor. We often play on antiquated sayings to get a laugh. This brand of clever doesn't work more than once, as the novelty dissipates almost instantly, but this particular brand of clever tends to stick, mostly because no one wants it to. We call this the Kill Floor as a twisted reversal on the kill floors of all those slaughterhouses that operated throughout the country before the Overthrow.

This floor does something strange to a person, even me, who understands why it looks the way it does. I can't imagine the effect on an individual dragged in for a confession. Every inch of this floor is black—the AA's favorite color. The floors are a gleaming expanse of black tile. The walls, which look like bare cinderblocks, and ceilings are merely painted with several coats of dark paint. This floor has no windows. The air smells vaguely of blood and sweat.

Kill Room Five is the only guarded room out of thirty. We don't keep prisoners overnight in the Complex. Executions come after the completion of the interrogation so, though we have quite a few interrogation rooms, we maintain neither a long-term nor a short-term holding facility.

I stop in front of the man guarding Kill Room Five. He doesn't look too enthusiastic to be the only one on duty. If the floor's empty of all prisoners, these agents spend their time in the lounge upstairs or in the gym. I show the man my identification. Unnecessary—I'm well-known at the Complex—but it's proper procedure.

The agent gives a cautious smile but doesn't remove his hands from behind his back where he has them locked together. "I haven't seen you on the Kill Floor lately, comrade."

I ignore his comment. Idle talk has no place in the AA.

"The prisoner was left untouched?" I ask.

The agent nods. "Of course."

"No interrogation?"

"No."

I nod, satisfied. "Open the door."

He punches his code into the keypad—these change daily on the Kill Floor—and steps aside.

FOUR

The Kill Rooms are all the same—black, soundproof walls, bare light bulb suspended from above to provide the harshest possible light, giant one-way mirror along the wall furthest from the door, table and chairs, and a drain in the middle of the cement floor to simplify clean-up. The drain is the most frightening thing about a Kill Room. As soon as a prisoner sees it, there's no end to the frightened whimpering, the bargaining, the pleas for mercy. The drains are concealed underneath the table for this reason, but prisoners often end up on the floor.

The temperature in the room stays a chilly sixty degrees. Once the torture begins, it tends to get quite hot in here. No cameras on the walls or ceiling. Only the one-way mirror provides access to the goings-on of an interrogation. The AA's always watching, even itself.

The straggler's seated at the wooden table in the middle of the room and staring at himself in the one-way mirror, perhaps assessing his injuries, perhaps ignoring the massive poster of the

Party Chairman glaring down at him from the wall opposite. He watches me as I approach. The air smells faintly of gasoline. He clearly did not sleep at all the night before.

That makes two of us.

I can see he recognizes me. His wide, blackened eyes are fearful, but also relieved, as though he hoped I'd be the one to came. I don't waste time on dark smiles or stroking the butt of my gun. Merely being on the Kill Floor's intimidation enough.

I sit opposite him and he leans back in his chair, putting some distance between us. The chairs are purposely uncomfortable, even the one for the interrogator. This discomfits the traitor while, at the same time, reducing the patience of the agent asking the questions, thus heightening the intensity and brutality of the examination.

I spend a few moments taking inventory of him while he does the same to me. My packmates and I did a number on him. Surely, those close to him would barely recognize his haggard, battered face. I turn away from this thought. Certainly, he has people close to him—a wife currently crying her eyes out with worry; a gaggle of children anxious over the empty place at the breakfast table—but thinking about them does little for me past making matters unnecessarily difficult. These people are traitors and must be treated as such. Another crucial aspect of AA training involved learning to bracket details of a criminal's life beyond the offense at hand. If a person's friends and family didn't provide sufficient enough reason to prevent him from breaking the law in the first place, why should their existence be a concern of mine? I flip an internal switch and my wondering about whether his loved ones would recognize his puffed and pummeled face comes to an abrupt end.

"I am agent 687," I say in a clear voice that makes him jump.

"You're so young," he says, voice quavering. He carefully intertwines his fingers on the table. A smear of blood on the back of his left hand. Three digits on his right lack fingernails. His left index finger is clearly broken. Small crimson dots on the flesh of both arms, either from the proprietor of the speakeasy or the bouncer. The light, thinning hair framing his face stiff with dried blood and sweat. He watches me cautiously, perhaps concerned about angering me. It's unnecessary. No one has ever named me especially emotional, even as a young child, but what emotions I possessed upon arriving at AA training, I learned to control completely, shifting them from liability to asset. They no longer ebb and flow on their own. I use them strategically, if at all. At this moment, they are of no use to me.

"Why wasn't I killed with the others?" he asks.

I raise a dark eyebrow. "You wanted to die with that woman?"

His expression turns pained, as though the torture hadn't really begun until this moment. "I hardly knew her." A single tear slides down his cheek. A broken man with no illusions left at his disposal. Hope doesn't exist on the Kill Floor. The drains beneath the tables carry it away long before the blood.

I don't intend to comfort him, but I am interested in conversing without the use of intimidation. This may not be a realistic goal. I'm either speaking to agents concerning agency business, or out on the street conducting said business. I spend my hours away from the AA alone. Any talent I once possessed for communicating with another person outside of my professional life has evaporated.

"Did you know anyone else?" I ask.

He shakes his head. "It was better that way."

The Overthrow was vicious and unforgiving, but the long years of Reconstruction truly changed the nature of the individual, how he comports himself, and his relationship with all others. It isn't rare to have a family member or friend go missing and never return. It isn't rare to work closely with someone for years only to report to work one morning to find him permanently absent. Often no explanation is given, leaving the imagination to fill in the blanks. On rare occasions, a traitor's family receives a certified letter stating that the traitor gave a detailed confession, but, again, the imagination must furnish the missing information.

Meat consumption isn't the only thing that diminished in the years since the Overthrow. Companionship is also a dwindling commodity. A wise person remains self-contained—an island unto oneself—as one cannot count on another's continued presence, not in this new era. Nor can one count on another's fidelity. Family members turn in family members and friends turn in friends on a daily basis. We joined the human hand with the hoof, with the paw, and with all nonhuman animal appendages just as the forcefully compelling boy promised we would at the beginning of AA training, but now human hands no longer touch. For an agent, this gap between the self and all others yawns even wider. The elastic cloth of our armbands make them quite easy to put on, but what it stands for, what it demands—duty, self-sacrifice, solitude—is almost too heavy a burden to bear.

"Tell me how it works," I say. The straggler seems confused. "The speakeasies."

It's quite difficult to get undercover AA agents enmeshed in the speakeasy culture, even superficially, but I know the basics. To gain access to a club, an established speakeasy patron must first give an unsolicited invitation. Speakeasies are set up and maintained by a network of close friends and trusted business associates. These people are highly selective and suspicious of those who seem too eager to join. Suffice to say, the AA has yet to pass an agent off as a genuine carnivore or gain entry into a speakeasy. Our intelligence runs quite deep, but without an undercover operative, we barely scratch the surface. I personally don't think we ever will. Current AA procedure won't allow it. Even if an agent gained access, he'd immediately give himself away by refusing to eat meat.

The straggler slumps forward onto his elbows. He rubs his long fingers together, save the broken one, and sighs.

I say nothing. Many agents can't allow the time for silence—this new era no longer values patience as a virtue—but I know the importance of it. The man's preparing himself for a trying speech, which means he intends to speak the truth. Interrupting to inject threats and needless force would cause him to recoil into himself, leaving me with nothing. The man's fate is sealed. We both know it. No good reason exists to make the situation any worse by repeatedly flaunting my authority.

The straggler looks at the one-way mirror before putting red-rimmed eyes back on his twisting fingers. "They called me Mr. Dublin." His voice is remarkably steady given the circumstances. For this, he earns back a scrap of the respect that disintegrated when I smelled the sickening stench of flesh on his breath. "We didn't use our real names."

I know all this but nod anyway. Aliases are vital for secrecy, as a person cannot trust his own mother not to turn him in for treason in this age and day. Still, I don't interrupt. I'm more certain than ever that he has something of interest to tell me. Something I need to hear.

"She was Ms. Berlin. The girl." He pauses, perhaps to remember her shining hair or the way she clung to him when the gasoline began to flow. Another tear runs down his cheek. He continues without wiping it away. "The first time, I went with a friend from work. I'd known him since before the Overthrow. We went to school together." He offers a tired grin that hangs rather grotesquely on his wan face. "He's dead now. Captured by the AA. But by then I couldn't stop."

I fight a sudden urge to glance at the mirror. Is anyone listening, I wonder? Perhaps not. This impromptu chat between cat and mouse wouldn't be on the official floor seventy schedule, therefore it wouldn't make sense for a team of agents to assemble behind the glass to listen, record and, above all, watch. The AA doesn't interrogate criminals involved in speakeasy activity. I find this to be a mistake, as we lose potentially crucial information with each traitor killed. But right now, I'm hoping the trend continues and no one takes an interest in this interview. I want to be frank with this man in a way I've never been with anyone else in his position. I think of the woman—Ms. Berlin—and how she trembled in his arms like a small bird. He gave comfort to her. Their hands touched. He bridged the gap between them. I want to know how. But the AA's always watching. I have no idea if I can proceed without consequence.

"I wasn't the person you see in front of you when I was in that place. I became different. Everything became different. Like before."

I take him to mean before Reconstruction. I agree. Things were different then. I can't say whether they're better now, but I can say they get better with each passing year. We're stamping out the remaining resistance, doing away with hypocrisy, and truly giving equality to all sentient beings. It's bloody, unforgiving work. And time consuming. Expecting immediate results is unrealistic.

"There were a lot of rules," he says, keeping his tired eyes from mine, glance traveling regularly to the one-way mirror. Anything, it seems, to avoid the poster behind me. "It was dangerous even being there. We all knew it could mean our deaths, but there was so much lighthearted nonchalance." He looks at me for a second—his eyes intensely blue—before dropping his gaze. "Restaurants were being raided left and right, but no one stopped. We were reckless and loving it."

I have so many questions, but keep them to myself.

"I knew I'd be caught." He smiles a wintery rictus of a smile, face very pale beneath the bruises and blood smears. "It was inevitable. But I couldn't stop." He watches his twitching fingers and speaks after a long while. "I'm an ordinary man. I have a job. A family."

I shift in my seat at this but think of the innocent nonhuman animal murdered to provide this man's fleeting gratification and contempt stomps out my pity.

"But inside the club, I was a man completely of my own making. Mr. Dublin. And things could be as they were before the world changed." He gives me the wintery smile again and his drooping, bloodshot eyes. "As long as I followed the rules, it felt like it could go on forever."

I neither nod nor speak. He's going deep and I want him to go deeper. I want to understand the novelty of connection. I did once, but lack of use coupled with immersion in the AA make it impossible to remember. I want to understand how hands can touch in a time when there's room for compliance to Party doctrine and little else.

He sighs and slumps deeper onto his elbows. He smells of gasoline and smoke and will die smelling of these things. "This was supposed to be it, you know. The end." He manages another smile, this one bitter. "I don't think I could've quit. I didn't want to. But I told her about it. And once she knew—"he shakes his head as tears slide through the grime and dried blood on his face.

I keep my expression serenely blank—another effect of AA training. I called my packmates hyenas, and I with them, but that isn't the complete truth. They trained us to behave as a pack and thrive on instinct, but also trained us to be as cold and flat as intelligent robots. Emotion is useless unless one can control it. An agent must be able to turn it up to fuel actions such as the ones I performed at the raid and also turn it off completely when it serves no useful purpose. I'm interested. He said *she*, and I know he doesn't mean the birdlike Ms. Berlin, but it won't do to allow that interest to become an expression. My face remains blank and pitiless.

"She was horrified when she discovered what I was really doing on nights I claimed to be working late. She begged me to stop. By her tears I thought I could quit." He wipes away his own tears with the backs of his hands. His sweating is worse. He looks at me and the frankness in his eyes alarms me. I'm intrigued to realize he believes he's sensed something sympathetic—or at the very least receptive—in me despite my vicious smiles and unforgiving sidearm. I know as I stare expressionlessly into his teary eyes that he wants me to do something for him.

"I was going to quit. I swore to her that when I returned home last night, I'd never put myself in harm's way again." He breaks down sobbing now. Such displays normally sicken me, but today I watch with quiet interest. He murmurs something softly into his hands, which rose to cover his face. He's an enigma. A lucky enigma, at that. If he'd caught me just weeks ago, I wouldn't have had the heart to humor him. I don't know if I have the heart now. What I do know is that he's setting me up for something and is being rather transparent about it. I just don't know what that something is. Fortunately for him, my only remaining vice is curiosity.

I feel a touch of pity anyway, training or no training. It isn't completely one-sided—I smelled something on him at the raid as well, something so strong it made me go against regular procedure and pull him out of immediate danger. I want him to explain this smell to me and why I found it so compelling.

He doesn't wait to get his tears completely under control to speak. He wipes his face as clean as he can get it and soldiers on. "She wept, and now I weep." He looks at me with glassy eyes and I can feel the tug of his character. "Do you weep?"

I blink involuntarily but am able to put a stop to the expression right there. It's a strange question and I've heard my share of questions, most of them as sharp as a punch to the gut. *What kind of monster are you?* is a popular one. *Don't you have a conscience?* is another favorite. This one, however, is new.

"I don't know what you mean," I say.

"The things you do," he says, and shakes his head. He's not chastising me. I can see this much. He's trying to understand, to connect something about him with something about me. "I do things. I weep."

Comprehension snaps into place. He broke a promise to this girl, so now he weeps. Perhaps he's trying to connect our consciences. An impossible task—from each of our respective stances, the other's actions are morally reprehensible. I suspect we both understand this and are trying to work past it. Pitting our opposite senses of morality against each other will prove a worthless endeavor. I'll always win that kind of contest, as I have the law on my side and the law is everything.

"Do you consider yourself a liar?" I ask.

He flinches, as though I accused him, and nods miserably. He doesn't hide his teary eyes the way he did earlier. He's sharing his despair with me, giving me this strange intimacy little by little. It alarms me, but I'm not willing to end it just yet. I've never had an interrogation go in this direction, as I've never allowed the control to slip from my fingers. My answer to his question? I don't weep and haven't since I was much younger.

A long list of rules comprises the AA and one has to know all of them. The most important of these concerns how we view the agency. The AA itself is a complex, living body and each agent is but a single cell in that body. When an operative descends upon a criminal, the criminal doesn't see a cell approaching, but the entire black clad body of the AA. Every agent is a piece but, at the same time, every agent is the whole. I am but a cell and, yet, I am also the black clad body of the AA. This awards me the instant obedience of the citizenry on the streets, even when I approach a group of them alone. It's never just me they see coming. They see the whole of the

AA and tremble. An agent must never do anything to cause the everyday citizen to glimpse a disconnect between himself and the agency he represents.

"She'll never know," he says, sniffling and wincing at the pain in his nose, which I broke the night before. "I meant to keep my word. She should know I meant to keep it."

"Your promise?" I ask. This much is obvious, but I'm trying in my limited way to make it easier for him. I don't know how to break through his lingering hesitation. I often play the rogue cell to satiate my curiosity, but, true to form, he only sees the looming body of the AA when he looks at me. Can he trust the disembodied smile of that corpus when he's so unsure of the location of its hands?

I smile a bit then as the straggler gives me a troubled look because even I have no idea of those hands' whereabouts or if those eyes are watching as the posters promise.

He relaxes visibly when the tidy smile leaves my face. "I disappeared. She'll remember me as a liar." His tears are starting to abate. I don't visibly relax as he did, but I count the lack precipitation a relief. I'm not as fond of tears as some agents.

"It didn't bother her that you ate meat on a regular basis? That you were, in fact, breaking regime law whenever you saw fit?" I ask, hoping to knock him off balance. Once flailing, perhaps he'll let slip the identity of this woman. Wife? Daughter? Girlfriend?

He flinches at this. "You don't understand. That isn't what it was about."

"The meat, you mean?"

He nods, brightening a little. Perhaps he thinks I'm extending my sympathies, which I never would. "That's never what it was about. Not for anyone. I was a vegetarian before…before all *this*." He motions to the poster of the Party Chairman, disgust sharpening the broken contours of his face. "I stopped eating meat as a teenager because I thought it was wrong. This was years before the Overthrow. I don't like the taste of it. Don't like the idea behind getting it. But I like the idea of this even less." He gestures to the Kill Room. "Things haven't improved. We're protecting nonhuman animals and that's great. But at what cost? The price is so high, we can't even afford to touch one another anymore. Companionship disappeared along with the meat. That was what we had in common, why we went to the speakeasies, what made them so attractive. Being inside a club was like being in the world before the Overthrow. You could reach out and actually connect with another human being without fear or hesitation. That's what I couldn't give it up. The meat was inconsequential."

A sudden surge of anger ignites my unsuspecting insides. I quickly put it in check.

"Inconsequential?" I say with a touch of ice-cold humor in my voice.

"It didn't hold us together."

I cross my arms over my chest. He watches the armband—the double A's—as though entranced. "What did?"

"Companionship. Protest."

I don't know what to make of this. I've never heard such things from a criminal's mouth, but keep lips sealed and expression clear, preferring not to speak unless absolutely sure of what to say.

"She agreed with me on that. The protest. The things that go on in the streets are wrong. Meat *is* murder, but what is just plain murder?" He pauses and I say nothing. This is bait I don't intend to take. "All manner of atrocities against fellow human beings have become acceptable. The government fills our days with mindless busy work to keep us from seeing how cold, impersonal, and sterile things are. This has made us busy, not better. And to survive, we have to turn away from the part of us that makes us human. The part that can feel and connect with others. Closeness is no longer valued. Only obedience is valued. Opening one's mouth in protest has ceased to be an option. But that doesn't quench the urge."

I raise my eyebrow again and he says, "The urge to open one's mouth anyway and to find people who will open their mouths as well."

I let loose a little titter that echoes off the black surfaces. He recoils from me as though I reached to strike him.

"So you opened your mouth and filled it with meat?" I ask.

His eyes, though still glassy, become cold. "The enemy of my enemy is my friend." He leans over further, perhaps to whisper what he means to say next directly into my ear, but his ankles are cuffed to his chair and the chair itself is bolted to the floor.

"In this regime, the meat-eater's the enemy. But it doesn't stop there. The enemy is also the free-thinker, the rogue, the one who believes in civil disobedience and liberty, the one who wants to love his fellow man freely and easily. It just so happens that most of them are meat-eaters because that's the most pointed protest one can find nowadays. A protest behind closed doors is still a protest. So I befriended the meat-eater." He drops his voice and I'm fortunate to hear what he says next at all. "And I ended up in Rome."

I rest my elbows on the table, meet the man's gaze, and mirror his low tone. "You merely did as the Romans do."

He nods.

Something's spinning in his eyes that's magnetic. I can feel it tugging at me. He hasn't asked anything of me, but I can feel it coming on. Within me, a new feeling blossoms—warmth stirring at my core. I have only a faint memory of the last time such a hot flame flickered there. The coldness of which he speaks I know intimately. I'm the face of the regime on the streets. When I wear AA black, no one dares to touch me, to meet my eyes, to stand too closely. I don't mind it, because things are very much the same even when I don't wear AA black. That unbridgeable gap is a side effect of order. Agency work takes the place of companionship, of touching, of the warm sensation stirred by friendship and family. I don't clearly remember those feelings. But I know the absence of them very well.

The man's passion reaches me. I open my mouth to ask something I never thought I'd ask this straggler or anyone else in his position.

"What would you have me do?"

His eyes don't leave mine, even as they widen with surprise. I ready myself for him to start begging for his life. If he does, I'll leave the room, and this strange spell will break.

He thinks a long while before speaking. I don't rush him, though I certainly have urgent business waiting for me at my desk. I pay this man the greatest courtesy I can muster at the moment: keeping my mouth shut. His explanations leveled the playing field. He is my equal. His actions disgust me, but not his motives. These I understand. It's passion, after all, the lifeblood of every AA operative.

"Look in on her," he says, voice so low, the recording equipment we use would have no chance of capturing it. If the equipment's on, which I don't believe it is.

I lean closer. "Look in on whom?" I ask, though I know. But if I hear it from the straggler's mouth, perhaps I'll do it.

He bends over the table as far as his shackled ankles allow, his voice a smooth whisper near my ear.

"*Lara.*"

FIVE

When I start home on foot, the sky's dark, the air clear, the streets empty. It's well past ten. Most citizens find it wise to stay in after eight-thirty or nine. I take comfort in this—the public solitude, the quiet glow of the streetlights, the feminine purr of the intercom.

Voluntary curfew is in effect. Meat is murder, comrades. Mandatory Alliance for Animals forum tomorrow at two, four, and six. See to it that you attend one of these. This week's lecture: How to Spot a Party Traitor. Freedom from cruelty is true freedom. Dairy is rape. The sanctity of life is the sanctity of all life.

I walk quietly, as though on tiptoe, hunching my shoulders into the silence. The Complex is centrally located, at the heart of the city, as well as the heart of the AA's vast corpus, a maze of skyscrapers surrounding it, shooting up to line the cloudless sky.

After our odd chat, I arranged for the straggler's execution. I didn't do it myself. He was on the Kill Floor and it wasn't my place. The supervisor on the floor dispatched an agent whose job consists of executing those unlucky enough to undergo an interrogation at the

Complex. I stood in the room behind the one-way mirror, watching in silence. He didn't beg for his life. He didn't weep. The gun left the agent's holster with calculated slowness and the straggler leaned into it as though receiving a gift. When it was over, I reported to Sup3 that the job was finished.

My mind refuses to stay on the day's business. I usually spend the brief walk to my flat in the Dormitories considering what I did today and what needs doing tomorrow. Sup3 pulled me aside at the end of the night and gave me three fresh speakeasy sites to hunt down. No matter what we do, more sites always crop up. One has to be partially impressed with the meat-eater's tenacity, if nothing else. As the senior pack leader on the floor, I'll oversee each raid. I'd normally already be ironing out the details, but don't have the head for it. My mind wanders. It has business, but not AA business.

Lara.

The straggler spoke the name in a whisper…and then he whispered other things. I now understand his connection to her and why he worries so. I also know where to find her. He wanted to communicate this information to me from the beginning and so caught me in a net using my own curiosity as bait.

And though the warmth I felt stirring within me at the sound of his passionate speech has dissipated—replaced by that familiar, cool emptiness—I have the memory of it, as well as proof that places made cold by single-minded work and self-sacrifice can be made warm again, if only for a moment.

I take quicker steps. Around me, all stays empty and quiet. Inside of me, the same.

*

AA business consumes the next few weeks, leaving no time for idle thought or action. Three suspected speakeasy locations loom over my head. More traitors to apprehend and execute. More paperwork to fill out and reports to compile. Each raid takes a day of solid planning on my part, so I spend my nights at the Complex and keep breaks to a minimum. The raids must take place mere seconds apart so the criminals won't have time to warn patrons at other clubs. Speakeasies comprise an intricate network. The ripples at one club are experienced at all others. They also share clientele, contacts, and vendors dealing in illegal meat. As far as patrons go, Intelligence provided an extremely promising number. Between the three sites, approximately one hundred traitors are suspected to be involved. These are big speakeasies compared to the ones we dismantled the night I apprehended the straggler. Sup3 doesn't have to express to me the importance of getting this job done correctly. We both know it. I also know one more thing: the outcome of these raids will make or break my career.

Necessity demands I remain at one location the entire night while remaining in constant contact with the other two, as the clubs are in three different boroughs. The logistics aren't terribly difficult to work out, but it takes several days to train the agents involved—six packs of seven agents, two for each location. I handpick the operatives myself, mostly ignoring personnel files and deciding their merits based on what I observed while working side-by-side with them in the thick of it. These forty-one agents are the best on their floors, and all from Blue Shift. After ironing out raid logistics, I meet with Sup3 several times a day for hours at a time. We scrutinize the plan from every angle, searching out holes and shortcomings, not stopping until we're satisfied the operation will go off without a hitch.

The raids occur a week after I received the assignment. Just before leaving the Complex parking garage, I gather the agents in a loose circle and make my final instructions clear. No traitors will escape alive. No confirmed speakeasy sites will remain standing. No one will act in a way that might put these raids in jeopardy. The men nod after each bullet point, their expressions appropriately sober. I assign my pack the largest of the three speakeasies. The other pack leaders will stay in contact using the tiny earpieces wedged into all our left ears.

It always begins the same way. An inhaled breath. Internal stillness. A sudden burst of passion that only this kind of mission can bring.

I call for radio silence as the forty-two of us move into position. We creep low into the shadows, becoming the night and the wind, the only noise the consistent whisper of the loudspeakers. They turn off at eleven. I wait for the final announcements—*meat is murder, comrades. Let us thank the Chairman for showing us the way. Voluntary curfew is in effect. Zero nonhuman animal reliance means zero nonhuman animal cruelty. Zero nonhuman animal cruelty means personal liberation. Tomorrow is another day closer to perfection*—then give the order to move in.

An agent breaks down the door and we flood the club, guns drawn, shouting for everyone to get down. No one escapes the site this time. No straggler to hunt only to have him turn the tables on me with his drooping eyes and passionate speech. Only three people attempt to leave when we burst in. Two of them stop the moment they're ordered to do so. The third continues running and is shot in the back.

In less than twenty minutes, we have the traitors grouped outside in a weeping, begging knot, the illegal meat documented, and the speakeasy in flames. Once my site's secure, I radio the packs at the other two locations for a full report. My preference would've been to set up the raids on three consecutive nights so I could oversee them myself, but this would've compromised our greatest asset: surprise. I needn't have worried. Everything went according to plan. All three sites are burning, all traitors detained. In total, we've caught and processed one hundred twenty-seven criminals who won't get the opportunity to offend again. I tell the other two pack leaders to dispose of their detainees however they see fit. Tonight, setting our own captives on fire just doesn't interest me. There's already enough burning with the speakeasy in flames. Behind my itchy, burning eyes, a headache throbs in time with my elevated heartbeat. More smoke would only make it worse. I position the men on one side of the trembling, shrieking, begging group of defectors and instruct them to open fire. No loose ends. As simple as that.

I leave my packs to clean up the mess and drive to the other locations. At both, the speakeasies are little more than smoking piles of blackened debris. The agents at the first location chose to cook the traitors while the ones at the second also employed a firing squad.

I release the men at three-thirty in the morning. Soaring high on adrenaline, most are ready for the next assignment, but I order them home. We have an early report time in the morning. Instead of following these orders myself, I spend the remainder of the night at the Complex, curled up on one of the cots we keep in the packroom closet. Staying here gives me a jump on tomorrow's paperwork. I want it completed by early afternoon, which means a lot of work for me. The agency gives us seventy-two hours to submit our reports, but I prefer to finish it sooner—usually within twelve hours.

I think of the straggler before collapsing onto the cot in front of the window wall and going to sleep. His insistence, the warmth I felt, and that single whispered word.

Lara.

I hoped plunging myself into work would erase the memory of the peculiar connection I felt with him. And it had. But now the work's over, and that strange interaction in Kill Room Five has come back to me. The events play out in my head, not so much the words he used to explain his actions, but the way those words made the cold, steady place in my middle bloom with tingling warmth, like a thing brought back to life. Still keyed up from the raid, with sore muscles and a sour stomach, my mind is nowhere close to the calm fuzziness that normally soothes it right before sleep. The thoughts tick in my skull, buzzing instead of resting quietly. I reach for sleep, knowing I need it, that the next day will be difficult if it doesn't come to me, but remain awake and staring at the dreaming city beyond the window.

I don't know what to do about this, but it's clear I'll have to do something. The straggler keeps coming in at odd moments—during our division's morning meetings, during my short, obligatory showers, right before bed when I usually think of AA business or repeat cadence—*honor when it is easier to do the opposite; integrity when those around us lack in entirely; loyalty to those unarmed innocents above all else*—until sleep comes, bringing with it gentle, unimportant dreams I don't remember in the morning. This sudden, sporadic loss of control dismays me. I'm a machine—a cog in the automaton that is the AA—and have been so for years. In my work, I'm cold, efficient, unhesitating. But these errant thoughts are forcing me to consider issues beyond my work, which has consumed my time for more than a decade.

I close my eyes, shutting out the clouds and stars. In my head, the straggler lingers, his whispered words echoing like a lullaby until, finally, sleep arrives.

SIX

I leave my apartment in street clothes though I feel more comfortable in uniform. The building in which I live is owned by the AA. Known as the Dormitories, this group of barracks houses all junior and mid-level agents in the Capitol City. There are five of them: Liberationist Hall, Capitol Hall, Goldstein Hall, Anderson Hall, and Triumph Hall. Three of the five are double occupancy barracks, meaning agents share rooms and each floor has a communal bathroom and kitchen. The two remaining halls are apartment style and house more senior agents. I live in such a room in Lib. Hall. My flat includes a combined living and dining room, a small kitchen, and a single bedroom with en suite bathroom. For this, I pay nothing.

Once an agent surpasses ten years of service, he can choose to transfer to the Executive Dormitories—though these are difficult to get into if one has less than fifteen years of service and a personnel record that's anything less than exemplary—or move offsite to an approved neighborhood. Not many agents choose the latter option. The convenience of living in the Dormitories far outweighs whatever benefits moving off AA property might offer. All one's living expenses are covered in government housing. The agency does provide a small stipend to eligible agents moving elsewhere in the city, but it doesn't pay for all expenses. Our salaries aren't very competitive considering the high cost of rent and utilities. While AA pay is low in comparison to the salaries of others, we receive numerous benefits not offered to civilians: free medical care, a small stipend for food—or unlimited free access to the AA cafeterias here at the Dormitories in Cap Hall or at the Complex on floor one nineteen; we also have free access to the cafeteria in the Plaza if we happen to be there on official agency business—a yearly clothing allowance for our uniforms, and fare for the city's extensive mass transit system. I have no interest in living offsite. I enjoy the camaraderie of living in close proximity with my fellow agents. Though I spend my leisure time alone, deep in thought, or engaging in prolonged sessions of repetition, I welcome the noise created by others while spurning their actual presence.

I'm not going into work today. Under normal circumstances, AA agents receive no more than four off-days a month. But these are not normal conditions. Incensed by the number of speakeasies still in operation throughout the country, Chairman Goldstein, head of the Animal Liberationist Party and Commander-in-Chief of the Animal Alliance, reduced the number of off-days by half over a year ago. I expect to see them decreased even further if we don't gain the upper hand in the situation sometime soon.

This counts as one of my two off-days for the month. When allotted four, I never took more than one—two if I had some mandatory personal business to attend to, such as my yearly physical or psychological examination. I'd avoid taking off-days altogether, but Sup3 decreed that all agents on floor one ten take at least one personal day per month. I spend such days wandering the city, casing suspected speakeasy sites, or doing other agency work that can be completed away from the office and without the AA uniform. Sometimes, I visit the Plaza or the Bureau of Propaganda. Less often, the Loop. Though necessary, reeducation is a frightening, secretive procedure. Visitors can only learn scant generalities about the process, which, frankly, seem more terrifying in their indistinctness than they could ever be if stated outright. It's important to understand as many aspects of our post-Reconstruction government as time and interest allows and, though the means of keeping citizens in line with the country's goal of zero nonhuman animal reliance often unnerve me, I appreciate their necessity.

During the day, I can't play the shadow, but without AA black, I'm even more dangerous. The anonymity gives me the freedom to lurk about wherever I wish without attracting attention. It takes a special kind of agent to do the work I do, but I could also work for Intelligence if I had the inclination. And while these plainclothes operations appeal to my love of sneaking and secrecy, it's enough for me to moonlight as an Intelligence agent on my off-days. I always make sure to set something up for myself the evening before an off-day so the mandatory time away from the Complex is useful, both for myself and the government that employs me.

I leave my building without giving the doorman the time of day. The man's AA, but effectively useless, hence his position as security guard for the Dormitories. The lobby is small, with a desk for the guard pushed against one wall and two cameras positioned at the front and rear of the room. The keypad to gain entry to the residential areas is beside the steel doors along the back wall. This door leads to the elevator, stairs, laundry room, and housekeeping office. Full cleaning services are available for no charge, but I don't partake in this, having no interest in strange people nosing about my room. The service people working the buildings and grounds aren't AA, but they see me leave and come in from work and know to save their jokes or attempts at small talk for some other, more receptive agent. When they look at me, they see the corpus of the AA and steer clear. Today, I don't even intend to be a cell.

I think of the straggler as stroll down the sidewalk. I've yet to decide a lot of things. Four weeks have passed since our conversation. Sup3 said very little when I told him I'd gleaned nothing of interest from the prisoner. Strictly speaking, this isn't a lie. The straggler told me nothing worthwhile in terms of AA business. My division's concerned with speakeasies and the straggler didn't provide anything pertinent. I did tell Sup3 about the underlying protest involved in illegal meat consumption.

"He insinuated it was about more than wanting to eat meat," I said.

Sup3 regarded me with a breed of flat interest that's uniquely his. "He considered it a protest?"

"He called it civil disobedience."

"Do you think other traitors think this way?"

"It's hard to say. We won't know if we don't start talking to them, but I don't believe he represented the typical defector."

"Will this make a difference in the way you handle future offenders?"

"No," I said, meeting his eyes so he could see I meant it. "But this kind of insight into the motivations of the criminal needs further exploration."

"How so?"

"We have to begin questioning them."

"That's a job for Intelligence," Sup3 said.

I shook my head against this bit of red tape, refusing to be held back by it. "They aren't on the streets with us."

"I'm just telling you what those above me will say when I bring them this suggestion. The gathering of intelligence isn't the concern of Enforcement."

"We can question them preliminarily on the street and bring only those with promise to the Kill Floor for examination by Intelligence agents."

"That would require much more training for Enforcement agents."

"I'll undergo all the necessary training myself and then provide it to my division. I'd undertake this training during my off-hours, of course."

"Of course," Sup3 said, smiling.

Midmorning, but the street's only mildly busy. In this new age, everyone works. Unemployment's as unacceptable as the consumption of meat. Those who refuse to work are sent to the Loop for reeducation and reintegration. We're a new people now— hardworking and of sturdy morals. The regime can spare no place for a lazy, irresolute individual who won't do his part to bring Party goals to fruition.

The loudspeakers buzz at full volume.

We do not have the right to use nonhuman animals to satisfy the caprice of our palates. We will not discriminate along the arbitrary line of species. Speciesism is a disease. We have found the cure: treat all living things with respect.

I walk by without paying much attention. After years of exposure, I'm used to them. They play on the streets and in the hallways of government and private buildings. When it's quiet, I hear their looping messages in my head. I wake with them on the tip of my tongue. My first words in the morning are likely the ones I heard the night before on my walk home. I hum them to myself as I prepare for work.

"Meat is murder, comrades."

Brush and spit.

"We will do our part to annihilate Speciesism in all its forms."

Toss warm water onto face.

"It is never a question of availability and ease, but a question of right."

Apply shaving cream.

"In equality is liberation."

Comb hair into place.

People wander this way and that beneath the soothingly calm chastisement of the loudspeakers. Some purchase bagels from street vendors. Others munch on fruit from the corner market. All take part in the midmorning commute, refusing to make eye contact while keeping attention securely pinned to their own affairs.

I watch all this in my precise way, taking in particulars that most miss and scribbling mental notes. I catch bits of conversation as I pass, listening for the red flag of suspicious speech, always prepared to take someone into custody if given a reason.

For most of the day, I'm no more than an automaton programmed to conduct AA business, but I find great pleasure in my first walk of the day. It holds so much mystery, so much promise, those virgin hours ripe with possibility.

I take the stairs to the metro. We have a great transit system here, which eradicates the need for a personal vehicle. Not many can afford such a luxury, as one must apply for a special license and these are difficult to get. The Clean Air Act severely limited the amount of cars allowed in one city. Most permits are given to top government officials or taxicab companies. Perfectly satisfied with the transit system, I use it whenever disinclined to travel by foot. The train's quick and avoids the inconvenience of parking a personal vehicle and the severe fees involved therein. My lack of desire for a vehicle also reflects my disinterest in the outward signs of success. I merely want to move up the AA ladder. The hearty congratulations from my superiors mean more to me than a plush downtown apartment or a vehicle ever could.

It's second rush hour, but midweek, so I have little trouble reaching the turnstile. I show my government pass to the subway attendant and step onto the platform. The loudspeakers play beneath the city, just as they do above. The voice is the same, but the echo in here gives it an otherworldly quality that's somewhat disturbing.

We will not sacrifice moral uprightness for our appetites. We do not wear the skins of others as though they are our own, comrades. Let us join the human hand with the paw and hoof. Let us taste true freedom instead of the flesh of another. Meat is murder. Mandatory Alliance for Animals forum tomorrow at three, five, and seven o'clock. See that you attend one of these. This week's lecture: The Hierarchy of Being is a Myth.

I lean causally against the tiled wall, watching as the eastbound train pulls into the opposite platform. After it pulls away, I'm left staring at a black poster that encompasses the entire wall opposite me, its red letters making a grim pronouncement.

The AA is Always Watching.

We are indeed.

I step to the yellow line when the westbound train comes into the station. People push in closely on either side and I say nothing. I never take the subway to the Complex—it's only a fifteen minute walk—but I sometimes do during the day. When in uniform, others give me a wide berth as they play at being on their best behavior. I could put my arms out spread eagle and not touch another person, even during the mad rush of the early morning or late afternoon commute.

Right now, I welcome the anonymity my plainclothes allow me. I don't mind the easy glances of the other passengers or the way their shoulders or hands accidently brush mine. This is touch, though illusory, as they don't know the first thing about me. I'm accustomed to the power the black armband lends my words and actions, but grow weary of the cautious, frightened glances or the way people trip over themselves to demonstrate how loyal they are to the regime. A citizen understands that he can be brought in, interrogated, or executed on very little probable cause. So, in front of an agent, he's always acting, always pretending to be law-abiding to a much higher degree than he actually is. Part of the reason an AA operative can't touch anyone is that no one exists to be touched. While in uniform, my world is peopled with actors on a stage, citizens merely mimicking behavior, all the while hoping it's the behavior I expect. So, I make it a point never to leave my flat on an off-day wearing AA black. This doesn't change the fact that I've lost the ability to touch, but it does make it easier to forget.

I squeeze into the packed metro car, just a city dweller in jeans and a nondescript black jacket, on his way to work or a late breakfast. The ride across town takes awhile. I don't fight the motion of the train as it starts and stops. I study my train-mates. This is my job: observation, inventory, quickly processing that information. I think of the straggler, but fleetingly. He disappears by the time the train reaches my stop.

I melt into the current of bodies surging to exit. This current leads me from the train to the platform, down the platform to the stairs, from the stairs to the gates, through the gates and onto more stairs, up those stairs and into sunlight.

This part of the city is more residential than the downtown area in which I live. It's more for working families. I don't spend much time here—AA business keeps me busy elsewhere—but I've diligently studied intricate maps of each borough and can find my way around anywhere.

The metro station's one block away from my destination. I go slowly, telling myself this is merely a fact-finding mission, that I'm only trying to confirm what the straggler told me. But, in reality, I don't entirely know what this is. I trust my instincts as much as, if not more than, I trust my capacity for logical thought. This little field trip will satiate my curiosity—the only vice to survive the rigor of life in the AA—so I let my instincts bear me forward.

The loudspeakers whisper in this corner of the city as well.

Kindness to all animals, human and nonhuman, is a mandatory virtue. We must do our best to fight Speciesism in all its forms. On the other side of this prejudice lies liberation. Tomorrow is another day closer to perfection. Meat is murder, comrades. Let us thank the Chairman for showing us the way. No one has the right to consume the flesh of another.

I take in deep lungfuls of air as I walk. The city center always reeks of bodies and sweat, sewer water and exhaust fumes—though it's minimal with the permit system and increased environmental laws and restrictions. In these primarily residential areas, the fresher air feels crisp against the face, even in summer.

I reach my destination much too soon and don't have the head to circle the block to burn the additional time. There's a deli directly across the street from the building I want. I go in, order a bagel with vegan cream cheese and a black coffee, and sit near the window. On the wall opposite, a rather large poster of the Party Chairman scowls at the few customers in the cramped dining room.

I eat the bagel in silence, eyes trained on the building across the street and the large sign hanging right beside its immense metal door. *Support Your Local Branch of PETA!* the poster demands in bold, black letters made more severe by the white background and an equally intimidating artist's rendering of a glowering, high-ranking AA official pointing directly at the viewer. The official looks like a young Chairman Goldstein, though he was never AA.

Of the few people on the street, most are elderly. None are school-aged, as it isn't Sunday. Children attend eleven hours of school—not including two thirty minute meal breaks in the very early and late afternoon—six days a week, eleven and three quarter months per year. Students receive the countrywide week of Celebration free of lessons and that's all. This rigorous schedule teaches Party loyalty and instills the healthy work ethic necessary for success. I don't plan to have children—it doesn't fit with the desire to devote one's life to the AA—but even the childless can appreciate the results of the regime's improved educational system. The children leaving school at sixteen are ready and willing to work. Many enlist in the AA. Those who don't have college to attend—perhaps followed by a lucrative career in the Liberationist Party—or seek immediate employment elsewhere.

The buildings here aren't as tall as the ones near the center, so the sunshine touches the sidewalk much earlier than it does in my corner of the city. It will be a mild day. Summer's tumbling into fall, bringing with it the cooler temperatures I prefer.

The people passing by don't look upset in the least, even with the PETA poster looming across the street and stern posters of the Party Chairman on every corner. I grant that the new laws are strict, but the ends justify the means. I must believe this, or what is this all for? The loss of touch, the breakdown of companionship, the forfeiture of trust? It all serves an end. People have to be forced into things, especially when those things are good. A government isn't meant to be the citizen's friend but, rather, its unconditional ally, willing to steel the citizen's resolve when he's too weak to commit to what's morally right.

I finish my coffee, still watching the building across the street while the murmuring of the loudspeaker fills up the empty spaces in the background. At exactly ten forty-five, the large metal doors crack open slightly and a young woman steps onto the near empty sidewalk. A man in a suit walks by her and she gives him a shy look as she shrinks against the door, clasping thin arms across her chest.

She looks left and right, seeming terribly frightened to be alone on the street, even in broad daylight. This is the girl. *His* girl. Lara. She's alone now, perhaps for the first time in her life.

She sticks to the door for several minutes before it opens against her. She scurries out of the way of an elderly woman pulling a small reusable grocery bag on wheels. As soon as she passes, Lara collapses against the wall, clutching purse to chest and peering down the sidewalk, dark hair spilling over her shoulders.

Watching this pitiful scene, it's no wonder the straggler feared for her even in the face of his own execution. I'm curious as to what she thinks happened to him. These days, people often disappear without explanation. Perhaps it would help her to know he meant to keep his promise? That his last thoughts concerned her welfare?

I clear my recyclables and leave the deli. I pause on the sidewalk, eyes on Lara. A man sidesteps past me, cursing loudly about assholes in this city never watching where they're going. I don't respond, though a small smile creeps onto my face at the thought of how differently our exchange would've gone had I been wearing AA black. I'd still be an asshole in the man's way, but I doubt he'd dare to voice the thought. I doubt he'd do much more than step around me with a polite and accommodating *excuse me, comrade.*

So consumed by fear, the girl doesn't notice me blatantly watching her from across the street. According to the straggler, she has a job at a boutique a block from their apartment and must report at eleven sharp. I glance at my watch. It's nearly eleven now. I have a sudden urge to take her by the elbow and lead her safely down the street. But she isn't any of my concern. I'm only here to quench my itching curiosity. Nothing more. I smile a little, recalling what I said to the straggler on the night of his arrest.

Curiosity killed the cat.

Perhaps. But I understand satisfaction brought him back. If I can satisfy my curiosity without jeopardizing AA business, I don't see the harm.

But according to what I told Sup3 about the interrogation—which I'm confident wasn't recorded, as I told my superior a number of boldface lies and haven't received demerits, nor am I currently in the Loop—I shouldn't even know of this girl, where she works, or where she lives. Making contact with her is a mistake. Discussing the straggler with her is a mistake. Simply being here might even be a mistake, though I've yet to cross a line.

And if I decide to approach her? What could I possibly say that wouldn't terrify her? How could I bring up the straggler's promise without revealing the details of the man's apprehension, interrogation, and subsequent execution?

She begins striding down the sidewalk, as though drawing from some hidden cache of courage, dark hair rippling over her back as she goes. I have to walk briskly to keep up. She makes it to her place of employment and goes inside. She works in a pet shop, which are very popular these days. The Party encourages people to spend extravagantly when it comes to their pets, equating money spent with how much a nonhuman animal is loved. Having a pet is quite costly, even if one doesn't spend a fortune at boutiques. One must receive an annual license to cohabitate with a nonhuman animal from the Department of Nonhuman Animal Services located in the Plaza.

I cross to the shop, pausing at the door but not opening it. This will constitute crossing the line, fact-finding or no. But it's too late to turn back now. I didn't exactly make a promise to the straggler per se, but I agreed to something, albeit tacitly, and feel strangely compelled, as though he passed the girl from his hands to mine. I can at least verify that she's not too shattered by his absence.

I walk into the store, which is empty, and the tail end of a lecture going on near the register. A severe woman with thick arms crossed over an ample bosom—the proprietress of the shop, I imagine—is talking loudly to Lara, who's huddled against the counter, nodding and chewing her lip. I feign interest in a combination food and water dish. The woman never lowers her voice, though the bell above the door chimed when I entered.

"I'm not entirely sure when it became commonplace to come to work late," the woman says, creaky voice matching her sneer. "Today it's only five minutes, but you've been showing up late for weeks. It's unacceptable."

"I'm sorry," Lara says, her entire demeanor captivating in its helplessness. "Since my father disappeared, I haven't—"

The older woman raises her gruff voice to cover over Lara's breathy one. "That was weeks ago. And I don't see how his whereabouts are any concern of mine. I have a business to run." Her sneer turns contemptuous. The law-abiding citizen—or the citizen masquerading as law-abiding; often, there's no way to decipher between the two at face value—exhibits disdain bordering on hatred for those suspected of breaking the law. The government cultivates and rewards this attitude, as it encourages those who obey the law to turn in those who don't even when receiving no reward. Most don't hesitate to report suspicious behavior, even when the execution of the offending party is guaranteed. The need to please is strong in the citizen, as is the need to make sure all around him know that he follows Party law to the letter.

The proprietress's lack of compassion is hardly unjustified. All disappearances have explanations. No one vanishes into the night for no reason. A sudden absence means wrongdoing and wrongdoing means a certain kind of fate—arrest and execution.

The crone persists in her lecture, still undaunted by the presence of a customer in her midst. "You'll either arrive on time or find another job."

"Yes, comrade," Lara says in a wavering voice.

I choose an inexpensive item—a collar for a cat or small dog—and approach the register. Neither woman turns to help me. I clear my throat loudly, drawing their attention. Lara meets my eyes, the color high in her cheeks, then looks at the floor. Her eyes—a deep blue, almost luminescent in their vibrancy—are nothing like the straggler's. They give a striking impression with her pale skin, soft features, and dark hair.

The proprietress, clearly annoyed by the intrusion, glares at me.

I hold up the collar and speak with authority. "I'd like to purchase this if you're quite finished berating this young woman."

Lara gasps and sneaks another look at me before glancing sideways at her employer, perfectly imitating a dog that's used to being kicked by its foul-tempered master.

The woman's broad face darkens, her cheeks and forehead filling with hot blood as she makes an indignant sort of noise. She opens her mouth to argue, but the flatness of my stare stays her tongue. Even without the uniform, I convey authority to which people must respond.

"Yes, of course," she says, but nastily.

If this is the tone she takes with all her customers, it explains the lack of business in here while other pet boutiques around the city are booming with sales. I consider reminding her that the party credo—*Equality for all animals, human and nonhuman*—also extends to one's employees, regardless of how late they report to work. But stoking this woman's anger won't get me what I desire—time alone to speak to Lara. Also, she's likely to pay any anger I stir up forward to Lara after I leave. I know the type and this woman's as transparent as they come. Despite her threats, she'll never fire the girl because it's infinitely more enjoyable to punish her without reproach.

"Ring him up," the proprietress growls at Lara, who nods obediently. She pushes past, grumbling as she storms through a door at the rear of the store.

Lara meets my gaze briefly and I flash a small smile, careful to keep it from turning vicious. It feels strange on my face. I don't often have need for friendly smiles.

"Excellent customer service, that one," I say with forced good cheer.

She looks down at the collar I set on the counter, her cheeks a deep red, and nods. Her dark hair is shiny and straight, though the ends curl around the buttons of her jacket, which she didn't get the chance to remove before the woman started in on her.

"I've been coming in late recently," she says quietly. She then rings up the collar and whispers the price, as though it's a secret.

I pay with my identification card. Cash no longer exists. All business is done with the credits on one's ID, which must be carried at all times.

"It sounds like you have good cause to," I say.

She looks at me, glassy blue eyes wide, appearing shocked that I'd speak so. I can sense her delicacy as easily as I can see the trembling of her chin.

Clarity seizes me, sharp as a slap to the face. I can't tell her about the straggler. Her open, hopeful expression, the clear way she's looking at me—it would all crumble at the horror at my actions. I didn't kill her father, but I captured him and watched as another agent ended his life. And if I color my description of his last twelve hours alive by telling her I punched him in a way I knew would break his nose? That I ordered him doused in gasoline, meaning to burn him to death? Or that I was the one who dragged him to a Kill Room?

Looking at her, I feel my place in the AA acutely. To her, I wouldn't be a cell—rogue or not—but the hands that throttled the life from her father. She wouldn't see that I did it to keep order, that the straggler was breaking one of our most fundamental laws. She'd only see those hands stealing his life away.

"Thank you for your purchase," she says, flashing me those deep blue eyes again. She looks at the rear of the store and back to me again. "And for sticking up for me." She gives a sheepish smile, really no more than the slight upturn of the lips, but it ignites the warmth just above my stomach, the same place I felt it when the straggler whispered his passionate, compelling words—a single point of tingling, alien heat blossoming in a sea of icy, dead things.

Taking the collar, I return the smile. "My pleasure. Have a nice afternoon."

"Please do the same," she says.

I leave the store with a deeper understanding of the straggler's motives. After this brief interaction, even I'm concerned with her welfare.

That strange warmth's gone by the time I reach the metro station, leaving me as cold as always, though now I miss whatever was kindled twice in the span of a few weeks. My mind turns to the straggler, to the question I asked him.

What would you have me do?

It seems so obvious now. I have to let her know he kept his promise. I have to see about that warmth, about rekindling it on my own terms if such a thing is even possible.

SEVEN

On Friday, my packmates and I, as well as a few others from floor one ten, walk over to the Loop. We missed the AFA lectures on Monday and Wednesday and so have to make this one, which starts in twenty minutes. The walk to the Loop is short if one cuts through the courtyard between the four buildings of Headquarters, but one must be seated no less than ten minutes before the forum starts. We have an abundance of work to do, but Sup3 had no choice but to release us for the hour long meeting. I routinely put the forums off until the last moment. This meeting begins at seven and is the last one offered for the week.

I see the merit in such meetings for the general public. Citizens become complacent and lazy without forums and other mandatory events during the week to vigorously remind them of Party principles and the horrible atrocities visited upon nonhuman animals throughout the preceding regime. But I don't see why AA agents need to attend. Our loyalties are apparent each time we slide on the black armband. We prove ourselves faithful Party members on a daily basis. For us, the forums only interrupt important agency business.

We enter the lobby of the giant building that is the Loop and move down a cavernous hallway. The convention center's through here—it holds all mandatory public events. The public has free access to the first ten floors of the building, where the Bureau of Thought Reform hosts various activities. The other floors require increasing levels of security clearance. Reeducation and re-assimilation take place in these restricted areas.

People give us a wide path as we walk through the hall. I enjoy the power the AA black affords me—on occasions like this, it gets us to the front of the line, as we can't be expected to put off official business to wait around like normal citizens—but I care less and less for the skittish way people's eyes skirt just around my own and then down to the floor. Dressed as I am, I can't touch people. I think of Lara, of her clear eyes and flushed cheeks. I *touched* her. Or she touched me, rather. But it was fraudulent. She doesn't know me. If she did, she'd recoil like all the rest.

A series of turnstiles block the entrance to the convention center. Alongside each is an area to slide one's identification card. The regime issues each citizen over ten an ID card stating name, address, number, and place of employment or schooling. It also has a magnetic strip along the back for swiping in various locations throughout the city. The turnstiles at the convention center don't allow entry until one swipes his card. The Bureau of Thought Reform compiles electronic lists of the citizens that have and have not attended forums. At the end of the week, they issue a list of those who missed. A special division of the AA deals with these offenders. If one has a legitimate excuse—hospitalization, a family member's illness that requires around the clock care, death—no further action is taken. If not, three points go onto that citizen's ID card. Receiving more than five points in a two-year period means a two week cycle of reeducation at the Loop. Accumulated points disappear from an ID card at the rate of one point per six-month period.

I slide my card, magnetic strip out, and step through the turnstile. My pack follows and we go to our seats. An area near the front of the convention hall is always reserved for AA agents in uniform. I sit next to a man I recognize from a raid a few months earlier.

"Evening, comrade," he says to me.

I return the greeting as other agents exchange terse words and nods. The uniform allows automatic though superficial brotherhood which requires a greeting or nod of the head when two agents come together. This rarely extends to actual conversation, at least not in my experience.

The atmosphere in the convention center remains hushed, even as the seats fill up. Many citizens procrastinate as I do, and Friday meetings are always busier than the ones on Monday or Wednesday.

The mechanical sound of the entrance doors sealing shut quiets the light conversation, plunging the hall into complete silence though the meeting won't start for ten minutes. The lights dim in preparation. An agent behind me whispers about the monotony of these meetings. I agree, but don't voice the opinion, preferring to keep my own counsel unless I must speak my mind.

When the lights go off completely, I stifle a sigh and mentally prepare myself for the next hour. The stage lights come on and out walks the Chairman of the Bureau of Propaganda, Chairman Zander. As he steps to the lectern, the audience claps appropriately. All noise ceases at the high whine of the Chairman's microphone reverberating as it comes to life. He taps it as he always does and smiles broadly, as though surprised to find it living. The screen behind him is displaying PETA's logo in bold colors—a red flag with a human fist raised in solidarity with a nonhuman animal's hoof and paw, all three in silhouette.

"Good evening, comrades," he says, voice cheery. No responds. "Thank you for joining me for this week's final Alliance for Animals forum."

Another sprinkling of polite applause.

Chairman Zander's monologue concerns the speakeasies—he doesn't mention them overtly, but the title of the lecture is *The Greatest Offense Against the Party*—a tiresome subject for me, as I deal with it on a daily basis, but I can't resist nodding when the Chairman makes various points. He shares with us the ins and outs of this insidious offense, identified only as the continued desire to consume nonhuman animal flesh, while pictures flash on the screen behind the lectern. The first shows a burning speakeasy. The Chairman only remarks that this was once the site of illegal activity, but any AA agent would recognize it for what it is. The second image shows a freezer filled with black market meat. A number of strangled cries issue from the audience. The third image shows a knot of AA operatives leading a large group of traitors outside a speakeasy at gunpoint. The hall erupts with hearty cheers and thunderous applause though the Chairman's still speaking. Most of the audience has no way of knowing why these criminals are being detained. Chairman Zander quiets this raucous show of support with a wave of his hands and a patient smile.

"We must remember, comrades, that it's our sworn duty to protect the weakest and most innocent among us: the nonhuman animal. In this noble duty lies our *liberation*. This is a freedom from the whim of our palates as well as from incorrect and immoral ways of living, which is damaging to selfhood."

The audience is a sea of nodding heads and mumbled assents, myself included. I understand the phenomenon of mob mentality, but it never does much to aid me when I feel it coming on. I must nod, shout, growl at the horrid pictures shown to me, or pledge my loyalty at the top of my straining lungs. The PETA Chairman's a powerful speaker, his words setting traps in which the listener is only too happy to become caught. Chairman Zander is second only to the Party Chairman in this arena.

"We must look upon those who disobey the law with contempt. We must not hesitate to turn them over to the AA. No place exists in this regime for those who sneak across Party lines to consort with the enemy—with the *meat-eaters*—and those who value chaos above the ordered peace of freedom."

The audience hisses vehemently.

"Who among us has the right to indulge in Speciesism?" Chairman Zander asks, looking about as though honestly seeking an answer.

We forcefully shake our heads and begin to scream our responses. I let out an energetic *NO ONE!*, my words lost in the volley of shouted replies from fellow spectators, many of them red-faced and shaking their fists.

Chairman Zander smiles at us paternally and quiets our shouting with another wave of the hand. More pictures flash on the screen, disgusting images of animal cruelty, each one more grotesque, more inhumane, than the one before it. We scream our outrage at the cows hung upside down from one leg, their slashed throats spilling fountains of blood. Pigs led to slaughter and electrified with stun guns. Animals caged in sterile laboratories with wires hanging from their skin. Chickens packed into small cages, pecking each other to death.

I scream until my face burns, so high does my blood boil. The room steams with communal outrage. We watch the parade of pictures, becoming only our anger, our contempt, our venom. This intense experience—of being one mind recoiling in horror, one heart beating furiously—is a comfort. The camaraderie creates a warm feeling at my core where coldness dwelled only moments before.

As the pictures continue, the outrage, the unmitigated, murderous fury, reaches a soaring pinnacle. This is how we touch. We no longer achieve it at the level of the individual, only in a group. The rage running through the audience builds until it reaches a plateau, then the pictures become worse. The violent, frantic energy fueling us reaches an even higher level. The remainder of the meeting is spent in this way, with all of us trembling and shouting, overcome with the brute strength of our emotions.

Finally, the horrifying slideshow comes to an end, replaced by a soothing image—the Party Chairman patting the head of a young calf. I find myself smiling at the screen, though the fervor of the last couple of minutes has exhausted me. The picture changes, showing a line of AA agents standing at attention in front of the Complex. My pride swells.

"This is our obligation as higher-order sentient beings, comrades. We will protect nonhuman animals as we would our own human families. And why?" He pauses, the silence deafening. "Because we are *all* family."

Chairman Zander stands motionless, his friendly grin in place, as we give him a standing ovation. The picture on the screen transforms into the PETA flag. We cheer this with both hands and feet. My throat's raw from so much screaming, but I can't stop pledging my loyalty in a shouted string of words, arms pumping with the enthusiasm of my applause. My quickly moving thoughts come up against a wall, crowding and shooting upwards. I suddenly must shout whatever I'm thinking. It's glorious when those around me do the same. The Chairman raises his hands, encouraging us to shout the same words together. The heat in the room, the heat within, reaches a startling degree, but I beat my feet and raise my voice.

"*Meat is murder! Dairy is rape! Fur is sacrilegious! Meat is murder! Dairy is rape! Fur is sacrilegious!*"

The letters flash in black across the screen.

Now white.

Now red.

Another picture of Chairman Goldstein, only this one stern. The shouting turns disjointed, then dies away completely as the applause grows wild and carries Chairman Zander off the stage. The lights come on above us, ending the cheering as though someone in charge flipped a switch in us as well.

The sound of the doors opening gets us moving, but it's slow going, a stream of disoriented individuals making its way up the theater steps to the exits. Exhausted and lightheaded, throat raw and hands sore, I go along with the others. The warmth drains away quickly, leaving me cold, calm, and empty. The group of us from floor one ten returns to our packrooms. I work, the disorientation lifting steadily as I apply myself. Four hours later, I leave for the night.

*

I give the next Monday division meeting in place of Sup3, who's occupied elsewhere. The possibility of his promotion has become certainty. I'm pleased for him, of course—he's an exceptional agent—but am more pleased for myself, as I'll replace him as Third

Shift super. The promotion won't happen until the week of Celebration—less than two months away—which is fortunate. Sup3's responsibilities greatly outnumber my own and I'll need a significant amount of training to ensure my success at the new post. The perpetual activity within the AA leaves no time for the type of formal training I received after enlistment. This schooling will work around other floor business, rendering it mostly catch-as-catch-can. The logical place for me to try my hand at the new position is the weekly division meeting, which never lasts more than twenty minutes or so, its purpose to lay out the tentative itinerary for the following week, applaud agents who gave exemplary performances during the previous week, and punish those who faltered.

I'm used to positions of leadership. Here on floor one ten, I'm senior pack leader as well as backup super for Third Shift, meaning I'm responsible for all division matters whenever Sup3's unavailable. During initial training, I was my company leader. I welcome the challenge of this promotion, even with the tripled workload. The increase in pay is negligible. My aspirations rise higher than simply busting the heads of those citizens dining on nonhuman animals. The AA can't continue to be purely reactionary. A proactive element must come into play. To catch the criminal whose cleverness increases with each passing day, we must understand him. Hence the importance of conversing with those we apprehend before executing them. Understanding their motives will furnish the illumination necessary to bring all citizens in line with Party doctrine, if not in thought, at least in deed.

Despite these aspirations, I'm satisfied with my current position—the hours spent on the street, keeping order and crawling through shadows. I'd be quite content to remain where I am. But if I hope to encourage the AA to make the shift from reactionary to proactive, upward motion is required. Only an agent with a privileged position and an exemplary service record could push for such a thing and succeed. I have the latter, but the former will mean a few more promotions.

I spent last night preparing this meeting. It took longer than it should've, mostly because Lara kept invading my thoughts. I'd write down key points of the speakeasy problem only to find myself thinking of her smile and what her eyes did to that part of me I believed long dead. All pointed, rational thought fell away at the memory of the high color in her cheeks and the heat that jumped directly from her eyes to my chest. I have no business even knowing who she is. But her face. The soft insistence of her helplessness. That single smile. All this foolishness resulted in a late night and several cups of coffee on my way to the Complex. A dull headache now throbs at my temples, a consequence of all the caffeine.

The meeting room on floor one ten seats all one hundred forty agents. Each pack sits at one of twenty tables. I'm standing at Sup3's usual place—behind the lectern and in front of a freshly scrubbed dry erase board—reviewing my notes as agents filter in. The meeting's at ten sharp. I check my watch and see with annoyance that ten has come and gone and still agents are trickling in. I'm no pushover, but neither am I Sup3, whom these agents have come to respect over the years. I'll have to forge my own way as the new shift supervisor if I want to earn their respect, and it has to start today.

After all have taken their seats, I read off the agent numbers of the eight men who sauntered in late.

"Tardiness is just as unacceptable today as it was last week when Sup3 gave the division meeting. The agents matching those numbers will accept two demerits. If that puts anyone over five, mandatory physical training is tomorrow at five a.m. on floor one nineteen and will continue for the rest of the week. I'll send your numbers up after this meeting."

I receive shocked expressions from three of the tardy agents. They must be the unlucky few who will be at PT in the morning. The gym on floor one nineteen has weights, an indoor track, and various cardio machines. The AA encourages everyone to partake, but it isn't mandatory unless one receives five or more demerits in a two month period. If this occurs, an agent goes on PT for the next seven days—including off-days—working demerits off at a rate of one per week.

"If this continues, I'll double the demerits. Are we clear?"

Heads nod. Most also add a *yes, comrade* for good measure.

"Also, this is the last time any agent will ride above zero demerits. From this day forward, I'll issue PT for any demerits received. Clear?"

More nodding heads.

"This will be a short meeting, as it concerns a familiar issue. Intelligence has given us three more speakeasy locations." I hold up the fresh report Sup3 handed to me the night before. "If I can rely on your diligence, brothers, I have no doubt we'll eliminate these the same way we have countless others."

Each black clad man nods his head with conviction and answers in the affirmative, even those who now have a mandatory week of PT.

"The sites are spread across the city and only two of the three are confirmed. We must tread lightly with this third site. If we burn it to the ground on bad intelligence, we all know the result."

Such blunders, even when based on incorrect or shoddy information from Intelligence, always fall onto the shoulders of the agents conducting the raid.

"I'll put three packs on each confirmed location. The orders for those packs are obvious. Level them, and we all know what to do with the traitors."

The boys smile, looking less like hyenas than sharks in bloody water. Their identical expressions unnerve me. I attribute this to lack of sleep combined with the guzzling of too much coffee.

"I want four packs on the third site, including my own. Training will begin in the afternoon. The raids are scheduled for midweek. I won't go into detail at the moment, as only members of the chosen packs need concern themselves."

An agent raises his hand, stopping me in my tracks. When I give him my full attention, he looks unsure as to whether he should've interrupted.

"What of the other packs, comrade?" he asks, unsure expression turning into one of concern. I know the feeling. It's horrible to receive no action whatsoever.

"Neighborhood watch," I say, and a number of shoulders slump.

Neighborhood watch is glorified street duty. Agents pair off and patrol a specific area, usually a five block radius. I don't mind the work, provided I pair with an agent who doesn't feel the need to talk throughout the entire assignment. It's soothing to be out in the steady hum of the loudspeaker and starlit shadows. There's very little action, which is why the duty repels most agents. But, for me, this too has a certain allure, as it allows quiet time for thinking. I wouldn't mind putting my own pack on neighborhood watch and me with them, but that's out of the question. I have to be at the most delicate spot—the unconfirmed site—because this is my operation.

"The pack assignments will go up later today. I'll confer with Sup3 on my choices, but doubt he'll change anything. Those with mandatory PT are excluded, of course."

Only a few sets of shoulders slump this time, but no one speaks a solitary syllable.

"That's all for midweek," I say with some finality. "I have the weekly assignments for neighborhood watch and double duty posted in each packroom." I pause, reviewing my notes. To be safe, I've followed Sup3's format for these meetings. I'll work out my own way in due time. "Is there any other business?"

No one speaks.

"Meeting adjourned."

The agents leave in silence. Only my immediate packmates hang back, clearly waiting to discuss something.

I collect my notes and walk to where they're standing in a loose knot in the corner. I raise my eyebrows but say nothing. I've worked with these men for years. They know my little idiosyncrasies and so don't hesitate to get right into it.

"Does midweek mean Wednesday?" the lead boy asks. He doesn't call me comrade. Anyone who has worked with me closely knows I despise it. I refer to all my agents by their numbers, but this one I call Deux to indicate his position as my second in command. He'll take my place as senior pack leader when I move into Sup3's position. He watches me with eyes that are dark blue. I think of Lara.

"Yes," I say. "We move Wednesday evening at nine-fifteen. This stays between us." I meet each pair of eyes with a steely gaze. Only Deux dares to nod. I suppress a smile. I like very few of the agents I've worked with over the years. This doesn't mean I dislike them, but I don't make a habit of warming up to anyone. Deux's different, young—no more than twenty-one with four years in the agency already, not to mention three years of Junior AA in school— and reminds me of myself at newly seventeen when I enlisted. I sense something favorable in him. I imagine it's similar to what Sup3 must've sensed in me in the beginning.

"May I take lead position?" Deux asks, a hopeful shine in his eyes but face blank. I've already begun grooming him for the new position. Part of what he must learn includes a suppression of one's emotions, as these foster weakness. The AA teaches us to show blank faces to the public, but I extend this to everyone with whom I have contact.

I nod and Deux gives a small, triumphant smile to his comrades. He erases the expression when he looks at me again but doesn't thank me. We both know he wouldn't have lead position if he hadn't earned it.

"We'll be the lead pack onsite. I expect no mishaps."

Deux nods. He's the only one who dares respond to me half the time. The rest of the pack hangs back and lets him deal with me. They already defer to his authority, though he's the youngest agent in the city with a pending senior pack leader assignment.

I dismiss them, wanting time to think in silence. I return to the packroom slowly, bones weary and thoughts drifting to unfortunate locations.

For well over a decade, my life has been my profession, leaving my personal affairs a nonexistent void. But now I find myself looking forward to my next off-day—the first in over a month. I already know how I'll spend it. I haven't seen Lara in weeks. If she's thriving, I'll leave her in peace and let that be the end of it. But if she's struggling, I'll confess, somehow making her understand all this. Though the warmth she kindles intrigues me, I know any attempt at touch is folly. I am the AA and the AA is me. No room exists for anything else.

EIGHT

My next off-day comes after the raids.

The third location turns out to be a speakeasy masquerading as an evening society for the welfare of undomesticated nonhuman animals. We burn the three sites to the ground, seize and destroy all the illegal meat, and execute the traitors without questioning them.

I receive accolades as acting Third Shift super and senior pack leader, the AA Chairman communicating his congratulatory remarks via an underling. Sup3 assures me no one has any doubt as to my ability in the new position. Unfortunately, I don't share his confidence. My thoughts travel in strange directions whenever I'm not occupied by neighborhood watch, a raid, or busy work that keeps me hunched over my desk in the packroom, such that I fear my wandering, grasping mind will soon affect me professionally. My place in the AA is everything. I am its beating heart, its open ears, its watchful eye. It, in return, is my resolve, my purpose for being, the recipient of every shred of loyalty I have to give.

*

Early afternoon on my off-day finds me at the deli across the street from her building, eating a sandwich I don't really want. I've watched for an hour already, thinking over what to do. If she's better, I won't say anything at all. I'll just walk away. The desire for that tingling warmth draws me closer, but it can't last, that feeling. It disappears on the wind, as do all things once real and now illusory. Heat of that type is over for me, for everyone.

Eleven o'clock comes and goes with no Lara. Perhaps she reported to work early. I dump my mostly uneaten lunch into the trash and leave. It's Sunday, so traffic on the street and sidewalk is heavier. The government employs most people in one way or another, and Sunday off-days are common. Children don't attend classes today either. Throughout the regime, Sunday means time spent with family. If one still has one.

The ever-present voice of the loudspeaker trails me down the sidewalk.

Speciesism is insidious and illogical. We do not discriminate along the arbitrary line of species. Be kind to your fellow animals, be they human or nonhuman. Let us practice moral uprightness. Hypocrisy in all its forms is to be looked down upon. Tomorrow is another day closer to perfection. Meat is murder, comrades. True freedom is freedom from harm. All life is sacrosanct.

I cross the street to the pet shop. Instead of Lara, I discover the middle-aged proprietress at the register, engrossed in a magazine of some kind. This will be PETA issued material. The agency controls all media besides *The Capitol City Chronicle*, published by the Animal Liberationist Party. The bell over the door chimes as I step into the store, but she doesn't look up. This obvious disinterest in the basic tenets of customer service again makes me wonder how she manages to stay in business.

I walk to the register, position myself above the woman, and clear my throat. She cuts her eyes to me, unattractive face alight with smoldering annoyance. She doesn't close the magazine, which I can see is the latest issue of *PETA Weekly*. The contempt boring into every wrinkle of her face is general. She doesn't remember me, which works to my advantage.

"Comrade, I'm looking for one of your employees—"before I can finish, she interrupts with a brusque retort.

"I only have one. What do you want with her?"

I pull out my AA badge and place it on the counter between us. If this doesn't cut through the layers of her belligerence, nothing will.

She looks down as though expecting some insignificant timewaster, then gasps, her small eyes going from chips of ice to the beady eyes of a nonhuman animal when cornered. She glances at me again, fear settling over her broad face instead of contempt.

"Now, if I may finish," I say in a flat, no-nonsense voice, and pause, interested to see if she'll contribute another stinging, disrespectful barb. "The girl who works here. Where is she?"

The woman shakes her head, her tight, fuzzy curls and jowls jiggling. I haven't collected my badge just yet. Her eyes keep sneaking down to it. She knows I have the authority to take her into custody and shut down this poorly run business. I consider doing it out of spite. But that would be a blatant abuse of power. More troubling still, this sudden desire to see the woman ruined stems less from her rudeness towards me than from my outrage at the glee she took in her poor treatment of Lara.

The proprietress stumbles over her words in her hurry to answer my question. "She has Sundays off, comrade. Always has. She'll be back Monday afternoon." Though her expression remains appropriately timid, her dark eyes burn, betraying her true feelings. "Has she done anything wrong?"

I put my badge away with calculated slowness. Her eyes stay trained on it until it disappears into my pocket. "I don't believe that's any of your business."

She recoils as though slapped.

"The girl isn't in any trouble," I say, revealing this only because I wouldn't put it past the woman to punish Lara herself by firing her. Nowadays, a wise person ceases association with those bringing AA interest upon themselves, lest he also be implicated.

"But I do need to speak to her about another matter. I trust I can rely on your discretion, comrade."

She nods emphatically, jowls and curls nodding as well. "Yes, of course."

"Good. The girl…"I let my voice trail off, hoping for the exact response I receive.

"Lara," she says, more than eager to interject. "Lara Miranda. She lives down the street." She points in the correct direction. Most find the urge to provide pertinent information to an authority figure overwhelming.

"She's never been much trouble," the woman says, now rambling quite irritatingly. The urge to take her in for questioning and perhaps a short stay at the Loop washes over me again. I dismiss it. "Her head's in the clouds. And there's the whole mess with her father, but the girl can't be faulted for that."

I nod but not sympathetically. I have the information I need and am not terribly interested in listening to this woman carry on.

"What's happened to her father?"

The proprietress trips over herself to spit out the sordid tale. I can see the glee in her eyes, the way she enjoys this. She fears me, but not enough to avoid engaging in this gushing narrative.

"Disappeared weeks ago. The girl was hysterical. He just went out one night and didn't come home. I never liked him myself. He wasn't right." She drops her voice and leans closer, which is completely unnecessary given the utter lack of customers in the shop. "But you know how that is."

I give no indication as to whether or not I do. Not that she requires a contribution from me to continue speaking.

"He was up to something illegal, if you ask me. He had shifty eyes. I never trusted him. Not sure how he managed to raise such a gentle, pliant daughter."

"Well, I thank you for the information, comrade. I'll dispatch an agent to speak with Miss Miranda next week."

The look in her eyes turns to cold merriment. "Will the agent come here? She reports to work at eleven and we're open until eight o'clock."

Her desire to please is merciless. I normally find this tendency in citizens convenient, but it seems especially despicable here. Just moments ago, she made a great show of convincing me Lara is a decent, *pliant*, law-abiding citizen, and now she's in a sick sort of ecstasy at the prospect of seeing the girl in trouble. I chalk this up to yet another example of how little we touch each other these days. If we reach out a hand, it's always only to accuse.

"Your silence is compulsory," I say, and wait for her to nod before continuing. "The girl hasn't committed a crime."

The high shine in the woman's eyes dims but doesn't disappear completely. There's still hope of a punishment for the girl, after all, if only she answers certain questions in an incriminating manner.

I leave without bidding the woman good afternoon. It would only take a phone call to get her on the Kill Floor. I clench my jaw against the urge, letting it roll over me and disappear as so many others have done. Isn't she the example of a commendable citizen? Isn't she simply performing her civic duty by telling me everything she knows of Lara? The amount of delight she takes in the telling is irrelevant. Her conduct is what the regime desires in all right-thinking members of our meat-free society.

The maternal voice of the loudspeaker calms me as I walk to Lara's building.

We must not allow those around us to engage in illegal activities. Meat is murder, comrades. There is no shame in reporting a fellow citizen if he has lost his way. The truly innocent are the only ones deserving of protection. Let us eradicate all avatars of Speciesism. Let us be free from deficiencies. No one has the right to consume another.

I mumble along as I go. The slogans are on a rather large loop that replays monthly. I spend a lot of time on the street. After a few years, one becomes quite familiar with the order of the messages. Even after the loudspeakers go off at the night, I can hear them in my head, repeating until sleep silences them.

I step inside Lara's building and pause in front of the directory. An H. Miranda is listed as living on the fifth floor in apartment fifty-seven. I realize I don't know the straggler's first name. I didn't ask and he didn't offer the information. I'm lucky to have extracted the last name so effortlessly from the proprietress, as, without it, I would've been hard-pressed to locate the girl at all. The AA computers could provide the information, but I didn't dare use them. A specific branch of Intelligence monitors computer activity. I'd prefer no one knew about these little visits.

I take the stairs, jogging up five flights without encountering anyone or becoming winded. The AA gives monthly physical exams, so it does one well to stay in shape. I keep trim by running on the treadmill in the small living room of my flat, which occupies the place a television should be. I do eight miles a day while listening to pertinent Party news on Regime Radio. I also work out in the Complex gym on the days I don't sleep in my flat.

I stare at the tarnished gold numbers on the door to apartment fifty-seven for a handful of minutes, immobile, realizing that I have no idea what I'm going to say to her. I'm here to tell her the truth—or a very close cousin of the truth—but also to see her blue eyes again. They held real warmth at the pet shop, real feeling. Feeling so strong, it sparked something inside me as well, just as the straggler's passionate speech did.

I knock on the door before I convince myself to beat a hasty retreat back to the stairs. Talking to her will be difficult. I no longer engage in true conversation. I have no friends. No family. No casual work acquaintance with whom to exchange a friendly word. I only open my mouth to give orders, issue threats, conduct an interrogation, or repeat cadence in the dark solitude of my flat. Reaching out, opening myself—I haven't done it in years. It's easy to forget how much one misses such simple things. This is what the straggler's passion fostered in me: an understanding of my own emptiness. An understanding that the ability I once possessed to truly touch another person or engage him in conversation for conversation's sake has been misplaced and, perhaps, lost forever.

Footsteps on the other side of the door.

"Who's there?" she asks, small voice apprehensive. The door has no peephole. The regime outlawed those during Reconstruction.

Who exactly am I going to be for her? I can't very well be agent 687 and demand she open the door. I'd gain entry to her flat, but at a cost I don't wish to pay. Everyone fears the AA. It's the way the regime wants it and it makes doing my job easier. But eliciting

Lara's instant obedience would render touch impossible. I want to truly converse with her, not simply frighten her into answering my questions.

"I have a message for Lara Miranda."

"I'm Lara. What is it?"

"This can't be said behind a door."

She falls silent. I start to wonder if she isn't sneaking out the window and down the fire escape, so long does it take her to respond.

"How do I know I can trust you?"

"The message is from your father."

She gasps. I wonder what her clear eyes look like, if her tears have started already. I don't want to gain entry into her apartment by lying, but if she asks me pointedly who I am, I'll have to provide a convincing fiction.

The metallic snap of locks turning fills the hallway. I count seven sets. The door opens and the smell of her flowery perfume rushes into my nostrils. Straight away, I see she doesn't remember me. Another fortunate turn of events.

"You know my father?" she asks, glassy blue eyes enormous and pleading, chin trembling as we stare at one another. Her dark hair frames her face and tumbles down over narrow shoulders. Her garments are simple, her pale, blemishless face free of makeup.

"I knew him, yes."

Her face contorts at my use of the past tense. A tear falls from one eye. She wipes it away quickly, her cheeks bright red. She looks past me, scanning the empty corridor, then steps back and motions for me to come in. She closes the door behind me, flipping over three of seven locks. She comes around to block the entryway leading further into the apartment, her body language sending a clear message that I'm not to leave the foyer.

I don't inspect the flat, which goes against all my training. An agent must always be cognizant of his surroundings in case evasive action becomes necessary. But that would mean taking my eyes from hers. I don't smell meat and wonder if she's ever visited a speakeasy. Perhaps she possesses valuable information, which would mitigate some of the inappropriateness of this visit.

She speaks, as if with great pain. "You *knew* my father?"

I nod.

She drops her gaze to the floor and I take note of the gentle curve of her cheek. The fragile spot where her jaw meets the slope of her neck. The urge to touch her—and not just figuratively—slithers over me, much stronger than the compulsion to drag the ill-tempered proprietress to the Loop. I ball my hands into fists to keep them to myself.

Her eyes lift to mine again. She's crying openly, but her gaze is steady. "Is he alive?"

"No."

She lets out a little whimper and I merely stand there, watching, hands hanging limp at my sides, face expressionless.

"How?" Her pained expression is tragically beautiful.

"He was captured by the AA."

Her shoulders drop as her silent tears quickly accelerate into sobs. She covers her face, every inch of her trembling.

I watch, having no idea how to comfort her or if I even should. The straggler's death was my doing. While I feel no guilt at this—he broke the law—a sinking feeling is slowly settling over me. I purposely avoid thinking of those connected to the criminals I apprehend. For me, offenders are starkly individual, as much islands unto themselves as I am. I have no friends or family, and transfer this solitary condition to those I take into custody. This keeps feelings out of it, but seeing Lara's desperate tears topples this carefully constructed simplicity, leaving me alone with the brutal truth of the world. Protecting the most innocent among us leaves no room for touch, for closeness. I accepted this long ago, but perhaps that's my own deficiency.

"He's dead?" she asks in a sob.

"Yes."

She sinks to the floor, falling heavily to her knees, hands shielding her face from view. I take note of the wood floors as the dark fabric of her skirt spreads atop it like a flower in bloom. She weeps and I stand above her, always watching, never touching. In or out of the black uniform, I'm but a cell in the body of the AA. I'm no longer myself. I'm not even entirely certain what kind of thing *myself* is, so tightly am I bound by my chosen profession. I am my training, my instincts, the double A's on my uniform, a small piece in the giant puzzle that is the regime. But a government is little more than rules and structure. It doesn't touch. Or feel. Or love.

I kneel to her slowly, expecting the betrayal of my legs as they instead lead me out the door. I'm close enough now to kiss her if I so desired. The thought fills me with unspeakable terror.

"Lara." Her name feels like the first true word I've spoken in years. I don't understand her effect on me. She is fragility incarnate, a girl broken by the absence of the straggler.

She drops her hands, exposing a tear-soaked face and cheeks rosy with embarrassment. Her eyes are the straggler's—passionate, intense, steady. Though they don't mirror his exact color, they hold me as easily as his did.

"Was it the speakeasies?" she asks.

I reach to wipe a tear from her cheek with my thumb. She doesn't recoil from me. Having forgotten the sweet simplicity of touch, it amazes me how quickly the knowledge comes flooding back once one takes a single, resolute step forward.

"He gave me a message for you," I say.

She takes my hand and squeezes. I look down at our fingers intertwined, heart thudding against my ribcage, and feel my estrangement from the AA acutely, throbbing like the ghostly sensation of a lost limb.

"How did you know him?" she asks.

"I came across him at the speakeasy."

Her hand clutches mine more tightly.

"It was raided by the AA." Her face contorts and her breathing grows more rapid. I say the only thing I think might calm her. "He gave me a message for you. Would you like to hear it?"

"Please." She's struggling to regain control of herself—wiping tears, swallowing sobs, making a grim line of her mouth. I understand grief. I lost my own parents some years ago. The AA filled that gap, serving as mother, father, friend, lifeblood, and sustenance.

"He wanted you to know he intended to quit that night, to keep his promise to you."

She buries her face in her hands. "I begged him," she sobs, shaking her head so dark hair cascades onto her shoulders. I touch a curling lock without her notice.

"I begged him to stop." Her face is a trembling canvas upon which pain paints in broad strokes and vibrant colors. Even in the grips of this agony, she's lovely. I feel a sudden hatred for the straggler. He left her, and for the worst reasons.

I reach to wipe away another tear and she falls forward, clearly meaning for me to catch her. It's a rigid, panicky sort of embrace at first, but then she works her face into my chest and my lips find the top of her head.

"I'm sorry," I say into the thick softness of her hair and mean it. I'm not apologizing for my actions that night—I acted well within my authority—but for the choices the straggler made. His insistence on meat eating has destroyed this young girl. He had his rebellion, his points to make. He thought of her, but only afterwards, when it was already too late.

I have no idea what to say once her tears stop. I delivered the message, but am reluctant to let that be the end. She knows about the speakeasies. Does she have other information? I'll never know unless I ask. But this isn't the only thing keeping me here. I want her close to me. Perhaps I can work it so I get the toasty feeling as well as vital information to report to my superiors.

"Did he say anything else?" she whispers.

"No."

She nestles further into the embrace, sweet and supple in my arms. I understand the straggler's actions even less now, having met her.

"How did you escape?" she asks.

I almost tell her no one escapes the AA but think better of it. I marvel at the straggler's influence on me even now, after he himself is dead. This business of his started a chain of duplicity. I lied to Sup3 and am now lying to Lara. But it's too late to backtrack now if I want her to stay as she is: fragile, trusting, and in my arms.

"I'm not entirely sure," I say and, fully consumed by the depths of her grief, she believes me.

NINE

Intelligence has nothing for us the following week, which means long hours of neighborhood watch for Third Shift. A less experienced agent might believe our steadfast eradication of speakeasy sites has been successful, but I know better. More sites will be discovered in due time. If the underlying reason for the clubs is rebellion and not simply the desire for nonhuman animal flesh, the traitors will find a way.

Tonight, we have the southwest borough, three sets of two agents patrolling the area. This recent round of watches is on a sixty hour rotation. Ten hours on, five hours off, until sixty hours pass. This is the beginning of our third rotation, which leaves us thirty hours, including down time. It's not so bad. I can function on as little as two hours of sleep per day.

I prefer to do neighborhood watch alone, but the AA frowns on this. Pairing off makes the streets safer for both agents, though in all my years in service, I've never needed backup on watch duty. During the day, we see little more than citizens on their way to and from work or school. At night, we occasionally discover some law-breaking, but it's rare. After voluntary curfew, the streets stay mostly barren. I use the time spent on this docile, thoughtless duty to plan raids or prepare the next department meeting. Today, I use it to sort through my muddled thoughts.

Pairing agents off is Sup3's responsibility as Shift super, but, busy with his own training, he has left all routine duties to me. Of the few agents on the floor that I can stand working neighborhood watch alongside, Deux's my top choice. He can get chatty—always only about AA business—but when I ask him for silence, he complies and doesn't need to be told again. Many agents ramble on about their personal lives, films they've seen, good restaurants, and other things about which I couldn't care less. When I ask them for shut-mouth, I only receive short periods of begrudging silence and so must as again later.

Deux and I walk side-by-side. It's ten forty-five and well past voluntary curfew. The tranquil voice of the loudspeaker is the only sound on the street.

Dairy is rape. Voluntary curfew is in effect. We respect the right of all beings to life. Defending this right is of utmost importance. Meat is murder, comrades. Do not succumb to the immoral caprice of your palate. All life is sacrosanct. Let us thank the Chairman for showing us the way. Freedom from harm is true freedom.

"Do you think we'll see any action tonight?" Deux asks, voice low. These are his first words during the cycle, which began two hours ago.

I shrug but don't speak. The streetlights dim after voluntary curfew, lengthening the shadows and making it easier for us to patrol undetected.

We turn a corner to find more nothingness. I cross the street while signaling for Deux to remain opposite me. This will discourage further conversation. He walks with a hand on the butt of his gun. I do the same.

My thoughts, ever stubborn, refuse to abandon Lara. It troubles me that I nearly assigned the pack neighborhood watch in her borough. I know what's necessary—that I have no further contact with her—but not if I want to do it. My feelings are ice cold, much like everything else unless I'm close to her. I've always been the type to know what needs to be done and then to do it without hesitation. I have no interest in becoming a new animal, even if that animal is warm inside and able to touch. Change means compromising my life in the AA.

Deux motions from across the street, touching his right ear and then pointing in the direction of an alley about one hundred yards away. I cross the road quickly and soundlessly, drawing my weapon as I fall into step with him. Sounds of a hushed conversation are emanating from the dark confines of the alley.

I gesture for Deux to fall back behind me and we move into the alley's still shadows. It dead-ends further back. From where we stand—heads cocked, listening—I can see the outlines of two people, their discussion only a slight whisper above the night wind. I'll have to commend Deux later for the sharpness of his ears.

We step behind the conversers—two men with their backs to us. I motion for Deux to cover me and don't turn to make sure he complies.

"Voluntary curfew is in effect, comrades," I say in a loud voice.

The men spin around, the one closest to me issuing a muffled yelp as they look frantically from me to Deux, obviously identifying us for the AA agents we are.

"Identification cards," I say. I sniff at the air as they fumble in their pockets. No meat smell. They hand their cards to me. I reholster my weapon, pull the flashlight from my belt, and inspect the IDs. The addresses on both reduce a substantial amount of my suspicion. They live in the immediate borough—right down the street, to be exact.

I point the flashlight at the first man, aiming for his eyes. Blind and frightened, he can't find my face behind the light. I do the same to the second man, who reacts in a like manner.

"Are you aware of voluntary curfew?" I ask, speaking with deliberate patience. I don't think these men have done anything wrong besides indulge in foolish behavior.

They nod like children trying their best to please.

"Yes, comrade," one man forces out, the younger of the two. "We were just heading back to our flats."

The other man nods vigorously but keeps silent.

"What are you doing here, if I may ask?" I say.

The men exchange a worried glance. Already believing them innocent, I take this for what it is—not a tacit admission of guilt, but a hesitance to get oneself into trouble by offering unfortunate information to an AA agent. There are operatives who drag people in for stern and sometimes deadly punishment for relatively minor infractions, including flippant responses. I don't punish people simply for being out after curfew—it is voluntary, after all—but I do inquire as to what they're doing and then advise them to get off the streets.

The same man answers. "He lives this way." He points to the left, then to the right. "And I live that way. He left his ID card at my flat. We met here because it's off the street. I don't like going out after curfew if I can avoid it."

This makes sense. A citizen can't do much of anything without his identification card, including using public transportation, gaining access to government buildings, making a purchase, or clocking in at work.

"I advise you to return home before you meet an agent who isn't as understanding as we are, comrades," I say.

Nodding, the men speak in unison. "Yes, comrade." They rush off and exit the alley in opposite directions.

I click off my flashlight and turn to Deux.

"Did you believe them?" he asks.

"Yes."

"Well, alright then," he says, and we walk out to the street.

The loudspeakers are shutting down for the night. This is the last recording until five a.m.

Voluntary curfew is in effect. Meat is murder, comrades. Dairy is rape. Fur is sacrilegious. Hubris should be avoided at all costs. Let us celebrate the nature of all life as sacrosanct. Equality for all animals, human and nonhuman. Tomorrow is another day closer to perfection.

The speaker beeps and goes off. It will be a long night now, in silence.

*

I spend a series of nights alone in the packroom. I've always found a delightful sense of solace in the emptiness of my flat in Lib. Hall, spending nights reading, engaging in long sessions of repetition, or exercising as I watch the city through my window. It's just enough space for an individual who cares very little for material things and never has acquaintances over. I enjoy the off duty hours when I can be alone in this silent sanctuary.

But now I see her face there.

I see her face everywhere, to be exact, but can keep occupied with other things while at the Complex.

I don't pull out the cot I frequently use on my nights in the packroom, as I'll merely lie there, staring into darkness and thinking about the single lock of hair I held in my fingers. I stay at my desk, working long after the other Third Shift agents leave for the day. I pore through a stack of reports from Intelligence, trying to pick out something they might've missed, working until exhaustion carries me into blissful, unthinking oblivion. If I dream of her, I don't know it. I ceased remembering my dreams long ago.

No matter where I sleep, she's my first thought upon waking. I have no right to know her. I have no right to the warmth that blooms in my center when she reaches out to me. She doesn't know me—how dangerous I am, what I've done to others who once trusted me.

Reconstruction made touch perilous. Betrayal became a necessary component of remaining a law-abiding Party member. She must know this. But, still, she reaches out.

Work is my only respite from troubled thoughts, provided I stay busy. Pausing to stretch or rub my eyes is idleness enough for my head to meditate on the blue of her eyes, the way her trembling body felt against mine, the urgency of her tears, our fingers intertwined. I toil through the quiet evening hours until my eyes drift shut. And still, at the brief moment before wakefulness tumbles into sleep, she's there.

Knowing her is bad enough, but I did other things to which I had no right. Before leaving her apartment on the day our hands touched, she clung to me, begging me not to abandon her, not now, when she has no one else. Her wide, teary eyes were hypnotically blue. Caught up in the tiny spray of freckles on her cheeks, I spoke without thinking.

"I'll come back, but I can't say when."

The warmth she shared in her tiny foyer turned cold the moment I stepped into the corridor. As I regained the sidewalk outside her building, I turned to see her face in the window, watching me. She raised a hand in farewell. I did the same, an odd feeling seizing me. This feeling followed me home, where I spent the rest of the day on the treadmill, trying to outrun that strangeness, trying to become exhausted enough to erase her final words from my head.

You are all I have in this world now.

Her trust in me is both burden and blessing, unwarranted and unquestionable.

*

I sit alone in the far corner of the Complex cafeteria. Third Shift has a day of meetings that started at eight o'clock this morning. Two before lunch and three more afterwards. The AA Chairman's giving the last one of the day. He has a certain talent for public speaking, though he doesn't hold a candle to the Party or the PETA Chairman. Each shift will go through these meetings sometime during the week. Fourth Shift went yesterday. Second Shift goes tomorrow. First Shift, the day after that.

The pleasure I take in my three small meals a day is a testament to my simplicity. But, today, eating is as much a chore as the day's meetings. I'm not excited about most meetings as a general rule—now that my responsibilities have increased, the wasted time is an even bitterer pill to swallow—but the ones during the AA's annual self-assessment are usually enjoyable. This period comprises a two week long event involving both agent and agency evaluations, held in conjunction with the country's yearly Celebration. The meetings involve passing out accolades on the pack, floor, division, and shift level, as well as officially announcing promotions.

During the day's final meeting, Sup3 and I will formally receive our new positions. I know this is a great honor and excellent for my career, but find it difficult to locate my excitement. This is what my entire life in the AA has been building towards, but the cold places within me throb with emptiness. I haven't had an off-day in weeks. My thoughts are with Lara.

Celebration culminates with a parade through the downtown area surrounding Headquarters, the Victory Luncheon, and speeches by Chairman Zander. At the end of the afternoon, a live video feed will broadcast a speech by Chairman Goldstein throughout the regime, as each city and town has its own events planned for Celebration. All top government officials will make appearances, except the Party Chairman who is rarely, if ever, seen in public. Even the week's mandatory AFA forum reflects the festivities with a lecture titled, *Freedom Through the Liberation of Nonhuman Animals: the Anniversary of Our Noble Regime.*

I look up from my tray of half-eaten food as Sup3 drops into the chair across from me. He's smiling, which is rare. I suppose he has reason to be pleased. Not only is he receiving his promotion at the end of the business day, but the official announcement went out this morning that Third Shift earned high honors this year, meaning we've toiled the hardest and our agents received the largest number of accolades over the previous twelve months. This is our fourth year in a row. For me, this only applies additional pressure, as it's now on me to continue the tradition. A few weeks ago, I wouldn't have seen this as a problem. But now my head's different—constantly swimming or floating when I need it grounded firmly in reality.

Sup3's my superior, which means it's inappropriate for us to do anything together after hours—not that I do things with anyone, superior, equal, or subordinate—but I consider him a friend. He knows me as well as anyone. Communication is easy between us, but we don't talk about personal business. Speaking to him about Lara would be a costly mistake. Friend might be too strong a word. He's an acquaintance.

"Our hard work's paying off again," he says. He leans over his tray and begins to eat the way he does most things, with methodical efficiency.

I stare at the double A's on his uniform. We're the same. Our passion, our faith, the short lines of our presents and futures—even our pasts—all belong to the AA.

"Yes," I say after a long moment.

He looks at me closely, dark eyes conveying nothing though I know they see everything. He, too, is a product of training. "You've been spending nights at the Complex."

My comings and goings are documented by ID card swipes and scanned thumbprints.

"Are you feeling sound lately?" he asks. This easy concern is why I count him among my very short list of acquaintances. No one else at the Complex would ever ask this question. Training teaches an operative to tend to his own affairs. Connections are dangerous. I'd never inquire into the health of an underling, unless it could jeopardize a mission.

"I haven't been sleeping well," I say. This much is true. I increased my working hours, trying to snap my mind and realign it— as the Bureau of Thought Reform would say—and, as a result, my sleep has suffered. Ironic, considering that sleep is the one place I can best hide from her.

Sup3 nods, the expression on his face knowing but not sympathetic. He finishes his sandwich before speaking again. "We'll have some interesting business again after Celebration."

"Speakeasies?"

He starts to shake his head, thinks for a moment, then nods. "Yes and no. The hours you spent sorting through reports led Intelligence to a suspected site. There's also some double duty for the northeast borough."

I keep my gaze even and expression blank. Lara's borough.

"There's a third matter, one that should please you greatly, but that's for later," he says. "What kind of assistance will you need?"

"None for the latter business." I never take more than my own pack for double duty. "I'll want my pack and perhaps two others for the speakeasy."

Sup3 flashes another broad smile. He's positively giddy this afternoon. "After today, this will all be at your discretion and your pack will become Deux's."

"Congratulations on your promotion," I say, as now it feels obligatory.

He bids me the same and we finish our lunches in silence. The all-day meetings have put me in a reflective mood. My thoughts hover over the meetings that have been, the ones that will come, and the business for the following week. What would happen if Lara caught sight of me in uniform during my double duty assignment? I picture her warm eyes freezing over until they're as cold as the absence in my middle.

The intercom buzzes above the cafeteria, cutting off the maternal voice of the regime whispering Party slogans. In ten minutes, the next round of meetings will begin in the large meeting room on floor fifty. A dark puddle of agents exit the cafeteria. Sup3 and I wait for the rush to die down, then leisurely go to the elevator. We're given immediate access, though several agents are already in line.

We arrive in the meeting hall and sit in seats flanking the one for the AA Chairman. My mind does not snap. It does not realign. It wants very much to wander. I hold it steady with thoughts of duty, the meetings I must attend, and my impending promotion. It's hard and constant work, but, for the moment, I succeed.

TEN

When Intelligence has nothing for us Enforcement operatives, we occupy our time in two ways. Neighborhood watch is one, but we also conduct random searches of the homes and businesses of private citizens. *Private citizen* is a bit of a misnomer. The regime considers all people the same way—as animals that can only be trusted when continually watched, threatened, and berated. I use the term to differentiate between civilians and AA agents. But no one is above the law. Operatives have their rooms searched at least once per week at random intervals, as do citizens working directly for the Animal Liberationist Party, PETA, and the Loop. Rumor has it even the Party Chairman's residence and offices are checked regularly.

Privacy is neither a right nor a privilege. Those in charge can give or take it at will. Probable cause is an archaic concept. Warrants are a thing of the past. Any citizen can have his flat, workspace, or person searched at any time and for any reason.

An entire floor of Enforcement—floor one fifteen— conducts these searches twenty-four hours a day, seven days a week.

Though it's a larger than usual floor—thirty packs—additional agents are required from other areas to conduct the random searches scheduled for a given day. This city's the largest in the regime. To avoid backlog, packs are sent out to perform searches whenever Intelligence fails to provide other assignments.

I rather enjoy these searches. We rarely find anything, but it's a nice break from the monotony of neighborhood watch. The majority of Capitol City citizens wholeheartedly support the Party credo—*equality for all animals, human and nonhuman*—but there are always those who attempt to undermine the regime, be it out of disrespect or rebellion. Because no one can be trusted at face value— one's outward appearance often belies the lawlessness or immorality beneath—such searches are necessary.

During the week of self-assessment, AA business slows to a crawl. Whole floors are put on neighborhood watch or door-to-door duty, more commonly called double duty for the two D's in door-to-door. The senior leader on the floor gets to choose between the assignments. As we've recently come off two sixty hour cycles of neighborhood watch, I pick double duty. It's a good break for the boys and we might see some action. Citizens still largely cleave to the illusion of privacy in the home, so searching a residence reveals the truth of an individual in a way that simply encountering him on the street cannot do. The streets are dangerous and people take care while in public. But this is a mistake in judgment. Every place in the regime is dangerous for those who break the law.

*

It's two in the morning and I have lead position. We're in full riot gear, my packmates and I—helmets, flak vests, lightweight, fully automatic assault rifles—though no one does much rioting these days. The appearance of the AA inspires complete cooperation in most people, but if not, the automatic rifle certainly does the trick.

We travel up the stairs in a tight, soundless knot, me in the lead and the others going two-by-two. This is our sixth location for the night out of the twelve we received before leaving the Complex around seven o'clock. Double duty is a long detail. Each search takes at least thirty minutes from start to finish, but can last longer depending upon the size of the residence or business. After three searches, we get a fifteen minute break.

The flat we're after is on the seventeenth floor. A woman carrying a laundry basket comes out of her apartment as we flow from the stairwell in an orderly line. She turns on her heel, panic lending her face vibrant color, and darts back into her flat, the lock turning over on her front door the only sound in the hall. She isn't our target. The apartment we want is at the end of the hall.

I pause by the door, breathing deeply, listening. Shuffling on the other side. Voices. A muffled cough. It's odd to find working citizens awake at two in the morning. This will be slightly more difficult than the last search. That flat was empty. People mean complications. Many an innocent civilian is critically injured because an agent misconstrues a panicky gesture for a threatening one.

"Going in, brothers," I say, and they know to prepare themselves. I steady my weapon, then kick the door in.

A woman screams as we rush in, flooding the flat like spilled ink. The tiny foyer leads to a tiny living room. A man, woman, and small boy are huddled on a couch, watching us with wide, terrified eyes, the woman crying and clawing at her son's shoulders, the man with his arm protectively around her, the child anxious at his mother's odd attention.

I step forward to confront them, lowering my weapon so it points away from the child, who lets out a gravelly cough. "This is a lawful property search. Do not attempt to hinder it in any way."

The woman emits a screeching wail, muffled by her husband's chest, where she's pressed her face. This starts the child crying too. He doesn't look old enough to understand what's happening, but I imagine he finds his mother's sudden panic quite unsettling.

"Please, comrades, we are law-abiding Party members," the man says, as though I can simply take his word for it. "My son is sick. Please."

"Don't expect a second warning," I say, and signal my packmates. We all have our jobs. The most junior agent stays with the residents, keeping a gun on them to make sure they stay out of the way. I don't expect any problems on this one—when a child's involved, the chance of resistance greatly diminishes. The rest of the pack splits up, one or two to each room. A small flat like this shouldn't take more than twenty minutes to search.

Six locations and six searches without incident. Finding nothing is a bit of a letdown, but it means people are obeying the law, which is the goal.

Wrapping up a search is the responsibility of the pack leader. I face the family again, weapon pointed at the floor and finger off the trigger. The woman, no longer crying, stares blankly at the wall opposite, trembling violently. The child's asleep in his father's arms. The search took approximately thirty minutes. The second child's bedroom was vacant. When asked, the man explained that the boy's coughing keeps everyone up at night and their daughter chose to stay with her grandparents across town. A phone call confirmed this.

"Everything appears to be in order, comrade," I say to the man. "The regime appreciates your fidelity."

He nods, relief flooding his face. He isn't completely at ease—this won't happen until we leave—but at least he knows we won't execute his entire family or drag them to the Loop for thought adjustment.

We leave the messy flat without another word. My pack goes through personal belongings methodically and conscientiously, and though we don't leave complete destruction in our wake, there's always a mess to clean up. We have the authority to tear a location apart, breaking, ripping, and destroying things if need be. I don't allow this unless and until an item of contraband is found.

We go to the stairs. On the way, one agent expresses his disappointment at the uneventful night. A second man reminds him we still have six locations left. A third reminds them both that people should be loyal, law-abiding Party members. Finding nothing is a good thing.

"Boys," I say, just sharp enough to express my distaste for the conversation. I prefer pack silence in public—a group of black clad hyenas seen but not heard. Under no circumstances should we be overheard bickering or complaining about law-abiding citizens. Each uneventful raid is another victory for the regime.

We load into the jeep. That was our sixth search, which means a fifteen minute break. The boys could use some coffee. So could I. We'll finish the rest of the searches before sunrise. I put the jeep in gear and take off in the direction of the nearest coffee shop.

ELEVEN

I see Lara again before Friday's culmination of the nationwide Celebration. We don't have an off-day, but are dismissed from our shifts early due to overall inactivity, giving me an extra three hours to kill.

I normally spend the night before the final day of Celebration in my flat going over AA business or on the streets in plainclothes, keeping a watchful eye. Today, I return to the Dormitories on foot, change out of my uniform, and take the metro across town. It's seven fifteen, just a touch before nightfall. The proprietress said the shop closes at eight on weekdays. But I don't intend to visit Lara there. Bad enough the insolent woman knows I'm AA, but no agent ever materialized to question Lara.

I catch sight of her in the shop as I walk from the metro station. She's tidying merchandise on the shelves, her back to me. I pass without pausing, the loudspeaker providing the beat by which I walk.

The Capitol City's anniversary Celebration parade will take place tomorrow at noon followed by the Victory Luncheon in the courtyard. Freedom from carnivorous lifestyles is personal freedom. Tomorrow is another day closer to perfection. Meat is murder, comrades. Do not be a slave to your palate. Protect the most innocent among us. All Alliance for Animals meetings will resume their normal schedules after Celebration.

My usual haunt—the deli across from Lara's flat—is closed at this late hour. I find a coffee shop just down the street and order a tall cup, black, though it will make me jittery. I sit by the window and consider the new sign on Lara's building. Black with bold white letters that read, *Freedom from Meat is True Freedom for All Animals.* Below this, written in smaller but no less inflammatory letters, *And if you value your freedom, you WILL NOT eat meat!*

I drink without much enthusiasm despite the fact that my day was a banner one. I'm officially Third Shift super—another rung up on the AA ladder—but my satisfaction feels just out of reach, more concept than actual emotion.

At five to eight, I toss my cup into the recycling bin, leave the café, and cross the empty street. The fall's coming on gently with air that's crisp without being cool. I prefer the chillier temperatures of late autumn and winter. I step into the patch of shadows to the left of the hulking double doors and disappear. Those passing on the sidewalk don't notice me. I wear black even when not in uniform, all the easier to nestle into darkness.

Lara comes up the street slowly, walking beneath a loudspeaker and glancing up at it with obvious trepidation. It tells her of the importance of being a good Party member, how true freedom is achieved, and how many days closer we are to perfection. She looks at it as though not quite trusting that maternal voice, the one that so soothes me when my mind runs riot.

She's only wearing a light jacket to protect herself from the night's mild weather, dark hair cascading over her back and shoulders. She puts her hand on the door to the building, apartment key at the ready.

I step from the shadows, coming up behind her as I once did to the straggler. The smell of her is fresh and feminine—flowers and spice. I touch a curling tip of her hair.

"Good evening, Lara."

Gasping, she spins on small feet. Her fearful expression melts quickly into one of almost frantic relief. She jumps into my arms.

"It's you!" she cries.

I go rigid in her embrace. I scan the streets. No one watching us, at least no one I can see. I usher her into the building, not wanting to draw attention to ourselves.

She burrows farther into my chest. "I thought for sure…"

An odd feeling grips me, but I hold her until she's ready to let go.

"I thought maybe you were AA."

My face stays neutral, but my heart begins to thud in my ears.

"My boss told me an agent came, that they want to question me, that I might be in trouble." Her delicate chin trembles. Her lashes flutter. At the sight of this desperate fragility, I hate the straggler.

He isn't the only target of my wrath. I told the proprietress to keep silent. Perhaps a few dark weeks at the Bureau of Thought Reform will teach the woman to follow orders given her.

"It has to be about my father and the speakeasies," she says, small voice wet and trembling. "What else can it be?"

I hear feet on the stairs and cover her mouth. "Upstairs, Lara. Don't speak of such things out in the open."

She nods and leads me upstairs past the man I heard descending. He doesn't pay us any mind. We're locked safely in Lara's apartment before I realize she led me the entire way by the hand.

She pulls me into her tiny living room. From what I can see, this apartment's smaller than my AA one, which is intended for a single occupant. I wonder how Lara manages to pay for this place on her pet shop salary, which must be low. I doubt the proprietress pays a penny more than the minimum required by law. Any money from the straggler stopped after his execution. The state denies executed persons death benefits—insurance doesn't pay out, nor does a pension that might have assisted a grieving widow or orphaned children.

I spy many family pictures on walls and shelves. Only one has a woman in it as well as straggler and daughter—the mother, presumably. In this picture, Lara's quite young. It was just her and the straggler for years. A dark feeling seizes me, not guilt exactly, but a brand of gut-wrenching regret for the straggler's poor choices.

I sit on the small couch at her invitation and she sits beside me, very close.

"I don't know what I'll do if they really are after me," she says, her expression a deeply troubled one.

"What exactly were you told?" I ask.

"My boss said an agent came looking for me at the store. He wanted to question me, said I might be in some kind of trouble." She's crying again, but it doesn't stop her words. "She said she can't have that kind of embarrassment at the boutique. She's paying me less, for the inconvenience. I'm lucky she didn't fire me altogether."

Fury ignites every cell in my body. For one moment, it completely consumes me. After this, I go cold again, but the anger persists. As I can't tell her this is all make-believe on the proprietress's part without revealing myself as the agent visiting the pet shop, my first inclination is to inform her that the AA doesn't wait this long to question a witness or suspect—I spoke to the proprietress three and a half weeks ago—and that, if we can't find you at work, we go immediately to your residence and vice versa. But how to explain my knowledge of such things without admitting to being AA?

My profession doesn't shame me, but I've never had this compulsion to hide what I do for a living, not even from my parents, who begged me not to enlist. I think of my mother's tears and heartbreak, the way she and my father learned to recoil from me. It would be worse with Lara because of the straggler, perhaps as bad as it was with my father—screaming, threats, shaking me by the collar, laying me flat on the front lawn, demanding I leave and never come back.

"I only hope they've changed their minds about me," Lara says in a shivery whisper. "It's been weeks. But what if they haven't? I don't know anything besides what my father told me. I never went to those places! I didn't even like speaking about them." With her hitching breath, every word sounds like she's forcing it out with great effort. "I don't want to go to the Loop. I don't want to disappear like he did!"

I touch the tears on her face with my fingertips, taking time to wipe them away. This magic—this touching—warms me from the inside out. It can't last, because it's not real, even if she thinks it is. I regret the little ruse I put on for the proprietress. My disgust at her impudence sears my insides as well, flaming so hot I know I'll have to satiate it to know peace.

"I've known people taken by the AA," I say, speaking slowly, as though to a bewildered child. "They wouldn't wait weeks. They'd come immediately and not rest until you were in custody."

She looks at me, her blue eyes captivating, even when red-rimmed and puffy. "I hadn't thought of that. It makes sense. Why would they wait? If they know where I work, they must know where I live."

"Undoubtedly."

She smiles and squeezes my large hand between her small ones. "Thank you."

My dark eyebrows pull together slightly. That's the extent of my expression. I don't necessarily have to hide them from her but it's a hard habit to break.

"You're welcome, though I'm not sure what I did."

She leans in for another hug. "I was so scared. My father disappeared, probably at the hands of the AA, and I was so I'd suffer the same fate. But I think he sent you...to care for me."

I don't say anything to this, though it's exactly what the man did. Somehow he knew I'd be taken with her, that I'd realize the flat echo of my current existence I've always associated with selfless duty is actually loneliness and that this loneliness is all-consuming, no matter how busy I keep myself.

Lara seems to sense my secretive nature. She doesn't pry into what I do for a living or demand other personal information. I gave her my first name weeks ago—the neglected word rolled off my tongue so awkwardly, I questioned whether it was indeed my name at all—but she has yet to call me by it.

She sits up again, catching me in the intensity of her gaze. "Can I ask you about my father?"

"I didn't know him well."

"Were you with him at the end?"

"No."

"Can you tell me what happened?"

I must tread lightly here, lest I reveal my AA ties, but I also can't pretend to have been a patron of the speakeasy. She can never know the way the straggler died, that he leaned into the gun with a sigh of relief and a beatific expression on his face. That I watched.

"He spoke of you," I say. "He worried about the promise he never got to keep."

Her open, attentive expression is new. Those I encounter in my capacity as an AA operative aren't attentive. They listen, but they fail to *listen*. I am but the mouth of the agency, issuing orders and making threats. They respond by nodding their heads, wide eyes fearful, minds reeling with the bloody, horrible things of which they believe me capable. The men with whom I serve are no better. They fear me because I don't enjoy their company, laugh, or take part in their chatter. I'm still the embodiment of the AA to them. In short, I don't touch people. My hands and words stay as cold as my insides and I keep all three to myself. But Lara and I touch. Her eyes send sparks that kindle the empty places in my chest and gut, electrifying me with short-lived feeling. Too bad it's fraudulent. As soon as she sees me for what I am, all this is over for me, for us.

"He thought he was being so clever, said the speakeasies were an act of civil disobedience." She gives a bitter laugh. "I asked him who he was rebelling against, the government or the nonhuman animals he consumed."

"What is there to rebel against at all?" I ask.

She gives me a sharp look. "The atrocities against the human animal."

"Atrocities?"

"The chief atrocity is the devaluation of human beings," she says, eyes flashing with intense confidence. I can see the straggler's poison boiling inside her—the need to rebel, the ability to find fault where no fault is present, the penchant for troublemaking.

I keep silent and she continues. "The nonhuman animal has become the focus to the detriment of all else." Helplessly intrigued, I can clearly picture the hours she spent talking with her father, sharpening their shared arguments. Here is the mind of one with whom I am constantly telling the AA we must become acquainted. The straggler's rebellion started as an innocuous string of arguments that eventually led to action. Lara has the arguments already. How long will they simmer before she feels compelled to act?

"I was very young before the Overthrow, so I don't remember much of the preceding government. All I know, I learned from my father. Basically, it was human-centered."

I don't interrupt the smoothly moving train of her thought. With every word she speaks, she becomes infinitely more interesting.

"The focus was skewed, I agree. Any hierarchy of being is bogus. We all have a right to life and freedom from torture. But this regime's no better than the one before it. The focus is just as skewed, only conversely. We went from human-centered to nonhuman animal-centered. This reversal of the old hierarchy has only caused the human animal more suffering."

"What part of that suffering's worse?" I ask, voice even, expression calmly blank. "The lack of available meat? Or the prohibition on cruelty to those who don't share our blessed capacity for reason?"

She gives a small shake of her head. "I was raised vegan, even before the Overthrow. My father was an Animal Liberationist way before it was fashionable or compulsory. I've never tasted meat in my life and don't want to. That's not what this is about. We need equality of species, not one group standing a rung above the other on the ladder of existence. This reversal of the hierarchy put humans at a constant disadvantage, even law-abiding ones. We're no longer free to speak against the travesties we see."

The Chairman called the reversal of the hierarchy of being a *leveling of the playing field*. Once the field's level, we can achieve true equality. I don't argue this point. Those in positions of power understand the facts for what they are. Others can be made to understand through persuasive force.

"Have you read much Spinoza?" she asks, lifting an eyebrow.

"He's been blacklisted."

She offers a cold smile. "Of course he has. Who hasn't been?" Her smile turns playful. "My father was a philosophy professor at the university before the regime blacklisted his life's work along with the work of all the philosophers he admired. He ended up teaching classes on Speciesism and regime history, but his interests stayed the same as before the Overthrow. He shared those interests with me. I always loved Spinoza." She takes a deep breath, clearly reaching back into her memory. "*The most tyrannical of governments are those which make crimes of opinions, for everyone has an inalienable right to his thoughts.*" She waits for me to react, but I don't. "Does this sound familiar? Spinoza speaks of *our* government and of every government that extends itself over and above those it should serve and protect."

"Lara, this is treason." I'm now well within my rights to drag her into the Complex, process her, and send her to the Loop for thought adjustment.

She flashes a spirited smile. "Will you turn me into the AA, then?"

I don't speak immediately because I'm considering it. I'm duty bound to take anyone making seditious statements or admitting to illegal activity into custody. We've now left the territory of playful line-crossing for more dangerous country. It's happened before. The threat to my AA career, then only burgeoning, compelled me to take action. The lengths I took obliterated my past. I escaped with my career intact, but I escaped alone, cutting all family ties. I can clearly see this will also end badly. I don't want to turn my back on Lara, but I can't compromise my post, not after what I've done to keep it.

"It isn't wise to speak so," I tell her. "The AA's ears are always open."

Her expression turns suddenly sober. "Oh, yes, I know. They're always watching, aren't they? At least that's what the spooky posters all over the city tell us. My father says—"she winces but doesn't backtrack to correct her use of the present tense—"that a government should fear its people and not the other way around."

I don't want to be drawn into such a conversation. The days of feeling the need to support my position are long over. I prefer to allow the double A's on my sleeve to speak for me.

"There's nothing to fear so long as one follows the rules."

"You sound like one of them," she says.

"I am one of them, as you should be."

"Yes, I suppose I am," she says, sighing. "Who has a choice? I agree with the regime's founding principles, I just don't condone the methods my government employs to keep us all in line. To me, it makes no sense to say: meat is murder, comrades, and we'll punish anyone we catch eating meat by murdering that person on the spot. That's unconcealed, unforgivable hypocrisy. It's as foolish as smacking a child to teach it not to hit."

I smile at the simplicity of her comparison and immediately turn it to my advantage. "Yes, but it works, doesn't it? And why? The punishment appeals to his sense of self-preservation. Even if the child doesn't see anything wrong with hitting others because he doesn't value them, he'll keep his hands to himself. He doesn't hit because he now knows how badly it hurts. He also knows a hearty smack awaits him if he raises his hand to another person. The meat-eater is the same. If one doesn't want to die, then one should not kill." This is the most I've said in defense of my government in years. I agree, its laws can be severe, but they aren't unfair. A person only has to follow the rules to ensure his safety.

Lara's glassy eyes are offset by the defiant set of her chin. "Do you think my father deserved to die?"

"He knew the consequences of his actions when he broke the law."

"It was civil disobedience."

"Thoreau has been blacklisted as well, Lara, and civil disobedience is hardly an acceptable defense against murder."

A tense moment of silence shivers between us. I think she might lash out at me, so fierce is her expression, but she softens and collapses against my chest where her sobbing begins once more in earnest. I breathe in the sweet scent of her shampoo, saying nothing as she weeps in my arms.

Tomorrow is the culmination of Celebration. I have to get my head straight again, my mind clear, my thoughts moving in logical, controlled order. And I must set free the weeping, fluttering bird I hold in my arms to either fly or perish. I can't concern myself with her welfare. I kept my promise to the straggler, though I didn't mean to make a covenant with him. This business is over and done with.

I press the side of my face into Lara's thick hair for the last time, the warm sensations within me already beginning to fade.

*

In the small bedroom of my flat, I put on my dress uniform and confront the mirror. I'll wear this tomorrow during the culmination ceremonies. A new pin gleams on my left breast, signifying the promotion from senior pack leader to Third Shift supervisor. I look at the double A's on my armband. Touch the gun on my hip.

I returned home from training wearing this uniform. My father didn't want to let me in the door but, at that point, Mother still argued on my behalf, though it didn't please her to see me in AA black. She thought operatives heartless, merciless, and bloodthirsty.

"I am the black clad body of the AA," I whisper. We stand for honor, integrity, and loyalty. We do the things that must be done.

I look at my gloved hands, which have done so many things, Mother's high screams ringing in my ears. Father's hands at my throat, squeezing as he demands to know what I did, why I'm covered in blood.

Other agents are in the hallway, laughing and talking. With Celebration ending tomorrow, tonight means parties and lightheartedness throughout the city. I don't look away from my reflection. The longer I stare, the harder it is to see my own face.

I go to the living room and stand by the large window, left hand on my gun as I watch the city lights pouring in from outside.

"I am the black clad body of the AA," I say. "Honor when it is easier to do the opposite. Integrity when those around us lack it entirely. Loyalty to those unarmed innocents above all else."

I watch, unmoving, as the city begins to sleep. If the loudspeakers were still on, I'd go to the dormitory courtyard to listen until my mind emptied of all but Party slogans.

My comrades buzz in the halls. And Lara? Is she holding tightly to one of her blacklisted books and reading beneath the lamplight? Her fate will be the straggler's if she's not careful.

"Honor when it is easier to do the opposite. Integrity when those around us lack it entirely. Loyalty to those unarmed innocents above all else."

There's comfort in this. I repeat it for hours. It isn't as good as the loudspeaker, but it soothes me and cleanses my thoughts of Lara and her father.

I touch the new pin on my uniform.

"I am the black clad body of the AA."

TWELVE

The last Friday of the two-week long Celebration starts early for the shift receiving high honors. We report to the Complex before sunrise for a short meeting to discuss the events of the day. The parade takes place late morning. The Party Chairman hosts a public luncheon after that in the large courtyard here at Headquarters though, of course, he won't really attend. Events like these happen all over the country. He appears at them via satellite. No one actually knows where he'll spend the holiday. His location changes often. The strength of his resolve holds the country together. We can't afford to lose him.

After the Victory Luncheon, the message from Chairman Goldstein will broadcast. Those who can't make the luncheon can listen via the loudspeakers and Regime Radio or watch it on all three television channels. A few dozen activities are scheduled at various locations throughout the city for the remainder of the day, including speeches from Chairman Zander of PETA and Chairman Anderson of the AA, as well as amusing activities for the youngest Party members.

The culmination of the day's events is a spectacular fireworks display over the city. My boys usually watch from our packroom, taking advantage of the breathtaking view. The agency discourages drinking on duty, but we break protocol to enjoy a glass of champagne during the celebratory fireworks. I don't care for the taste of alcohol, but the champagne means we've again received top honors, so the single glass tastes like concentrated victory.

*

I'm standing by the window, watching the sun sneak through the thick, early morning clouds when Sup3 comes into the packroom. I'm always the first agent on the floor. Sup3's always the second. Deux occasionally shows his face before all the rest—a trend I suppose will continue given his recent promotion—but not often. Celebration complicates matters. The constant parties in the Dormitories leave agents groggy in the morning. It isn't appropriate for someone holding my position to attend these gatherings, but even as a young agent, I rarely partook. When I did, I never stayed out so late it affected my performance the following morning.

Sup3 clears his throat. I don't turn. I know him and he knows me. He doesn't do things like make small noises in order to get my attention. If he clears his throat, it's because it needed clearing.

He stands next to me at the window. We're about the same height—he's a bit taller—and build. If I'm the left hand of the AA, he's the right. The camaraderie I feel in his presence, the respect, neutralizes the silence between us. We have a mutual understanding of the power inherent in speaking fewer things than one leaves unsaid.

He has something to say, most likely of a personal nature, since he never hesitates when his comments concern AA business. I wait for him to begin, eyes on the sleepy city below. The loudspeakers are on—that gentle voice vibrating in every particle of air—but no one's on the street to listen.

"Are you still having difficulty sleeping?" Sup3 possesses the rare ability to voice his concerns without inciting me to recoil the way I would from anyone else attempting to pry into my private affairs.

"Yes," I say. My interaction with Lara has compromised my concentration, leaving my mind perpetually wandering. Sup3 must have noticed this lack of focus.

He shifts position, clearly uncomfortable. Many lines exist in this regime besides the one I crossed to make Lara's acquaintance. One lies between the two of us. On one side, we find AA business. On the other, our personal affairs, which are strictly off-limits. It's worrisome that Sup3's crossing the line for the second time in two days.

"See that you take care of it," he says. "Lack of appropriate sleep can interfere with the duty day."

I look sideways at him but his eyes are on the building opposite. This is a warning. I don't have time to respond before the boys begin to enter the room, chattering, rubbing puffy eyes, and shuffling to their desks.

Sup3 addresses the entire packroom. "All right, brothers, to the meeting. Make it quick. There's a lot to cover and a short amount of time in which to cover it."

They go, their exodus much quieter than their entrance.

*

"Celebration ends today, comrades," I say, positioned behind the lectern at the front of the meeting room. Sup3's next to the door, arms folded and dark eyes on me. He doesn't look the least bit concerned, despite our earlier exchange. At moments like these, my focus comes when I call it, thoughts of her scattering as though in a high wind. The agents watch me expectantly. This morning, I'm the mouth of the AA as well as its hands.

"Just as in past years, receiving high honors means nothing today. Our duties remain the same—protect law-abiding citizens, sniff out those who endeavor to ruin Celebration in some way, and uphold regime law."

The agents form a sea of nodding heads.

"Minimal staff will be left at the Complex. No one from this floor, of course. AA presence must be strong today. Have a good time, brothers, but don't neglect your duties. After the Victory Luncheon, report to a location where you can listen to the Chairman speak. It's a rare opportunity.

"On the rear wall of each packroom are the day's assignments. Most of you have assignments for the Headquarters area. The rest will be a few blocks out. No one here has parade duty." This is spared us as recipients of high honors. The parade route is only through the downtown area, but it lasts for more than an hour. Though the weather's cooling as fall progresses, the afternoons are still quite hot, especially for an agent clad in head to toe black. Our dress uniforms are made of multiple layers of heavy material and include gloves. Those on parade duty must also march in them. During cold winter months, the uniform's ideal. At any other time, it turns an agent into a pool of sweat.

"Any questions?" I can tell by the tense silence that these boys want out onto the streets. Each still has a meeting to attend in his respective packroom before leaving the Complex. When no one speaks, I look at Sup3, who nods without uncrossing his arms.

"Dismissed," I say, and the agents file out. Sup3 catches me at the door.

"I won't be available today. This operation is yours."

I nod once. "I'm ready."

Blue and Red Shift supers spend the final day of Celebration with the AA Chairman. This will be the first time I act as Third Shift super without Sup3 standing directly behind me. I don't doubt my ability, but Celebration isn't the ideal time to cut one's teeth on a new position. If something goes wrong, the consequences will be catastrophic to my career.

I push these thoughts from my mind with the simplicity of a man removing a large but physically light barrier from his path. When Sup3 dismisses me from our impromptu meeting, I stride from the room, prepared for the day's events.

THIRTEEN

I don't technically have a pack. As the new senior leader on the floor, Deux now leads my old one. But as Sup3 did before me, I'll keep ties with them as long as possible. I assigned us the best duty—patrolling Headquarters, specifically the courtyard area, location of the Victory Luncheon and the Party Chairman's televised speech.

I give the meeting in my former packroom instead of Deux, who I don't feel has the training to appropriately rally the boys. He seems relieved not to shoulder the burden. Afterwards, we report to the courtyard where we'll patrol until eight o'clock this evening, right before the kickoff of the fireworks display.

The Headquarters courtyard can seat several hundred people comfortably, making it the top choice for festivities like Celebration. In the center of the meticulously landscaped patch of land sits a giant water fountain. From this, four paths radiate, snaking through grass and gardens to the rear of each government building, which flank the courtyard on all sides, giving it a diamond shape. Many government employees take their lunches here, me included, amidst the simple beauty of flowers, trees, and winding paths. Today, the park shines at high gloss. The party colors—red, white, and black—adorn every available surface by way of banners and ribbons. Each agency's flag hangs at the top of its respective path—the black flag of the AA, the red flag of PETA, the white flag of the Bureau of Thought Reform, and the Party flag, which combines all three colors.

A stage is pushed up against the broad rear of the Loop, which stands directly across from the Complex. Hundreds of seats are arranged here for the Capitol City's dignitaries to recline during the Chairman's speech later in the afternoon. Ordinary citizens are also welcome, though they must apply for seat space, which is on a first come, first serve basis. But those unable to reserve a seat needn't despair. A large area behind the final row of seating is cordoned off for standing room only. I'm spending the day on my feet—only the highest ranking agents can partake in the day's activities—but will remain in close proximity to the large screen just behind the stage. I don't intend to miss the Chairman speak.

Every AA agent in the city is on duty today. The higher ups suspended all off-days three weeks ago in preparation for Celebration. My next one's scheduled for the following week if nothing goes awry, but I plan to turn it down. The temptation to visit Lara might prove too great. Unbeknownst to her, I said my final goodbyes the other night, so perhaps it's best if I decline my off-days for the next few rotations, at least until I'm nothing but the pulsing, beating heart of the AA once more.

The loudspeakers are buzzing as sweetly as usual. Once the activities begin, they'll stop broadcasting slogans until just before voluntary curfew. The final day of Celebration is the only time the loudspeakers forsake their duties during daylight hours.

Meat is murder, comrades. Today is the closing day of Celebration. Let us celebrate freedom from harm. The Chairman speaks at two p.m. The Victory Luncheon starts at noon. Only ticketed citizens allowed. The parade begins at ten thirty a.m. Its route is as follows...

I cross to the far side of the courtyard. The Victory Luncheon will take place here behind the Bureau of Propaganda, which is opposite the Plaza, which is between the Loop and the Complex. I can hear the excited noise of people on the streets. It's wise to get one's place secured for the parade early. Most Capitol City residents will be out and about today and the parade is a much loved part of the merriment.

Deux's approaching rapidly from the opposite side of the courtyard, moving awkwardly in his dress uniform. He clearly starched it a little too enthusiastically the evening before. I have to suppress a smile. At moments like these, the tender weakness of his youth is glaring. Fortunately for him, his passion burns more intensely than agents twice his age, which does a great deal to compensate for lack of experience.

"The area's secure," he says.

"Where are your agents?" I ask, circumnavigating the urge to call them *my agents.*

"I positioned four of them at each entrance to the courtyard. The last man is patrolling the outer perimeter of Headquarters."

My promotion left my former pack's number at six. I make a mental note to recruit another agent to fill Deux's position now that he's taken mine. It won't do to have the pack undermanned for too long. Bad enough it's shorthanded on a day like today. To remedy this, I decide to take the place of his seventh, though this will cripple his authority a bit.

"Where will you be when the parade begins?" I ask.

"I'll take lead position on the street during the parade. After, I'll patrol the courtyard for the remainder of the day."

"You're one man short. I'll take position seven."

He smiles, relieved.

"I'll also take lead position."

"Yes, of course," he says, and sounds more grateful than he looks. I understand his hesitation then, as well as the awkward way he's fidgeting in his excessively starched uniform. His first duty assignment as senior pack leader coincides with the country's most important event of the year. A blunder on this day would harpoon his career. It might even send him to the Loop. I've seen it happen.

"What should I do?" he asks. His shoulders have relaxed, sinking down to a more natural level.

"Take position at the rear of the courtyard." I point for emphasis. "During the parade, watch the street, then continue with your plan to patrol the area. The other agents can keep to the perimeter."

He nods but doesn't move.

"Are the others in position?" I ask.

"Yes."

"You might join them."

He dashes away as though I threatened him with demerits if he didn't take action swiftly enough. I watch him exit the path behind the stage and check my watch. The parade starts in an hour. It won't hurt to take another cursory walk around the courtyard, followed by one around the outer perimeter of Headquarters, all the while checking in with floor one ten agents to verify they're on task.

I sigh.

It will be a long day.

*

The parades don't change much from one year to the next. Each begins with a large banner held by several school-aged children that proudly announces the anniversary year of the country. The number is the only thing that truly changes. I suppose the faces of those in the parade are also different, but it's like looking at a group of AA agents—we're different people, but we embody regime ideals and have the same hands, the same sneering, unforgiving mouths. Watching the parade, one sees the same Party flags, the same banners bearing the stern face of the Party Chairman, the same Capitol City dignitaries riding in the same flashy cars, the same animals paraded about—cows, dogs, sheep, chickens, rabbits, all led or cradled by black and red clad youths—marching bands playing the same triumphant music.

I busy myself with the crowd. It, too, seems like every other crowd. The people clumped in loose groups wear the same rapt expressions, clap their hands, and cheer in the same way. When banners pass that scream *Meat is Murder* or *Freedom From Harm is True Freedom* in bold red letters, their applause becomes thunderous and their cheers unsettling. No eyes fall on me as I prowl the sidewalks behind the shrieking mob. I'm a phantom in the light of day, watching but not being watched.

Riotous bursts of applause explode from the crowd as the Chairman of the AA, of PETA, and of the Bureau of Thought Reform pass on their respective floats. The Party Chairman is absent, but the Animal Liberationist float bears his likeness. Its appearance elicits hands over hearts and bowed heads from the crowd. I marvel at the obvious power of this man. Even the mere sight of him on paper produces a potent response. My pride swells despite the parade's blatant monotony. We are one people and this man is our leader. I place my hand over my heart and silently recite my oath.

Honor when it is easier to do the opposite. Integrity when those around us lack it entirely. Loyalty to those unarmed innocents above all else.

I stand behind the cheering crowd, watching the Party Chairman's float disappear. This marks the end of the parade. Most stay on the street, talking excitedly. The music is still pulsing from the loudspeakers, a proud rendition of the Party anthem played by brass instruments and a thundering drum line.

I haunt the streets, waiting for the crowd to disperse. Some citizens head towards the courtyard, others in opposite directions.

Events are happening all over the city, though the ones at Headquarters are the central focus.

A woman speaks loudly as she walks past, seemingly oblivious of the AA presence at her shoulder.

"*What* a wonderful *display*," she says, emphasizing the oddest words in the sentence. The man beside her nods in vigorous agreement. They're clad in Party colors from head to foot. I watch them cross the street and enter the courtyard. He's holding her by the elbow, but gently. The smile she points up at him appears genuine. They touch. The gentle sucking sensation returns to my midsection, emphasizing the emptiness there, the aching. I feel the turning tide of my thoughts then—*Lara*—and the emptiness within me sucks harder.

I follow the couple's path, Party music blasting on the now empty street. The excitement of the busy courtyard surges over me as I enter it, killing all rogue reveries.

*

I make my rounds during the Victory Luncheon, keeping eyes open and mouth shut. Much like the parade, this event rarely changes. The tables are filled to capacity. The chatter is happy and self-satisfied. The loudspeakers hum state songs instead of purring Party slogans.

The boys follow my lead, all of them moving through the crowd unnoticed, lips sealed and eyes watchful. Hordes of citizens have descended upon the streets, which normally spells trouble, but a singular energy permeates the day—one of pride and satisfaction. The country's flourishing. The harsh years of the Overthrow and

Reformation are becoming blurred memories of a distant past, even for those old enough to remember the way things were before. I recall less and less of those times as the days pass. Certain things cannot disappear from memory, but I make a conscious effort to push such thoughts away when they come. Staying busy helps, as does the constant flow of information from the Bureau of Propaganda. The government speaks to us unceasingly, the loudspeakers whisper sweet things, and the posters, television, and radio announcements buzz and flash in our eyes and ears. The room new information takes in our heads shuffles out what was there before it. But the most important facts stay with us—we're prosperous, free and, above all, morally upright. If we can't celebrate this, what can we celebrate?

I keep my distance from the people making merry at the luncheon tables, watching disinterestedly as they consume the grand meal and discuss Party business in loud voices. If a smiling person happens to glimpse my blank face and vacant eyes, he loses his cheery expression for just a moment before going back to regarding his fellow comrades positioned around the table. This is my effect on people. I don't drop my hand to the butt of my gun or flash a vicious grin, but anyone with eyes knows me for what I am—the harbinger of the AA's wrath, a phantom that can come at any time, indiscriminately touching citizens on the shoulder with icy finality.

The cloudless afternoon is unforgivably hot. I remind my packmates to drink plenty of water, which is available at a small station in the courtyard to those in AA uniform, as we're given no breaks. There's never been any trouble during the two weeks of Celebration—not even the ones directly following the Overthrow—especially not on the final day, but if problems arise, agents must be ready, not catching a break in an air conditioned packroom or the cafeteria. This long stretch of duty combined with the heat and heavy, dark attire makes proper hydration imperative.

I cross the courtyard, aiming for the drink station, and have my hand on a bottle of water when, from the farthest edges of my peripheral vision, I become aware of eyes assessing my person. I turn sharply, left hand dropping to the gun at my hip. It freezes there, clutching the butt of the weapon, as my face twitches and tries to replace its blank expression with a more bewildered one. I don't let it. My face no longer belongs to me. It's AA property and so must remain steely and pitiless, giving nothing to an onlooker.

But, at the table, peering up at me in wide-eyed surprise.

It's Lara.

FOURTEEN

Lara's watching me, a fork suspended halfway between the plate and her open mouth. I mirror her motionlessness, watching her with careful eyes, blank face giving no indication as to the emotions surging within me. What is she doing here? I fancied her alone, without resources, incapable of conducting her daily life without collapsing into a puddle of tears. But somehow she managed to obtain an invitation to one of the most prestigious events in the Capitol City.

Those at her table are trying to engage her in conversation, but she keeps her eyes on me, even as the man seated to her left taps her lightly on the shoulder. His smile slowly evaporates as he waits for her attention. Nonplussed, he turns to the man on his left.

I never considered this—that she might show up here—which is further evidence of my inexcusable preoccupation. The music pouring from the loudspeakers combines with the happy sounds of feasting citizens, spiraling into a nightmarish cacophony. I can clearly visualize the end of my career. It will only take Lara voicing an allegation, and there are so many from which to choose—the straggler, the deceptive way I made her acquaintance, the details of our final conversation, packed full of sedition. The knowledge that she can destroy everything for me is maddening. This is far worse than mere line-crossing. I've put myself in real danger.

She sits.

I stand.

Lara's fork drops, and her paralysis breaks. She stands, eyes pinned to mine, and stumbles away from the table. The man next to her looks sharply up—in her haste, she stomped on his foot. She pulls her purse free from the back of her chair, neither apologizing to the man nor sparing him a glance. The handbag comes into her arms ungracefully, but she pays this as little mind as she did the gentleman seated next to her.

My paralysis snaps as she spins on small heels and hastens for the exit nearest her. She hurries down the path, heedless of other citizens, dark hair rippling in the breeze, her escape glorious though she's running from me. I follow on nimble feet, easily closing the distance between us. Much like all else in my life, I calculate the approach, not wanting to catch her inside the courtyard. I have no idea what she'll do or say. It's important to avoid a scene at all costs, not just for me but for her. Surely, she must understand this. Perhaps it's why she elected to dash off rather than confront me.

I come upon her once we're safely outside the courtyard. People are wandering about, but no AA. It'll have to do. I can't stray much farther from my post.

I pull her to a stop with a gloved hand on her shoulder. She spins away from me, the high color in her cheeks matching the furious shine of her eyes. The cacophony that was so overbearing before—the conversations and laughter, the Party music flooding from loudspeakers—falls away in the intensity of that gaze.

"Lara," I say, but don't continue. How to proceed? I have questions—*why are you here? What are you going to do?*—but no clue as to her responses, so I don't voice them. Another side effect of AA training—never travel a path unless you have an idea what waits for you at the destination; observation trumps action until the consequences come into clear focus.

She wraps her tiny arms firmly around herself, mouth working but not producing sound. I focus on the hair lying over her shoulders, a thick and wavy brunette sheet.

"You're a liar," she says, not forcefully, though the wounded tone and wet eyes turn the words into an accusation. I misread her. She isn't angry—not yet, at least, but I suppose that will come later when I invariably choose the incorrect response—she's hurt. I understand anger and how to deal with it. But this is alien territory.

"No," I say, voice flat and expression flatter.

She makes a tragic little gasping noise. The dismay that seized me in the courtyard upon spotting her is widening into a deeper feeling very much like sinking. I touched her once and now cannot even imagine how I might make contact with what's standing right in front of me. The shaky bridge built between us has crumbled into the chasm that separates me from all others.

Her wide, wet eyes are icing over quickly. Her gaze drifts to my black armband. This strip of fabric means different things to different people. To me, it stands for honor, integrity, loyalty, and self-sacrifice. To Lara, it represents only ugly but necessary things— ruthless violence, torture, brutal executions, the disappearances of family and friends, the cruel, unfeeling hand of the government bearing down and strangling into submission those who might stray from the straight and narrow.

Standing at the foot of the steps leading up the Complex, the shadow of the AA flag falls upon us. She looks at the gun at my hip. My armband. The medals on my chest.

"You lied," she says, her eyes finally finding mine. It's an accusation, but not in the regular way. Her unorthodox behavior makes me think of the straggler.

The things you do…do you weep?

"No," I say again, and add a decisive shake of the head. I never lied about being AA. It's something about which I would never lie, as I'm AA first and foremost, flowing as easily through the agency as lifeblood flows through the body, making it animate. The AA is my lifeblood—it makes me animate—and vice versa. I would never lie about what provides my sole reason for living.

Her face contorts, as though my response injured her. She steps back, leaving me alone beneath the shadow of the AA flag.

"My father," she starts, but doesn't finish, the look on her face excruciating. I can't act, can't even begin to imagine what to do next. "I don't want you near me."

I didn't mean for her to discover what I am by seeing me in uniform, but regardless of the way she found out, the outcome would be the same—*I don't want you near me.* I think of my father with his threats and his fists, screaming in my face that I was no longer welcome. My mother's hysterical sobs, how she dropped to her knees and begged me. The sinking feeling becomes a terrible, sucking vacuum. The shadows in which I stand seem to bind my hands and arms, keeping me from going to her. These shadows are the agency, and that I cannot fight. I accepted everything—its credo, its fervor, its solitude—and the first casualty of that decision was touch.

She takes another step back, gaze wandering from gun to armband to eyes to looming silhouette of the Complex, all malice and polished glass.

"Aren't you going to say anything?" she whispers.

I never know how to respond to this question. Experience tells me it's better to say nothing than to shoot from the hip, letting words come as they may. This only leads to trouble as those words tangle around hands and feet like ropes of irretrievable discourse, crippling me. Silence seems the lesser of two evils. But surely, she must construe my reticence as others do—cold disinterest—instead of what it really is—a debilitating cluelessness.

Her eyes stay pinned to the double A's on my upper arm for a long moment. When they lift to mine again, I can see she's well past angry. I formulate a plan for the scenario in which she becomes loud and/or violent. I'll have to restrain her, possibly even knock her unconscious—whatever it takes to avoid attracting attention.

Tense in my AA black, I wait for her to move. There are a few options besides knocking her unconscious. I could report her as deranged and remand her to the Loop for reeducation. I could even execute her on the street. It means a sheaf of paperwork, but that's the extent of the inconvenience. If I tell her this, perhaps she'll decide to leave quietly. But perhaps not.

Every second I refuse to speak is only upsetting her further, but she's at that precarious point where the wrong word from me could shove her over the edge. And, by the look of her, just about any word I select will be the wrong one. I have a gift for viciousness, for creeping through shadows, for producing fright in those crossing my path. I can shoot a traitor in the head without a single misgiving. I can work until I collapse from exhaustion and get up an hour later to do it all over again. But becoming the solitary creature my government required stripped me of the ability to speak soothingly, to apologize, to even feel sorry at all.

When her shoulders slump, I know she won't yell or pelt me with harsh words and tiny fists. But the look on her face is its own kind of assault. A physical attack would be better than the teary way she's staring at me, as though I broke something important in her.

The music from the loudspeakers reminds me of my obligations. I can't let this go any further. It's Celebration. The Victory Luncheon will end shortly and I should be in the courtyard before the Chairman's speech begins. I need to canvass the area, yes, but I also want to see his face and let his words fill the empty sucking in my middle.

"I don't want to see you again," Lara says.

The blank expression on my face doesn't change, though the sinking feeling intensifies, spreading from stomach to chest.

She fixes me with one last measured glare, her expression playing hard at being hateful, then takes several steps back, keeping her eyes on me, as though I might suddenly pounce. She turns and dashes to the metro entrance at the far end of the block. The sinking feeling worsens the further she moves away from me, not disappearing when she does.

I return to the courtyard. The luncheon's winding down. Only an hour and a quarter until the Chairman speaks. The strange sucking feeling diminishes a little as my excitement surges. My focus returns with remarkable speed. Cadence helps—*honor when it is easier to do the opposite. Integrity when those around us lack it entirely. Loyalty to those unarmed innocents above all else.* Packmates coming to me for orders help. The lack of her presence helps.

I circle the courtyard, observing without taking anything in. I think of the look on her face—*honor when it is easier to do the opposite*—her horror at finding me in uniform—*integrity when those around us lack it entirely*—and the soft, trembling words she spoke to me—*loyalty to those unarmed innocents above all else.* It takes great effort to cast her out of my head. To rein in meandering thoughts, I immerse myself in the courtyard's buzzing activity, becoming little more than my power of observation. I slink through the crowd, miraculously invisible, and don't think of her taking the train across town with tears on her cheeks and head hung low. I wait for Chairman Goldstein's speech, my newfound focus sharp as a knife.

*

The Chairman's speech is one of the few things about Celebration that changes, getting better as the years pass.

He says nothing of speakeasies. Nothing of the traitors who hide among us, reaping the benefits of the regime while also working to destabilize it. The speech is uplifting and optimistic, a renewal of faith—faith in the government, faith in our resolve, faith in ourselves. Celebration isn't about chastising us—that's more appropriate for a citizen's bi-annual self-criticism session. Chairman Goldstein speaks openly, congratulating us for another banner year and challenging us to make the next one even better.

At the close of the Luncheon, the banquet tables are replaced by seats facing the stage and the large screen arranged atop it, instantly creating room for close to two thousand people. I stand to one side, my command position affording me a choice spot near the action.

Chairman Zander of PETA gives a small speech before the screen onstage shifts from the Party colors to a live shot of the regime's leader. He bids the crowd good afternoon and goes through a list of important events that took place in the country over the past year, all the while cracking jokes that draw enthusiastic laughter from the crowd. Chairman Zander plays the clown more during his Celebration speeches than he ever does in an AFA forum, most likely to avoid outshining the Party Chairman.

While Chairman Zander warms up the crowd, I think of other things. Lara at home alone, curled up listening to the speeches on Regime Radio. The sinking feeling overtakes me again as my thoughts gain speed—her blue eyes, how stony they were in comparison to how hopefully she looked at me the last time I visited her.

The rising crescendo of Party music cuts into my brooding, forcing my attention back to the present, where the cheering of the crowd and the flickering of the giant screen coming to life hold it hostage. The long, angular face of the Party Chairman obliterates all but the present moment. I'm a pair of ears, a set of eyes, anticipation itself. The crowd falls into reverent silence as the charismatic drone of the Chairman's voice pumps through the loudspeakers. My head, empty of its own thoughts, seizes every word.

Afterwards, I don't remember much, though my mind reels in paroxysms of ecstatic agreement. My hands hurt from applauding so enthusiastically, but I can't stop. The Chairman can't see us; it isn't necessary to applaud, but we're doing it anyway. I cheer until my throat's raw, unable to hear my own voice beneath the shrieking crowd, who've risen to their feet to better clap and shout. It doesn't matter that I can remember very little past the measured expression on the Chairman's face and the pictures displayed on the two smaller screens to either side of the larger one—smiling children in Party colors, AA agents standing at attention, citizens in plain clothes raising their fists in camaraderie with their nonhuman animal brethren. After the screens go black, I applaud with the others, trembling, hot, and unsure about what just happened.

In the several minutes it takes for the cheering to die down, the audience looks as disoriented as I feel. Some are rubbing their heads, others their bright red hands. Most women have tears on their cheeks. Even some men do. The crowd begins to file out of the courtyard. The loudspeakers come to life, the triumphant music casting out the awkward silence. I watch people depart, a headache digging in just behind my eyes. The peculiar fervor I feel after such speeches is fading, surrendering room to that that sinking sensation. The black band's tight on my arm. I become aware of the heat and the thick fabric of my dress uniform.

A packmate approaches from across the courtyard, seeking instruction. We have several hours between now and the fireworks display. There are no more structured activities in the courtyard, though citizens can stay to enjoy the ambiance, short films, and light refreshments. Celebration is a long day for an AA agent, but not a hard one. It consists mostly of walking around while hot. After conferring with my packmate, I hurry to begin my patrol as thoughtlessly as possible.

FIFTEEN

I can't get out of my next off-day. I planned to spend it dealing with some recently neglected AA business, but Celebration went well and Third Shift received a mandatory off-day on Sunday. Sup3 usually bends the rules for me, granting me the freedom to work for several months with no time off, but this isn't one of those times. Demerits will follow if I dare report to the Complex.

I wake early and spend the morning on the treadmill, inducing exhaustion with a twelve-mile run. The intense burning in my legs and the too-loud drone of Regime Radio playing on the shelf next to me makes thought impossible. I shower and eat breakfast, then launder, iron, and hang up my uniforms for the week. I tidy my already immaculate apartment. I spend thirty minutes standing at the window repeating cadence. I pass an hour going over Party material and AA training manuals. I attempt to read a chapter from Chairman Goldstein's autobiography, *What it Takes to be Human*, but it barely holds my interest. I fleetingly think of joining my fellow Third Shifters in the downstairs lounge, but the idea fails to appeal to me.

By early afternoon, I've exhausted just about every opportunity for amusement in my flat. Though it's safe here—she's absent—I decide I must get some air. Lara's never been here—I'd never be so careless; there are cameras everywhere, even inside my apartment—but her absence hangs in the stuffy emptiness. I tell myself a walk will do my riotous mind some good, so I leave my building, go directly to the metro station, and take the train across town, my mind miraculously free of thought.

After exiting the train, I follow the trickle of passengers out into the midafternoon sunlight. Lara doesn't work on Sundays, so I go to the deli across from her building for a late lunch. The loudspeaker accompanies me, as always.

Let us celebrate freedom from harm. Violence against nonhuman animals indicates a weak and destructive character. Meat is murder, comrades. Do not hesitate to turn over traitors living in our midst. Tomorrow is another day closer to perfection. All life is sacrosanct.

A new sign decorates the glass door of the deli. *Veganism is for the Civilized*, it reads, with a small PETA logo stamped in one corner. I order a bowl of soup though the weather's mild and sit at the window to watch her building. No one enters or leaves as I empty the bowl in front of me by the spoonful. Not many people are on the street, which is typical for the weekend after Celebration.

I sit back after finishing lunch and coax thought forward—not the solitary loop of reflection that simply whispers her name, but a logical working out of the issue at hand. I know Lara through an unauthorized conversation with the straggler. She's a traitor-sympathizer, if not a full-blown traitor herself. She has possession of unknown amounts of blacklisted materials. I know what needs to be done. Confiscate and destroy the illegal materials. Send her to undergo thought adjustment and reintegration in order to forcibly break and reverse her misplaced sympathies for law-breakers. But before she could go to the Loop, I'd have to turn her in.

I leave the deli and hesitate beneath the loudspeaker, barely hearing it. I should take a train back across town and spend the remainder of the day in my flat. I know this, and still I cross the street and go into her building.

There's a new AA poster in the lobby, black with angry red letters. *Sympathizers Will be Treated as Harshly as Those Breaking the Law.* I look at this for several seconds, wondering if perhaps the agency knows about Lara and this whole unfortunate mess. Impossible. No one else even knows she exists. But they watch. And though I've treaded carefully, incidents like the one outside the courtyard could easily bring disaster.

I climb the stairs to the fifth floor. A black and red ribbon partially obscures the gold numbers on Lara's front door, placed there in observance of Celebration. Only after knocking, do I consider the very real possibility that she might not open the door to me.

"Who is it?" she asks, voice escaping through the crack in the door.

"Me," I say, and wait through a few beats of silence. "Lara, open the door." I could simply kick it in, but that would create more problems than it solved.

"Please go away."

I consider doing as she asks. If I simply leave the building now, we have no reason to ever run into one another again.

"I don't want to see or speak to you," she says, clearly crying now. I think of the softness of her hair and the way she crumpled against me, dependent and trusting. As AA, I'm not meant to touch anyone. But the feel of her against me. How her tears looked on her cheeks. I want to see her once more and then never again.

Minutes pass as I keep my silence and she keeps hers. The corridor's empty, which I count fortunate. I don't want to be seen out here, waiting. When the locks turn over and the door opens, I don't adjust my vacant expression.

Here she is, exasperated and teary. I came in plainclothes but, much like everyone else, she'll only see the AA when she looks at me. I tell myself this is good and necessary. It will make things easier. But the sinking starts deep in my chest and I know I'll miss the open expression she once gifted me along with her trust.

She hangs behind the door, shielding herself. I can see the fear in her eyes, the hesitation. Does she see it in mine? This small-boned girl with the shivering chin shouldn't have any effect on me at all. A blur of nameless, faceless criminals accosted during my career have yelled at, admonished, and cursed me without arousing a single emotion.

"What do you want?" she asks.

I can't answer. I don't know. The art of conversation eludes me.

Her face contorts without becoming ugly. "Did you come here to stare at me? Or to arrest me?"

"No," I say. No one's lingering in the hall, but one never knows who's listening behind closed doors. I step forward, just wanting out of the open before someone notices me.

Lara gasps and jerks back, allowing me passage. I think she might scream, but she only stumbles into the foyer as I close the door and flip over two of the locks. I turn to find her pressed against the wall, her eyes radiant with fright.

"We can't speak in the hall," I say, explaining only because she's so upset, as though I'm the first step in a process that ends with her disappearance. I want to tell her no one knows about the blacklisted books or her sympathies. I'll keep it this way though it compromises my loyalties. She's already lost enough.

She's trembling like a wounded animal, her face so pale against the dark auburn hair hanging over her shoulders. From this distance, the spray of freckles on her nose and cheeks is too light to see. She looks at me and doesn't see honor or integrity. She sees the black clad body of the AA. She sees her father being killed—*murdered*. She sees beatings, heartless, merciless torture, and the unforgiving face of Chairman Goldstein, the agency's Commander-in-Chief.

"Did you murder my father?" she whispers.

"No one murdered him. He knowingly committed a crime punishable by death."

She grimaces. "Did you do it?"

"No."

"Did you capture him at a speakeasy?"

"Yes."

"So you were the catalyst in his death, then?" she asks in a voice best described as heartbroken. It's clear she wants an apology for her abandonment and the straggler can't give one. The next best person is me, only I'm not sorry.

"He was his own catalyst."

Her eyes narrow as she twists arms around her slim torso. "You don't feel any guilt at all?"

"I've done nothing wrong." I attempt to rest my left hand on the butt of a gun that's not on my hip. I tuck my thumb into the pocket of my jeans instead.

"Would you do the same to me?"

"If you committed the same crime, yes."

"What about the blacklisted books?" she asks, expression hardening into defiance.

This bating's unnecessary. "Burn them."

"They belonged to my father."

"Do you wish to share his fate as well as his reading material?" I ask, but don't wait for a response. "You can't keep them, just as you can't continue to voice fellow feeling for those trying to overthrow our government."

"*Our* government?" she asks, incredulous and beautiful, tears streaming but face still so sharp. "It isn't anyone's government. It has a mind and a mission of its own, not working for us but against us. Can't you see that?"

"Such talk is treasonous."

"Only a tyrannical government fears a citizen voicing her opinions."

"Your opinions are incorrect."

"How can an opinion be incorrect? It simply is!" She's absolutely vibrant—the high color in her cheeks, her impassioned speech. We're very similar, only I employ my passion in service of my government and she employs hers against it.

"Sedition used to be called our First Amendment right to freedom of speech," she says. The familiarity of this argument opens a door in my memory. As a young agent, only one person challenged me. She can't know she's resurrecting his arguments, but this doesn't reduce the effect on me. The sucking emptiness expands.

"I shiver in the face of this regime. My father shivered. What about you? Do you shiver?"

Do you weep?

Her eyes flash, confident and intelligent—the straggler's eyes. "Are you familiar with the writings of Jefferson?"

"Familiar enough to know he was blacklisted during Reconstruction."

She sighs, impatient. "Of course he was. Anyone speaking of true liberty is eliminated, even a founding father." She gives a bitter, barking laugh. "My own father was very partial to Jefferson, as he was to any thinker wrestling with ethics and freedom. He thought philosophy should show us how to live a good life." Pain softens her face, but doesn't steal the steam from her argument for long. "Do you know what Jefferson would say about a hypocritical regime that speaks of true freedom being freedom from harm as it murders its own citizens left and right?"

I don't even blink my eyes, lest she consider it a response to her question. Years have passed since I felt it compulsory to defend the laws of my government. I no longer have the patience for it.

"*When people fear their government, there is tyranny. When a government fears its people, there is liberty.*" She smiles knowingly, as though the quote possesses the power to elicit something in me other than disgust. "A government should act as a servant to its people, not the other way around. My father believed this and so do I. But this government…" she pauses, brow furrowed. "This government has always only been our master."

"These words are treacherous, Lara. And dangerous."

"The regime is treacherous. Can't you see that? Don't you care? Or are you so blinded by your post that you—"

"Don't," I say. "I've already broken vows to keep you safe, but I can't continue to shield you from the consequences of this recklessness."

"My father could've used some of your mercy."

"He didn't deserve any and neither do you."

She recoils, blinking, though I haven't advanced a single step. "How dare you—"she begins, voice rising. I cut her off.

"Since you adore the subject of liberty so, I'll speak in terms of it. You don't have the liberty for this brand of seditious folly. Burn the blacklisted books, cease voicing your philosophical arguments, and play the part of a loyal Party member."

Shock has stolen the passionate heat of her expression, but I doubt she's seriously considering what I've said. When a person believes he has the moral high ground, it's impossible to make him see reason. I've tried this once before and it ended badly. I won't do it again with Lara.

At the sight of her shattered and lost, the sinking sensation worsens. Silently, I repeat cadence—*honor when it is easier to do the opposite. Integrity when those around us lack it entirely. Loyalty to those unarmed innocents above all else*—in an attempt to distance myself.

"Is there nothing at all between us?" she asks in a tiny voice.

I stand uncomfortably straight, hands safely in my pockets, cadence on a continual loop in my head. "No."

Her blue eyes move over my face in the ensuing silence. I've never felt such a weighty pause between words. I think of my empty flat where I go for hours without making a sound. I accepted loneliness as my lot in life years ago, but never has it affected me so. I am the black clad body of the AA. I am emptiness and violence, law and order. Closeness can't exist in the aftermath of selfless service. It isn't a matter of not wanting touch, but of no longer possessing the ability. The memory remains, but the how-to, the understanding, is lost.

"Why?" she whispers, the word a delicate surrender, an appeal made only to me. Some small part of her must understand the straggler broke the law, but his disappearance snatched the traction from her. The hungry look in her eyes tells me that she expects me to set her right again. "Why does it have to be like this?"

I keep my face blank, giving bewilderment no chance to rise to the surface. "I'm AA."

Inexorably seized by her confusion, her defeat, that sinking sensation metastasizes so it's no longer confined to my chest or stomach. Now it feels like I'm slowly falling through the floor. The pain in her eyes is enough to annihilate a weaker man's resolve.

Honor when it is easier to do the opposite.

"Is that all that matters?" she asks. "The AA?"

Integrity when those around us lack it entirely.

"For me," I say.

Loyalty to those unarmed innocents above all else.

I can see she doesn't understand—not many do—and this is surprising. Like me, the straggler placed his beliefs above all else. It's what drew me to him in the first place—that he was willing to die for his convictions—though his actions disgusted me. Lara must not have understood that either.

"And for me?" she asks, chin trembling, and it isn't only the weaker man whose resolve would crumble at this.

I reach for the gun at my hip. Not there. I repeat silent cadence until my wayward thoughts evaporate.

"Lara—"I say, but she cuts in.

"My father's gone," she says, and her body convulses as though a terrible pain shot through her. "But he sent you."

I shake my head but it doesn't stop her from going on.

"And you've done horrible things."

If she only knew the half of it.

"I don't care." She shakes her head hard, the way a child does. "I mean, I do, but we're linked now."

"No," I say.

"We could have each other to take care of, to depend on," she says, blue eyes shimmering with teary hope. "My father was all I had. But he's gone and here you are."

"No."

"The regime isn't awful because it attacks its citizens or devalues the human animal. The real horror is how it keeps us from connecting with one another. Companionship is dead. Trust and love is a distant memory. I had all that with my father. I thought, maybe, with you—"

"No," I say again.

She succumbs to harsh sobs while I watch, frozen, expressionless, unsure of what to do. Repeating cadence doesn't help. I think to speak comfort to her, but the words won't come. My mind's clogged with Party credos and agency speech. Here she is before me, heartbroken, human, and I can only watch, the black clad body of the AA, an automaton with no heart beating in its chest.

"Why did you come at all?" she asks. "Did you think you owed him? Owed me?"

"I owed no one. I was curious."

"But he asked you to come and you did."

I nod though she didn't ask a question.

"Why did you come today?"

I speak without hesitation, but don't tell her the complete truth—that I wanted to see her, to hear her voice one last time.

"You needed the warning."

Her eyes harden. "I told you how I felt because I trusted you. I had no idea you were…" The look on her face makes plain what she thinks I am—one of *them*. "Report me if that's what you need to do. I won't hide the books or my opinions." She lifts her quivering chin, defiant as ever.

"I have no intention of turning you in," I say. She seems completely unaware that implicating her shines unwanted light on my own actions, which is fortunate.

"I trusted you," she whispers.

"I gave you no cause to do so."

She smiles sadly. "No."

Time to leave. I flip over the locks while she watches me. I step through the door and she calls me by name. I shudder at the sound of it but turn to face her again.

"What happens now?" she asks.

The sinking sensation worsens, throbbing at my temples, demolishing cadence when I try play the words in my head.

"You forget I exist," I say. "And I'll do the same for you."

I leave before she can draw me in with the compelling magic of her words, her sobs chasing me through the hall. I charge down five flights stairs, the momentum carrying me out onto the street. Lara's living room window faces this direction. If I turned, I might catch her watching me.

I walk, ignoring the loudspeaker and the people on the sidewalk, focusing instead on my footsteps and repeating cadence. Once safely seated on the near-empty train bound for my side of the city, I huff a relieved sigh. Perhaps now my life can return to normal.

SIXTEEN

Third Shift has another off-day on Monday, this one voluntary. I didn't sleep well the night before, so early morning finds me already situated at my desk. Behind me, a gym bag stuffed with uniforms and toiletries. I think it best to spend the next several days getting my head straight, and hours of unbroken poring over AA business or sweating in the gym usually does the trick.

Third Shift packs occupy several floors, with only the most elite on floor one ten. Today, the floor is barren, as is my old packroom. I'll leave my desk here—Sup3 did the same when he became Shift supervisor—instead of moving to the office now at my disposal. Sup3 used the space for storage and I suppose I'll do the same. This pack will always be special to me, and the chatter of the other boys keeps unfortunate thoughts at bay. I also generally enjoy being around them. The camaraderie between AA agents is the only kind of solidarity available to me anymore. But there's a potential downside to my staying in the packroom. If Deux's behavior during Celebration is any indication of the future, my mere presence will routinely usurp his authority. I never had this trouble with Sup3, though I too was young when I took over as senior pack leader. Worse comes to worse, I can always move to the office at the end of the hall. Being alone most of the day wouldn't be the worst thing. Solitude suits me. And I'd get so much more work done without the distraction of the other boys.

I have my reports filed and packroom tidied before the sun begins to show its muted colors on the horizon. I watch for a moment before bending over another stack of files, my measured breathing, the scrawling of pen on paper, the tap of computer keys working like white noise.

The silent morning drapes a blanket of calm over me that directs my thoughts away from my tired, achy body and niggling turmoil. AA business sets me straight, gives me control over both mind and body, the agency offering me exactly what I offer it—consistency, loyalty—as long as I serve its purpose.

The morning and most of the afternoon disappear in a flurry of work. I only realize the lunch hour has come and gone when the janitor walks by with the buffer, filling the corridor with droning noise. The janitorial staff knows my habit of working late and alone. They won't attempt to clean the packroom until I've left.

A few hours later, I go to the cafeteria, ravenously hungry. I purchase a few items and return to the packroom to eat. Afterwards, I work late into the evening before falling into a dreamless sleep at my desk.

When I start awake hours before sunset, she is my first thought.

I go to the gym, run on the treadmill until I can barely remain standing, and hobble to the showers. I return to the packroom, prepared to do it all over again.

*

Less than forty-eight hours after the voluntary off-day, I move my things into the empty office down the hall set aside for the Shift super. I do this without giving Deux a bit of notice. He might ask me not to leave. I don't believe I made a mistake in choosing him as my replacement, but his reliance on the authority my mere presence fosters can't continue. With luck, moving will solve this little dilemma. If not, I'll have to appoint a different senior pack leader, which would reflect poorly on both of us.

Funnily enough, I actually prefer the office. It's smaller than the packroom, but eight of us shared that space, if you count Sup3, who was there most of the week. I have a large desk, a couch—much nicer accommodations than the rickety cot back in the packroom—a radio, and a television. The picture window behind the desk opens the office to the city beyond. My thoughts revolve around her as the planets do the sun, but the office is my own. I don't even feel the gaping hole that is her absence. Truth be told, I don't feel anything at all. I set my mind to work and go for hours without a rebel thought interrupting my progress.

At noon, a knock at the door tosses me out of the steady rhythm of my work.

"Yes?" I say.

Deux opens the door but seems hesitant to enter the office. I don't speak to alleviate his distress. I was enjoying the solitude. This sudden spike of anger at being burst in upon concerns me. My emotions have never been much of a problem—not even in earliest childhood—but AA training taught me to control my passions so well they now lie completely dormant, no longer even threatening to ignite unless needed—on a raid, for example. I put my anger away, extinguishing it as easily as I would the flame of a tiny candle. I must watch this. Operatives who can't control their emotions don't last long.

Deux hangs in the doorway, an odd look on his face. Any other agent would've already begun to brief me on his predicament, but Deux's young. I gesture for him to come in or get on with it.

"The boys are on the brink of mutiny," he says, wringing his hands, showing me nothing but the top of his blonde head. His nervousness invades the room, expelling the peace and eradicating my patience. Holding firm to a blank expression, I wait for him to continue. His eyes flick briefly to mine before retreating to the floor. "They aren't happy with the pack assignment."

A dull spark of rage ignites in me at this. All Third Shift packs are on neighborhood watch per my orders. Intelligence hasn't given us anything definitive since before Celebration. Yes, high profile assignments are exciting—rounding up traitors, kicking in doors, burning down speakeasies—but they only represent a small percentage of the job. Most of our work involves simply walking the streets, letting the AA presence be known. No assignment, no matter how dull, gives a man the right to question the authority of a senior agent.

"Tell me who." I say.

Deux's face loosens with gratitude as he recites several agent numbers.

I stride past him and down the hall. A torrent of angry voices welcomes me to the packroom. The boys fall silent as soon as they notice me standing against the wall. I motion for Deux to shut the door. None of the boys will meet my eyes.

"I understand there's a problem with the pack assignment," I say loudly, speaking as I might to a room full of traitors. I love every man in this room for his selfless service and loyalty to the agency, but right now I consider them all subversives. No one questions authority. No one. As far as these boys are concerned, an order from Deux is no different than one from the AA Chairman himself.

I look at the man closest to me, engaging him against his will. "Do you have a problem with the pack assignment?"

He shakes his head, eyes pinned to the double A's of my armband. He isn't one of the boys Deux identified. Three of the six members of the pack—I filled the open position immediately after Celebration—voiced complaints, but this doesn't make the others innocent. The new man—I rescued him from the monotony of Intelligence work one short week ago based on his agency test scores, physical fitness report, and class placement in initial training—can't shoulder the same amount of blame as the other two, who remained silent when the agitators attempted to undermine Deux's authority. An AA agent follows rules unquestioningly, never challenging authority or disobeying a direct order. The regime encourages solidarity, but only amongst the law-abiding. Subversives deserve neither friendly consideration nor camaraderie. I love these men, but would turn in any one of them at the slightest sign of treachery. I'd expect them to do the same to me.

Lara, my mind whispers, the hypocrisy thick enough to taste. But that's different. And things have ended between us, if they even started to begin with.

"Who does have a problem?" I ask. After no one speaks or meets my eyes, I recite the three agent numbers and look around, skull pulsing with a headache slowly reaching its pinnacle. The smoking embers of my anger reignite. This is Deux's job, not mine. I should be in my office, listening to Regime Radio and working through the tall stack of files on my desk in unmolested peace.

"Mark those numbers," I say. "You boys have just received three demerits for insubordination."

No one dares to speak a solitary syllable.

"That means three weeks of mandatory P.T. to clear those demerits."

A few mouths draw into tight lines. A couple pairs of eyebrows rise, then draw together as though their owners are undergoing torture. This is painful, only not for them. Sup3 never reprimanded the pack on my behalf in all the years I commanded it. I shouldn't do it for Deux, but I still believe he can lead these men if I quash this small rebellion before it goes any further.

"Insubordination will not be tolerated," I say, and the boys nod their vigorous agreement. "If this happens a second time, I'll triple the demerits." Any agent carrying five demerits in a single quarter must report immediately to the Bureau of Thought Reform. These forced periods of reeducation last roughly one to three weeks. Afterwards, if he is able, the agent returns to his post. Too much time at the Loop can break a person, leaving him unfit for government service.

I glance at Deux and am relieved. In his steady gaze, I glimpse a bit of the man I saw on raids, the one I trusted as my second in command. His light eyes shine with renewed confidence, as though he simply lost his way but has once again found it.

Deux gives the men a stern expression. "Are we clear, comrades?"

The boys answer in the affirmative.

I leave the packroom without another word.

*

I work doggedly for the remainder of the afternoon, skipping lunch and keeping my head steady with the sound of my own breathing. I file reports. I investigate several possible assignments from Intelligence. I write up Third Shift pack assignments for the following week. In the late afternoon, I take a short break to stare at the city whilst repeating cadence, a loop that lasts five minutes. Then I get back to work.

Hours later, the sun sets, but I don't turn to see it. I'm organizing a meeting for my Third Shift senior pack leaders when someone knocks on my door for the second time today.

Sup3 comes in before I can respond and closes the door behind him. This means he intends to have a serious discussion. I don't offer him a chair. If it suits him, he'll sit. He hovers near the door for a single beat too long. I know him. He'd like to lock the door, but this is my office and he has always respected my authority and autonomy.

"Do you like the office?" He has the weathered expression of a man run ragged.

I nod once. "Staying in the packroom was compromising Deux's authority."

We watch each other for another moment. Sup3 doesn't do this often, but when he does, I know he's about to question a recent decision of mine.

He inhales deeply before getting on with what he came out of his way to say to me. His new office is three floors up. As Blue Shift super, he has a larger set of responsibilities with which to occupy his time, leaving little reason to be on floor one ten, especially at this late hour.

"Why did three agents receive demerits this morning?"

"Insubordination," I say, but don't elaborate.

Sup3 moves his right index finger in a small circle, meaning I should continue.

"Those men questioned the day's pack assignment. Deux came to me. He used the word *mutiny*."

"And you felt it necessary to intervene?"

"Insubordination cannot be tolerated," I say simply.

"I agree. But perhaps Deux should've given the demerits."

My inner workings hum, serenely devoid of anger. I understand his purpose now. This is my first disciplinary action as Third Shift super. He's testing me.

"He wasn't in a position to do so," I say.

Sup3 lifts a dark eyebrow. "Does that concern you?"

"No. My immediate action reinstated his authority. I don't foresee any further problems."

"What if these demerits resulted in one of your former packmates being remanded to the Loop?" he asks.

"So be it."

As senior pack leader, I never allowed my men to ride above a single demerit. Anything more meant mandatory P.T. Directly before my promotion, I shifted to a zero tolerance rule for my packmates, meaning no agent was to have a demerit on his record unless actively engaging in P.T. I plan to make this the rule for the all of Third Shift, which I'll announce at my first official meeting as Shift super. I imagine this will upset a number of agents, as those above the zero demerit cutoff will need to report to daily physical training immediately.

Sup3 gives the small smile that means he's pleased with me. This is the man to whom I am closest, and yet we aren't very close at all.

"You never disappoint. Watch Deux closely." He doesn't need to say the rest. If the boys question Deux's authority again, he'll need to be replaced. I don't expect this, but already have a replacement in mind and a plan for Deux—I'd send him to Intelligence.

Sup3 appraises my office, taking note of the bare walls—save the one in front of my desk, adorned with a large poster of the Party Chairman—and lack of personal effects.

"You're authorized to move to EQ now," he says. EQ is short for Executive Quarters. These two buildings are farther away from the Complex than the Dormitories, but accommodate fewer agents in single rooms much bigger than the ones at the barracks, large enough, in fact, to house a family, though no agents have them. AA agents don't take vows of celibacy—we aren't pre-regime priests—but we do pledge to live a single life that precludes marriage and procreation. Many agents date openly, some even have long-term relationships. I don't see the point in this. Relationships merely supply an unnecessary weakness in an otherwise competent agent, another distraction that interferes with the mission. Most of these relationships end up failing anyway. No civilian can truly understand what it takes to wear AA black—the things we do, the hours we keep, our solitary natures, our fierce loyalty to the regime. A smart agent simply learns to accept the necessary loss of touch that comes with the job. It takes a special breed of human animal to pledge his life to such work. I know many competent agents, but very few possess the passion essential to do the job well. Sup3 possess such passion, as do I. In all my time with the agency, I've remained single, never initiating a relationship with anyone, be it a girlfriend, a fellow comrade, or what family might remain to me—I'm not exactly sure who's still living. For this reason, I couldn't keep pretending with Lara. I can't be friendly or open, not just with her, but with anyone.

"You only need to report to the housing office for a room assignment," Sup3 says. He moved to EQ shortly after taking the post I now hold. The housing office is on floor two along with all the offices handling administrational matters—payroll, housing, relocation, clothing orders, etcetera.

I nod, though I have no interest in moving. It seems an unnecessary headache, especially considering that I barely possess enough belongings to warrant my one bedroom flat in the Dormitories. I care nothing for material goods. My life is the AA. I need little more than uniforms and some regime-endorsed reading material to make me a content little comrade. A two or three room flat at EQ would be wasted on someone like me. The only obvious bonus to moving might be the ambiance. I'm likely to be one of the youngest, least decorated agents in both EQ buildings, thus the incessant partying that goes on in the Dormitories would be minimal, if it occurs at all. What a welcome change to live in complete silence. But barrack rooms are issued according to seniority, meaning I'd probably receive a flat on the first or second floor. At Lib. Hall, I have a room on the top floor and my lovely view of the city is the sole thing I covet. But my office has an even nicer view, so I could probably survive a second floor flat for a few years while I climb the AA ladder. Still, I'll probably wait to move until my rank makes living in EQ compulsory.

The communicator on Sup3's belt vibrates. He unclips it and reads the message flashing on the screen. He taps the screen a few times, eyes moving rapidly from left to right, and snaps it back onto his belt.

"It's going to be another long night" he says, and leaves without waiting for a response.

I sigh as the door closes and return to work.

SEVENTEEN

Winter in the Capitol City is like the regime itself—cold, unfeeling, yet beautiful in spite of all this. I enjoy the season's coarse cruelty. The temperatures dip so low, they become as deadly as an AA agent. Never particularly susceptible to freezing weather, the bitterness of winter has suited me since childhood.

Every season is busy for the AA, but winter sets us all scrambling. Cold weather means a decrease in outdoor regime-sponsored activities. A decrease in outdoor activities means an increase in leisure time. Citizens with too much free time often come up with unwholesome ways to fill it. Fortunately, the regime provides a variety of extra activities to keep a citizen's plate full as soon as the weather begins to cool. Social and political groups, additional forums, athletic exhibitions, city and nationwide pride events, and compulsory physical training. Add in a job or school, and a person's day is packed full from morning until voluntary curfew goes into effect.

Winter changes AA agents as much as it does civilians. The cold weather flips a switch in an operative, initiating hibernation mode, rendering them sluggish and bleary-eyed. Decreased sunlight encourages sloppiness and lethargy. Sup3 compensated for this by taking away the better part of his subordinates' leisure time. I do the same. For month eleven, I put Third Shift on mandatory P.T. After the start of month twelve, physical training will increase to twice per twenty-four hour period, including off-days.

As soon as the cold weather sets in, I see a spike in disciplinary actions. Still in the nascent stages of my supervisory position, I don't hesitate to take a firm hand, doling out punishments for even the smallest of offenses. This doesn't increase my popularity, but does earn me the respect of my subordinates. Respect equals obedience. I'm determined to make Third Shift—specifically floor one ten and, even more specifically, my old pack—the most obedient, the most physically fit, and the most productive. In this way, I also eliminate most of my own leisure time.

*

I leave the Complex well after voluntary curfew and step out into the bitter cold. I enjoy this walk regardless of the season, but especially in winter. There's just something lovely about my breath wafting out thick as smoke, the crisp air breaking over my cheeks, reddening them, the tingling numbness in my toes, fingers, and the tip of my nose. In winter, I experience the truth of my existence—I freeze, therefore I am. I like to plunge through chilly streets with my head down, repeating cadence while my steps keep rhythm—*honor when it is easier to do the opposite. Integrity when those around us lack it entirely. Loyalty to those unarmed innocents above all else.*

Warmth seems to radiate through the armband, allowing me to disregard the numb and tingling fingers in my AA issue winter gloves and the frozen feet in my cold weather boots. At my core lies the passion that has keep me warm since I signed my name on that dotted line, pledging my remaining days and nights, the cells in my body, the breath in my lungs.

I walk slowly, in no hurry to reach Lib. Hall despite the high wind. It's very late by the time I approach the vicinity of the small cluster of buildings that make up the Dormitories. In between repeating loops of cadence, I think of the scalding hot shower I'll take once inside.

At a distance of a few hundred meters, I spot a cloaked figure hunched directly beside the sidewalk that snakes along the courtyard between all four barracks buildings, dividing it in half. I quickly conceal myself behind an exaggerated storefront. My initial alarm elevated my heartbeat, but this surprise smoothly melts into calculation. I chance another glance at the dark figure.

This loitering individual's out hours past voluntary curfew, which isn't in itself cause for suspicion—many citizens work late hours, though they wouldn't simply loiter in the street at the close of their shifts—but the hooded cloak hiding his face certainly is, along with his position directly outside the entrance to the Dormitories courtyard. Civilians have no business hanging about idle anywhere— regime law strictly forbids it—but in particular around government buildings and lodging facilities.

I creep back in the direction I came, sliding through the storefronts' thick shadows and keeping my eye on the mysterious figure. After voluntary curfew, the city's streetlights go dim to save power. Between the lack of light and my uniform, I become darkness. This person, whoever he is, can't be a professional. Only a novice would take such care to conceal body and face beneath an elaborate cloak while boldly standing beneath a streetlight in full view of AA lodgings.

I slip into a nearby alley and dash soundlessly to the street parallel. The barracks courtyard has two entrances—one behind my mystery man, the other on the opposite street. Before leaving the alley, I poke my head around the corner to make certain a second man isn't staking out this entryway. Finding no one, I run to the other entrance and dissolve into the shadows of the courtyard.

Whilst negotiating the terrain, I remove my gun from its holster. I just cleaned it the evening before. If fired, I'd have to clean it again, but that would give me something to do in the early hours after sleep abandons me.

I approach, moving silently at top speed. My mystery man becomes aware of my presence only when I press the gun into the back of his head. He's quite a few inches shorter than I am.

"It's after curfew, comrade," I say. "And these are government lodgings. Explain your purpose."

He gasps, the sound unexpectedly feminine. This is a mystery woman. I holster my weapon, tear the cloak back, and spin her around by the shoulder. I have to swallow my own gasp.

Lara.

The furiously swishing heartbeat in my ears steals the words from my mouth. She gazes up at me, blue eyes darker than usual, expression a mix of fear and relief. Beneath my hand, she's shivering hard, her teeth chattering. I break physical contact still struggling to catch my breath. Her vitality is just as real to me as the breath shooting from her lips in jagged, seemingly painful bursts.

I take her by the arm, ignoring her bird-like cry, and drag her into the much less conspicuous courtyard where the shadows conceal us. As soon as I release her, she takes a step away from me.

"I'm in trouble," she whispers.

I glance around the courtyard, combing it for movement. Nothing. Some lights are on in the surrounding buildings, but most drapes are pulled closed over windows. We're alone, for now.

"Why did you come here?" My words aren't cold, but neither are they toasty. It's been months. Clearing my head of her was an excruciating process that took many hours of working, repeating cadence, exercising to the point of passing out, and little else. Now that my head has returned to my control, here she is.

Her face contorts at the lack of warmth in my comment and I feel that familiar sinking sensation. Not just in the pit of my stomach, but deeper, spreading so it envelopes my entire body. In an attempt to steel myself, I focus on the freezing air burning my lungs, which keeps a lid on my rising alarm.

"I didn't know where else to turn," she says.

"I can't help you."

"But don't you even want to know what's wrong?"

"I can't help you."

The words burst out of her in a strained whisper, "*I'm wanted by the AA!*"

"Lara, I am the AA."

She begins to sob then—as if she didn't know this—not loudly enough to attract attention, though I realize it could escalate very shortly if I don't mind what I say next and how I say it.

"Explain," I say, voice flat and comfortless. This interest in her situation visibly calms her. I need to encourage her to leave as soon as possible. It's only a matter of time before someone happens by.

"I overslept," she sputters, wiping her tears, more impatient than embarrassed. Thanks to the dark, I can't properly decipher the tragic look so at home in her large, expressive eyes that only makes the sinking worse. It also makes me want to touch her, which is no way to be thinking.

"I overslept," she says again. "It made me late for work and my boss came looking for me."

I bristle at mention of the proprietress. No surprise that she has some involvement in all this. I never took action against her, feeling it would only exacerbate the severity of my misconduct to condemn a woman guilty of little more than being fantastically unpleasant to a round of reeducation at the Loop. Those flexing their power unwarrantedly are no better than those routinely breaking the law. Still, I can't help but think that if I'd only taken care of the proprietress, Lara wouldn't be standing here right now expecting help from me.

"I fell asleep on the couch. She has a key to the door, in case." She waves her hand instead of explaining in case of what. "She found me in the living room. I'd been reading." She stares at her feet as my jaw tightens. "Thoreau. The book had fallen on the floor and slid almost all the way underneath the coffee table. She wouldn't have even seen it if she hadn't stepped on the corner. She reached to pick it up and threw it down again, like it was poison."

I almost tell her that, according to Party laws, it *is* poison. On the wall behind her, a rather large poster of the Party Chairman silently reproves me for holding my tongue, but the last thing I want to do is start her crying again. The game we played for weeks—the one that merely obliterated my focus but caused us no real danger—is over. Having attracted the attention of the AA, she stands before me as good as dead. According to agency protocol, I'm duty-bound to take her into immediate custody.

"I begged her not to turn me in, told her the books belonged to my father and I couldn't bear destroying them." Her streaming tears catch the dim light and sparkle on her cheeks. "She laughed in my face and said she was calling the authorities."

Another inappropriate flare of anger sears my insides. To extinguish it, I go over the facts. Lara was warned. She's an adult and responsible for her own actions, regardless of the straggler's negative influence. The proprietress is simply performing her civic duty. It doesn't matter how much satisfaction it gives her.

"I panicked and ran. I went to the park across town where my father and I—"she can't continue until the fury of her rising sobs calms. "I stayed there all day, convincing myself she'd keep my secret. I've worked for her since I was a teenager. So I went home."

It seems Lara is one big lapse in judgment. I knew the proprietress back to front upon our first meeting.

"I was down the street from my building when I saw them." She drops her voice, leans in. "*AA agents.*" Blinking, she straightens, as though once again viciously slapped by the reality of my uniform, armband, and weapon. Her eyes hesitate on my chest, and I wonder if my new rank is flashing in the weak light. Or perhaps she senses the sinking feeling her presence causes in me.

"There were two agents outside and I could see at least one more in my living room window. I ran." She breaks down again, weeping into her hands.

I wait as long as I can, giving her the opportunity to calm down on her own before I hurry her along. "When did this happen?"

She wipes her eyes as she answers. "Five days ago."

"What has transpired from that day to this?" I ask. I expected her to tell me all this happened earlier today. This unexpected resourcefulness both intrigues and annoys me. If she can survive on her own, why is she clinging to me?

"I know of a few safehouses. From my father."

This is the most interesting thing she's said all night. Intelligence has long suspected the existence of safehouses—traitors have to go somewhere once wanted by the AA—but has never had a confirmed report of one. Travel in and out of the Capitol City is impossible without an identity card. Places must exist where wanted criminals can lay low while waiting for forged papers and safe passage outside the city and then the country. Receiving confirmation of not just one safehouse but *a few* is thrilling. It's a challenge to restrain myself from burying Lara beneath a deluge of probing questions.

"I could only stay a night or two in each location. There's no getting out of the city right now. I don't know what I'll do once I exhaust my resources."

"Where are these safehouses?" I ask, keeping the words casual. Information of this caliber could mitigate the damage caused by this nonsense. Finding and obliterating these safehouses might redeem me for this long string of indiscretions.

"All over. There are a few of them in every borough of the city."

I silently repeat cadence twice before asking another question. *One or two in every borough.* Not seeming overly eager is key.

"What happens at these places?" I ask.

"They provide safety for those wanted by the AA as well as a way out of the city." She watches me for several moments. "Should I leave?"

If she were anyone else, she'd already be in a kill room.

"If you want to live," I say. This clandestine existence won't resemble the life of privilege one enjoys here in the Capitol City, or anywhere else in our lush, successful regime. If one escapes the AA—which I personally feel is impossible to do forever—the only way of life left open involves going underground or, worse, out of the country and into the heathen wild.

She drops her shoulders. "I'm afraid."

"You should've disposed of the blacklisted materials."

She doesn't respond.

"How did you find me?"

"I asked a man at one of the safehouses. I told him I needed to get in touch with an AA agent I knew, a friend, and asked where to look apart from the Complex."

I clench my teeth against hot, rising fury. "You compromised us both by coming here."

"No," she says, shaking her head. "I didn't mention your name. I didn't mention anything about you. I only said you were AA."

"And you don't see the danger in that?"

"I didn't have anywhere else to turn. The people at the safehouses are kind, but they don't know me. You're all I have. And you made a vow to my father."

My rage, already sizzling with her easy, thoughtless audacity, expands until it fills my entire body, making muscles rigid and breaths pointedly shallow.

"I have but one vow and that's to the AA." I don't stop, though she starts to cry again. She'll have us both remanded to the Loop over her precious Thoreau and Spinoza. "I've been well within my rights to execute you for months, or at the very least take you into custody. I can't say what exactly stayed my hand, but that hesitation ends now. Whether or not you mind my advice to leave the Capitol City is of no concern to me, but you must never attempt to contact me again."

She lifts her chin defiantly. "Execute me then. What good is it to live if I have no one?"

"No one has anything but his resolve and his undying love of order and law."

"It doesn't have to be so lonely. You could come with me."

"No." I've taken part in a dance like this once before. My mind wanders before I can snap it neatly back into place, summoning the shrill screams of my mother at the sight of me covered in blood and the way my father pushed me out the door, as though I might attack the two of them next.

She touches the double A's on my armband with her long fingers. I have to swallow the impulse to step away from her.

"This is the most important thing to you," she says, the resignation in her voice both encouraging and excruciating. "More important than companionship? Than love?"

"I gave my life to the AA. I can't just take it back."

I rest my left hand on the butt of my weapon. It would only take one clean shot to end this mess right here and now. I'm very quick. I excelled at marksmanship in training, but it would hardly take an accomplished sharpshooter to get a clean shot at such close range. She wouldn't feel a thing and my difficulties would come to an end. Win, win.

My fingers twitch on the gun. No one would even question my actions. A civilian poking around on government property—a *wanted* citizen. All I would need to do is fabricate a convincing story of why I found it necessary to kill her. It wouldn't even need to that convincing, truth be told. The AA doesn't care what happens to people once they've defected.

"Don't you care for me?" she asks.

"Anyone else would be dead or in the Loop at this moment." I drop my hand from the gun. "You shouldn't have run. Your crime didn't warrant execution, only reeducation. You could've explained away ownership of the books."

She issues a tired little laugh. "And torture's so much better than being killed?"

"Reeducation would've allowed you to have your life back."

People are bound to be along shortly. I have to end this, but not the way I know how. And Lara's right—I made a promise to the straggler and, for some reason, feel oddly compelled to honor it. I haven't considered another person in years. I'm sure I did it before my enlistment, but the AA has a way of making one fall completely inside it. Once in, the present becomes all that exists, which fosters an all-enveloping loyalty that obliterates past action unless beneficial to the task at hand. After training, all but the fuzziest memories of my past disintegrated. I never fought it. The past is useless—it's what the regime says it is. The future is but a flickering mirage on the horizon, always changeable. The present is all that matters.

"I can't be alone," she whispers.

I don't share this weakness, nor do I possess the tools with which to comfort her. We stand a foot apart, but it might as well be several hundred miles.

I speak only because it's clear she means to stand there staring expectantly with her mouth agape.

"I can't compromise my position in the agency any further."

"I had to see you."

"And you've done so." The cold's freezing the marrow of my bones. Silently, I repeat cadence. I'll say it hundreds of times in the dark emptiness of my flat after I hustle her out of here. I'll erase all traces of her existence inside my head with Party credos and late nights spent at the Complex, piling on exhaustion. This ends now. If she doesn't leave voluntarily, I'll draw my weapon and make the decision for her.

She swallows audibly. "And if I want to see you again?"

I don't hesitate with my answer, though I don't know if it's true. "I'll execute you on the spot."

She flinches, gasping and shaking her head. I regret everything. This is as new a feeling as the sucking absence violating the tenderest parts of me, and one I could've gone without remembering. I should've shot the straggler on sight. I should've let him burn to death with the others.

The step she takes away from me puts the poster of the Chairman between us. This reflects life as it should be—the two of us on opposite sides of the spectrum—the one who keeps law and the one who breaks it. I can hardly blame Lara for all this. It was my error in judgment, not hers. As such, I must be the one to correct it.

"What you believed to exist between us is over," I say, body as rigid as my voice despite the unbearable cold. My extremities and face are numb and tingling, but I have to show her a front as decisive and solid as my resolve.

Lara crosses her arms, breath floating on the winter air. Now at the edge of the wall, a shard of light cuts across her face, revealing trembling lips and one reddened cheek. The light also turns one of her eyes a vibrant, unnatural blue, eerily iridescent. I know I ought to leave before she opens her shivering mouth and spins a web to trap me, but I'm in that chasm that exists between the understanding of a thing and the actual doing.

"What did you think was between us?" she asks, voice as tender as an apology.

I can't clarify exactly how I feel about her, but the fact that I do feel something—sinking or otherwise—is a problem.

"Enough for me to advise you to leave the Capitol City instead of taking you into custody." I pause, but not for long. "And even that's too much."

When her tears start—much worse than before—I grow acutely mindful of where we are, the windows lit all around us, the hundreds of agents that could happen upon us at any moment.

I spin away from her, hunching my shoulders into the bracing wind, and walk across the frozen courtyard, my crunching footsteps and her weeping the only sounds in the dark. If she chooses to remain here, the AA will apprehend her. I don't worry about her implicating me. She knows my first name, but that's very little in itself, certainly nothing remarkable.

Walking into Lib Hall, I don't glance back at the large windows to either side of the entrance doors. Cameras are everywhere, including the dorm rooms. I have enough understanding of AA surveillance to know cameras in private residences are only watched a few minutes out of every day. Common areas—the streets or halls, lobbies, and waiting rooms of buildings—are of more interest to the government. The average citizen doesn't know this. They believe the posters that tell them the AA is *always* watching.

Once in my room on the top floor, I repeat cadence in an even, flat voice, letting the rhythm soothe me. I peel off my uniform and shower, making the water as hot as I can stand and then making it hotter. I scrub my skin raw, then dress and turn out the lights. I sit alone in the dark, repeating cadence. The steady sound of my voice carries me through, unthinking, until morning.

EIGHTEEN

Over the next few weeks, I avoid my flat altogether, spending nights at the Complex, all to ensure I don't run into Lara again. Fortunately, we have the work to warrant these long nights, not that anyone ever enquires into my habit of spending days at a time in my office. As Third Shift super, Sup3 didn't allow agents more than a few consecutive nights at the Complex. He was lenient with me because he knew I truly used the time to work, but even I couldn't spend more than five nights in the packroom unless compelled to do so. But now I control that particular aspect of my schedule.

I spend this extra time pulling together information on the possible existence of safehouses gathered from agency reports filed over the past ten years. No one has ever undertaken such a broad investigation. It takes many hours of scouring reports, taking detailed notes, and cross-referencing hundreds of facts gleaned from interrogations and witness statements to begin to make significant headway. According to reports filed by numerous interrogators on the Kill Floor, quite a few traitors have mentioned safehouses. I reread the transcripts of these interrogations to the point of memorization, then connect bits of promising information from reports originating from packs on a variety of floors, Intelligence as well as Enforcement.

After two straight weeks of late nights, I've exhausted every resource available to the AA. I move on to other agencies, combing their databases, searching for any mention of safehouses and underground ways out of the city. Unfortunately, I only have limited access to reports originating from outside the AA. I'll need Sup3's approval to lay hands on anything more, but I don't want to involve him just yet. For now, I want to travel this road alone. It might not lead anywhere. If it does, I'll involve my chain of command.

I draw detailed charts and fill a notebook with notes, diagrams, and musings. I spend long hours staring thoughtfully into the face of the Party Chairman. I hang a map on the wall and plot possible points, first marking the spots of all confirmed speakeasies located in the past eleven years. It seems illogical to have a safehouse in close proximity to a speakeasy, so I eliminate those areas. I focus on the borough in which Lara lived. No confirmed speakeasy sites in that neighborhood during the entire history of the regime. It would be a choice spot for a safehouse or two. It also makes sense that Lara would know about safehouses in the immediate area of her flat.

By the end of a month of long nights and days, I have several probable areas marked upon the map, and not just in Lara's borough. At least this one silver lining has come from the giant storm cloud that was Lara's intrusion on my otherwise orderly, predictable life.

I'm duty-bound to turn all leads over to Intelligence, much as I'd rather continue investigating on my own. So I compile a detailed report and shoot it up the AA ladder.

*

The role of senior pack leader has begun to suit Deux. The boys have bent to his will as their superior with little need of serious disciplinary action. The typical boundary testing occurred initially, as it does whenever power changes hands—showing up late to morning roll call, whispering to a packmate instead of keeping silent while the pack leader's talking, mumbled retorts when sealed lips are more appropriate. I was even younger than Deux when I became pack leader, and so went through all this myself. Others misconstrue youth as weakness and attempt to exploit it. But adequate motivation can overcome all obstacles, even lack of experience. To offset the handicap of my youth, I became harsher in tone and manner, building a reputation for giving out severer punishments than my elder AA colleagues. It didn't take long to see results.

Deux seems to be following my example, at times becoming a mere carbon copy of me as senior pack leader. Once he's earned his packmates' respect and unwavering loyalty, he'll have the liberty to cultivate a leadership style that suits him. My own style never changes. I stay consistently harsh, though not unfairly so. Deux seems to favor a more diplomatic route. He's quick to poll his subordinates for ideas, a kind of testing of the waters before selecting a course of action. I attribute this idealism to two things—his youth and the fact that he joined the AA well after Reconstruction. Spared the hard, bloody work, he has only ever seen the maintenance aspect of the agency, not the side that had to topple the preceding government and bring resistant citizens around by violent force. But despite his various weaknesses—youth being the chief among them—I have no doubt Deux will grow into a highly capable leader.

*

It's been weeks since I slept in my flat, but Sup3 doesn't interfere in my daily routine. In all the time I've spent at the Complex, I haven't spoken to him much outside of obligatory Blue Shift meetings.

The AFA forums have become a persistent thorn in my side. These increase in late fall and then again in winter—four compulsory attendances per week for all citizens. At least the time of each forum decreases, going from an hour to forty minutes. To avoid confusion, attendance times are assigned electronically and mailed to citizens on a weekly basis. Though an AA agent's workload increases during the colder months, we're not excused from additional forums.

I spend my days racing from task to task, neglecting sleep and meals in equal measure. Meetings occupy the majority of most days, leaving me the quieter evening hours to compile reports, indulge in repetition, and draw up pack assignments. Despite this, I pile further tasks onto my capable yet exhausted shoulders. But nothing takes my thoughts very far from her clear blue eyes. The instant my mind has a moment's respite, I see her trembling chin, her open, hopeful expression. Weeks have passed since I found her outside the Dormitories courtyard. A pause in my work brings her voice snaking into my office, begging me to come with her, to leave the city. She reached out to me, but every ounce of what makes me human already belongs to the AA. I don't have anything else to give.

Plowing headlong into agency business doesn't help the way I'd like it to. There are just too many solitary nights spent in silence. The instant I come up for air, reflection seizes me with cold fingers, initiating that sinking feeling. My thoughts rise up, becoming so large they overwhelm me. I must beat them back to find focus again. I don't believe my duties have begun to suffer, but objectivity is the first thing to slip when one's concentration has been compromised.

I spend my days as I have for the last eleven years—a cell in the giant corpus of the AA, every breath a gift of the agency. An agent is neither thought nor independent action. An agent is a nod, an answer to a question, a springing to action that's calculated and clean of the paralysis of contemplation. No one understands this better than I do, and yet I'm thinking of her, wondering if she made it out of the city. The AA hasn't caught her. I know this much. Every citizen has his current likeness, fingerprints, and DNA on file. Querying this database for information on new captures has been a daily habit of mine for years, so I doubt my continued interest will arouse suspicion. I don't know what I want more—for her to be caught or for her to get away. Either way, it's out of my hands.

NINETEEN

On Mondays, I meet with Deux to discuss floor business. Sup3 did a similar thing when I was senior pack leader and he Third Shift super, but never as rigidly defined as I've made it. We met when the opportunity presented itself, usually very early or very late, as we were often the first or last agents on the floor. Though this worked well, I prefer set times so my various pack leaders arrive prepared. I meet with Deux weekly for at least thirty minutes—though we end up meeting for shorter intervals multiple times a week besides this— then he meets with the other floor one ten pack leaders. I do the same with the other senior leaders. Together with floor one ten, these five other floors and the packs they contain comprise the whole of Third Shift. On a normal week, I have a meeting per day with one of my senior pack leaders. It's only been a few months, but the system appears to be running smoothly.

"We have a very important assignment from Intelligence," I say to Deux, voice low though my office door is closed and locked.

Deux nods his blonde head and leans forward, his permanent state of being one of attentive readiness. Ever the observer, once he sees or hears a thing, he doesn't forget it. His willingness to accept direction without ever taking offense is a key factor in his eventual success in his new position. Older agents lack pliability. They have set ways of doing things and aren't likely to change them, even under a direct order.

I continue after a lengthy silence in which Deux made no attempt to interrupt me. Yet another example of how youth trumps aged experience.

"Speakeasies have long been our sole concern, but now we have a new one. Safehouses."

Deux's light eyes widen but, leaning farther forward, right eyebrow lifted, he holds his tongue.

"We have a location." I pause to let this sink in. Safehouses being a bit of an agency fairytale—no one knowing whether they truly exist—I couldn't very well reveal my source without exposing the whole mess with Lara, but sitting on the information proved difficult. No agent has ever uncovered indisputable evidence of a safehouse, but simply presenting the facts to Intelligence would've aroused suspicion. I had to insulate the information behind hours spent hunched over maps and agency records, lending credence to the truth only I knew. No use claiming I received the tip during an interrogation, as we always kill those apprehended at speakeasies outright. I've watched upwards of one hundred people put to the bullet without the agent in charge asking a single question.

I understand the AA's zero tolerance rule for those caught breaking our most fundamental laws, and I wholeheartedly agree that confirmed speakeasy patrons should face swift execution, but not to the detriment of crucial information gathering. True, interrogations—whether on the street or the Kill Floor—can produce a wealth of desperately false information, but a modicum of truth often runs beneath the lies. Reconstruction is long over. The agency must begin to evolve with the times, starting with this specific policy change.

Deux flashes a vicious, triumphant smile. "How many packs will move on this?"

"Three," I say. "Yours will be the only one going into the flat. The other two will provide support and aid in the processing of any prisoners you find onsite."

"And executions?"

"You'll have lead position from beginning to end. I'll join your pack for the raid, but only to observe."

His smile turns satisfied. The hard work of the AA has yet to tarnish the shine of his exuberant naivety, but no agent can retain his youthful idealism for long.

"I trust I don't need to express the importance of this raid," I say.

Deux nods, so I don't waste time reminding him what an honor it is to receive such an assignment. I pull out the dossier I received the night before from a senior Intelligence agent. Within me, mixed feelings battle to the death—the empty sensation that reverberates like an echo in the center of my body versus a passionate, fiery contentment I haven't felt in years. This assignment demands the full benefit of my attention. I can't think of Lara, if she secured safe passage out of the city, if she's alone and frightened. She chose her fate just as I chose mine.

"The safehouse is in the southwest quadrant of borough three."

Lara's borough. Even she couldn't be thoughtless enough to take shelter in a safehouse nestled within her former neighborhood. But her carelessness led to the discovery of the blacklisted materials and directed her to seek me out at AA lodgings, though she's a wanted traitor. Seeking shelter in her immediate borough might not be a simple matter of carelessness. It's entirely possible she doesn't know of any other safehouses. If they work the way speakeasies do, no single individual knows of more than one or two locations, thus minimizing the damage done when a patron is caught and interrogated.

I go to the large, detailed map on the adjacent wall. "All reports indicate the location is in a residential building on the corner of this intersection." I indicate the place with a single finger. Two blocks from Lara's flat.

Deux nods, his expression serious, attentive, deadly.

This mission might be a complicated one. Those seeking refuge in a safehouse have nothing to lose. There isn't a man or woman among them not wanted by the AA for outright treachery— an executable offense. These are desperate, dangerous criminals. Regime law forbids the possession of personal weapons, but this doesn't mean places don't exist where one can go to procure one. Meat is also illegal, but that doesn't stop criminals from eating it.

The tide of my thoughts turns to Lara again, and the straggler, a man I barely knew, yet felt such an alarming affinity with. I put everything in jeopardy by allowing this to begin in the first place and only made a poor situation worse by not ending it when I had the opportunity. And there were so many opportunities, the last being the night outside the Dormitories. I'm still holding my breath on that one. It happened weeks ago, but sometimes Intelligence is purposely slow to act, merely waiting for a person to make another, more serious misstep before pouncing. With no evidence to the contrary, I assume I'm in the clear. I received this high profile assignment, which confirms the agency's faith in my loyalty to the regime.

Deux shifts in his seat, his young age apparent in the trembling of his body, as though the excitement building within him will burst forth at any moment. He clearly wants to say something. I raise a single eyebrow as I take my seat, giving him the go-ahead.

"Who else knows about this?"

"A single cell in Intelligence, Chairman Anderson, and Sup3."

He doesn't flash a smile, which he might have done to show his pleasure just last month. Every assignment, training exercise, and meeting proves my choice in him to be a fine one, which is fortunate. A poor choice would've killed my career as well as his. If an agent's instincts can't be trusted to choose members of his own team, they can hardly be trusted out on the streets where the situation changes in a matter of seconds.

"When can I tell the boys?"

"The day of the raid," I say. "We can't risk a leak."

Disappointment sullies his contented expression and I can see he wants to argue this point with me. I know the boys in question are upright—I wouldn't have chosen them for the raid if not—but orders are orders.

"Of course," Deux says, smoothing his furrowed brow.

"Keep the pack on its feet with training from morning to night, including mandatory PT until the day before the raid."

He nods obediently.

"I'm also removing your pack from neighborhood watch rotation."

His light eyebrows twitch. "How will I explain that to the rest of the floor?"

"Don't. Point the finger in my direction." I pause for any further comments and continue when there aren't any. "I'll tell the other two packs nothing for the time being. On the day of the raid, they'll be told your pack is in need of backup but not why."

He nods once more, though he appears mildly unconvinced. Shaking his blonde head a bit, his expression clears, leaving his face as blank as my own.

"How much time do we have?" he asks.

"Two weeks."

"I'll begin preparing the boys immediately."

I nod.

Deux smiles. "Tomorrow is another day closer to perfection."

*

I take lunch in the courtyard, needing the freezing wind to clear my head and sharpen my focus. The upcoming raid means everything. I trust in Deux's competency as Sup3 trusts in mine. Beyond this mission lies my success or failure in the agency. I am now the one who must sink or swim.

The loudspeaker whispers to me sweetly.

Zero tolerance for nonhuman animal cruelty equals personal liberation. Speciesism is a disease. Veganism is the inoculation. Meat is murder, comrades. Let us join the human hand with the hoof and paw of our nonhuman animal allies. Traitors to the Party are not to be tolerated. All life is sacrosanct. Equality means moral uprightness.

I unwrap my cafeteria sandwich with gloved fingers. The day's beautiful—crisp and bitterly cold, the clear sky full of muted sunlight. I'm sitting on a bench in my winter street uniform, regarding the barren courtyard as I mechanically chew. The sandwich gives me little pleasure. I'm not sure whether to attribute this to its substandard construction or the cold needling into my gloved and booted extremities.

Shed of its summer greenery and the fall colors that adorned it so prettily during Celebration, the courtyard is dismal, nearly colorless. The Capitol City doesn't often get snow, and today's light dusting has already turned muddy.

My bench is directly across from the Plaza. The broad rear of the building displays a new poster of Chairman Goldstein, his expression severe as a loaded weapon, the Party colors forming the backdrop—red, black, and white in flowing ribbons. I meet his flat eyes with difficulty, a mix of guilt and alarm upsetting my softer bits. Under that perpetually disappointed glare, it seems impossible to do anything that might aid the regime.

I finish my lunch without anyone entering the courtyard from a Headquarters building, the winter wind keeping me company. Along with it, as ever, the loudspeaker.

The AA is always watching. Mandatory AFA forum tomorrow at two, four, and six. See to it that you attend one of these. This week's lecture: Liberty through Equality. Let us celebrate freedom from harm. Tomorrow is another day closer to perfection. Let us thank the Chairman for showing us the way. No one has the right to eat the flesh of another.

My insides buzz their emptiness, the sucking I felt in Lara's presence still there, plaguing me, but agency business fills up what's missing, as it always does, giving me enough present with which to occupy myself and spiriting the better part of my past away.

In the presence of the Chairman's printed glare, my focus snaps rigidly into place. This raid is the culmination of my AA career, of the success of the regime itself. I know I can't singlehandedly influence the thrust of the regime either backwards or forwards, but it's how heavily I weight every AA mission.

I put elbows on knees, balling the sandwich wrapper in my fist, and consider the days ahead. Preparing the packs is primarily

Deux's responsibility, but I should oversee the training. It's his first high profile raid and the most significant of my career. There can be no mistakes.

I stand under the winter sun and don't mind being merely a cell in the giant corpus of the agency. Many cells make up the colossal organism of the AA, but only a few are absolutely essential. At times like these, I feel I'm one of them.

*

Sup3's waiting when I return to my office, casually seated in front of my desk, not even turning his head as I come in. He's the only person whose uninvited presence doesn't stoke my instant annoyance.

I sit.

"You spoke to Deux," he says.

I nod. He doesn't talk to Deux, just as I no longer talk to Deux's subordinates. No one goes more than one level up or down the ladder. I have Deux to converse with those too far below me and Sup3 to converse with those too far above.

"He understands the raids importance." Not a question.

I nod again. It's my office but I always follow Sup3's lead. We could be in my flat and I'd conduct myself the same way. He gives me a smile finally, tight as it is small.

"My superiors need constant assurances."

"Of course," I say. The silent room seems heavy. On the wall opposite, the poster of the Party Chairman stretches from ceiling to floor. There's one just like it in every office and packroom in the Complex.

"We move on this in a week," he says.

I keep my face blank, though one eyebrow lifts slightly, and don't question him. He'll give me whatever explanation he deems necessary. This development does annoy me, however, as I just took time out of a busy morning to brief Deux on a raid I mistakenly believed would happen in two weeks.

"I didn't tell you this earlier because I didn't know myself."

I nod and he continues.

"Deux will find this out raid day. No threat of leaks that way."

"We already have a training schedule in place," I say.

"Expedite it." He gives a shrug as though this will be the easiest part of the plan and fixes me with a stern glance. Most would avert their eyes. I do not.

I nod to show my understanding. He looks ragged, but we aren't friendly enough for me to inquire into the matter, though he's done so for me in the past. He's a man of great strength and exceptional character, so I see little reason to trouble myself with his welfare. We all must tend to ourselves in this new age. Responding to an outstretched hand conveys weakness. Outstretching one's hand makes one vulnerable.

"How will your preparations change?" he asks.

"The same level of training, just in a shorter period of time," I say. It's simply a matter of re-strategizing to account for the seven day loss. I planned to spend the last week at the Complex working out issues and making arrangements, so I'll simply start tonight. Conveniently, I keep a few uniforms and various toiletry items on hand at all times. I'll return to my flat for a few hours the night before the raid. I don't hold much stock in superstition, but I always spend some time before an important mission in my living room, repeating cadence until my mind empties, until my focus becomes as sharp and lethal as the blade of a knife.

"Very good," Sup3 says, and stands. "One more thing."

I lift my dark eyebrows.

"Your pet project, the desire to question individuals we take into custody for execution."

I nod.

"Just after I learned of the schedule change for this raid, I also learned we'll be able to process those found at the safehouse and transport them back to the Kill Floor for interrogation before execution."

I blink but that's as far as it goes. "Well, then," I say, surprised, but pleased.

"Indeed." The communicator buzzes on his hip. His smile turns resigned. If a man exists in the Complex who works longer hours than I do, it's Sup3.

After he leaves, I stare at the poster of the Party Chairman for a long time before returning to work.

TWENTY

Deux doesn't ask why I want the men pressed so hard, he simply presses them. Mandatory PT, twenty hour training days, a week of overnights at the Complex. This raid embodies everything we've worked for—the years of obedient diligence, the nights spent casing speakeasies in the cold and the rain, the unyielding training, the permanent loss of self. All of it is finally coming to fruition.

I look up at a knock on the door, naturally expecting Sup3, who drops by once per day. But it's the AA Chairman who enters and promptly shuts the door. I've served the agency for over a decade—most of that time here in the Capitol City—and have never spoken to Chairman Anderson face-to-face.

I jump to attention. "Comrade."

He waves a hand in seeming impatience. "At ease, 687."

I sit.

The AA Chairman's tall—well over six feet—but plain, possessing neither the good-natured personality of the PETA Chairman nor the smoldering charisma of the Party Chairman. All agency heads wear suits, but his left arm bears the double A's, same as mine. I respect this, if nothing else.

He drops into a seat across from mine. "Tough work ahead, comrade."

I nod, a bit discomfited by this approach. Small talk isn't typical in the duty day. Some agents get casual when dealing with those of similar rank, but I wouldn't expect that from the agency Chairman. Many operatives would fall over themselves to indulge Chairman Anderson, blathering on about the weather and other such useless timewasters, but I remain silent. Part of this stems from my inability to engage in small talk, the rest from the suddenly tense atmosphere clouding my office. The man wouldn't have come without a reason, so I sit quietly and wait for him to reveal it.

"Your supervisor says you have everything under control."

I nod once. Here's the conversation with Sup3 all over again, except I have no history with this man, no working relationship. I also don't have the time to assure each of my superiors of the impending operation's merit. It's Sup3's job to assure those above me. I should never even speak to the agency Chairman.

"This raid can't fail."

I answer in a voice devoid of feeling, the expression on my face impassive. "It won't."

His eyebrows fold together as he takes stock of my flat response and disinterested countenance. I've always been peculiar in this way—much to the shared chagrin of my parents—but these tendencies only became more ingrained with AA service. And because I've been this way for years, I recognize the look blooming on the Chairman's face as he takes my inventory. He's pondering the anomaly of a subordinate not contorting himself in an attempt to please. But I don't need his faith. If I plan it, it will be a success. Sup3's behind me. Deux's capable. The men are trained and ready to go.

"Do you understand what will happen if this operation fails? To you? To floor one ten?" His voice is light, almost playful, but his face twists with a sharp emotion I can't identify.

I have to suppress a chilly smile at his motivation laid bare. His purpose is to threaten me. Sup3 doesn't operate this way, nor do I. A well-placed threat can sometimes prove beneficial, but it should never take the place of appropriate training and respect for one's superiors.

I nod for a third time, not dignifying his threats with a response, my face serenely neutral. An expression is also a response.

He waits for me to respond. Once clear I'm going to do no such thing, he stumbles into additional conversation alone.

"Your personal dossier is impressive."

I don't take my gaze from his. This is yet another source of discomfort for an interlocutor—I never break eye contact. I find myself attempting to focus on the poster of the Party Chairman while also looking at the broad, shiny face of Chairman Anderson. Sup3's presence never feels like an intrusion or an attack, even when he's testing me, but this man congests the office with his pomp and his threats. I hold my tongue only out of prudence. His position as AA

Chairman entitles him to a certain level of respect even if his actions don't.

The Chairman's saying something about trust and accountability. I hardly follow, though I do make sure to nod when he appears to come to the end of a sentence. The picture of Chairman Goldstein fills the wall behind him, fuzzy in my peripheral vision. Chairman Anderson continues to speak and I continue not to listen. The minutes tick by, minutes that could be used for making this operation a success. Though this appears to be the Chairman's central concern, he won't leave me to it. The raid's tomorrow night. So much remains to be done.

"Don't you agree?" the Chairman says in a pseudo-amiable tone, his expression expectant.

I nod my agreement, but to what, I don't know. He seems satisfied, but is by no means finished. I pull my focus from the poster and make an honest effort to listen. I haven't slept in seventy-two hours. Prior to this latest stretch of work-induced insomnia, I didn't sleep more than two hours for well over ninety-six hours. I'm not complaining. The boys and Deux have done the same thing. Tonight, we'll all get a full night's sleep. My subordinates think this reprieve a reward for reaching the halfway point in raid preparations and that they must prepare to do it all over again next week. I'll tell Deux the truth a half hour before I instruct him to tell the boys. He'll put the other two packs on a heightened neighborhood watch, restricted to a one-block radius, and give them additional instruction on a need-to-know basis.

Chairman Anderson clears his throat. I haven't taken my attention from him, at least not fully, but perhaps he can sense the wandering nature of my thoughts.

"This operation's very important to the regime." He pauses, creating a small steeple beneath his chin with his fingers. He raises an eyebrow as I often do when inviting a subordinate to speak, only it's apparent he doesn't want to be interrupted, even in silence. "Your supervisor assures me you're the ideal agent to oversee a mission of this caliber. His confidence in you engenders confidence in the rest of us." The thinness of his smile renders it disingenuous.

Not possessing the head for such things, especially not now, I don't return the smile. Agency business more pressing than making a lasting impression on the AA Chairman occupies all the available space in my mind. I also have a throbbing headache, eliminating any interest in playing bureaucratic ball.

"Of course," I say, speaking only because it seems overly awkward not to, though I despise the meaningless fumbling of empty speech.

Chairman Anderson seems confused by my response, but nods anyway. I need uninterrupted silence to complete my numerous duties, but can no more direct him towards the hallway than Deux could me if I were the one talking his ear off and wasting valuable time.

He stands and I follow suit, standing at rigid attention.

"Tomorrow is another day closer to perfection," he says.

"Yes, comrade." We don't salute in the AA.

He exits the office, leaving me standing before the poster of the Party Chairman. I stay at attention—hands at my sides, chin raised, shoulders back, chest thrust forward—and speak in a steady voice.

"Honor when it is easier to do the opposite. Integrity when those around us lack it entirely. Loyalty to those unarmed innocents above all else."

The dissatisfied expression on Chairman Goldstein's face doesn't change.

I repeat cadence.

My headache intensifies, burrowing in behind my eyes.

I repeat cadence.

I won't rest tonight. Thoughts of the raid will consume my attention, alleviated only by long sessions of repetition. And Lara? She's nowhere and no one. Once I obliterate the system of safehouses in the Capitol City, the speakeasies will fall. The heavy boot heel of the AA will crush the entire underground movement out of existence and eliminate all defectors. But to do this, I must forget how her auburn hair curls at the ends. I must forget the rich blue of her eyes, how they shimmer when brimming with tears. I must forget *touching* and the sucking sensation it caused in my dark places.

I consider the Party Chairman, who surely knows more about sacrifice and selfless service than anyone in the regime.

I sit behind the desk again, prepared to pour every last drop of myself into my work until I'm no longer an individual at all, but merely the agency.

*

I walk to the Dormitories in the biting cold. It isn't quite ten thirty, so the loudspeakers follow me home.

Voluntary curfew is in effect. Personal freedom means freedom from harm. Reliance on nonhuman animal resources indicates a weakness of character and an inability to conform. Traitors must be dealt with directly. Let us join the human hand with the hoof and paw. Meat is murder, comrades. The sanctity of life is the sanctity of all life. Speciesism is not to be tolerated.

The maternal voice trails me as I step into the Dormitories courtyard on numb, tingling feet. I can't feel the fingers in my gloves. My nose and cheeks are nonexistent.

I walk to Lib Hall and ascend to my warm, empty flat. I shower to wash the cold away but don't turn on the light. I wash my hair, letting the shampoo burn my eyes.

Any feeling is feeling.

I rinse my face and cut off the water. I keep my showers under five minutes. Water conservation is everyone's responsibility.

I walk through the steam without drying off. The beading water on my skin is feeling. A headache throbs at my temples, but not intensely. Even the sinking sensation in my chest has subsided.

I put on a pair of boxers and go to the living room window still dripping. My one joy, my gateway to the city. But besides the aching in my head, I feel nothing.

Below me, the city sleeps. The loudspeakers have fallen silent. If anyone's touching, I can't see it. There must be those who continue to reach out, to touch, to find comfort in companionship, even if the regime makes it difficult. I touch no one. I feel nothing. I am the black clad body of the AA, a clockwork representative of a regime that holds me close. But the regime cannot touch.

I think of Lara on the final day of Celebration.

"I am the black clad body of the AA."

Mother slapping my face and tearing at the double A's on my arm.

"I am the black clad body of the AA."

Father, who raised his fist but couldn't strike.

"I am—"

My voice breaking as I whispered to them, *I've done something terrible.* Father did not stay his hand then. Mother did not stay her tongue.

The sensation in my chest—that empty sucking—returns with renewed force, hampering my breathing, strangling me. Weighed down by cottony silence, I peer out at the slumbering city. Solitude is the only constant in a regime without touch.

I try to repeat cadence but the words won't come. Still, calmness returns with my even breathing. The past is what the regime names it—bloody, thoughtless, without compassion. Lara's right about one thing—the regime is also without compassion—but she's wrong about motivation. This isn't about cruelty. It's about inoculation. A forthright system of ethics is bound to have some casualties—companionship, a meeting of minds and hands and hearts, love. We no longer touch, but thoughtlessness has been eliminated. Once hubris meets the same end, perhaps we'll see the revival of true compassion. And after compassion, we might even bear witness to a resurrection of the altruistic touch.

I hear voices in the hall, laughter, but it doesn't touch me. My body's dry, my resolve firm. Every muscle seems to vibrate and hum. The tightness in my chest loosens. Quite suddenly, I have the urge for chin-ups.

"Honor when it is easier to do the opposite." I clench my fists. "Integrity when those around us lack it entirely." I clench harder, fingernails biting into palms. More feeling. "Loyalty to those unarmed innocents above all else."

I touch the place on my arm where the double A's should be. There's nothing except skin touching skin, but that doesn't count.

TWENTY-ONE

I wake to dull thudding behind my eyes that gives my head a raw, scooped out feeling. This doesn't subside as the day rushes towards its pinnacle, but anticipation's a drug, and flying high on waves of nerves and focus, I bury my discomfort beneath all the things that needing doing on raid day.

For the first time in years, I take the metro to the Complex. It's a short walk but a faster train ride, and I need the noise of the subway and the crush of the people—faux touch—to divert attention from my escalating headache. I'm in uniform but no one has any choice but to touch me. It's morning rush and the trains are packed. My fellow patrons don't meet my eyes as they make a great show of attending to their affairs, putting as much space between my body and theirs as humanly possible.

*

I go straight to my office without uttering a word to anyone. If, as I swiftly pass, an agent extends the typical greeting—*morning, comrade*—I merely nod and move on. No small talk today. I've already planned what to say to Deux when the time's right. We're meeting at nine fifteen tonight. The boys and I will leave the Complex no later than ten o'clock. I want the door kicked in at the safehouse by ten thirty.

I open my office door and Sup3 turns from his standing position in front of the poster of Chairman Goldstein. I sit but Sup3 doesn't. He rests his hand on his gun, not coming any closer.

"Are the men ready?" he asks.

"Yes." I always answer him, even when my responses don't seem to make much sense given the question asked. With all others, if a nod or shake of the head will suffice, I don't bother with a verbal response.

"What about Deux?"

I shrug—evidence that I'm more relaxed with Sup3 than anyone else. I'd never shrug in front of the boys. They see one face, Sup3 another. This doesn't mean I let my guard down, but it's easier to relax a bit, like faux touching in the subway station.

"He's ready."

"The men respect him?"

"Without question," I say.

Sup3 nods, but something's obviously troubling him. He steps closer to the desk and crosses his muscular arms, stretching the fabric of his uniform over his broad, muscular chest. I repeat cadence or run to the point of exhaustion to keep steady. Sup3 lifts weights.

"And you?" he asks. "Are you sound?"

I watch him a moment before speaking. This must be about my admitting to difficulty sleeping some months ago. Perhaps he's also noticed other shortcomings of which I'm unaware. I understand his concern for what it is—professional, not personal. No one has the right to let his private troubles affect a mission.

"Yes," I say.

He clearly wants to say more on the matter, but the set of his jaw tells me he won't.

"Will you take part tonight?" I ask.

"Minimally. I'll follow up after the action." He pauses, dark eyes settling on my lighter ones. "This is your mission."

His faith is more valuable to me than any empty praise from the AA Chairman.

"When do you speak to Deux?" he asks.

"Nine fifteen."

Sup3 looks slightly more assured than he did five minutes ago. I forgive him this unease—even Chairman Anderson felt the need to threaten a subordinate over this operation. Neither disquiet nor hesitation troubles me. My plans for tonight are seamless. We will obliterate the safehouse, bleeding all traitors for information before they're sent for execution. Tonight, the regime will have its victory.

*

Deux appears at nine fifteen on the dot. I speak to him in a low, measured tone, expression flat, hands resting on the desk. At first, his light eyebrows tighten sharply, but eventually, his face drains of all expression. He mimics—another useful side effect of his youth—

everyday fashioning himself into something better. He embodies the spirit of the regime—hard, precise, ever-changing.

The talk lasts no more than five minutes. Deux asks no questions. He merely nods at various points, keeping his eyes on mine. Everything's the same, only happening a week earlier. I dismiss him with strict instructions—gather the boys and share the news, giving the senior pack full disclosure and the backup packs partial.

Five minutes to ten finds me in the parking garage beneath the Complex where we house our pack jeeps. High-ranking AA officials can also keep personal vehicles here at no cost. A substantial perk, considering the high cost of parking elsewhere in the city.

I meet the boys near the jeeps. The senior pack bristles, ready to go. The other two packs stand close by, confused, inquisitive. Neighborhood watch never involves this much secrecy, preparation, and cooperation with other packs. It's also never limited to a one-block radius. If they have questions, they stay their tongues. These boys know me and we all know the agency. One learns what one needs to know only when one needs to know it.

The boys form a loose half circle with Deux and me in the middle. I nod, giving him the lead. Sup3 called this my mission, and it is, but these are Deux's men.

"You've all been briefed," Deux says, hand moving to rest on the butt of his weapon. He has a magnetism about him that I noticed from the first. When he speaks, others lean in to listen.

He calls two agent numbers. The men step forward—the leaders of the backup packs.

"You men have your instructions." This isn't a question, but both agents nod.

"Yes, comrade," one man says, showing deference though Deux's his junior by ten years or more.

"You're dismissed to your vehicles then. I'll be in the lead jeep. Follow me until the splitting off point and begin your patrol. I'll contact you if we need assistance."

Fourteen agents go to their pack vehicles and load up without a word.

Deux speaks in a lower voice to the eight of us left behind. "This is our shining moment, brothers. These traitors are the lowest of the low. They've kept their hiding places hidden for years, but we have them now."

The boys cheer and Deux dismisses them.

I ride in the lead jeep. The vehicles accommodate up to nine individuals with equipment. Normally, we carry a fair amount of gasoline, but not tonight. The site's a medium-sized flat in a district comprised mostly of apartment buildings zoned for families with children. Fire's only authorized after locating evidence of illegal meat, but never in a private residence.

It takes approximately fifteen minutes to reach the southwest quadrant of borough three. We have sirens but never use them for raids. Where's the fun in thwarting the surprise?

I stay silent in the passenger seat, eyes forward as Deux navigates through dark streets. The jeeps are unmarked, cargo concealed behind tinted windows, but everyone knows the speeding black trucks for what they are. We encounter no other vehicles. So few people own cars and no one's out this time of night.

All three jeeps park in an alley two blocks from the location. The packs on backup immediately begin neighborhood watch detail. The two pack leaders have communicators clipped to their belts so Deux can send word if we need assistance processing defectors.

A brief flash of contentment warms me despite the chill in the air. Things are finally going the way I've always felt they should. After processing, we'll transport the traitors to Kill Rooms for brutal interrogations. I don't expect to find many people at the site. Too many people in an apartment draw the attention of nosey neighbors and constitute a serious offense, even if the individuals aren't wanted criminals. Rewards are offered to those turning in lawbreakers. The meager credits awarded aren't why anyone snitches on a friend, family member, or stranger. The real reward comes in the form of recognition from the Party that one is loyal and upright. This acknowledged loyalty is beyond valuable, as it issues in continued peace for a citizen and his family.

I come around the jeep on silent, booted feet. The relief packs are wearing street uniforms. The rest of us are in riot gear. One man moves to the rear of the main jeep and begins passing out assault rifles. Many hands visibly itch to use them, including my own. These traitors sicken me, no matter how beautifully Lara and the straggler articulated their arguments about the desolate climate of the regime. Once each man receives a weapon, he turns to the pack leader. I stand next to Deux, but slightly behind, clearly indicating who's giving the orders. All this derives from pack mentality training in AA boot camp. Body language, positioning, facial expressions—it all comes together to create a rich, unspoken language.

"No screw ups, brothers," Deux says, words a cloudy puff on the winter air. "You all have your jobs. Capture alive who you can, but don't hesitate to eliminate troublemakers."

I watch predatory smiles stretch across six faces. I keep my own face blank, as does Deux.

"Masks, brothers," he says. "And helmets."

Each man slides a cotton mask over his face and then puts on a helmet with the plastic visor firmly closed. Deux and I follow suit.

"Honor when it is easier to do the opposite," one man says in a voice too low to risk drawing attention to our position in the alley.

"Integrity when those around us lack it entirely," Deux says.

"Loyalty to those unarmed innocents above all else," the rest of the men say, myself included.

"Move out." Deux takes lead position, I take second, and the rest of the boys fall in behind us. We file out of the alley, eyes scanning the empty street, ears cocked to catch anything suspicious. We pass beneath a loudspeaker as we stalk up the street, silent as the night itself.

Let us celebrate the downfall of anyone who refuses to be free from harm. Meat is murder, comrades. Voluntary curfew is in effect. Let us not succumb to blind hubris. Dairy is organized rape. We do not eat anything with a face. Let us thank the Chairman for showing us the way. Mandatory AFA forum tomorrow at two, four, and six. See to it that you attend one of these. This week's lecture:

Speciesism and Its Unfortunate Consequences. Tomorrow is another day closer to perfection.

The soothing voice of the regime keeps us company as we creep along the deserted sidewalk, our breath visible in the chill air, our guns at the ready. We reach our mark—a small, three-story building containing fifteen flats.

Deux holds up a gloved hand, signaling that we're going in. I see no flaw in his form, no reason to interfere. Until I do, I'm just another junior packmate, a pair of eyes to watch, a mouth to keep quiet, and a head to nod when given an order. We trickle into the building. The downstairs corridor's barren.

Deux moves to the stairwell. We follow, the men close enough to breathe on each other's necks, but no one steps on the heels of the man in front of him. The pack moves up one flight of stairs as a unit. We step into the second floor corridor and encounter no one.

The flat's right next to the stairwell. The riot gear makes the sweltering air much worse.

"Going in, brothers," Deux says. Strange to hear my own words coming from another mouth. We ready ourselves, the tension communal.

Deux kicks the door in, the sound of it slamming open and splintering the frame booming in the air around us. We run in, still not knocking into each other, screaming for everyone to get down, to shut up, to not move or we'll open fire. Screaming greets us. Lots of it. The last packmate in line stands in the open doorway, hindering escape. We already know the floor plan of the two bedroom flat. An adult couldn't fit through any of the windows. No other doors lead out. Deux stands in the middle of the living room facing two people, a man and a woman pressed against the wall.

"Do not move a muscle," he says in a menacing tone, gun pointed in their direction. The boys scatter, each with his own job to do.

I take the first bedroom. Another man takes the second. Another takes the dining room, another the kitchen, another the bathroom, and the last man holds firm in the corridor, discouraging runners.

I enter the bedroom and instantly hear soft whimpering from the closet. I check the rest of the room—inside a large dirty clothes hamper, under the bed, behind a dresser that's positioned oddly in front of a corner, leaving a large space behind it—before addressing the obvious.

I throw open the closet door, step back, and aim my weapon, prepared for the concealed individual to spring out at me. Instead, I find a man in his early thirties or late twenties crumpled upon the carpeted floor like a chastened child. His sobs rising, he begins to beg for his life.

My revulsion is immediate. "Be silent."

He stops his pleas for mercy, though the weeping only gets worse. He covers his head with trembling hands as though this might protect him from a bullet. My disgust intensifies.

"Get up." A volley of loud voices fills the flat, both from agents and criminals. I prefer not to shout if I can avoid it. Being patient and deceptively kind gives a much more interesting effect. I smile a lot, not that I bother doing that tonight with my mask on. In my real life, I don't smile. It's only when I'm putting on a show for these traitors that I allow myself the liberty of false expression.

The man stands, but backs further into the closet, shaking his head and snatching at the moisture beneath his nose with the heel of his hand. He's more boy than man.

"Please—"Whatever he planned to say disintegrates into sobs when I aim the gun at his face.

My head's pounding an unceasing rhythm, excruciating in its precision. The air in here isn't much cooler than it was in the hall. Sweat's beading at my hairline and dripping down my back. I can't wait to shower after this is all over.

"Step out of the closet slowly, hands up, and go to the living room."

Blubbering like an infant, he complies. I doubt he'll be much trouble past refusing to dry his tears. His lack of composure disgusts me, but I've grown used to the sight. Adult men weeping, women wailing in hysterical fear, children sobbing as black clad operatives drag their parents away at gunpoint—as a rule, we don't execute traitors in front of their children—I've seen it all.

The man's sniveling is getting worse instead of better. He must know his fate. Even if he isn't a wanted criminal himself, he's guilty of aiding and abetting. The records show a married couple as

the tenants of this apartment along with their newborn daughter. I
don't know why anyone with a child would take such risks.

The straggler leaving Lara to fend for herself.

I blink and my mind snaps back into place. This is more
despicable. The girl's so young. Such thoughtlessness carries a charge
of willful endangerment of a minor child. That's if they're charged at
all. Formal charges don't often materialize unless Regime Radio
needs a bit of filler. The normal course of things goes: capture,
interrogation—if time permits—and execution. Constant broadcasts
about criminals and their misdeeds no longer tickle the airwaves.
Crime supposedly decreased in the years following Reconstruction
when it was commonplace to see executions in public squares and on
television. No good comes of people believing the streets are teeming
with crime. But high profile offenses work to the regime's advantage,
enraging everyday citizens, uniting them in the heat of shared
outrage. But these high profile crimes are few and far between. On
the whole, the AA works against insurgents in silence while the
regime continues to show the public a competent, untroubled face.

I stick the gun in the man's back. "The living room. Now."

His sobs reach a sickening crescendo as we travel the short
distance to the living room. I don't want to hear his bawling, but
prefer it over the begging, the desperate justifications, the deal-
making.

"Over there, with the others," I say.

The packmates gather in the common room, save the agent
watching the door. He stands in the middle of the foyer, gun pointed

at the captives clumped together in a corner. I watch the sniveling, pathetic man take his place with the others.

"How many?" I ask Deux. Even with the mask, I can tell him by his stance and the way he holds his weapon.

"Eight," he says. "No sign of the newborn."

This is a bit of luck, as it makes the absent child someone else's responsibility. Children complicate matters. Taking a suspect into custody almost always means execution. Since adults teach children what they believe morally correct—not simply in word, but in deed; case in point, Lara and the straggler—orphaned children of defectors undergo a year of re-education and thought reformation. Those under two are immediately placed with a law-abiding family, while the rest go to the juvenile division of the Loop. After that first year, a child's fate depends upon his age. Those under ten find homes with childless Party members known for their loyalty to the regime. Those between ten and fifteen attend a boarding school three to five years in duration where they learn skills valuable to society. They can then find government work as tradesmen or groundskeepers. They may also enlist in the AA. Orphans above the age of fifteen go directly to the AA for training, the duration doubled or tripled to offset the child's questionable upbringing and tender age—normal enlistment for the AA is seventeen and above, though a sixteen year old can be accepted if he shows promise. Regardless of age, the Party red flags every orphan, as his origins include a tendency for treachery. If a stray steps out of line once reaching adulthood, he finds himself on a fast track to a Kill Room.

I nod to express my approval to Deux. The other packmates are hindering my view of the captives. I want to see them, to experience their distress, though I can't frighten them with my harsh grin and dead eyes. I step through the boys, who give me a wide passage. They know me by the way I comport myself, same as I do them.

The captives are huddled together on the floor as captives always are. I point my gun at them, finger near the trigger, ever eager, but don't fire. They have no mercy for the nonhuman animals they slaughter or the regime they weaken with careless law breaking, but they never stop expecting mercy to spring from the arbitrary classification of species we happen to share. *We're all human!* they scream, as though it means something.

The man and woman we encountered after bursting into the flat are clutching at each other while my blubbering man melts into near hysterics in the corner. Another man pats him on the shoulder, whispering something I can't hear. It always amazes me how they can comfort each other as though it matters, as though it will lead to some alternate outcome. They are dead men conversing. Two more women sit behind the original couple, hugging and dry-eyed. The blubbering man could learn a lesson from these two. Of course, this silence doesn't guarantee they won't descend into inconsolable hysterics later on. Another man sits against one wall, seemingly oblivious to the activity around him. He could also be trouble later. Silence is suspicious. A final shape is curled on the floor near this man, face hidden. A woman, by her long hair and small build.

The color of these tresses, their curling ends, quicken my heartbeat. Could it be Lara? I start to order her to sit up but stop myself. Lara knows my voice. A flash of dark anger consumes me. She shouldn't even be in the Capitol City, let alone nestled within this sniveling group of traitors. Didn't I warn her?

I aim my weapon at the feminine shape curled in the fetal position, my finger moving onto the trigger. I can take care of this quickly. As the senior agent on the floor, no one will question my actions. They'll believe any story I choose to give.

More agents flood the flat, these without riot gear. The rest of us could remove our masks, but no one does. I won't until I verify this girl's identity. I don't fire only because I can't be certain.

The men coming in are from the relief pack. Deux must've radioed them after we cleared the flat. These men will now tear through the apartment looking for contraband and contact the Bureau of Child Services to locate the missing child.

I watch the huddled figure. She's either weeping or having trouble breathing. I contemplate forcing her to reveal her identity by poking her with the barrel of the gun, but the others will panic if I bring my weapon too close. I can't risk it.

The flat hums with activity, boys chattering or searching the premises with the enthusiasm of the recently victorious. Agents crash through the flat, knocking things to the ground, ripping items from walls, and tossing objects out of drawers and cabinets to be crushed underfoot. Even during routine double duty, an agent can tear apart a citizen's residence if he sees fit. I never do this, nor do I train my men to do it, unless and until a piece of contraband is found.

Deux stands at the center of the excitement, still wearing his mask, the barrel of his weapon pointed at the floor as he speaks with the two leaders of the relief packs and gesticulates wildly. I can't feel pride for him right now, not when I'm certain the girl weeping bitterly on the floor is Lara.

A hand falls onto my shoulder. I turn sharply to face Sup3. He's wearing a helmet with the visor flipped up and no mask.

He grins. "I've already let Chairman Anderson know of the raid's success."

I nod, keeping my face blank though it hardly matters with the mask on.

"Where's Deux?" he asks, eyebrow lifted, the rest of his face blank.

I point to an agent directing a group of subordinates. We approach. Sup3 rarely speaks to Deux directly, but if he does, I'm always present, as though needed to perform translations so the agent on one level can understand the agent on the other. The men standing around clear out at the appearance of Sup3, leaving the three of us to our business. It seems strange—two of us wearing masks and the other one not—but the oddity doesn't appear to affect Sup3, who's used to speaking to blank faces.

"Have you processed the captives" he asks.

Deux doesn't answer. The question was directed at me.

I didn't actually see anyone processing the traitors, but as my second in command on many-a-raid, Deux knows procedure.

"Yes," I say. "Deux has the details on that."

Deux nods, but stays mute, following the advice I often received as a child—*do not speak unless spoken to.*

"Did you find any contraband?" This subject change shows Sup3's confidence in me. He doesn't need the details on the processing. He knows I'll have a report on his desk before morning.

I don't confer with Deux before answering. "Not to my knowledge, but the search is ongoing. Any findings will be reflected in my report."

Sup3 nods. "I'll expect it before sunrise." Not an order, just a mere stating of the obvious given my history. I'll complete the paperwork before doing anything else, including eating, sleeping, or showering.

"Of course," I say.

"The Complex then."

I nod. "The Complex." We both spend the night after a high profile raid at AA headquarters. This is our way of saying, *until we meet again.*

"Excellent job, comrade," Sup3 says, addressing Deux.

Deux nods once, but I can clearly imagine his self-satisfied grin spreading beneath the dark cloth of his mask.

I direct my attention to Deux after Sup3 strides out of the flat. "You processed the defectors."

"Yes, of course."

"The results?"

"The man and woman are the registered residents." He points behind me at the captives.

I take the opportunity to inspect the pathetic, sobbing group, though I clearly remember the frightened couple. The girl's face still isn't visible.

I look at Deux. "And the rest?"

"Fugitives, the lot of them."

"Crimes?" No one's actually going to stand trial, but when an individual earns fugitive status, charges are entered into the system, allowing the agent in pursuit to know what he might face upon apprehension.

"Sedition, peddling of black market meat, possession of contraband, aiding and abetting, willful endangerment, eluding authorities, irreverence."

I nod at these common charges. The possession of contraband could be Lara, although even the tamest of items can be construed as illegal goods when paired with questionable activity. Each fugitive has probably been charged with possession, sedition, and eluding authorities. The peddling of black market meat is a separate charge involving speakeasies, which I doubt concerns Lara, although she could've become involved in anything after going underground.

"Contraband?" I ask.

Deux shrugs, clearly disappointed. "A few blacklisted books. Also, there's not one picture of the Party Chairman on the premises."

That explains the charge of irreverence—a crime punishable by a few weeks in the Loop. Most citizens find it prudent to have a picture of the Party Chairman in every room. AA agents don't need to worry over such details—all rooms in agency housing come equipped with such posters, as does every room and hallway in the Complex.

"Nothing else, besides that."

"Next?" I ask.

Deux thinks a moment, though he must already know the answer. I often take a few seconds to consider my own answer before speaking, and he mimics.

"I'll instruct the leader of relief pack one to stay onsite as senior agent while the search continues. The leader of relief pack two and I will transport the traitors to the Complex for interrogation. After that, I'll return to pick up my agents and document any further contraband. We'll then report to the Complex for debriefing."

"I suggest you begin," I say. There's no hurry. I simply want an excuse to see the mystery girl's face. I'm not certain what I'll do if she turns out to be Lara.

Deux rounds up the other pack leaders and briefs them quickly. He then calls together the six members of his own pack and gets them into position. I stand to one side, watching Deux, who's masterful as he leads the men. Agents crowd around the captives, pulling them to their feet and handcuffing them. I can't see any of their faces clearly. Three agents shout at the captives to double time it through the small foyer and out into the corridor. I study the face of each traitor as he marches past.

The last one is Lara.

TWENTY-TWO

I watch the procession, my mask camouflaging any rogue expression.

Her arms are handcuffed at the wrists, her head down. When an agent crudely jams the barrel of his gun into her back, she looks up, her eyes wide with panic. Time slows. My respiration slows. Even she seems to slow. This synchronicity only lasts a moment.

An agent begins to force black hoods on all the traitors. Lara shakes her head from side to side, her fearful expression excruciating. I merely watch the struggle to put the hood over her head, my regret as suffocating as the air in the flat. The sinking feeling spikes suddenly and I expect to drop through the floor. She has no business being here. I told her to leave the city. Recklessness appears to run in the family.

The agent succeeds at his task, transforming Lara into a faceless traitor in a line of faceless traitors. I watch them stumble into the hallway. Deux and the leader of relief pack two follow them.

I remove my helmet and tear off the mask, breathing deeply for the first time in an hour, my hair sweat-soaked and warm, my skin slick and crawling. Agents buzz in the vicinity, asking questions I ignore. I should've put a bullet in Lara's head that night at the Dormitories. My mind skitters—her face before the black bag made it ordinary; the tears I couldn't wipe from her cheeks.

I pull off my gloves and touch my face with calloused fingers. Faux touching, same as always. No sinking feeling blooming in my chest, no warmth. Agents are clamoring for my attention, but they don't touch me.

An hour passes before I walk back to the Complex, turning down the ride offered me by the leader of relief pack one. I need the cool air to clear my head after so much sweltering heat inside the flat. A headache only lightly troubles me, as it's become a common occurrence. I used to attribute it to nerves, but perhaps it has more to do with age. I haven't yet reached my mid-thirties, but this work takes its toll. In the end, the regime takes everything—time, youth, motivation, strength.

Deux gives the debriefing after all three packs return to the Complex. I watch him, barely listening, thinking of Lara, wondering if, in a perfectly vicious twist of fate, she ended up in Kill Room five.

I complete my paperwork in less than two hours. Reports as detailed as this needs to be often take other agents a full day to author but I plow through it, needing something to anesthetize my riotous mind so it will lie quietly. Once I have the printed report in my hand—eight pages long, not including supporting materials—I check the clock. Four fifteen. Forty-five minutes until I meet with Sup3.

I leave the report on my desk and take the elevator to the cafeteria. I haven't eaten all day. My sour stomach and headache kept me from ingesting anything heavier than a cup of black coffee. I try to keep Lara out of my thoughts. The time has passed to take care of this matter on my own. If I couldn't shoot her when I had the opportunity, I doubt I'd do it now, even if left alone with her on the Kill Floor, which won't happen. Better not to dwell on it.

The cafeteria's barren. The late hour will find agents on neighborhood watch, double duty, or raids of their own instead of here at the Complex.

I take a bottle of juice and a premade sandwich with hummus, lettuce, and tomato from the counter. Hot meals aren't available between midnight and seven. I eat my meager meal in silence, unsure whether to call it dinner or breakfast. It doesn't really matter, but puzzling it keeps my mind off other things. Lara won't go to the Loop. On the Kill Floor, the future becomes short and visible. Interrogations are brutal, the damage they cause irreversible. If a traitor's lucky, the end comes swiftly, but very few are lucky.

Oddly, I don't consider my own welfare. Lara will tell her interrogators everything she knows. It's unavoidable. She may also admit to a number of untruths. Still, worry barely troubles me. This is foolishness of the highest order, but what can I do save await the repercussions? Lara doesn't know much about me, but she knows enough. Everyone will recognize my description, and those with access to my file will also know my less than original name. Giving her father's name will run a direct line from the straggler to me. AA records list me as both the apprehending and interrogating agent. I feel a dull disappointment at my own carelessness, but it falls short of actually moving me to action, not that any action could change what's coming.

Sup3's waiting for me, sitting this time, his presence expelling the cozy emptiness of the office.

I look at my watch. Ten to four.

"The report's finished," I say, sitting behind the desk. He doesn't normally collect paperwork. I hand deliver it. I push the dossier across the desk for his perusal, but he doesn't touch it. His odd expression lifts slowly, leaving exhaustion in its wake.

"The raid was a success," he says after a long silence, voice lacking the enthusiasm it had back at the flat.

I nod but don't speak. This feels like a confrontation. Lara ripples to the surface of my mind before I cast her out again. Why waste energy worrying? Either I'll be punished or I won't.

"The Kill Floor's conducting interrogations."

I raise a weary eyebrow. This is indeed about Lara. Sup3 came alone, perhaps to give me a warning. Will he tell me to leave the city? I hope not. I wouldn't do it for him.

Sup3 shifts in his seat, clearly uncomfortable and wishing to be elsewhere. My refusal to engage in the nascent stages of the conversation seems to be affecting him in a way it never has before.

"Let me be frank," he says.

"Please," I say.

"There are concerns."

The truth of the situation seizes me. Lara has spilled everything and then some—one can hardly help it in the face of serious torture. A deep and sudden hatred burns within me for the straggler. Had he been a dependable Party member, I never would've met Lara in the first place. I put a stop to this line of thought in a hurry. I'm responsible for my own actions.

"Do you have any idea what I'm talking about?" He lifts his eyebrows, his expression earnest, clearly hoping I'll say no.

I keep my face blank and don't answer. This technique is taught in initial training—asking broad questions in the hope that a suspect will incriminate himself while answering. But I've had the same training and know a person should never begin his confession when the accusation itself remains indistinct.

Sup3's expression turns uncharacteristically exasperated as he continues without me. "A girl, in her twenties. Blue eyes. Auburn hair."

"Discovered at the flat," I say.

"She knows your name."

I blink—the extent of my visible physical response—and my hands twitch in my lap, concealed beneath the desk. "My name's far from unique."

He makes an impatient gesture with his hands and I suddenly understand. This is more than simple annoyance at the rash actions of a subordinate. He's worried.

"Have you been compromised?" he asks.

"No," I say with real conviction because I don't believe I have been. I merely sated my curiosity.

"Are you certain?"

"Yes."

"This was a serious misstep." His dark eyes study me. "If the opportunity presented itself, would you be willing to prove your loyalty to the agency and the regime?"

"Of course."

He nods, but I can't tell if he's convinced.

"Take the night off. We'll speak again soon."

*

I fall into a light sleep easily enough after reaching my flat.

I hear them coming in the dark.

The sound of the door crashing open shakes the air. I have an instant to note the time—six seventeen—before dark shapes flood my bedroom. No one speaks. My eyes adjust to find guns drawn. A masked agent moves towards me—the pack leader, and not AA. Hands fall onto my arms from either side, placing my wrists in handcuffs that clasp too tightly. I don't ask questions or struggle. I feel a sharp pain at the base of my skull and the room, already dark, becomes darker.

TWENTY-THREE

I open my eyes to the dark, muscles tense, head throbbing, cheek tingling against cold cement. I touch my face. No blood. No broken bones. Not yet, at least.

I stand on bare feet and nearly fall from dizziness—an odd sensation to have in the dark. I sit down again. The air's cool. Frowning into the darkness, the realization slithers over me slowly.

I'm in the Loop.

An influx of brute alarm makes parts of me warm, but not for long. My dull surprise proves just as short-lived. No one's safe from this. Anyone can be taken at any time. I considered myself immune— to a point, I still do, though I'm now imprisoned in the Bureau of Thought Reform.

I lean over onto all fours and begin to slide across the floor, pushing with frozen toes and holding out a shaking hand to feel for the wall. My knowledge of the Loop is limited. I've only visited the convention center and the activity rooms, all below floor eleven. The rest are secure floors, closed to the public. It's rumored there are floors beneath the ground where especially difficult citizens go to be broken. I have no way of knowing where I am. I haven't been beaten—my head's throbbing near the base of my skull where I dimly recall being struck with a blunt object—but it'll come at some point.

The tips of my fingers touch a cement wall as cold as the floor. I stand up, bracing myself, as the dizziness rushes in and then recedes. I take inventory. Bending arms and legs to check the joints. Opening and closing my mouth to test the jaw. Running my tongue along the inside of my teeth to confirm none are missing. Wiggling all ten fingers and toes. Rotating head on neck. Bending over, back straight, to touch the floor and assess the spine.

It only takes seconds to review all I know of what goes on in the Bureau of Thought Reform. I don't even know what agents of the Loop look like. As for the aims of the agency, I know even less. Those leaving the Loop after reintegration don't speak of what happened to them. This silence is what elicits true terror.

I glide carefully forward, not moving too quickly lest I slam my bare foot into an unseen obstacle, keeping one hand on the wall and the other stretched out in front of me. I must create a workable strategy if I hope to get through whatever I'll face here. It's trouble how little I know about an agency so essential to the regime. I've lived my life as a contented little AA cell, ignorant of anything that doesn't concern my agency's business while, around me, the whole of the regime stretched, unknowable.

A person goes into the Loop one way and comes out another, if he comes out at all, returning to his life a shattered individual, his mind forcibly broken and realigned with Party doctrine—a visibly devastating process. I've sent many men to the Loop for weeks at a time. When they come back, their ability to be diligent agents is severely compromised. Loud noises—guns firing, boots in the hall, doors slamming—send these men into paroxysms of hysteria. Recovery from the Loop lasts the rest of a person's life. An agent returning from thought adjustment will never find himself placed in highly stressful positions, making upward motion in the AA impossible. But upon a condemned agent's return to his post, I never asked him what happened in the Loop. I never cared.

I reach another wall in twelve steps and have to breathe deeply to steady a surging sensation of helplessness, a thing I've not felt since childhood.

I repeat cadence until calmness returns—*"Honor when it is easier to do the opposite. Integrity when those around us lack it entirely, loyalty to those unarmed innocents above all else."* I must retain my wits. Without knowledge of what Lara confessed, I don't know what I'm up against. Every thought seems useless. I don't know this agency's means and measures. Even knowing the accusations against me wouldn't bridge the gap of my ignorance.

I continue along this wall as the room seems to grow cooler around me. I know a great deal about torture from initial training, but none of it has to do with reeducation. I'm familiar with the brand of torture most useful to me onsite and in a Kill Room—how to pull fingernails and teeth, where to punch to cause the greatest pain but the least internal injury, how to administer a beating that will leave a person conscious and able to confess, how to break bones, how to flay skin. But the AA doesn't have use for sustained techniques or in-depth psychological torture.

I meet the other wall in ten steps and continue on, eventually finding a steel door with no handle and no cracks along the frame to shed light into the cell. Feeling around, I locate a slot near the bottom, mostly likely for delivering food and water. Presently, it's closed. There's no way to open it from the inside.

I walk to the final wall, coming back to where I started. I drop slowly to hands and knees, then travel the length of the cold cement floor, making broad, sweeping motions with my arms to find anything not attached to the wall. I give up after several minutes, finding no more than a cold metal toilet pushed into one corner. If I'm going to die, it won't be in this room—no metal drain in the middle of the floor. The blow to my head seems to have dulled my already lackluster emotions. Torture will come eventually, but it hardly troubles me.

I sit back, legs drawn up, and rest my head in my hands. In the dark and the cold, waiting's all I can do.

*

First I lose my hold on time, minutes, hours, days all melting into one another. They took me into custody in the early morning, but I don't know how long I was unconscious. I count out sixty seconds to make a minute, then count out sixty of those to make an hour. I travel the length of the room and count again, the constant stream of numbers keeping my head occupied. I can't stop shivering. The room's getting colder by the second.

I count out an hour. Time only exists when I put my hands on it like this, fleshing it out, naming it with a parade of ascending numbers. I don't doubt they're watching me, but if I can't see the cameras, they might as well not exist. There are no noises past the ones I create. In my daily life, I prize silence, but now I long for sounds not originating from me. I miss the loudspeaker, the maternal mouthpiece of the regime that accompanies me on city streets, in Complex corridors, or in the halls of the Dormitories. That voice is normalcy and order. The absence of it, chaos.

I repeat cadence, curling up on the cement, knees against my chest, shivering. Hard to keep warm with bare feet. The cold seems to be coming up from the floor to infect the air. Trembling, I count out another hour. Time slips the instant I stop whispering numbers. Certainty doesn't exist here. Only I exist.

I repeat cadence.

I count out an hour.

A sharp ache stabs my stomach. How long since I last ate? I remember the sandwich in the Complex cafeteria, the exact taste of it. I remember the conversation with Sup3 and the expression on his face—concern in exhaustion's clothing. Had he warned me? No. He wouldn't risk his post. And if he'd meant it as a warning, what did he expect me to do? Defect? I never would've gone underground. Only cowards run, only those who choose their whims over the stability of their government.

Hunger makes it hard to keep track of the seconds and minutes ticking by in my head. I whisper cadence. I crawl to the door and push on the slot. Nothing—no movement, no sound.

When regime slogans pop into my head, I say them aloud.

"Equality for all animals, human and nonhuman."

I cross the room, touch the opposite wall.

"Meat is murder, comrades. Dairy is organized rape. Fur is sacrilegious."

I cross the room, scuttling on hands and knees.

"Tomorrow is another day closer to perfection. We do not eat anything with a face."

I circumnavigate the cell, my reaching fingers desperate for something different.

"The sanctity of life is the sanctity of all life."

I sit down cross-legged in what I estimate to be the center of the room.

"Personal freedom means freedom from harm."

The cement's uncomfortable, which I suppose is the point. Nothing swells within me at the thought of Lara, no sensation of sinking, no stirring of a heart I can't say I still possess. Only contemplation lacking emotion. She's surely dead by now. The goal of the Kill Floor is to extract information on other fugitives and illegal activity—the bitter irony of the situation, that I initiated my own downfall by insisting on the interrogation of captives before execution, elicits no emotion in me—not to send a person for thought adjustment. I don't know what she told her interrogator, but

I must be alive because my foolishness stopped just short of recklessness. True, I shouldn't have known her in the first place, but what did I actually do? Nothing seditious. That's the important thing. Keeping my mind on that will get me to the other side of this, if an *other side* exists. When the torture starts, I have to keep from confessing things I didn't actually do. In training, each trainee underwent torture in order to test his level of pain tolerance. Mine was the highest. But they didn't break bones or pull teeth in training. They didn't cut very deeply or beat too forcefully. The pain was intense, but I never feared for my safety.

Lara received no training to prepare for what they did to her. Executions are only swift on the street. In a Kill Room, they can last hours, with confessions taken down between screams. I try to imagine myself screaming as my arm is twisted out of the socket or broken. A filmy picture forms—agents beating me bloody while I spit teeth and blurt whatever they want me to say to make it stop. The horror's all around me, but I feel nothing but hunger.

I sink down, pressing my face against cement, damp clothes sticking to my skin. I count out an hour to forget about the food I want. Everything aches from lying on the floor. I twist over onto my back. This is no better—it relieves the pressure on one part of my body only to increase it on another. Nothing helps this wrenching, empty yearning. Not just in my stomach—I feel it in my bones, in my pounding head. I close my eyes and it's as dark as when I have them open. I don't know if it's night or day. Is this the goal? Disorientation? A loss of that inner anchor that keeps one's sanity

from drifting, unmoored? The Bureau of Thought Reform is so
detrimental to the regime, but I have no firm idea about its goals, its
methods and procedures, its limitations, if any. I know the AA. It's
not encouraged to know more than one's function.

I whisper cadence to the floor, my feet flat against cement. I
rub my hands over the gooseflesh on my arms. It does nothing. Just
cold skin touching cold skin. I smile in the dark, grim and invisible.
Faux touch exists even here.

*

I sleep in what feels like snatches, but there's no way to tell. The slot
in the door does open, but follows no real pattern. I never hear boots
approaching or voices in the hall, only the click of the slot. A dim
sliver of light, never enough to touch me or uncover a bit of the cell's
mystery, something drops to the floor, and the slot closes again. The
first time, I'm lying in a heap in the corner for warmth, dangling very
near sleep. The noise sends me shrinking back against the wall, ready
to spring to my feet and defend myself though my strength's
diminishing rapidly. The thin shard of light appears, as though by
magic, and an object hits the floor before the slot closes again, sealing
out the light.

I crawl to the door and find something soft. Bread. I devour
it without thinking, the hunger stronger than my better judgment.
Only after eating it do I think of poison, but still I'm feeling around
for more bread. When I don't find any, I retreat to my corner.

The next time the slot opens, it's an orange. I eat it rind and all, no thought of poison worrying me. They won't kill me before I'm interrogated.

After the orange, a small bottle of water. I drink it greedily, my thirst rising rather than being sated. The slot opens again.

"Send the bottle through," a firm voice says.

I do and the slot closes. No sound of boots walking away. The room must be soundproof, just like a Kill Room. The air's cold, perhaps sixty degrees now. Exercise would make me warmer, but I shouldn't waste energy needlessly. I don't know when the slot will open next. I stare into the darkness, my eyes unable to focus, and make a list of my choices. I can crouch in the corner for warmth, and I can wait. Nothing else exists.

*

The high whine of an intercom blasting to life tosses me out of sleep too light for dreaming. I look up, blindly searching for speakers that sound positioned in every corner of the cell. The Party Chairman speaks, repeating the same phrase.

"To lose you is no loss. To keep you is no gain. To lose you is no loss. To keep you is no gain."

His voice bounces off the walls, echoing, assaulting my ears.

"To lose you is no loss. To keep you is no gain."

I spin into a tight ball, trembling hard, my body numb and sluggish with cold. Teeth chattering in my head, I open and close my hands to make sure I still can. The air in the cell is just warm enough to ensure I don't freeze, just as the food I receive is just enough to keep me alive.

"To lose you is no loss."

I shut my eyes, but can't shut out Chairman Goldstein's voice.

"To keep you is no gain."

I see his face burning with disgust, the biting glare of his dark eyes, the indomitable squaring of his broad shoulders. He has intimate knowledge of all my failures. Shame and regret dance just out of reach, as though someone else is having the experience and simply relaying the idea of the sentiments to me.

I repeat cadence, trying to cancel out that accusatory voice.

"Honor when it is easier to do the opposite."

"To lose you is no loss."

"Integrity when those around us lack it entirely."

"To keep you is no gain."

"Loyalty to those unarmed innocents above all else."

"To lose you is no loss."

I understand the regime, at least as much as any man can be said to understand. It stands for the collective, even to the detriment of the individual. It must be this way, because individuals are weak and impulsive. I myself have been weak and impulsive. When I act as I ought—a cell in the enormous body of the AA—no difficulty arises. It's only when I go my own way, when I see fit to defer to my whim as opposed to Party doctrine, that a problem arises.

"To lose you is no loss. To keep you is no gain."

I try to curl up more tightly, cement scratching bare skin, the intercom invading my ears. Occasionally, it gives off a piercing shriek of feedback so sharp I flinch. I asked for a break from the silence, but now I want silence back. The Chairman's voice obliterates all comfort. I see her face and blue eyes, feel her hair between numb fingers. I wipe away a single tear before it travels over the fine peppering of freckles on her cheeks.

She's dead.

That's the best-case scenario. The worst? She has her own cell and her own waiting game.

I give myself over to Chairman Goldstein's voice. Unable to sleep, body aching and trembling, I count out an hour, only making it halfway. When I try to recite cadence, my words mimic the Party Chairman's instead. His voice is the only objective thing in the darkness, booming through shadows. We speak the same words together.

"To lose you is no loss. To keep you is no gain."

I repeat it until my voice begins to fail, until the words rub my throat raw. In the endless, empty dark, only two things exist—the Chairman's voice and mine.

*

The intercom never stops. It gets louder and the room grows colder. I often wake to mist settling on me from above, leaving clothes perpetually damp. Aching, my thoughts running riot, there isn't a moment that hunger and thirst don't twist my insides. The sound of the slot opening and closing becomes the only objective proof of the outside world.

For me, sleep has always been dreamless and restful. Now nightmares descend, destroying any hope of rest. I don't dream of monsters but of the past. The regime took this from me, giving me such a fiercely brilliant present that the past seemed unreal in comparison. But it comes rushing back to me in the dark, all the things I never think about—my family, the things I've done.

I hear the Chairman's voice and know I'm no loss and no gain. I wake in a cold sweat to find the slot sealed shut. I press my hands against the floor, hang my throbbing head, and think of the straggler.

Do you weep?

I could've answered him. I don't weep and haven't for years. Not since I had to face them, to explain what I'd done. Mother wept when I told her of my AA enlistment. Father shook his head and said nothing. But the three of us wept the night I walked in from the rain, my uniform soaked with blood. It was the last time I confessed anything, the last time I wept and sought forgiveness. Mother attacked me, pummeling my chest with blows light as kisses. Father bloodied my nose before shoving me out into the rain. I didn't protect myself from either of them. It was my penance. I accepted his rage and my mother's sorrow.

You aren't welcome here, Father said, and Mother couldn't speak through sobs. I lay on my back in the front yard, lightning electrifying the sky, and they shut the door to me. The pouring rain washed the blood from my uniform. Thunder shook the ground and I waited for lightning to strike me. When it didn't, I walked away with hunched and shaking shoulders. My brother would never come home again and neither would I.

To lose him was no loss. To keep him was no gain.

I haven't spoken his name in over ten years.

"*Josh*," I whisper, and the booming voice of the Chairman swallows it whole.

TWENTY-FOUR

A lock turns over and the intercom stops, cutting the Chairman off mid-sentence. Cowering against the wall, I whisper the rest.

"To keep you is no gain."

The door creaks open and weak light trickles in as agents in dark uniforms invade the cell. Hands take me by my upper arms and pull me to my feet. This hurts my shoulders. My legs and back ache. My knees buckle but the agents keep me standing. I raise my eyes as a cloth hood is pulled over my head, shutting out the light from the corridor. No handcuffs. These men must know I have no energy to escape or fight. Walking is its own dilemma. After a few moments of awkward shuffling, I want to double over, hands on knees or, better yet, fold onto the floor in a heap, gasping and shivering.

They lead me down the hall. The waist of my AA issue pants is loose around my hips. I don't have a belt—they took it, perhaps fearing a suicide attempt. No one speaks to me. The hood keeps out the light. I loved shadows before, but now I truly live in the dark. I'm not forced to go quickly, but my sore, swollen joints make walking exceedingly difficult. I stumble and the agents don't let me fall.

The hands on my arms pull me to a stop and bring me sharply around to the right. My head rocks, light on my shoulders. It's dark, but I can tell when my vision goes black and comes back again. I lose my balance and the agents drag me instead of setting me right again. I make a dismayed noise as they suddenly push me into a seated position, expecting to crash to the floor. I fall into a chair and bow my head, wiling my shivering to come under control. This room isn't as cold as the cell. I listen to boots on the floor, striding in and out of the door. My body's weak, but my hearing's as acute as ever. A single set of boots walks past, followed by a chair moving directly in front of me. A body settles into the chair. The door closes behind me. This is an interrogation.

"Remove the hood," the man across from me says.

I straighten in my chair. I know this agent.

I pull the hood off. Sup3's across from me, a table between us. This doesn't look like a Kill Room. The light's too dim. Still, if someone's going to end my life, I'd like it to be Sup3. A masked man in black stands to my right, holding an automatic rifle. Not AA—the uniform's similar in color only. Sup3 dismisses the man, and waits until the door closes to begin speaking.

For once, I don't have to work to keep my face blank. I don't possess the energy for an expression. Habit compels me to wait for him to begin.

He keeps dark eyes on me, his face conveying nothing. "Will you talk about the girl now?"

"There isn't much to say." My low voice sounds foreign from lack of use.

"I suggest you start somewhere."

"I told her my name."

"Why?"

"She asked me." I'm warming up, but the hunger and sleep deprivation leave me shaky, with a throbbing head and dry mouth. I could ask Sup3 for food, but refuse to sink that low.

"Do you know her name?" he asks.

I nod, blinking to clear my fuzzy, burning vision.

He raises both eyebrows as he spins an index finger. *Get on with it.*

"Lara Miranda."

"How did you come into contact with her?"

I run numb fingers over the stubble on my cheeks. I've kept myself clean-shaven since late adolescence.

"I captured her father at a speakeasy."

Sup3 shakes his head. It looks like sleep has been dancing away from him as well, though for different reasons. "For this you compromised yourself?" He sounds truly disappointed.

It's useless to tell him I didn't consider it a compromise. Someone does, clearly, or I wouldn't be here.

"Do you know how quickly she turned on you?"

"What was being done to her at the time?"

"Do you care?" he asks.

"No."

I can see my answer pleases him. "Explain your relationship with this girl."

The words take a great effort to summon. "It was fact-finding in nature. I took her father into custody. On the Kill Floor, he shared many things about the resistance that were previously unknown to me. He was concerned for his daughter, and so mentioned her to me. I thought I could exploit her recent loss to gather information of interest to the agency. She had no knowledge concerning speakeasies, but did know of some safehouses. Her information eventually resulted in our most recent raid."

I put my elbows on the table and lean onto them, trying to take the stress off my back. It doesn't work. Everything's sore and stiff.

"Why didn't you inform me of this fact-finding mission?"

"It didn't seem necessary until I had results."

"But once you did, why didn't you inform me?" he asks.

"I informed Intelligence, though not of the girl specifically. At that time, she was already wanted by the AA."

"Do you see the problem here?"

"Yes," I say, truly meaning it.

An expression passes over Sup3's face that indicates he doesn't think I quite grasp the gravity of the situation. If I didn't before, I certainly do now.

"You've always been a skilled, diligent agent, which makes this even more disappointing."

I nod but say nothing. Sup3 knows many things I don't—the details of Lara's confession, what I'm being accused of, if I'll be allowed to live. I could ask him to share this information and perhaps he'd tell me, but the answers might dishearten me more than the uncertainty.

"You committed the greatest misstep, putting yourself before the agency." He pauses, eyebrow raised, giving me an opportunity to defend myself that I have no intention of taking.

My eyelids droop in the warm air and it takes enormous effort to focus on Sup3. I can't sleep in the cell—the chill invades my bones and tightens my achy muscles. My head's pounding from exhaustion and hunger and my scattered thoughts keep wandering to what will befall me after this. Solitary confinement, minimal food, and sleep deprivation can't be the long and short of my punishment.

"Did you have a physical relationship with this girl?" Sup3 asks.

"No." I can't properly define what was between us, but I never considered brushing her lips with mine or, worse, taking her to bed. Perhaps my moderately gentle treatment stems from the fact that I didn't do these things. I can't be sure. Knowing what Lara confessed might help. Then again, it might not.

"What happens now?" I ask.

Sup3 fixes me with a flat stare. It's impossible to read his true feelings once he decides to hide them.

"The girl's confession has called your loyalties into question. Do you understand how serious this is?"

Men have lost their lives for lesser offenses.

"May I know what she said?" I ask.

"Does it matter?" he says, vacant anti-expression unchanging. "The issue is that there was something to say in the first place."

That's a definitive end to the matter. It would be helpful to know what I'm accused of doing, but he clearly doesn't intend to elaborate.

"Why are you here?" My headache's soaring to a sickening pinnacle. Even my squinted eyes are pulsing. The light, though low, is terrible. My extremities are warming up—nail beds going from purple to light blue—but I hardly consider this a consolation. I'm still in the Loop and will remain here long after Sup3 walks out into the sunshine, a man at liberty to do as he pleases.

His slight shrug gives me a glimpse of the old Sup3, the one I saw so often on nights after a raid, the hours creeping towards daylight.

"I wanted to ask you a few questions."

I raise my eyebrow, inviting him to continue without opening my mouth.

"Does this girl mean anything to you?"

"No." Very little does anymore. She is no loss. I am no gain.

"Are you still a loyal Party member, faithful to the AA and your government?"

"Yes."

"What are you willing to do to prove this?"

Keeping my eyes locked with his, I answer with as much feeling as I can muster. "Whatever I have to do."

Sup3 sits back in his chair. I sense the end of our conversation. Whatever he was after, he now has. I watch him leave without a word. Two black clad agents return, one training his weapon on me while the other approaches with the hood in his hands. As he lifts it above my head, I close my eyes, locking myself in darkness before he has the chance.

*

Days have passed. Or weeks. It's difficult to say. The slot has opened three times since I saw Sup3—twice for small bits of food and once for a few ounces of water. The room's colder, the intercom louder. Instead of the Chairman's flat, chilling message, it now broadcasts the slaughter of animals. A video accompanies the audio, projected from a place above the door, depicting all manners of cruelty. I saw such things in initial training. We watched the clips to get our blood up. It took less than five minutes to have us red-faced and screaming, hands balled into fists and feet stomping. Very Pavlovian in nature, except we didn't drool at the ringing of a bell. We instead became enraged enough to kill at the sight of nonhuman animal abuse or exploitation.

I shut my eyes to scenes of the most revolting butchery and try to cover my ears as well, but my trembling fingers do little to block the sounds, which are deafening. A horrible cacophony of bleated, inhuman screams, throats cut, the loud hum of nonhuman animals electrocuted, the blood and guts pouring onto kill room floors. My rage exhausts me. The air feels as cool as fifty degrees. Everything's damp.

A pig lets out a high squeal. I open my eyes in time to see it electrocuted by a metal wand, the picture so large it encompasses an entire wall. I flinch as a knife slices through the poor animal's neck, but am rapt with horror. More squealing shatters the air before disintegrating to gurgling as blood gushes from the wound.

I shut my eyes and attempt to count out an hour but can't concentrate past a few moments. The screaming is terrible. Even before the Overthrow and AA training, I watched these types of videos online and showed them to my parents, my brother, to anyone who'd listen. I can close my eyes to the sights but can't turn off my imagination, which fires vividly to life, providing pictures even more vicious than the ones flashing unseen on the wall. Cows hung upside down by a single leg that breaks under the pressure of all that weight. Pigs electrocuted anally or bashed on the head before receiving a knife across the throat. Chickens with beaks burned off so they can live five to a tiny cage and not peck each other, thus damaging the meat.

I scream but it doesn't stop. Everything comes in flashes just as clear as the video in front of me, though I refuse to watch. Calves in small cages, unable to move so the meat remains the whitish-pink of anemic flesh. Turkeys plucked alive when the stunning doesn't work correctly. Fully conscious pigs immersed in scalding water for hair removal. Male chicks ground into feed, as they can't lay eggs and the cost to bring them to adulthood is too high. Nonhuman animals forced to breed in disease-ridden pens until the body can no longer produce young—after this, slaughter. Crowded, manure-laden feedlots where animals are unnaturally fattened by the thousands to produce meat for some human's table, if they don't first succumb to cholera, pneumonia, or dysentery.

I scream my throat raw but the intercom just gets louder, the noise expanding, bouncing off bare walls, reverberating, needling into my skull. I begged for light and now I have some, though it brings such gruesome images. Keeping eyes sealed, I fold into myself, letting the noise break over me. The horrid, miserable sounds of torture. Of death. And for what? Hamburgers, lamb chops, steaks, fried chicken, veal cutlets, and the like. All for the caprice of our palates.

"We do not eat anything with a face!" I shout, words disappearing beneath the bleating and stunning. *"Freedom from harm is true freedom! Meat is murder! Veganism is moral uprightness!"*

The screaming makes my face warm, but everything else is cold. I twist my hands into fists, nails digging into palms. I want my gun. I want to administer justice to those responsible for this torture, to those ordering their porterhouse steaks and cheeseburgers and chicken fingers. These cowards order flesh without ever thinking of the animal itself. They depend upon pleasantries and clever turns of phrase—*pork* and *beef* instead of *pig carcass* and *dead cow*—to hide the fact of the matter: that it takes a murderer to make another sentient being into a commodity.

I howl Party doctrine at the top of my lungs, feeling my voice break but not hearing it, going over all the old arguments, my head dizzy with this intense surge of passion.

All animals are sentient beings.

All sentient beings deserve proper consideration.

The line between human and nonhuman animals is arbitrary at best, no different than the line between a person of normal mental ability and one who's severely handicapped.

Through all this—the nonhuman animals shrieking their suffering, the sounds of the knife and the stunner, the video that refuses to stop—I hear my brother laughing as he refutes my arguments with a steady string of his own faulty logic, his denial too thick to ford. I see his smile, smell the innocent blood on his breath.

The stink of meat.

My imagination pulses, sending picture after horrifying picture skittering across my mind. The stockyards where nonhuman animals stand ankle-deep in manure, shivering from pneumonia, perishing from dysentery, struggling under their immense weight.

He had meat on his breath. When I confronted him, he laughed and pushed me aside. I did what I had to do. The AA understood. It always does. Mother and Father were a separate story. They only saw the blood. I didn't get the chance to tell them about the meat on his breath, about sentient beings, about fairness.

My throat's shredded, my head pounding with an ache that refuses to relent. I lie flat on the cement, back aching, breathing heavily, body twitching. The surging, angry emotions running through me, making me warm, float slowly away. My blood's up, but my energy's depleted. I moan at the sounds of suffering, my screaming finished. The point of my life, of my career, is to prevent things like this from ever happening again.

I can't get comfortable on the floor, not with the intercom stinging my ears. I cover them to no avail and squeeze my eyes more tightly, praying for sleep I know won't come.

*

When I wake coughing and shuddering, my lucid dreams often continue in the dark. Sometimes I'm talking to Lara. Sometimes my brother. Sometimes I'm trying to explain what I did to my parents.

The slot hasn't opened in a long time. I stop expecting it, though I'm desperate for sustenance. This gets better with time, but sleep never comes easily. When the intercom's on, I want silence. When it goes off, I want it for stimulus. I haven't spoken to anyone since Sup3. I can't even guess how long ago that was. Time has lost all continuity. Only the most painful things remain immediate— hunger, thirst, the cold that grips me, the dampness of my clothes, my aching joints and bones. Sitting up hurts. Lying down hurts. Even breathing hurts. When I gather the energy to speak, my voice belongs to a rasping stranger.

Today I hear Josh.

I sit pushed into a corner—the one opposite the latrine— head down, hands slowly opening, then closing. My numb fingers feel full of broken glass.

Josh was the oldest. After two boys, Mother prayed for a daughter. One came, but she died in infancy before the Overthrow. I don't even remember her name. I do remember Mother's eyes forever glassy with tears, but I had my own affairs and Josh had his. Years later, I formally enlisted in the Animal Alliance—I'd been fully immersed in underground activities for years—and Josh's protests began to take over his nights and days.

"It's a matter of law and order," I whisper to no one, voice barely cracking the silence.

His response snakes through the shadows, so crisp and real that I can see his sardonic grin.

It's a matter of protest and liberty.

We went upstairs to have our fights, away from our parents, who couldn't stand to hear us assaulting each other with heated words, threats, and eventually fists. I already wore the AA armband out of solidarity though I hadn't yet submitted to formal training and wouldn't for months. He wore the old flag, with its stars and stripes—a protest in itself; the new government had initiated a process to abolish it. I called him a traitor. He called me a weak-minded conformist. Father came running when our discussions deteriorated into shouting or violence. Mother pleaded with us to find our places with them in the middle—I was too far right and Josh left. He was bigger by two inches and forty pounds. He'd always been bigger. When we fought, he pinned me to the ground or pushed me against the wall, twisting my arm behind my back and threatening to break it. I believed him because he had broken it once, when I was eight and he eleven. Only extensive training in hand-to-hand combat eliminated my size as a disadvantage.

The Overthrow reached its pinnacle and the Party moved into its permanent place. I helped with the underground movement and already had blood on my hands, though not innocent blood. The honor of the AA armband wasn't bestowed upon everyone involved in the revolution. Only those who proved themselves could take this first step into the black. Protesters abounded—holdovers from the dying government, which tolerated and encouraged seditious acts under the guise of freedom of speech. Josh became one such person. It was a constant source of embarrassment for me.

"You run your mouth," I said. "And when you aren't running it you're filling it with meat."

"Open your eyes. You kill for these people and you don't even care what they stand for. It's outright tyranny. They're repealing our civil liberties—"

"The liberty to murder the innocent? I'd hardly call that an ethical liberty. True freedom is freedom from harm—"

"You sound like one of their clones, *comrade*."

"And you're a Party traitor," I said, not raising my voice at all. I never lost my cool. My inability to display appropriate emotion always exasperated my family. Even when Josh broke my arm, I neither screamed nor burst into tears.

"I'll never be a Party member," he said, and I believed him.

"Then you won't survive."

He lunged at me and I stepped out of his grasp, delivering a swift punch to the soft part of his stomach. He caught me by the throat, tumbling us both into the wall. Father screamed at us from downstairs. He always took Josh's side, but this no longer mattered to me, as I had the AA. The agency became the only family I needed. Shortly after this fight, I enlisted and left for training, my mother's bitter tears bidding me farewell.

TWENTY-FIVE

They come for me in the dreams.

I open my eyes at the hands on my shoulders, wrenching me to my feet, the black hood already over my face. My bare feet slide on the floor, tingly and numb. The hands on my arms tighten, keeping me upright. Everything's weak. I don't remember the last time the slot opened. I barely recall my conversation with Sup3. My tired mind insists he was never here at all. This is all a dream, a nightmare. I remember Lara talking about the atrocities against the human animal, my brother whispering, *sedition used to be called freedom of speech.*

No one rushes me. I shuffle out of the cell at my own pace, my body fighting me constantly. In childhood, it was often my nemesis, succumbing to sickness after worsening sickness. For this reason, I understand the importance of one's health and have always taken excellent care of myself. Most of my work in the AA is—*was;* all that's finished now—very physical. So, I kept myself in excellent shape. Now I can't walk the length of the cell without collapsing in a breathless, shivering heap.

I walk carefully on sore feet, the hands holding me firmly on either side, the barrel of a gun pressed against my spine. If I resisted, would the man at the trigger fire into the skinny expanse of my back or the base of my skull, pretty, painless, easy?

The hands pull me to a stop. A metal door opens. The hands push me forward more quickly. One ankle twists with a sharp jolt, but I don't fall. When I can't regain my feet, the hands drag me, turn me around so abruptly my head spins, and shove me against a long board that reaches from head to toe. It tilts suddenly back into a horizontal position, the movement leaving me dizzier still. Straps cinch tightly at my ankles, knees, and chest. The air here is warmer, but breathing still hurts.

When the hood lifts, I squint through half-shut lids. The light's low, but even a little makes my headache worse.

I'm in a small room with one masked, armed agent positioned at the door and another standing closer, but not close enough to touch if my hands were free. My face is level with this agent's waist, which means I'm about three feet from the ground, more or less.

"We're going to have a conversation, you and I," this lead man says, voice low but jovial, dark eyes shining through the holes in his mask.

No expression rises to the surface of my face, though I understand I'm about to be tortured. My emotions have begun to swell and bubble over when I'm alone in the cell, but right now, they don't exist at all.

"Do you understand?" he asks, speaking to me in the nurturing way a father does his young son. Josh also spoke to me this way, though he meant it as an insult. The agent's friendly play doesn't disguise his true intentions—to get information from me. It will be best to cooperate fully, which means answering him aloud.

"Yes," I say, voice a rasping whisper.

"Then let's get started!" he says, speaking with real enthusiasm. A shiver runs through me at the thought of my own eagerness at the beginning of an interrogation.

I don't respond. My agreement or disagreement hardly matters. I try to breathe deeply, to prepare for what's coming. Since joining the AA, I've always been in control of what happened to me. I submitted to pain or discomfort in accordance with my whim. I submitted to the laws of the regime because I found them virtuous. I submitted to the rule of the Party Chairman because I found him righteous. I'll have to submit to this as well if I want to make it easier on myself. This is the will of the regime.

The agent produces a photograph from the front pocket of his uniform.

"Do you recognize this traitor?"

I have to wait for my vision to clear, but I know what I'm about to see.

It's a picture of Lara from the neck up. Both eyes blackened and puffy. A sizeable bruise spreading from her jaw to right below the eye socket on the left side of her face. A split, fat bottom lip.

Dried blood beneath both nostrils. A large knot protruding from the middle of her forehead.

My face doesn't change. Within me, no sucking absence initiates, no elevated heartbeat, no stirring of concern. I look past the photo at the agent's dark eyes.

"Yes."

"Identify her."

"She's Lara Miranda." Or, more accurately, she *was* Lara Miranda. This photo was likely taken minutes before her execution. Seeing her battered face is supposed to elicit sympathy from me. Or, better, anger. Perhaps this agent expects tears. Others clearly believe our relationship was a deeply romantic one.

"How do you know her?"

"I captured her father at a speakeasy. He led me to her." Interrogation protocol calls for these warm up questions, which Sup3 already asked. Loop agents must've monitored our conversation. These preliminary questions provide a rhythm that will end in torture if I don't provide satisfactory responses. My fingers twitch on the wooden board—the only sign of my rising distress, but even this feels cold and far away. My body's numb, my emotions number.

"Why didn't you alert your immediate supervisor of this?" he asks.

"I didn't think it was necessary unless and until something beneficial came of it." I want to see his expression, to measure it against my answers, but the mask keeps me from reading him.

My shaky mind summons an image of Lara's blue eyes swelled nearly shut, the knot on her forehead. How did they end her? A bullet to the back of the head? Bludgeoning? Strangulation? Starvation—have they had the time? Hanging? I've seen it all. My method of choice, a bullet to the head. If I want maximum suffering, I go for a slow-bleeding kill shot to the stomach. Impassively, I wonder which way they'll execute me.

"And did something come of it?" he asks.

"Yes. The safehouse location."

"Why didn't you alert your immediate supervisor at that moment?"

I close my eyes to clear the fuzziness from my vision and open them again before answering, exhaustion rolling over me in a thick wave as I struggle to focus. "I wanted to double check the veracity of the information."

He makes a weird noise, like a muffled laugh. "Explain the nature of your relationship with this Party traitor."

"I lied to her in order to glean information that might prove useful to the regime." I've also received extensive training in conducting an interrogation. One should only answer the question asked and keep it short. Offering additional information, explanations, or justifications causes trouble. Stories get mixed up. Lies get told that can't hold up to hours of tireless interrogation. I don't plan to lie, but I also don't plan to become hopelessly tangled in a web of superfluous responses.

"Drop him," the agent says.

My head plunges towards the floor while my feet shoot up where I can see them. But instead of my head smashing into cement, knocking me senseless, it plunges into freezing water. Breathless, I can't clear my nose when water rushes in, burning its way down my throat and into my lungs. I thrash against the straps, hands balled into painful fists, bare feet flailing uselessly. In training, I had an abnormally high breath-hold break point during waterboarding trials, routinely going for well over two minutes, even after repeated dunking. But I was also in perfect health. Now my lungs itch from suppressing a cough. Wheezing, I suck in water and can't cough it out again.

The board returns to an upright position. Sputtering, my throat a closed fist, I can't breathe. I fall forward with the strength of my coughs, water pouring down the front of my unkempt uniform. The wooden plank doesn't move. Finally, the air comes. I cough so deeply, my vision clouds, then goes black. My chest feels full of water. I can't unclench my fists, can't make my head burst to release the awful pressure.

The board rights itself, sliding down with terrible speed, leaving me flat again. The agent's standing above me, hands folded behind his back.

"One minute," he says, smile apparent in the tone of his voice. "It'll be a minute and a half next time. Shall we begin again?"

I must get my breathing under control, must prepare for the next drop. No use fooling myself. There will be more. I make hazy calculations, my mind refusing to move as fast as I need it to. The coughing will lower my breath-hold break point, but by how much? I was in top physical condition during training. Now breathing too deeply, holding my breath, or simply being conscious brings on a violent coughing fit. Self-control is of the utmost importance but I have no workable strategy to achieve it. My fuzzy, mutinous mind renders focus and planning impossible.

I manage to unclench my fists. Step one.

"You habitually exchanged seditious statements during your meetings with this defector, isn't that true?"

"No," I say between gasps, shaking my throbbing, helium-filled head.

"Didn't you read blacklisted books together as well?"

"No."

"Were you aware of the blacklisted materials?"

"Yes."

"Why didn't you bring this to the agency's attention?" he asks, voice rapidly losing its cheeriness as we approach the meat of the interrogation.

"It wasn't enough. I wanted a safehouse or a speakeasy."

"Drop him."

Instinct surges into my aching, empty spaces and takes care of everything. I breathe in with care—not too deeply—as the board tips backwards and immerses me in water up to the neck. I begin to count out a minute. In training, I routinely made two rotations without much trouble, but now a coughing fit itches in my chest near the end of the first minute, breath bubbling as it escapes my sealed lips. I'm straining too hard. I try to flatten my hands on the board, to relax, but can't. The coughing bursts free from my chest, tensing every muscle in my body. Sucking in a stinging mouthful of water, I thrash against the straps that bind me. The numbers—my tenuous hold on calm—drift away into icy water. I can't regain control. I'm going to drown while these men watch.

The board rights itself. I fight to bring up the water I swallowed and aspirated, hair hanging over my eyes, thick and dripping. Everything's wet—uniform, skin, thoughts. The immediacy of my helplessness breaks over me. I'm at the mercy of the regime and always have been. My presence here only makes this fact inescapable.

I cough my throat raw, chest alive with stabbing pains and head fit to burst. The air comes in snatches and gasps. I hang my leaking head, aching from coughing, from the taxing struggle for air.

As the board swings back to its horizontal position, I brace myself for a drop that doesn't come, an involuntary tremor racing through me.

"A minute and a half," the agent says, sounding both amused and impressed. "Next time, two minutes. What was your training record, comrade? Two minutes and twenty-six seconds?"

I turn my head to hack up more water. That was my exact record for repeated dunking and this man knows it.

"Shall we try for that? Or do you want to cooperate?"

"Yes," I say in a breathless whisper, meaning that I want to cooperate.

The agent crosses his arms over his broad chest. He's bigger than Sup3. My vision's too wet and blurry to see his eyes. The agent at the door is a dark blob. The man asking the questions is a bit clearer, but not by much.

"I'd like to know more about your relationship with this girl," he says, not bothering with pretense this time.

"We spoke on occasion. She mistakenly thought me a sympathetic ear."

"Fact finding in nature, yes?" he asks, confirming my suspicion that agents listened to my conversation with Sup3.

"Yes."

"That's all?"

"Yes."

"You never slept with her?"

"No."

"Never engaged in philosophical conversations that contained inflammatory remarks about the regime?"

"She spoke so," I say. "I did not."

"You expect me to believe that?"

Not a real question. I decline to answer.

"Drop him."

I barely have time to inhale before going under. I focus on counting, on numbers rising slowly, one at a time. I flatten my hands on the board to avoid thrashing. Unnecessary motion wastes breath. At the end of one minute, I start on the next. My throat burns, the coughing growing difficult to hold back. At one minute forty-five seconds, I cough, expelling all my breath in a single instant. The water rushes into my nose and mouth. I thrash as water fills my airway, losing all track of the numbers as my panic rises and throat squeezes shut.

The board swings upright and I throw up all the water I swallowed, water shooting from nose and mouth though my throat's still locked tight. I pull in air as soon as it will come, but the coughing only gets worse. I shut my eyes to the dim light and the black shapes watching me. I'll drown next time. Each drop is robbing me of something vital. My mind feels twisted out of joint. Fatigue clings to me with desperate fingers. The straps dig painfully into my chest. My hands twitch. My body shakes. My feet have turned to numb things disconnected from the rest of my body. Only a false confession will end this, and I refuse to give one.

The board flattens again. I open my eyes to murky, damp light.

"I lied, comrade," the agent says. "That was two minutes and fifteen seconds." He chuckles. "Shall we try for three next time?"

"No." I have to concentrate to get the rest out. "Try for five. We're wasting time. My answers won't change."

No order comes this time. I plunge into the water and don't have the opportunity to breathe in first. The coughing starts immediately. I don't turn to numbers to calm my uncooperative mind. This is over. Thrashing, I open my eyes to yawning, wet darkness and suck in water. I try to cough through a rigidly small airway, but can't. Struggling doesn't help but I can't stop. I want to drown. I coax the water in, biding it to fill my lungs, to end this on my terms. I fight until consciousness begins to slip, and then I fight some more.

*

I wake in the dark, feet flat against a wooden board and body leaned slightly forward so a strap burrows into my chest. It hurts to breathe and my feet are sore to the point of numbness. I try to take the pressure off them by bending my knees but this only causes the strap to cut more deeply into my chest, which hurts more than my feet.

I hang my head and cough until I think blood will shoot out instead of water. A deep and greedy breath only brings on another agonizing coughing fit. As a child, I suffered often from pneumonia. It starts this way—a wrenching cough that turns first to bronchitis and then to something worse.

I'm dry but the room's very cold. The empty hole of my stomach grumbles discontentedly, but I know I couldn't eat if given food. Besides the buzzing in my ears, the room's silent. But, no. If I listen carefully, I can hear whispering. Josh. Lara. My parents. The dark-haired boy from AA training. Sup3. I know they aren't here, but hanging from this board, straining to keep pressure off my feet and heaving chest, I hear them all. Lara reads aloud—her beloved Spinoza, Mill, Jefferson, and Thoreau.

Burn the blacklisted materials, I try to warn her. *Leave the Capitol City.*

But Lara's dead. I saw her face, her eyes, the bruises covering that fine spray of freckles. They slit her throat. Beat her to death.

Hung her by the neck. Or did a bullet slicing through the back of her head carry her sweetly from this life to whatever lies beyond, if anything?

To lose her is no loss.

To keep her is no gain.

She whispers about life, liberty, and the pursuit of happiness. All men are created equal, but she forgets about nonhuman animals. Equality includes all sentient beings, not just those who can reason and make hypocrisy look pretty. She laughs at me. Did I ever hear her do such a thing?

I cough—a gravely, sputtering sound deep in my chest—and spit a mouthful of phlegm onto the floor with a heavy splat.

Josh says my name aloud in his condescending way, doing it both to get my attention and to annoy me. But he's dead too. Or did the regime play a trick? AA service required a forfeiture of my family and so I gave them up. My choice, but is that true? Who can be said to choose anything? The regime alone tells each citizen what he can and cannot have. It told me I couldn't have Josh, couldn't have my mother and father, couldn't even have myself unless I pledged every waking moment to its service. The government stripped away my family, replacing them with brothers in black. It tells me what has and hasn't happened in my past. It shapes everything, turning events 180 degrees to fit its purposes. If it tells me Josh is alive, what then?

From the icy air around my head, my brother asks the old questions.

What are you willing to do? Become a mindless hypocrite like the rest of them? How deluded are you? How blind?

"You're dead," I whisper, voice barely there. Trembling from head to foot, my cough's the strongest part of me. Besides my feverish head, I'm freezing cold. I think of that last time—his hand around my throat and face close to mine, the stink of meat on his breath. I warned him. If I hadn't done it, he would've seen the inside of a Kill Room. Pulled fingernails. Bones crushed to powder. Teeth torn from his mouth. Eyes gouged out with sharp objects. Mother and Father didn't understand. I put my career on the line to do him a favor. And it was so quick.

Nonhuman animals aren't the only ones who need saving, he says, his passion hurting my tender head. *What about our inalienable rights?* He laughs and Lara laughs with him. *What about the atrocities against the human animal? Don't those matter anymore? We're all afraid to touch each other, afraid to be turned in as traitors. Each one of us stands alone now. Was that the goal? The regime's packed full of hypocrites who say all life is sacred but kill when it suits them. Are you one of them?*

He exhaled into my face, openly brandishing his speakeasy connections with the scent of meat on his breath. He made his illegal activities no secret and routinely challenged me to do something about it. His bold carelessness compelled me to take action. I gave him warnings, tried to suggest a voluntary surrender to the Bureau of Thought Reform for reeducation. His mind needed to be snapped and realigned. But once he came up on the AA's list of wanted traitors, I had no choice. As a young agent, I couldn't afford the constant shame his actions brought me. I showed him more mercy than anyone else would have.

He smiled and turned his back. He had to know what I would do. I cough until my lungs feel shredded. No gunshot splits the air. No blood or brains splatter on the wall. No body falls to the ground at my feet. I cried then but don't now. Coughing and trembling, I hear Mother's high shriek at the sight of me. I cradled his head as he twitched. I was young and he was my brother. My hands shook, spoiling my aim, turning a clean shot messy. He took his last breath, shuddering, and lay still.

"To lose him is no loss. To keep him is no gain," I whisper.

My knees buckle and I gasp at the instant pressure on my chest. The coughing starts again.

What have you done? Mother asks.

It takes everything I have to get to my feet. The pressure on my chest relaxes slightly, letting me breathe again, though it doesn't feel like nearly enough air.

I don't explain what I do to anyone. I never have. That night, I didn't try to justify my actions. I only wanted to explain what happened, that this was best, that Josh wouldn't listen to reason. Her hand was sharp against the side of my face. Father pulled her back, then hit me in the mouth so hard blood exploded onto my uniform. He called me a monster, told me not to come back. He took me by the throat and shook me hard enough to jostle the brains from my head. When he pushed me down the porch steps and onto the lawn, the rain started.

I wiggle cold, damp fingers and look up for raindrops, my clothes dry and loose on my shivering body. I hang my head, unable to respond to the voices barraging my ears. Sup3 wanting to know if I'm sound. The forcefully charismatic boy from AA training saying that there are going to be things about the new regime that are ugly, perhaps even morally reprehensible, but they have to be done. The AA will do them. It's what I whispered to Father when he asked, *how could you? Your own brother?* But how could he? The nonhuman animals were innocents.

I don't have the strength to whisper cadence. My unstable mind won't stand still, won't give me the words. Everyone whispers while I hang in the dark, inert and aching. I breathe and my chest rattles. If they don't kill me soon, this will. A wet head, exposure to cold temperatures while wearing inappropriate clothing. I know better.

You have a weak constitution, Mother whispers, patting my feverish head.

But Josh was the weak one. I listen to his whispered excuses. His justifications are always the same. Only the places are different. And I'm different.

*

I spend waking hours curled on the floor of the cell, shivering and coughing. I don't fall asleep—I lose consciousness. The slot opens, but I don't eat what they give me, don't even go see what it is. The intercom blares the Chairman's voice, but I can't follow what he says. It feels like something very large is pressing hard against my torso, cutting the breath I take in half and sometimes in half again. If I try to breathe deeper, I feel a sharp pain in my chest. My heart races. My head pounds. Covered in cold sweat, I close my eyes and feel dizzy lying down. But when sleep comes, it's deep. And if dreams trouble me in that murky darkness, I don't remember them.

TWENTY-SIX

I hear my father's voice and open my eyes. I'm sitting in a chair, dizzy, a headache pulsing in my skull. I lift a shaky hand to soothe my forehead where the pain's sharpest, but can't. My arms are handcuffed to either side of the metal chair. Another interrogation. How foolish to think my current illness was torture enough.

I lift my head slowly, not surprised to find two black clad agents—one front and center, the other positioned closer to the door, assault rifle pointed in my direction. What lengths would I have to go to in order to goad this man into fatally shooting me?

I give the agent closest to me the flickering spotlight of my attention, my throbbing head full of cotton.

"How about we pick up our conversation where we left off?" he says, voice friendly again, words seeming to come from far away.

I notice a drain on the floor near one of the man's large boots but can't lay hands on the proper fright. My thoughts are also coming from a great distance. I am my cough, my sweaty, feverish body, the headache that pulsates and pounds without end. The man who feels and can cry no longer exists. Only the most immediate things exist—pain, the phlegm I hack onto the floor, my shaking hands, the rattle in my chest, my feverish desire for death.

"In case you were wondering, I took your suggestion and we did indeed go for five minutes that last time. So that's a new record for you."

He's playing the same game I play during an interrogation. Each agent does it a little differently, putting his stamp on it, making it his. This man prefers a friendly approach at first before rapidly stripping away that ruse to reveal the cruelty beneath. I like to be overly polite, giving plenty of indulgent smiles before turning vicious.

My head falls forward of its own accord. I have to struggle to lift it again.

"Are you alert, comrade?" he asks.

"Yes," I whisper.

"I've read your personnel file. Very impressive. You were quite the agent." He pauses, presumably so I can digest his purposeful use of the past tense. He begins to pace, moving two feet this way and two feet back. It's dizzying to watch. "What made you turn your back on it?"

"I didn't," I say, then cough so strongly it doubles me over.

"Was she worth it?"

I keep my face as neutral as the coughing, body aches, and pounding head allow, not dignifying this with a response, verbal or otherwise. Stoking my anger might trick me into saying something incriminating but, within me, no emotion kindles. She's already dead. What does it matter what this man says about her?

He produces a metallic object that flashes in the dim light. "Do you recognize this?"

I have to blink to clear my foggy vision. Forceps. I see them clearly for one instant, and the next they're blurry, shiny, silver things.

I exhale miserably, returning my defective gaze to him, and answer in a thin whisper. "Yes." I know how to use forceps—it's taught in training—but have never resorted to them during an interrogation.

"Then you know what they can do."

I sit back, trying to ready myself for the pain to come. I don't possess the answers to satisfy this agent. In a way, I'm worse off than Lara. She had the unknown to contend with, which is a fear that has no boundaries, but I know exactly what's about to happen to me. Even still, I don't hate her. If she gave these agents false information about our relationship, it came as a result of torture. She lacked my training, my resolve, my willingness to die if the regime says it must be so. At this point, even I've been exposed to more than my training prepared me for. I don't know why no one has beaten me yet, but I'm sure it's coming. I have to prepare myself for broken bones, for spitting blood and teeth, for eyes swelled shut or lost altogether, for death.

"Your cooperation's appreciated, comrade, and will be rewarded," the agent says, his tone suggesting we're old friends simply having a chat. But old friends don't carry forceps or handcuff one another to chairs.

I nod to show him I understand and my head swims. For a number of seconds, my eyes roll back and my vision darkens. The room comes back slowly, the agent in front of me a smear of black. I try to rub my eyes, forgetting the handcuffs. I could slip into unconsciousness so easily. It would only take closing my eyes. I force a cough. The stabbing pains in my chest bring alertness rushing back. Just when I believe the drumbeat in my head has finally reached a plateau, it climbs to new, excruciating heights.

"The girl didn't hesitate to roll over on you," he says. "Do you understand?"

I don't chance a nod this time. "Yes."

"There's no reason to protect her."

His face is blurry blackness. I can't make out the eyeholes.

"I'm not interested in protecting her."

"Well that's good to hear!" he says with frightening enthusiasm. "Why did you help her hide the blacklisted materials?"

"I didn't."

"Why did you tell her to leave the Capitol City?"

"I wanted her to lead me to a safehouse."

He shakes his head and speaks with real regret. "It's going to be like this, is it, comrade?"

My head's full of painfully hot air and floating near the top of the room. My chest is a wheezing rattle, my heart dead weight inside a heaving ribcage. My hands belong to someone else. I possess absolutely no freewill, no ability to take myself in hand. My thoughts race in opposing directions. To catch one is to lose another. This man has nasty plans for me, but I can barely follow his words. My focus has no edge. I want to be attentive, but my eyes keep drifting shut.

He turns to the agent at the door. "The mouth prop." The other man rushes over to hand him an object I can't make out.

"Open your mouth."

I don't immediately obey. Not out of insubordination—that's beyond foolish—I just can't set the wheels in motion fast enough.

The second agent puts the barrel of his assault rifle against the side of my head. I'm so tender everywhere, even this hurts.

"Now, brother," the lead man says.

Despite my sore jaw and uncooperative muscles, I open my mouth. The agent takes hold of the back of my head and jams something hard and wedge-shaped into my mouth, forcing it all the way open. I cough but don't have the strength to clear my throat. Phlegm clogs my airway and I can barely breathe. I lower my head, hair falling over my eyes in sweaty clumps. I never wear it this long.

The agent grabs a handful of my hair and pulls my head sharply back. I moan as my headache rises three decibels. My vision flickers but returns in time to see the man holding the forceps up where I can see them, the silver gleaming menacingly.

"If you refuse to cooperate, you leave me little choice." He releases my hair and takes a firm grip on my forehead. "I may need help restraining him," he says to the other man. The forceps are cold as they slide into my mouth. I wrap my hands around the chair legs, squeezing until my fingers are numb, every beat of my heart echoing inside my skull.

The forceps tighten around a tooth at the rear left of my mouth. A wisdom tooth. I should've had them removed years ago but didn't want to miss the time from work. Oral surgery's a mandatory off-day, sometimes two.

I close my eyes and the room slips away. It would be so easy to sleep.

The pain brings me back.

The heft of the agent's body presses into the forceps, creating insupportable pressure. The ripping, wrenching, pulling tugs a string at the top of my skull that goes all the way down my neck. Grunting with the effort, the agent rips the tooth from gum and bone. I squeeze my eyes shut, groaning and pulling my arms uselessly against the handcuffs. I bite hard into the mouth wedge, spiking the soreness in my jaw, but don't scream. My mouth fills with blood. I gag on the warm, metallic taste. The man roughly pulls the wedge from my mouth, then releases my forehead.

I cough blood onto the front of my uniform, gums throbbing around the hole left by the absent tooth. A fresh sheen of sweat covers my face. My hair sticks to my forehead. Even now, I want a trim. I despise being untidy.

The agent's holding the forceps in front of me so I can see the shiny white tooth with its bloody root. One wisdom tooth down, three to go. I suppose it's possible this man will rip out all my teeth.

315

In the picture, Lara's mouth was sealed. How many of her teeth did they forcibly extract?

I hack up more blood, the taste of it turning my stomach. I want the sweaty hair off my forehead. I want my health back, my post, my quiet, contented little existence nurtured at the bosom of the regime. Mostly, I want five minutes alone with this agent who's holding my tooth like it's his crowning achievement.

"Just a wisdom tooth," he says, and releases it from the forceps. "Three more freebies before this starts to count. After that, I'll start at the front."

Money wasted on orthodontics, Father says. How true. This will make short work of my pretty pearly whites and a bullet blew Josh's from his mouth.

I cough for several minutes. At the end of this fit, I spit a mouthful of bloody mucus onto my lap. My tooth sparkles white on the floor. I haven't been attacked and injured this badly since AA training shifted the advantage of strength from my brother to me.

The agent begins to pace. I keep my attention on him, but my eyes keep closing. The taste of blood is making me nauseous. I lean over and cough until the empty socket in my gums screams along with my struggling chest and raw throat. I spit a clump of phlegm onto the floor and sit up, instantly dizzy.

"You seem ill, comrade," the agent says. "A simple round of antibiotics would clear up that nasty cough. Confess and you can have them."

I know a lie when I hear it. This man is as likely to secure antibiotics for me as he is to send me back to my flat at Lib Hall with a pat on the back and an apology. And how would receiving medication benefit me? I'd get better only to face additional torture. I'm not sure how long they plan to keep me here, but if I refuse all medical treatment, this will end quickly. Submitting to this sickness won't be difficult to do.

"I'm sound," I say, and spit again. Dark pink this time instead of crimson.

The agent crosses his arms with a silver flash of the forceps. "You're far from sound, but I'll take that as a sign of your eagerness to continue."

We both know my eagerness isn't a prerequisite for the continuation of the questioning, but I don't say so. If a person mouths off to me during an interrogation, I slap him across the face or punch him in the stomach. Right now, a blow to the face might knock my head from my neck.

"Do you know why you're here?" he asks.

"To assess whether I've been compromised."

"And have you been?"

"No," I say, and cough deeply. Unconsciousness threatens, air coming shallow and painful through a mouth that tastes like blood.

"That isn't what the girl says."

I take note of his use of the present tense but don't speak. He didn't ask a question. The rules are very clear. More than one line answers cause trouble. Answering statements causes trouble. Not answering at all causes trouble.

"According to her, your relationship was far from fact-finding in nature."

Another statement. He has yet to indicate what type of relationship Lara allegedly described. By stating vague accusations, he hopes to provoke me into self-incrimination.

"Do you believe you acted appropriately in this situation?"

"No," I say.

"Where did you go wrong?"

I take half a breath, treating my rattling chest with care. "I should've consulted my chain of command before acting." I bend to spit out more blood. Speaking a full sentence is exhausting.

"Going to bed with the girl wasn't wrong?"

"I did no such thing."

"Reading blacklisted books wasn't wrong?"

"I had knowledge of those materials but never saw them."

"How often did you exchange seditious statements about the regime and the Chairman with this Party traitor?"

"Never."

"Did the pair of you visit speakeasies together?"

"No." This word conveys the proper vehemence, but it costs me. The coughing fit doubles me over so suddenly my wrists twist in the handcuffs. I can't stop, even as the searing pain in my mouth becomes excruciating. The pounding in my head turns into concentrated pressure, so intense I expect my skull to split open. My chest feels stabbed and squeezed at the same time. Choking on a mixture of mucus and blood, I vomit. Over all this, the agent speaks.

"The mouth prop."

He waits patiently for my worsening coughs to subside, then rips my head up by my wet hair until it touches the back of the chair, my neck pulled taut. I open my mouth to cough and the wedge jams in past my teeth. In my peripheral vision, I see the barrel of the assault rifle very close. If fired, it would obliterate my head and face.

The agent flattens his hand on my sweaty forehead, holding me still. I can't put a single finger on my own calm. My chest, painfully tight, allows no air in or out. My heart is hot glass exploding in my ribcage and lodging shards in surrounding soft tissues. I close my bulging eyes, but the pain won't let me slip into the dark, unfeeling places unconsciousness brings. The forceps slide into my mouth. I gag on phlegm, praying for more vomit to calm my churning stomach.

The agent seizes the tooth in the upper rear right of my mouth and begins to pull. The wrenching, ripping sensation wraps around my entire skull as the tooth twists beneath the agent's weight. Sweat pouring, I emit a low sound thick with mucus, squeezing my eyes shut as the tooth tears loose from gum and bone. Blood pools in the back of my throat. I cough, spraying it onto the agent's mask.

He backs off, rubbing his eyes, the forceps clanging onto the cement floor.

Hacking up bloody phlegm, I bend over as far as my bound wrists allow, so far the throbbing in my skull arranges itself at the front of my head where I can feel my skittering heartbeat. I vomit blood and bile onto the floor, expelling the mouth prop, fuzzy black dots dancing before my eyes. After the coughing ends, I keep heaving chest against trembling knees, my mouth sick tasting. Sleeping sounds good. Not waking up sounds better. Anything to end this litany of questions I can never answer correctly. Now I understand the air of futility on the Kill Floor, the deadened, complacent eyes of the criminals. How many false confessions have I collected? How many hopeless individuals simply tell me what I want to hear so I'll make it stop?

I sit up, blood gushing from my mouth, eyes rolling back, heart threatening to leap from my chest. I want pull unconsciousness closer, to fall into the brilliantly feverish dreams it brings that I can never remember upon waking. But I cough instead. The agent waits, hands folded behind him. He's fuzzy around the edges, a black phantom that can do me harm with no repercussions.

My head rocks, riding an invisible current, vomit and drool dripping down my face, my unwashed, unshaven face. I can't wipe it on the shoulders of my uniform. Turning my head that far to either side might pitch me forward out of the chair. With no hands to break my fall, I'd do this agent a favor by snapping my front teeth off on the cement.

"That's two, brother," he says. "Shall we continue?"

I drift, as though on calm seas, head light enough to float to the ceiling. The room's not spinning, but it's not staying still either.

"My answers won't change," I whisper. Dizziness is a physical force. I sway but don't fall, blood draining out of my mouth because it hurts too much to spit.

"Do you deny these accusations?"

I look up, blurry vision flickering. The room's darker than before, the agent a crude shape.

"I don't know what I've been accused of."

"You don't remember what you did?" His voice is coming from incredibly far away.

The shivering worsens, invading muscle and bone. I'm dripping with sweat but frozen solid. Thinking is difficult and sparse. What thoughts I have revolve around finding warmth, getting my hands free, drinking orange juice until I throw up, stabbing this agent in the neck and then extracting his teeth while he twitches and writhes on the floor.

"I don't know what I've been accused of," I say again, not so far gone that I don't recognize a trick question when I hear it.

"This is going to be a long day for you then, comrade."

I bow my head, shoulders slumping, eyes closing, the dark comfort of sleep dancing just out of reach.

*

Interrogations and sickness are constants, the questioning stretching for hours at a go. At least it seems like hours. I have no firm concept of time. If I try to count out an hour, I cough or drift into semi-unconsciousness and can't finish. I have no wisdom teeth left, but he didn't take any of the others. *It gives me something to do later*, the agent said, laughing as I sat helpless, too weak to feel either anger or despair.

If I succumb to exhaustion, they wake me, depriving me of sleep, nourishment, and natural light. I spend long periods handcuffed to a metal bar suspended from the ceiling of my cell, swaying on tender feet, unable to sit or kneel. The interrogator promises medication often, if only I confess, but the questions never change and neither do my answers.

Dreams bleed hard into my waking hours. The agent speaks, but I can't hear it above Josh and Lara whispering. I never see them, but their voices are very clear to me. The agent sometimes hits me quite hard across the face to recapture my attention, resulting in pain the strength of which I've never before experienced. My swollen gums leak constantly. My head's a nest of throbbing, endless pain.

The intercom keeps me awake—the Party Chairman, nonhuman animals screaming in the slaughterhouses, a series of ear-piercing sirens that ward off sleep whenever it tries to come. The slot opens, but I don't care. Food's an abstract concept that no longer arouses my interest. Sitting up causes dizziness, coughing, vomiting. If I receive a glass of water in the interrogation room, I can't finish it, can't even come close. No one bothers with the hood anymore. I keep my eyes closed all the time, even on the trip to the interrogation room. Unable to walk, I'm dragged instead. I raised my eyes to the door of my cell once, just to see, and my vision cleared enough to read the sign on the metal door. *Bend But Do Not Break.*

I am clammy skin and a mouth that issues mucus-laced vomit and violent coughs. I am the ears that hear the dead speak. I am a whisper in the dark between coughs:

I am the black clad body of the AA.

TWENTY-SEVEN

Today I'll die of asphyxiation. Or so the agent says. I'm on my knees, bent so my forehead touches the floor, the cool cement a blessing on my skin. Thick rope binds my arms at the wrists and elbows behind my back. Attached to these ropes is another, thicker rope looped through a hook in the ceiling.

"Last chance," the agent says. He has the other end of the rope in his hands. I've never performed this particular technique, nor was I subjected to it in training—command deemed it too dangerous—but I know its name. *Reversed hanging.* I also know the ultimate result if done correctly. *Death by crucifixion.*

My body is sluggish with fever. The soreness and swelling in my gums has spread down the sides of my throat, leaving my neck painfully tender to the touch. I can no longer swallow. The last time I attempted to drink some water, it stood still in my mouth.

The agent pulls on the rope—an attention getter. My arms lift slightly and I sit up straighter, which causes a great deal of pain considering the state I'm in.

Unable to raise my head, I watch the man's boots through the hair hanging over my eyes. He has large feet. I cough—a deep, grating sound like my lungs are packed with gravel—and hack up a heap of bloody phlegm, my mouth a shot of burning pain in four places. My stomach joins the rising misery, threatening to empty itself though there's nothing in it.

The rope relaxes and my arms fall back onto my tailbone. I try to relax too. I know all about reverse hanging. Tying a prisoner's arms behind his back and lifting them as a unit forces them to support the body, causing severe pain. Dislocation can result, as the internally rotated, fully extended shoulder sockets are holding up his full weight. This procedure can lead to paralysis and extensive nerve damage. It can also lead to asphyxiation. The drastically stretched arms cause hyperextension of the lungs, which makes inhaling difficult. Adding drops after the detainee is suspended can cause further, irreversible damage, such as broken shoulders.

"Will you tell the truth now, comrade?" the agent asks.

I nod, dizzy. I can't feel my hands. The tingling numbness is spreading slowly up my arms to the shoulders. I close my eyes, feel myself floating, and open them again. Falling off my knees will pull my arms up. My own worry seems to come from a great distance. Nothing touches me—no thoughts, no emotions. The certainty of my existence derives solely from my constant pain. I'm a dead man shivering, a discarded appendage of the regime that still twitches and bleeds.

The agent asks questions.

I answer in a thin whisper.

When my responses aren't sufficient, he pulls the rope, jerking me up so my arms support my weight. Struggling for air triggers breathless coughing. I make an emaciated sound as my arms prepare to rip from their sockets. Black dots blot out my vision, unconsciousness hovering achingly close.

He sets me onto my knees and I press my head against the concrete, pulling in breaths that aren't deep enough. My chest rattles, ready to buckle under the pressure as my headache jumps to a sickening new level. I consider slamming my skull onto the floor until I don't feel anything at all. Only a complete lack of energy stops me.

"Don't you want to eat, to sleep?" he asks. "Don't you want the medication that will make you healthy again?"

I try to nod, but am slowly suffocating in phlegm and moisture.

"Then you must cooperate."

I've made these empty promises myself on so many occasions, always marveling at the thin gleam of hope in the eyes of those I interrogated. Now I feel such irrational hope. If only I cooperate, if only I provide the correct answers, if only I can please this agent. But I know better. If I promise food, drink, a bathroom break, medical care, a reunion with family or friends, I'm really only looking for information. Second chances don't exist in the regime. Lenience is weakness.

I try to answer but cough instead, hacking until I vomit and my vision goes foggy and thick with black dots.

My arms come up ruthlessly, lifting my knees off the floor. If I had the energy, I could simply stand. Instead, I hang from the rope, coughing and gasping for air.

"Do you want to change your story now, comrade?" the agent asks. His voice is cruel all the time now. I think this means something about how much longer I can expect to live.

My vision grows dimmer, consciousness slipping. I shake my head harder than I should and the headache spikes to a new, skull-shattering level.

"There's nothing to change," I whisper, voice so much smaller than my whooping coughs.

"You don't want to tell the truth?"

"I have—"the words disintegrate into harsh coughs.

"The girl was very truthful, though it did take some convincing," he says, chuckling darkly.

I imagine they're quite convincing here at the Loop. Lara hanging from her arms as I am, having her teeth extracted, sustaining punishing beatings, tilting backwards into a vat of water until she thought she'd drown. What else did they do? What else will they do to me? I don't ask these questions. The answers are meaningless. She's dead. Very soon, I will be too.

"She cried and begged. We told her she could save her own neck if she gave you over and she did it so much, we got tired of listening."

My eyes bulge in my head. He's not asking questions. I don't think he wants me to speak. He wants me to be scared. He wants me to feel hopeless and I do. A deep despair has spread its darkness within me, annihilating everything so I can't even feel despair anymore.

"To lose her is no loss," I whisper, sputtering. "To keep me is no gain."

"You're being quite foolish."

The coughing won't stop and the aching I feel all over overwhelms me so I can barely consider anything else. My shoulders are tight with agony. Their dislocation would be a relief, a release of pressure, the end of this.

He lets go of the rope, bringing me down hard onto my knees. Rolling over onto my side, shivering and gasping, I add this pain to the rest. My mind reels. Nothing I can say will end this. I hear him unholstering the weapon on his hip. Here it comes—the one clean bullet. Relief washes over me, a soothing sensation after so much horridness.

He kneels down, holding the gun in front of my damp eyes. "Are you ready to die? Or do you wish to cooperate?"

I nod my feverish, throbbing head. "I'm ready to die." With my flickering vision, he's fuzzy around the edges, the gun a dark shape with sharp lines and angles.

"Without confessing?"

"I've told you everything."

"Why are you so willing to die, comrade?" he asks.

"Without the AA, I am nothing."

He chuckles. "If only you realized that sooner rather than later, eh?"

I don't quite find the humor in his joke.

"If you confess, you don't have to die. We'll simply break you and remake you." He laughs again.

"I've told you everything." Repetition seems to be the key to learning with this one.

He presses the gun to the side of my head, the cold steel lovely against my hot skin. I fight for consciousness. This is important. I need to will the end, to live it, and not just as an end to sickness and torture. If I can't be a contented little cell in the body of the AA, I have no reason to continue living. Regardless of what this man says, it's clear I'm not here for reeducation. I'm here to confess and be executed.

I close my eyes and try to think of nothing—not Lara, not Josh, not my parents, not the things I've done and would've continued to do if given the chance. I haven't been happy, but I knew true contentment serving my government.

Once bereft of thought, I fill the vacant spaces in my head with cadence, the words relaxing my aching muscles. I'm ready for the bullet.

The barrel moves against my head, pressing harder. It'll be a clean shot, no pain, no twitching, no anguished shouts. I keep on with cadence, hoping the man will be quick about it.

At the click of an empty chamber, I flinch violently backwards.

No bullet.

I open my eyes, horrified to be conscious, alive. I want him to try again. But how to ask?

"I'm ready to die," I whisper.

"And you will," he says. "Just not today."

TWENTY-EIGHT

The voice of the regime tickles my ears, gentle as a cooing mother—*meat is murder, comrades. Moral uprightness is freedom from harm. Let us thank the Chairman for showing us the way. Tomorrow is another day closer to perfection*—mixing with the sound of several voices repeating cadence—*honor when it is easier to do the opposite. Integrity when those around us lack it entirely. Loyalty to those unarmed innocents above all else.*

My eyes flutter at the sound of Josh speaking. He's right beside my ear, telling me in his clear voice that I'm a catalyst for tyranny.

Harsh light invades the room, forcing my slitted eyes closed.

"Open your mouth."

Fingers against my lips, pushing things into the throbbing den of agony that is my mouth. I shake my head, the pain spiking, but can't stop. This is one of Josh's tricks. He'll make me eat something disgusting if I'm stupid enough to listen.

"Swallow the pills, comrade."

They sit still in my mouth, gigantic and tasteless. I cough, expelling everything. Fingers shove the pills back through my lips.

"Swallow."

Water floods my mouth. Coughing, sputtering, choking, I want to spit, but my mouth hurts too much. The blinding light seeps in through squeezed lids, piercing my eyes with fine needles. A hand presses flat against my lips, sealing in the water. I swallow and want to scream from the pain.

"Sedition," I say in a thin voice.

The government has made everything we say and think illegal, Josh says. *And you're making it worse.* Then he turns away. I put my gun to the back of his head. He doesn't move, doesn't tell me not to do it. The bullet roars, devouring the silence, obliterating his head and the ideals it contains, spraying my hands, my face, my open, gasping mouth with blood. I fall to my knees, cursing him, and myself.

I struggle to swallow the fist lodged in my throat. Are they pills? I can't open my eyes, can't make my voice work to ask. Water pours into my mouth and shoots up my nose. I swallow, the pain blooming in my throat. Coughing and struggling, I sink, descending into blackness. Everything seems so far away. Voices—the man telling me to calm down—and images—Josh bowing his head in acceptance of his fate, Lara crying in the rain…or is that my mother?

The choking brings me out of it. Hands pull at my arms, forcing me to sit. I lean over and throw up onto my lap. More pills in my mouth, more water. I shake my head. *No,* I try to say, but my mouth is full. I swallow. Gasping, I try to scream, but this turns to coughing. The hands disappear. I fall backwards and keep falling.

The sting of a needle electrifies my arm. His blood on my face, her tears on my fingertips. The falling intensifies and I let it take me into a place my dreams can't follow.

*

Soaking wet and shivering, I can't open my eyes. My head, under pressure and growing bigger all the time, prepares to explode, to paint the wall the color of brain matter. My mouth is hot and pulsing. I cough but none of the gravel shoots out of my lungs. I breathe in shallow pulls that make my headache worse, waiting for my heart to gallop through my ribcage.

Dying's like this—dark, painful, solitary.

Living's the same.

*

Mother mops the sweat from my brow. She sings songs, brings me water and soup, and keeps me company. She reads me books to make up for my inability to go outside and play. Josh skips through the halls, carefree, healthy, and Mother does what she can to shift the scales in my direction.

I clench my teeth, jaw aching, but not insupportably. I can feel her attending to me. Father's at work. Josh is outside causing trouble. Mother doesn't have the daughter she wants more than anything, but she does have her youngest son. Weak and sickly, I can't twist away from her as Josh has done. I nestle closer, needing her, my dependence binding us together.

Why would you want to join something like that? she asks when I come home from that first meeting and make my intentions clear. She lets her tears speak for her after I come home months later wearing the black armband, after I have blood on my hands, after I enlist. My dependence upon her evaporates from one day to the next, my sicknesses long over.

I will turn in anyone for treason, I say, and don't care how they shrink from me, all except Josh, who makes it his duty to challenge me.

If I'm very sick, I can have popsicles, but no red ones.

If you cough up blood, I want to know, Mother says.

I cough deeply, no blood spraying from my lips. No one's wiping the sweat from my brow. Is it the middle of the night? Where is she?

"Mother?" I say, voice raspy and unrecognizable. How old am I? Do my feet reach the bottom of my bed? Or am I still too small?

My desperate hacking can't mask Josh's laughter. The sicknesses make me soft and bitter. Josh is strong, always has been, and he lords it over me at every opportunity. Mother shoos him away but doesn't yell at him.

I tell him what he does is embarrassing, immoral, illegal.

If killing's immoral, why do you do it? he asks.

My hand twitches on my weapon. *I don't kill the innocent,* I say. He doesn't answer. He only turns around.

More pills. Fingers forcing them in my mouth where they're easier to swallow once water's poured in. My stomach complains angrily but doesn't send them flying back into my mouth.

"Good, comrade. Now sleep." A voice in the dark.

"I don't kill the innocent," I whisper. The sweat pours and no one wipes it away. I tremble and no one brings the blankets up to my chin, sealing in the warmth. I ask the dark for Mother, who never comes.

Josh doesn't speak.

Lara doesn't speak.

They're dead.

No loss.

I'm alive.

No gain.

*

Caught out in the rain again, water pours down from above, soaking my hair and skin. I'm on my back, eyes sealed shut. Is it the front lawn? The ground beneath me seems too solid to be grass. If Father pushes me hard enough, I could crack my head open on the front walk.

I don't hear him cursing me or mother's teary shrieks. No slamming door. No one accusing me, hitting me, shaking me by the collar. Only rain.

Hands slide over my arms, sitting me up, scrubbing my back and chest. I groan in disapproval, twisting but unable to get away. I open my eyes to watery, dim light. My feet slide on the ground until my legs are straight out in front of me. Shutting my lids again, I wiggle my toes in warm water. Too much to be rain. I want the thunder to shake the sky above and the ground below. I moan when a firm hand pulls my head back, but no mouth prop jams between my lips. I swallow water as the sharp edge of a razor drags over my cheeks, a hand on either side holding my head still. I try to explain being untidy, but my mouth fills with water, and my whispers are unintelligible. Do I still have blood on my uniform? Have I missed morning roll call?

"Relax, comrade."

"Josh?" The water turns the word into something else. I want to lie back and stare at the lightning. I want to give my parents the words that will let understanding bloom through all that anger. But the hands keep me up, hold my head still as the razor continues its work. Has Father come back? He taught me to shave in the first place. Has he realized I couldn't have done anything else? That it was mercy? I don't hear Mother's tears, don't hear her whisper, *would you do the same to us?*

"Treason is treason," I say, and no one slaps my face. No one screams at me to be reasonable, to measure my priorities, to be loyal only to what matters. I swallow, cough, and spit up water. The hands tighten on my arms.

"Steady, comrade."

Josh doesn't call me comrade. My trigger finger twitches in the water. I'll do it again. If I have to—if the regime desires it—I'll do it a thousand times.

Hands push me back, the sensation the same as falling. Father shoving me to the grass so the rain can wash the blood away. Lightning parts the sky, searing the air with electricity. I can't hear the thunder, can't open my eyes to see the angry, roiling clouds. Water pours onto my closed lids and clenched hands, bringing all the answers with it—where Josh is, why I can't hear Mother's screams or Father's curses.

I have no family.

I forsook them for the AA and now the AA has paid the favor forward to me.

TWENTY-NINE

I wake lying on a cot, wound so tightly, my knees touch the tip of my nose. Squinting at the soft light, I stick my tongue into the four holes in my gums. No pain. No swelling. My joints ache, but no headache surges through my skull when I widen my eyes. I swallow without wincing and enjoy the simple beauty filling my lungs with air, then letting it out again. I force a cough. My throat protests, but no phlegm, no gravel grinding in my chest. I feel my face with stiff fingers. Cleanly shaven.

I turn onto my back, groaning as my shivering muscles tense and relax again, arms and legs resisting as I try to stretch them. After counting out five minutes, I sit up under my own shaky power. My head feels pumped full of helium, but there's no dizziness, no faltering vision.

The room's nothing extraordinary. A cot in one corner, a toilet opposite. Beside me, an IV stand, the hanging bag attached to the needle in my arm. I pull it out and stand. Immediately dizzy, I stumble backwards and sit down hard, the cot groaning beneath my weight. I lower my head, waiting as the dizziness slowly fades. I count out another five minutes and stand again, this time carefully. The floor's lukewarm, as though heated from below.

I look down at myself. The boxers and white t-shirt appear clean, though they do hang on me. Bruises on my arms and legs. I don't remember what caused them. The rest of my skin is a pasty, lifeless gray.

As soon as I look at the steel door in the center of the adjacent wall, the intercom comes to life.

"Do not approach the door, comrade."

Locks flip over and the door swings into the room. Two masked, black clad agents enter, one with a tray of food—a steaming bowl of soup, a bottle of water, a bowl of fruit—the other with a small black bag. Neither man draws the weapon in the holster at his hip. An odd choice of procedure.

The first man hands me the tray. "Eat." His voice is familiar, though I can't quite place it. "Then dress in those clothes." He points to the bag.

Holding the tray above waist level is killing my arms. I clench my teeth, waiting for these men to leave, if that's indeed what they plan to do.

The second agent puts the duffel bag down at the foot of the cot. They leave without a word, closing the door but not locking it.

I set the tray upon the bed and sit down with a sigh of relief to be off my feet. I bend my arms at the elbows to relax the trembling muscles, feeling a stab of annoyance at the soft weakness of my body. But I should be content to be alive. I never expected to see my health returned to me.

I'm not hungry but eat anyway. My stomach's too hollow to do otherwise. I spoon the warm, tasteless liquid into my mouth, only eating a little, stopping when I feel full, though I haven't come anywhere near emptying the bowl. I take a small sip from the water bottle and feel a bit ill. How much time has passed since I last took nourishment voluntarily?

I bend slowly, supporting my weight with an elbow on the mattress, and grab the black duffle bag by the strap. I dump its contents onto the cot.

A full AA issue street uniform.

What's more, *my* full AA issue street uniform. Above the breast pocket is the pin I received after my promotion to Third Shift super. I touch it with an index finger, suddenly sure they restored my health so I could be completely cognizant for my execution. No other explanation makes sense. I'm still in the Loop. True, the door's unlocked, but I doubt they'll simply let me leave.

Inside the tightly rolled uniform pants, I find my armband and weapon. It's loaded. I hold the gun at arm's length—much heavier than I remember—pointing it at the door. Is this a test? Perhaps to see if I can resist taking revenge when the masked men return? I'd never fire on a fellow agent of the Party, not even the man who gleefully ripped the teeth from my mouth. And if I put the gun to my own head? Would agents come running? I could end this my way if I wanted. It's cowardly, but I have no desire to undergo further torture.

I dress—the uniform hangs on me, now much too big for service; I've sent agents home for pants that needed less alterations than mine do at this moment—preparing myself as I once did every morning before heading to the Complex. I cinch the belt tightly around my waist. Pants are tailored, so the belt's effectively ornamental, but now I need it to keep my pants from sliding off my nonexistent hips. I fuss with my uniform top for several minutes, my decreased size making it impossible to get it to hang the way it should. The baton, pepper spray, handcuffs, and communicator are missing, but I have the pistol. I draw it, aiming at the door. I could kill myself before they come for me again. That much I have control over. I return the weapon to its holster.

This room has no mirrors, but I know my uniform's in order, besides the necessary alterations. Also, I may not be ready to see my face. I don't remember beatings, but if I've been battered beyond even my own recognition, I'd rather not find out.

I push my hair back, again trimmed to the appropriate length, stand at attention, though my hands shake, and speak in a clear voice.

"I am the black clad body of the AA."

I touch the pin on my chest. If I must die today, I'm ready. I have my health, my AA black.

"I'm ready," I whisper.

The intercom engages, as though hearing me. "Leave the room and take a left, comrade. Fifth door on the right."

The corridor's long and silent. I walk it alone, arms loose at my sides, respiration even, my shuffling footfalls the only sound in the hall. The gun feels at home on my bonier than usual hip. I marvel at the oddity of transporting myself to my own execution, but don't consider running. I'll submit to whatever the regime has planned for me.

The fifth door down is slightly ajar. I take a deep breath and step inside.

It's an anteroom. Another steel door is three feet in front of me, only closed.

Footsteps behind me. I close my eyes and put my left hand back on my weapon where it feels the most at home.

I'm ready.

The door closes. Boots settle. A throat clears. I frown at this odd form. Instead of a bullet, a voice breaks the silence, one I recognize.

"Turn around."

I do.

My hand slips from its place on my weapon as I regard Sup3 wordlessly.

"Are you sound?" he asks, face blank in a careful way I've not seen before.

"Yes."

He gestures towards the steel door without a word.

It isn't easy to open. I have to force myself into the dark room beyond. Once I do, Sup3 closes the door behind me. I can hear thick, shallow breathing. This isn't my executioner.

The light comes on. A hunched figure is seated in the middle of the room. Another person I recognize.

Lara's painfully thin, her arms handcuffed to the chair, dark hair clipped nearly to the scalp. Her cheekbones poke sharply out of her gaunt, battered face.

She squints up at me and smiles, showing several missing and broken teeth. Her face is little more than a horrid road map chronicling the severity of her torture, her pointy cheekbones the elevation, the remainder of her ashen face the valleys.

"You," she whispers, then doubles over into a deep, wrenching cough, shuddering, struggling to swallow. She sits up again, her face wan and shiny where it isn't a patchwork of fading bruises. Dried blood beneath the misshapen lump of her nose. Bare feet with all ten toenails removed. I can't tell if she still has her fingernails.

I have no access to my emotions. These were removed, same as her toenails. The sight of this shivering, pathetic creature causes a great emptiness to expand within me, paired with the realization that I should feel something. Not necessarily sympathy or sadness. It could be anger—her confession, true or not, resulted in my time here. But there's nothing.

I watch her watch me. She keeps blinking, as though she can't get her eyes to adjust. I step closer and she flinches. I want to speak to her, but the words are as inaccessible as my emotions.

Her loud breathing fills up the room as she pushes her feet against the ground, trying to move backward. The chair doesn't budge. She has become a wounded animal, acting only on instinct. She keeps her flashing eyes on the firearm at my hip upon which I'm resting my left hand. For once, no tears cover her face.

All of this—her confession, the torture—has a purpose, even if it ends in my execution, which I believe it will. I've learned a valuable lesson. Or, rather, relearned. Touch cannot be. Reaching out creates vulnerability, which is exploitable. Josh found a way to do it, taking liberties with the law that were only possible because of his connection to me. But I didn't let that get far enough to injure my standing with the AA. With Lara, I was foolish in a way that has caused me great harm. And we share no connection. I only thought we might. It comes down to the same thing, at bottom. Even the solutions are the same.

I circle the chair to stand behind her. There are even bruises on the back of her neck. She doesn't try to look at me. She merely lowers her head, as though aware of what will come.

"Please," she whispers, raspy voice desperate. I think of Josh, turning his back.

I draw my weapon, the sound quieter than her labored breathing. This time, there will be no twitching, no nerves to spoil my aim.

I fire.

Blood sprays onto my hand and face. She slumps forward, her pain finished, but also whatever good might've come. I watch the hole in her head drip blood and brain onto her lap. This beaten, bloody, broken thing is no longer Lara Miranda.

My loose end tied up, I'm now prepared to receive my own bullet.

*

Sup3's waiting in the anteroom, his arms crossed tightly over his muscular chest. We regard each other in silence until I break it.

"I'm ready."

His eyebrows twitch—the full extent of his expression. "For what?"

"Death."

"You're willing to die if the regime says you must?"

"I've always been willing."

Sup3 gives a small smile. "And if the regime would rather you work tirelessly to protect it?"

"I'm willing to do that too." My legs are shivering gently with exhaustion, my entire body feeling soft and unused. My muscles have withered. My stamina is nonexistent. "What happens now?"

Another very small, very tight smile. "Things return to normal."

I have no words, no expression, though bewilderment seems appropriate.

"You've proven yourself," he says. "As I thought you would. You showed repeated willingness to sustain torture and even to die if necessary. After the things the girl said, we had to assess your loyalties. We also had to see what you'd do when faced with her again."

"I don't understand," I say.

"You went to the Loop to either prove or disprove your loyalties. Your confessions remained the same regardless of the torture you underwent, which was severe. You nearly succumbed to pneumonia and the gum infection."

My eyebrows pull together slightly. "This was a test."

"Partly."

I feel very little besides fatigue. All this was for naught—the torture, the rekindling of events surrounding the break with my family, the preparation for death, the sickness. I should be angry, but the ability to summon emotion eludes me.

"How long have I been here?" I ask.

"Fifty-nine days."

"Am I free to leave today?"

"A Loop agent will escort you to the street. You'll then report to the Complex."

This comes as a surprise—that I'll be allowed to set foot onto agency property again.

"Only be for a moment," he says. "Your agents need to see you. They believe you were undergoing voluntary testing at the Loop regarding maximum pain thresholds."

"What would you have told them if I'd been executed?"

Sup3 gives an easy shrug. "That you succumbed to an illness."

I don't possess the words to respond to this.

"Once you reassure Third Shift, you'll report to your flat for two weeks of mandatory sick leave. Then you'll return to work as usual."

Confusion throbs right along with the headache. Standing is becoming an ordeal. I expect my trembling muscles to pitch me to the floor at any moment.

"I had your things moved from the Dormitories to Executive Quarters. An agent of your rank is better suited there."

I think of the many nights spent alone in my flat in Lib Hall, cadence repeated to empty air, the treadmill in front of the window so I could see the city as I jogged to the point of muscle failure.

"What of my record?" I ask. All of these fortuitous developments amount to zero if my permanent record reflects the truth of my time here. Very lovely to allow me to keep my job as well as the respect of my subordinates—it's more than I dreamed possible in my icy, light-deprived cell—but advancement is impossible with these types of things marring one's personnel file. I suppose spending the remainder of my AA career in stagnation is better than execution, which I expected less than ten minutes ago.

"Your time here is officially recorded as voluntary testing, which will serve as an asset for your career," Sup3 says, raising a dark eyebrow. "And for mine."

"I'd like to sleep before going to the Complex," I say.

"As long as you understand the reason you're here."

I say nothing because I don't understand. Either I committed some crime or I didn't. I have my life back, but why? What purpose does it serve?

"Voluntary testing regarding maximum pain thresholds," he says, speaking slowly, as though to a child.

"Yes."

"Say it."

I do. Slowly, I come to terms with this new reality. No gun blast will expel the teeth from my mouth. No one will hold me while I twitch and bleed. A Loop agent won't throw my bludgeoned, lifeless body into an incinerator. But this doesn't comfort me.

"We'll talk again at the Complex," Sup3 says.

I give a slight nod, mind occupied with the promise of a nap. I want out of this building, but not as much as I want to sleep. I pray it will be dreamless, but I'm certain sleep will never again be a sanctuary for me. I have her blood on my face and his on my hands. My headache's cresting, growing too intense for logical thought. Sup3 must sense this, as he excuses me.

I walk alone to a room that's no longer a prison cell and collapse onto the cot without undressing. Sleep comes and for the first time in weeks, dreams don't trouble me.

THIRTY

The men on floor one ten welcome me back with claps on the back and vigorous handshakes. I have a short discussion with Deux, who seems even more devoted in light of my recent 'accomplishments' at the Loop. The naked admiration I see on his face—on everyone's faces—makes me tired all over.

I retire to my office with a pounding headache and am not surprised to find Sup3 waiting. I sit behind my desk, which feels very much like coming home.

"The men seem pleased to see you," he says.

I nod, but find it hard to reconcile my presence here with the certainty I felt for weeks that I was going to be executed. I don't remember everything that happened to me, but realize it might be some time before I'm able to realign my snapped and shattered mind back into productive patterns.

"Your two weeks start tonight. Don't come back to the Complex before they end. I don't know what all occurs in the Loop, but we both know what will happen in the AA if you can't get your head straight in that time."

The unofficial motto of the agency is *survival of the fittest.*

I nod to show I understand.

"You rarely disappoint," he says.

I speak after a prolonged silence. "I don't understand why I wasn't executed."

Sup3 smiles the small, wintery smile to which I've become so accustomed over our many years in service together. It conveys no contentment, this smile.

"You certainly might've been, but your actions didn't quite outweigh your stellar service record. I thought if you stated your true loyalties plainly, even under torture, things could return as they once were."

"How did you manage such an arrangement?"

"It was easy. I simply used my own career as collateral."

I blink. "You spoke on my behalf."

He nods, not smiling this time.

"You put your own career at risk."

He nods again.

"Why would you do such a thing?" It takes control to make my voice flat instead of accusatory. In the center of all that billowing emptiness blooms a hot kernel of horror. One isn't supposed to extend oneself for another like this. Altruism can only be directed at the most innocent among us. They alone deserve our sacrifices. Sup3 put himself in danger. I'm not sure I would've done the same for him. I can't even be sure I'd do the same for him in future.

"I knew your loyalties," he says. "It was hardly a risk at all."

"And if I'd failed? If, in my weakness, I confessed more?"

"Was there more?"

I shake my head.

"The gesture wasn't meant to offend." I can clearly see he means it. "It's merely indicative of the confidence I have in you as an agent."

My insides churn, anxious at his unshakable loyalty to me. I'm in Sup3's debt now. I suppose it's better than the alternative.

"Thank you," I say, the words feeling strange on my tongue, though I mean them.

"Nonsense," he says, flashing a playful grin that's wholly unlike him. "You saved yourself."

*

I take the metro to Executive Quarters. It's within walking distance of the Complex but I have no energy for the trip. At this odd hour, the train's barren. Even the loudspeakers are quiet. I have to admit, I miss them. The instant I close my eyes, sleep rushes in so completely, I don't wake at my stop. I exit the southbound train at the end of the line, climb the steps, and cross to the platform for the northbound one.

Two tall buildings make up EQ, surrounded by tidy landscaping. It gives quite a different impression from the

Dormitories, which are also tidy in their own way, but obviously for housing agents of a lower rank.

This entire day feels like an exercise in sleepwalking. I go through security in the lobby and can't even remember the details of the desk clerk's face. My room's on the twentieth floor—remarkable given my junior status in the building. I usually take the stairs for a bit of extra exercise—jogging up the thirty flights of stairs to my flat at the Dormitories always left my legs warm, especially when carrying groceries—but today I ride the elevator, glad for the break. The late evening at the Complex was too much.

I go straight to bed without undressing or taking inventory of the new flat. I do discover that I have two bedrooms now, but involuntarily, as, in searching for my bed, I choose the incorrect room initially. The rooms aren't much bigger than the one I had at Lib Hall. I find my bed neatly made and turned down, which hasn't happened since I lived at home.

My watch is on the night table. I put it on, synchronizing it with the alarm clock. The minutes and hours will no longer slip through my fingers like water. Order and logic have returned to the world.

I turn off the light, eyes on the window across the room, watching clouds and stars until my lids close of their own accord.

*

Hunger draws me out of bed before I want to go. I feel rested—I slept for over eighteen hours—but lament abandoning the warm comfort of my blankets.

The new flat glows in the muted gleam of early twilight. I prefer this. The florescent lights at the Complex were too much for my weak eyes. I have a headache, but from hunger this time. At the other flat, before the Loop, I kept my refrigerator and cupboards stocked with the basics—soy milk, bread, cereal, bottled water, soy cheese and patties, protein drinks, fruit, vegetables. I have no idea what I'll find here. Hopefully something. Everything else in the flat was arranged with care and concern—the turned down bed, fresh toiletries in the bathroom, all my belongings organized the same way they were in the old flat.

The kitchen's on the other side of the living room, which is much larger than my old one. My treadmill, radio, side table, and armchair barely filled up my previous living room. They seem pitiful in this one. Not that it matters. No one visits. We have random searches of our quarters, but these agents don't concern themselves with my poor interior decorating.

The kitchen seems about the same size as my old one, which is fine. I do very little cooking, usually grabbing breakfast on the way to the Complex and eating lunch in the cafeteria unless it's a mandatory off-day. Oftentimes, my days are so long I end up eating dinner at work as well. I keep basic items at home for off-days and emergencies.

I open the refrigerator. It's fully stocked, which I count fortunate, because I don't have the energy for a shopping trip. The several small grocery stores surrounding the Dormitories make shopping quite convenient, but I have no idea where to find anything in this part of the city.

I throw together a small soy cheese and lettuce sandwich and take it, along with a bottle of water, to the armchair in the living room. I fall into it, grateful to be off my aching feet.

My grumbling stomach bids me to devour the sandwich, but I need to reintroduce my system to solid foods slowly. I take small bites in between sips of water. It only hurts a little to chew and swallow. The back of my mouth feels tight. It's hard to open my jaw all the way. I saw a doctor before leaving the Loop. He listed all my injuries and gave me several bottles of meds. The gums were severely infected, he explained. I must continue oral antibiotics and work to open my mouth a little more each day.

I can only finish half the sandwich, but feel much better for eating. I go to the window. The pane of spotless glass takes up nearly the entire wall, drenching the flat in subdued evening light. After so many weeks in darkness, the view is restorative.

"I am the black clad body of the AA," I whisper in a paper-thin voice I barely recognize. Keeping eyes on the street below, watching busy people move, I use my tongue to work food particles out of the holes in my gums where wisdom teeth should be.

Within me, something's stirring. Not the sucking sensation, which I think is gone forever. It's more a sense of a thing that needs doing. It nags at me, as though I must double back to tend to something forgotten. If this feeling had a name, it would be *unfinished business*, but I don't quite know what to make of it.

In the next two weeks, I want to put on weight and start running again. I must be in top physical condition to lead my agents, not to mention my mental state needs to be sound. Agents can report to AA psychiatrists, but doctor-patient confidentiality no longer exists, so everything discussed is relayed to the agent's superior. I dodged a bullet getting out of the Loop alive. I don't wish to make any more trouble for myself. There's also Sup3 to consider. He linked his career to mine. If I fail, he will also. I can't allow him to receive his own bullet due to my inability to gain proper control over myself.

For now, the plan is to keep my feet pinned to the straight and narrow. No more satiating my curiosity. It killed the cat, as I said to the straggler.

EQ's very different from the Dormitories, whose halls are always alive with speech and laughter. Besides my breathing, there are no noises in my flat, no noises in the corridor. The silence, once so comforting, now sets me on edge. I can leave this flat if I want. I can step outside the building and lose myself in the crush of the city below. I'm no prisoner. But that's how I feel. Standing here, a free man, it feels like the Loop agents stripped away my ability to perform tasks under my own volition. I close my eyes and a black hood could be over my head again. I sway on my feet, dizzy with the thoughts swimming disjointedly through my head. Pneumonia released its grip on my lungs, but my chest seems permanently tight.

I turn away from the city. On the wall opposite is a large poster of the Party Chairman in full AA dress uniform. Fatigue washes over me, my lids heavy and knees weak. I shuffle to my bedroom in the vanishing light and collapse onto a mattress that's softer than the one at Lib Hall. When I begin to doze, no shrill shriek from an intercom pierces the air. I can do anything I like save relax.

*

The physical training's slow going. It takes days just to become accustomed to one decent sized meal per twenty-four hour period. If I force it, I pay dearly with prolonged bouts of heaving at the toilet.

I force myself onto the treadmill for five-minute increments—all I can stand at first. My untrustworthy body can be made reliable again. I've done it before. I can do it again. But my head's a different matter.

On the treadmill, my mind, occupied with my shivering muscles and gasping, irregular respiration, can think of little else. When I wake at odd hours so sick my body shakes, my mind concerns itself with how quickly I can reach the bathroom. But at all other times, my mind's so disordered that not even repetition can calm it. Once a steady friend to me, even when my body refused to be, my mind now seems a bitter enemy. Putting thoughts in order borders on impossible. I keep expecting the intercom, Josh's derisive comments, Lara's laughter. I wait to hear boots approaching, breath lodged in my throat and hands trembling. The Loop successfully completed one of its fundamental tasks while failing at the other— they snapped my mind, but neglected to realign it. This left me broken, my mind muddy with an incoherent flood of thoughts. I must bring myself back from this precipice, must remedy my frayed edges, or face execution.

THIRTY-ONE

The Capitol City flourishes as spring deepens and the AA keeps order with its iron fist and army of eager little cells. I am once more an eager little cell, my days of playing curious cat safely behind me. No one speaks of my time at the Loop, but my mind never strays far from those fifty-nine days. It took less than two months to destroy everything—all I was, all I worked for, all I could've been in the future. I continue to receive accolades from my superiors as well as my choice of high profile raids, but I'm not the same. My dreams mirror my waking hours, leaving me perpetually exhausted. I shy from sleep but it comes anyway, brining Josh, Lara, and the straggler, all three begging for mercy I never give. I hear their voices in my flat, framed in silence. They weren't innocent, but it all falls on me. They acted, and I was the consequence.

The chasm between self and others has grown infinitely broad—no one touches me and I touch no one. If I don't keep a firm grasp on my mind, it slips. I sit for hours in my office at night once my work is complete, staring at the Party Chairman and trembling. After one such incident, I looked down to find I'd written the same thing several times in my neat handwriting.

To lose you is no loss. To keep you is no gain.

*

Spring gives me the opportunity to take my lunch in the courtyard. I prefer being out in the open. Any kind of confinement tightens my chest.

I have an appetite again, though I'm still leaner than I was before. My body's trustworthy too. I can run for hours on the treadmill. I can stand before the window in my flat all night repeating cadence or whispering about losses and gains. I can sustain the physical pressures of any raid. Sound in body, but not in mind.

I sit on a bench directly below a loudspeaker. Cadence doesn't always calm me, but the soothing, maternal voice of the regime has the same anesthetizing effect every time.

Meat is murder, comrades. Let us inoculate ourselves against hubris, which is damaging to selfhood. Let us thank the Chairman for showing us the way. The most innocent among us require stringent protection. We must not hesitate to turn in Party traitors. No one is above the law. Dairy is organized rape. Let us not acquiesce to the caprice of our palates. Tomorrow is another day closer to perfection.

I eat my sandwich, basking in the solitude and mild weather while keeping my gaze from falling on the Loop lest it trigger an intense panic attack. These days, distress and disorientation go hand in hand. I feel them in the middle of the night when I surface from the depths of a vibrant nightmare. I feel them when the doors shut on an elevator, sealing me inside. I feel them when I face the building housing the Bureau of Thought Reform. Apart from these times, my emotions are so blunted, they're more like absences. I speak to people and feel nothing. I excel at AA duties and pride eludes me. I'm an empty vessel the regime can manipulate this way and that depending upon its whim. My hatred of those breaking regime laws, which once burned so vehemently—the unquenchable fire that fueled my actions—now eludes me completely, as all things do. Headaches are constant. Sleep provides some refuge, but the dreams wake me too often, leaving me struggling for breath against sobs that won't come.

I touch my clean-shaven face. Small things like this assure me that my will is my own. I can keep myself tidy, eat when I choose, and sleep when the dreams allow it. I keep the curtains in my bedroom thrown back morning and night. It helps. When I wake in a sputtering panic, my fear expanding into a paralyzing cloud, the view of the window tells me immediately I'm not in the Loop.

My trigger finger twitches in my lap. In my entire AA career, I've only performed two acts of mercy. One saved Josh from the terrors of a Kill Room. The other ended Lara's suffering. They acted. No loss. I was the consequence. No gain. In my dreams, I shoot my parents, Sup3, Deux, the Party Chairman, and still their voices torment me.

I keep my face blank. The entire courtyard's under surveillance, much like the Complex, the streets, the halls in EQ, and the flats themselves. After my time at the Loop, surveillance agents will watch me closely for months, perhaps years. I mean to arouse no suspicion. In training, they urged us to act like regime automatons. A machine works, but can't feel, can't even act without first receiving an order. Now I act the robot without meaning to, becoming nothing but a mechanical component in the giant clockwork universe of the AA. On my off-days, I walk the streets in uniform to discourage even the semblance of touch.

We do not eat anything with a face. We do not wear the skin of another. All life is sacrosanct. Speciesism is a disease that cannot be tolerated. Let us join the human hand with the nonhuman animal appendage. Let us not be slaves to a faulty hierarchical system of being. Violence against nonhuman animals is indicative of a weak and destructive character.

I want to close my eyes and just listen to the loudspeaker, but that would look highly irregular. So I go back to the Complex instead.

*

The woman lives alone and isn't home, allowing easy access to her flat. I pick the lock, enter, and lock the door again behind me. I remove the flashlight from my utility belt and conduct a cursory search. Tidy studio apartment with a cloth partition separating bed and night table from the living area and kitchen. This district's zoned for single individuals over forty.

Though acting alone in this, I have the blessing of the AA via Sup3. I no longer play the rogue cell. I believe this will allay that odd feeling—*unfinished business.* Afterwards, I'll write a complete report, not leaving out a single detail.

I lean against a kitchen cabinet to wait. She's due home very soon if her actions in the past three days are any indication. I focus on my breathing to stay calm. This place has no windows. How miserable to have no view whatsoever, even if the flat's only on the second floor.

Anticipation hums in the deepest, stillest parts of me, my mind mercifully engaged with what I'm about to do. Beyond this, I'm empty.

Footsteps in the hall. My hands tighten on the edges of the cabinet. I hold my breath, reminding myself these aren't boots approaching. No one's coming to do me harm. On the contrary, I am the threat. At the sound of the key in the door, I remove my gun from its holster and point it to the floor.

The door opens, letting in a shard of light from the hallway. A faceless silhouette enters the flat. I know her even in shadows, though a number of months have passed. She grumbles under her breath, perpetually ill-tempered. I never noticed—a testament to how dangerously preoccupied I was at the time—her back, curved with age, or her slight limp.

I aim the gun but stay otherwise still and silent while she closes and locks the door, then flips on a light.

"Move to the middle of the room," I say. Catching a person off-guard ensures cooperation. A criminal busy sorting through sudden confusion can do little else, including escape.

Yelping and spinning in my direction, the woman moves away from the door. She clearly doesn't recognize me, but I know her.

The proprietress. The long and short of my unfinished business. Lara made her own bed, but this woman didn't have to take such glee in finding the girl sleeping in it.

"What have I done?" she whispers, frightened but indignant. "I'm loyal to the Party!"

I fire the gun, catching her in the shoulder. She goes down screaming and I advance.

"Why are you doing this? What have I done?" she screams, cheeks blazing red but the rest of her face sickly white.

"You will be quiet," I say, emotionless as I aim the gun at her chest.

She closes her mouth, watching me with large, shining eyes. I can respect her lack of tears, though little else about her inspires the remotest feeling.

I flash the thin, vicious smile I've perfected during my years of AA service, though I don't feel happy or otherwise, this absence of emotion a black hole at my center. Keeping my eyes on hers, I fire twice more, both shots fatal. I have no head for drawing this out. This is justice, not revenge.

I leave, not surprised to encounter no one in the corridor. Rampant curiosity has a consequence, as I recently learned, to my sorrow.

I exit the building, hungry and exhausted. The sidewalks are busy with citizens on their way to lunch. I make for the metro, the crush of people parting to let my black clad body through unobstructed.

THIRTY-TWO

AA service turns life into a straight line—the agency, food, sleep, in that order. For over ten years, I walked it with no trouble, but sleeping's no longer an easy part of the equation. In the past, I worked hard and ate very little, so when I closed my eyes, sleep came quickly, plunging me into pleasant dreams I never remembered in the morning. Now my dreams have teeth, leaving me bitten up and bleeding when I wake from them. And sleep doesn't come easily, no matter how crushing my fatigue or how little I eat during the day. It's a fight to reach unconsciousness and a struggle to stay there.

The time at the Loop unlocked something in me, throwing wide a door through which my past comes screaming. Josh invades my waking hours whenever I'm not actively engaged in AA business. I did for him just as I did for Lara—killed all who knew him. That time, I didn't ask the AA. I was just out of training, the Capitol City my first duty assignment. After a long day at the Complex, I spent my nights hunting up the names I found in my brother's address book—how careless of him to keep such an incriminating piece of evidence—on his computer, and in his phone logs. It takes more than one person to be subversive. There's always a chain leading from one traitor to the next. So I started with the first link of the chain in order to get to the source. It took many weeks, but I eventually eliminated all who knew him. In my dreams, I can't keep the details straight. I creep through streets that make no sense to me, shooting the straggler, hunting my parents. I ride the elevator up to floor one ten and open fire with a cool, vicious grin on my face. I wake from these dreams soaked with sweat, panting and whispering that I need to kill all who knew them. But I've done that and nothing has changed. The nagging feeling of having more to do, something *unfinished*, plagues me. I shut my eyes and try to forget all the people I've killed. I can't take it back. But I don't feel regret. I don't feel anything at all.

*

I leave my flat early, bound for the Complex. I'm not due in until eight o'clock, but couldn't get back to sleep after waking from another nightmare.

The sky above shows no hint of the sunshine that's supposed to come later. I hope for a nice afternoon. I'd like to eat my lunch in the courtyard.

I walk in silence, encountering no one, thoughts my only company. The loudspeakers won't come on for hours. To say I'm lonely would be to misspeak. Better to say I'm empty, my chest and stomach sick with yawning voids. I can fill them with AA tasks, but only temporarily. This absence appears to be expanding, casting out any form of warm sentiment in favor of all that's cool and logical, alienating me from my feelings, from any enjoyment of the world around me. Save what's tied up with the AA, every aspect of what it means to be human is inaccessible to me. The regime joined my hand with every nonhuman animal appendage, but pulled it away from my fellow man, perhaps forever.

I take the elevator to floor one ten and walk down the empty corridor to my office. Today's a mandatory off-day for Third Shift, except for those in positions of leadership. I expect Deux in later this morning for a series of meetings with the other senior pack leaders. Sup3 and I also have meetings with various higher-ups. But for now, the silence is lovely.

I step around my desk to face the sleeping city through glass. I see myself moving through those same streets, a fire burning in the place where now only an absence swells and throbs, picking off Josh's friends and acquaintances. At the time, I believed my motives to be pure ones, but the completion of the task didn't bring satisfaction.

I see the face of the proprietress, stern even when her own death was imminent. Was she seditious in thought or deed? I doubt it. But her seeming patriotism sprang from incorrect motivations. She wanted to see Lara suffer for the sins of her father, long before the discovery of the illegal books. True Party commitment abhors the lawbreaker while celebrating those who follow the law without looking for ways to bring them down. True Party commitment lingers after everything else is stripped away. I'm the empty shell of

the boy who enlisted in the AA all those years ago, but my
commitment to the Party remains, even if my passion has waned.

*

The final meeting of the day is in the AA Chairman's conference
room on the top floor of the Complex. I've never been this high
up—these levels are restricted to those without official business. The
meeting includes the other three Shift supervisors, Sup3, the Red
Shift super, and Chairman Anderson. We sit at an oblong table, each
man with his own files filled to bursting with reports on every
pertinent subject, and wait for nearly twenty minutes before the AA
Chairman graces us with his presence.

"Sorry, comrades," he says, then takes his sweet time noisily
adjusting his chair at the head of the table. Arranges his papers. Pours
himself a glass of water, then takes a sip, slurping loudly. The rest of
us look on with blank expressions. Finally, he gets to it.

"All right, brothers. I'd like to hold these meetings quarterly.
Any objections?"

No one speaks. I feel this will be a monumental waste of
agency time. We already have weekly meetings at the agency, shift,
and floor level. I also have several impromptu meetings with Sup3
and my senior pack leaders on each floor. But I suppose if Chairman
Anderson schedules these meetings for off-days, they'll only waste
the time of those of us in the conference room and I've never really
valued my leisure time.

"Agency morale is at an all-time high," Chairman Anderson says. "Impressive, considering the loss of off-days. This trend must continue. When morale's high, so is productivity."

Heads dip into appropriate nods and I wonder if the Chairman means to do his part to keep morale high by threatening agents playing vital roles in high profile raids.

"Third Shift will receive accolades for its recent work with the speakeasies. Intelligence hasn't had a single lead concerning speakeasy activity in some time."

I exchange a flat, subtle look with Sup3. A lack of leads doesn't mean we've eliminated the speakeasy problem. It only means the traitors have new tricks. The black market peddling of meat hasn't ground to a halt simply because Intelligence is silent. I often pore over leads myself in order to pass on something promising to Intelligence so they can pass it right back to me with the official AA seal of approval, thus making it acceptable to act upon. Despite this, Third Shift agents will be proud to hear of the accolades awarded them. Of the four Shifts, Third is the most consistently superior, its members promoting faster and receiving more awards than those in the other three shifts.

"Additionally, agent 687 will receive the Quarterly Award for Excellence."

I feel a dull stab of surprise that quickly dissipates. Several months ago, receiving this award would've been a source of great pride, but now I can barely lay hands on my once fiery ambition. I find most things pointless, life the principal among them. As long as a person dedicates his life to the AA, what does it matter which position he holds or what awards he receives? I've become a bit of an unwilling legend at the Complex. No one else has 'voluntarily' sustained such high levels of torture at the Loop. Commendations now come regularly, as do high profile raids and choice assignments. As a young agent, I always hoped to find myself in such a situation one day, but my wandering, listless thoughts make experiencing contentment impossible.

The meeting lasts for another hour and a half. In the corridor, the other agents shake my hand and offer vigorous congratulations.

"Fine work, comrade," one man says.

Perpetually suffering from a lack of words, I only nod to him and the others, anxiety flaring at the sudden attention.

Sup3 accompanies me to floor one ten by way of the stairs. He clearly has something he wants to discuss, as his office is several floors above mine.

"Congratulations," he says after we take seats on opposite sides of my desk.

I shrug, face blank, unwilling to speak until I can be sure of his angle.

He gives his tight, humorless smile. "It's even more impressive, considering."

Within me, the sucking grows more virulent. Anxiety troubles me often, though I've come to experience it as less a feeling than a permanent state of being. I never speak of my time at the Loop. I try never to think of it either, but that's harder.

"Very few people successfully resume their lives after time at the Loop." He lifts an eyebrow, clearly meaning for me to speak. When I don't, his expression tightens into one I can't decipher, the gloomy visage of the Party Chairman looming behind him.

"The award you just received is a testament to the quality of your work." He pauses. Clears his throat. "But you've changed considerably."

I know this better than anyone. It's difficult to describe the sensation of recognizing oneself in the mirror, but being unacquainted with what one finds lurking *inside*. I don't see why this should concern Sup3. My job is the only thing I can still do correctly.

"I haven't neglected my duties," I say, voice as flat as I feel.

"That isn't what I mean."

I don't respond. Better to let him get to what he has to say without interrupting.

"You're different," he says after several moments. "Unsound."

The horror I should feel at this stays a great distance away. Sup3's reaching out to me, though it clearly makes him uncomfortable. People have felt concern for me before—Mother wiping the sweat from my brow as I shivered with fever, Father shouting a warning as I rode my bike into the street, Josh hitting a boy who threatened me on my first day of school—and it didn't end well. Sup3 keeps reaching out, keeps trying to bridge that gap. Doesn't he understand the danger, to himself, to me? I can never return that favor. We bridged the chasm between human and nonhuman animals, setting all sentient creatures on the same rung of the great ladder of Being. But this only created another chasm—between the individual and all others. Sup3's on one side of the gulf. I'm on the other. Instead of brotherhood, solidarity, there's only emptiness. I pack this emptiness with service to the AA, but service doesn't touch. It doesn't value an individual or make him special. If I serve the Party, no gain. If I fail to serve, no loss.

"I'm sound enough," I say.

Sup3 gives me a look—not quite concern and not quite pity—and shifts in his seat. "What does that mean?"

"It means certain parts have changed, but the ones valuable to the agency are in good working order." A headache pulses at my temples. The fluttering of my stomach tells me that it, as well as everything else, is empty.

"I need assurances," he says.

I clench my hands in my lap, wanting to feel something, even if it's only fingernails cutting into my palms. This sucking absence is the new normal. Nightmares stimulate fear and alarm, but it quickly fades to bleak emptiness once I wake. Feeling anything is a blessing, even pain.

"Of what?" I ask, though I know. Assurances that I'm not coming apart at the seams, that I'm still an able-bodied servant of my government. Perhaps *able-bodied* is the wrong word. Rather, *able-minded*. With concentrated effort, I can pin my mind to a task, but it wanders at the first opportunity. This internal struggle continues for as long as I'm conscious, though it has yet to interfere with agency business.

"Your health," he says. My attention wants to stray to the poster behind him. I spend hours in my flat staring at the Chairman's face on my living room wall, repeating cadence, Party slogans, or the ever-faithful *to lose you is no loss; to keep you is no gain.*

"Is it in question?" I ask.

"No," he says, giving me a strange look. "If that were the case, I wouldn't be here alone and you'd shortly be on your way to the Loop."

I clench my fists harder to suppress the tremor that starts at the mention of the Bureau of Thought Reform.

"I'm sound enough," I say. "My loyalty to the regime and the agency will never change." Though I mean them, these words sound empty. I suddenly feel very tired. Are all things to be empty now, not simply what's outside, but also what's within? If not for exhaustion and constant headaches, I'd truly be an unfeeling automaton, although I doubt a machine would feel a yawning absence where its emotions should be, nor would it wake sweat-soaked and shuddering from increasingly vivid nightmares.

Sup3 inhales deeply, the look on his face telling me this is as painful for him as it is for me. "Would you tell me if something was wrong?"

"No." Unstable agents are liabilities. If I can't do my job, I'm of no use to the regime. I have no family, no friends, no purpose beyond the agency. I gave it all away, never thinking twice about the sacrifice until recently.

He nods. "I shouldn't expect anything else." His lips twist, playing at that humorless grin. Things are still the same between us, even after the Loop.

"I'll continue to do my job with diligence and passion," I say. I wouldn't speak so for anyone else—even the AA Chairman—but this man wagered his career to return my life to me. If I can put his mind at ease, I'll do it. "You can expect that too."

He nods, drawing this uncomfortable business to a close. I still have his trust. Though we can never bridge that gap, I can always depend on that.

THIRTY-THREE

In my dreams, I don't pull my weapon. I tell him to run and go home with no blood soaking my uniform. No screams cut into the night. No blows rain onto my face. No one tears the double A's from my arm. When the rain starts, I'm inside with my parents. Mother doesn't beg me to leave the agency. Father laughs at the stories I have to tell. There's nothing to forgive because I haven't done anything. I tell them Josh is safe—*no loss*—that I let him go—*no gain*. Mother kisses my forehead. Father claps me on the back.

But Josh hasn't left. He stumbles into the house, a gushing wound in the center of his forehead. The blood splashes onto my uniform, coats my hands, my face. Screaming, Mother demands to know what I've done, but Father attacks before I can answer, slipping a black bag over my head as someone binds my hands. Lara giggles, ordering them to take me to the Loop for sedition. I shriek my horror, telling her it's free speech, that nonhuman animals aren't the only ones in need of protection. Josh laughs and calls me a narrow-minded conformist. They all laugh. I trip on the way out and go down hard onto wet grass, giggles ringing in my ears. Hands take me by the arms, dragging me away.

*

Breathless, unable to scream, I open my eyes. No black bag over my face. No hands on my arms. This isn't the Loop. I'm in my bedroom, alone.

I push sweaty hair off my forehead and lean forward onto my palms, legs straight out in front of me. The sheets are soaked. I kicked the blanket to the floor. It's hours until dawn. I rock back and forth, collecting myself. It feels like I've been sprinting instead of sleeping.

I go to the kitchen without turning on the lights, retrieve a bottle of water from the refrigerator, and walk to the living room window. This view can calm me faster than any breathing exercises or repetition session. I sit cross-legged on the floor and drain the water bottle, wincing at the burn of frosty water in my throat.

It's feeling.

Arms on elevated knees, I press my forehead against the window, wanting to be as close as possible to the city without actually being in it. I'm well-versed in solitude. The regime used it to usher in revolution and encourage conformity. But the Overthrow's long over. I've fiercely supported the Party's goals for years, but now Josh's words haunt me—*at what cost?* If the ends justify the vicious, unceasing means, when will we achieve those ends?

The view of the city works its magic, and the nightmare begins to fade. By afternoon, I'll have forgotten it altogether. The city snoozes, oblivious of my eyes upon it. Inside, a fluttering inkling troubles me—*unfinished business*. I mistakenly thought it had to do with Lara, but I know what I need to do now. I just have to summon the nerve.

At five a.m., the alarm rings in my room. I turn it off, dress, and make my bed with zero enthusiasm. Another poster of the Party Chairman wearing AA black hangs over my bed. *The AA Sees All and Knows All*, it declares in bold red letters.

Trembling, I retrieve the gun from beneath my pillow. I've taken to sleeping with my fingers locked around it at night. I won't go back to the Loop. If agents come for me in the night, I'll do myself the same favor I did Josh. Without the AA, I have no reason to live. The Party gave me a life, an identity. Without it, I'm nothing.

I tidy the living room and make myself a piece of dry toast, though I'm not hungry. I leave my flat, meaning to eat as I walk. The loudspeakers will be on by now and I need them to soothe me. So like a mother, that voice, but its hands are missing. It can't mop my feverish brow, can't hug me before I step out the door. The regime feeds and clothes me, but it doesn't concern itself with my welfare. It doesn't know my face, only my number.

I step out onto the street, relishing the crisp morning wind. Munching my undercooked toast as I walk, the loudspeaker accompanies me to the Complex as it has always done. But, really, I'm alone.

*

In the weeks leading to summer, floor one ten has plenty of neighborhood watch and double duty. So few raids take place that we all begin to wonder what, if anything, Intelligence is doing on the floors above. I join my old pack for double duty whenever Deux invites me, which is often. Sup3 and I even pair up for neighborhood watch when our schedules allow.

As the warmer months approach, I learn to survive on two hours of sleep. For the other twenty-two, the nagging feeling of *unfinished business* troubles me. Now that I know what it's about, I dwell on it constantly. But I put it off, keeping busy so I don't notice how tormented I am. I volunteer for extra duty. I attend Alliance for Animals forums twice a week instead of once. I forfeit all my off-days, which I can do as Third Shift super. I spend unavoidable free time scouring the streets for illegal activity, working until, exhausted, I return to my flat and fall into a few hours of turbulent sleep.

I continue to receive agency accolades and even garner Party recognition for the increase in my forum attendance, but this only gives me the notion of pride and accomplishment. The feelings stay inaccessible. I no longer experience happiness or sadness. Even true loneliness eludes me. Imprisonment at the Loop didn't hinder my capacity for reason. I can think, plan, and act as well as I did before. But the part that bridges the gap between the notion of a thing and the feeling of it was scraped clean away, leaving a desolate landscape in its wake.

The nightmares would be a comfort if they weren't so terrible, as they initiate the only instances of feeling I have left. I do experience the niggling sensation of this *unfinished business*, but that's not quite the same as being happy or upset. To remedy this, I pile on more work, more responsibilities, more exercise, bringing on perpetual fatigue on top of emptiness. Whatever I do, I find myself flailing. To keep my wandering mind in check, I constantly snap and realign it—a tiresome, precarious task. Only my loyalty to the regime strengthens me. It has always accepted me for who and what I am, even now when I barely know myself.

Neither regime rules nor my absence of emotion exists. Rules are nothing until enforced. An absence is nothing until it's filled. I exist—this much isn't in dispute—but when I look in the mirror, I don't recognize the stranger reflected there. He whispers—*I am the black clad body of the AA*—but even he can't touch me.

THIRTY-FOUR

I don't take another off-day until the year begins to edge into fall. Third Shift receives top honors again during Celebration—a sweet reward, considering it's my first full year as Shift super. But, for me, the contentment and pride are only half there. I understand these honors should evoke actual emotions, but can't manage any. The Party provides my reason for living and my devotion to it serves as my sustenance, but I stay as empty as ever—a sensation to which it's impossible to become accustomed.

*

Midmorning finds me underground. Another nightmare tossed me out of a turbulent sleep, so I showered, breakfasted lightly, watched the sun rise, and left my flat as soon as the morning rush hour ended.

I'm seated on a bench in the metro station, patiently waiting for the train. A large black poster hanging on the wall of the opposite platform informs me in bold red letters that *The AA Shows No Mercy to Party Traitors*. I look away, focusing instead on the maternal voice of the regime.

We must not be slaves to our palates. Let us be free from harm. Tomorrow is another day closer to perfection. Meat is murder, comrades. No one has the right to eat another. Mandatory AFA forum tomorrow at two, four, and six. See to it that you attend one of these. This week's lecture: How to Further Unify the Human and Nonhuman Animal. All life is sacrosanct.

When my train approaches, I walk to the yellow line. I enter the barren train car and take a seat. I watch my hands clench and unclench in my lap instead of looking out the window and contemplate the notion of anxiety and apprehension, both startlingly absent from my interior. I haven't traveled out of the Capitol City in a long time, as my jurisdiction doesn't extend beyond city limits. But this isn't AA business.

Over the next few stops, I keep my head down, focusing on my thoughts, on the voice of the regime whispering Party slogans, never lifting eyes to people watch.

My plans for the day are a mistake, but I pursue them because they might ignite some feeling. Even disappointment would be a welcome change from the stark landscape of my emotional state at present.

After forty-five minutes, I reach the end of the line. This train doesn't leave the city, so I exit and go to the platform of one that does. The ride takes thirty minutes. Right outside the city, the train leaves its underground tunnel and rises into open air and sunshine. I watch the scenery as it speeds by me.

I leave the train at my station, walk through the turnstile, go down a flight of stairs, and step out onto the sidewalk.

Not many citizens are on the street. I would've given up my own off-day, only Third Shift's top honors made it compulsory. Showing my face at the Complex, even to pick up paperwork, would result in three demerits and, by my own rule, three weeks of PT. So instead of staring out of my flat's window mumbling to myself while my boiling thoughts metastasize, I decided to tend to this *unfinished business.*

I know this neighborhood well, though I haven't visited in some time. Citizens living in this suburb who commute to the city for work must return here before voluntary curfew. There are a few more cars in these residential areas, as the cost to keep them is lower, though the Clean Air Act makes it just as difficult to get a vehicle permit.

I walk a few blocks, taking everything in, the changes and the constants, then turn onto a residential street. The AA made me adept at dealing with complicated situations, but today will be tricky for a much different reason. I pass beneath a loudspeaker and the regime's ghostly voice follows me down the street.

It is not a question of availability and ease, but a question of right. Let us destroy Speciesism in all its forms. Veganism is personal liberation. Meat is murder, comrades. No one is above the law. Only the innocent deserve protection. We do not eat anything with a face.

A collection of two-story, single-family homes make up this middleclass neighborhood. Living here has its advantages if one has a family. I see the house I want at the end of the street but feel nothing besides a pounding headache and the exhaustion in my bones.

I pause on the sidewalk, watching the target house for more than a few minutes. A Party wreath in black, red, and white hangs from the front door. A PETA flag flies from a pole in the lawn. No adornments representative of the AA.

My desire to see this finished—to feel something—propels me up the short walk to the front door. This cement path is new. It used to be just grass. The second step up to the porch still creaks under my foot.

I knock. After waiting through four sets of locks turning over, the door swings open, giving me a glimpse of a man I haven't seen in over a decade.

"Hello, Father," I say.

For a long moment, he only stares at me. The years have taken their toll. Wrinkles line his face and dark patches ring his eyes, as though he doesn't sleep. The vibrant color of his eyes has faded, leaving his once fiery gaze weak. I don't feel relieved at the sight of him, though I had no idea whether either of my parents was alive.

"What do you want?" he asks, voice thick, though not with anger.

I only thought about coming here, not what I wanted to achieve.

A third voice, coming from deeper in the house, breaks the silence.

"Who's at the door?" my mother asks.

I look down the corridor but can't see her. I settle eyes on my father again. He's a few inches taller, just like Josh.

"Will you tell her?" I ask.

"What are you here to do?" he asks, eyes narrowed, weathered face rock hard. Josh was a younger version of this man—everyone said so—and I look like my mother, though I don't act like her. I inherited my calm, reflective nature from this man, as well as my fondness for silence.

I answer truthfully. "I'm not entirely sure."

He sighs deeply, shoulders dropping and steps aside. "Come on, then."

Stepping into the small foyer, familiarity bombards me. The pictures covering the walls, catching Josh and me at various points in childhood. I have no family photos in my flat. Some agents do. With Reconstruction safely behind us, AA service doesn't necessarily require a pulling away from one's family. Sup3 has a picture of his parents on his desk. I, on the other hand, didn't even remember I had a family. Now, here I am, staring into the frozen face of my brother. The last time I did that was right before I shot him in the back of the head.

You do what you think is right and so will I, he said, back to me, and I tried to do both what was right and what was merciful.

I look away from the pictures to find my father staring at me. Does he see something on my face? Some shred of emotion decipherable to him, though I feel nothing? I follow him to the living room, stopping in the doorway to let him go in without me. My mother's fussing with her knitting, glasses sliding down the bridge of her nose. Her hair has gone completely gray and is much shorter.

"Who was at the—"Her words die at the sight of me. Eyes round, surprise written in every wrinkle, she drops her knitting needles and grasps the sides of her chair, squeezing hard, her knuckles going white.

"Hello," I say.

She's staring like she's just seen a ghost.

When I move to step over the threshold, they shrink away from me—a small movement, but they both do it, fear lighting up their faces. I stop cold in the doorway. Facing them again after a decade does little to stir my achingly vacant places. A disappointment, but not one I feel, only one I should feel.

"Why are you here?" Mother asks, voice as gentle as I remember. She seems to be struggling with a host of opposing emotions.

I try to rest my hand on an absent weapon. I wore street clothes today out of propriety, not shame.

"To explain," I say. "About Josh."

They wince in tandem, as though of one mind. As Father's face twists, I glimpse the old fire in his eyes, the one that flashed whenever we misbehaved. Mother sits in mute shock, too distraught for words. Tears fill her eyes. Trembling steadily, she pulls off her glasses and drops them onto her lap along with the knitting needles. Father puts a hand on her shoulder and fixes me with a challenging stare. My own words echo back to me through time and space—*I will turn in anyone for treason.*

Father speaks behind sealed teeth. "You have nerve coming here and speaking his name." This encounter could easily disintegrate into shouting and hitting. I've prepared myself for it. Whatever they want to give, I'll take.

"I know what I've done," I say, voice flat and face blank. "I just wanted to explain why I did it."

"There's nothing you can say," Mother starts in a wavering voice. She drops her head, the remaining words washing away in a flood of tears.

My parents are holdovers from before the Overthrow, when people could still attain companionship. He touches her and vice versa. For them, love is real, and it continues even after the regime takes everything—happiness, loyalty, children.

"Get out," Father says to me. "*You are not welcome here.*"

I blink at these familiar words. I don't know what I expected coming here—what unfinished business I intended to somehow finish—but I clearly won't have the opportunity to find out. The most I'll accomplish is starting another fight and ending up on the lawn, bleeding from nose and mouth.

I step backwards into the hall. Mother looks up at me, shaking her head.

"No! Tell me what you came to say."

Confusion softens my father's face. "He's upsetting you," he starts, and Mother interjects in her sweet, unoffending manner.

"Please, Tom. I want to hear it." She gazes up at him, teary eyes imploring.

He nods and she turns her attention to me.

I'd give anything just to feel something besides a greedy, expanding absence. Watching my parents touch only emphasizes how desolate I am. They touched me once too, though Josh's blood on my hands put a stop to that. This woman nursed me to health, gave assurances whenever the world treated me cruelly. But now? We're merely strangers who share blood.

"He was doing dangerous things," I say in a flat voice, trying to make this as straight forward as possible. "He came up on the AA's list of subversives wanted for questioning."

Father's face is turning the deep red I recognize from many years of pissing him off as a child. In the chair beneath him, Mother struggles with the strength of her tears.

"He flaunted his defiance at every opportunity." Here's feeling—anger at Josh—both inappropriate and short-lived. "He didn't seem to care about the consequences, not just for him, but his family as well."

"So you killed him?" Father says in a hissing whisper. "Your own brother?"

"Yes, I killed him," I say, and they flinch again, as though learning of this for the first time.

"Why?" Mother asks, tears pouring down her face.

"Because he was my brother."

Father clearly has a problem with this explanation, but he glances away from me without speaking.

Mother shakes her head, tears spilling onto the yarn in her lap. "They only wanted to question him."

"No one survives questioning," I say. "There would've been torture."

"And you work for these people?" Father asks.

I don't respond.

"Why didn't you warn him?" she asks.

"I did. He didn't appear to care about the risks, nor the damage he could do to his family. I went to warn him that night. The AA had just issued an order for his arrest. Once caught, he faced execution."

Mother hangs her head and weeps openly. Father gives me an ugly look as he attends to her. I've come this far. I might as well finish.

"I showed him his arrest warrant and begged him to leave the city. He refused. I told him in detail what would happen if he didn't go, but he laughed in my face and baited me with seditious comments. He took me by the throat so I could smell the meat on his breath." When Mother meets my gaze, I feel a pulling sensation in my chest above a churning stomach. Guilt?

Father refuses to look at me. Even he's crying now, making me the odd man out.

"You shot him?" Mother asks. "You shot him and left him to die?"

"I held him until he died. And then I came here."

I watch them weeping and can't join in. I know what they must think of me, but now maybe they'll find a way to understand my motives. My ordeal at the Loop pales in comparison to what Josh would've faced. Though the shot wasn't a clean one, it saved him from the horrors of the Kill Floor.

"You turned your back on your family," Father says. "And now you crawl back here looking for sympathy?"

I shake my head as Mother squeezes his hand to calm him.

"I accept responsibility for what I've done. I came to give an explanation, not request forgiveness."

"You aren't the son I raised," he says.

"No, I'm not." I step back into the hall.

Mother shoots up suddenly, the tangled mess of knitting and glasses falling to the floor. Weeping, her chest hitching beneath shuddering shoulders, she tries to cross the room. Father holds her back and I know why. He doesn't want her to touch me. I don't know that I disagree with him. I'm no longer the shivering, sickly little boy who needed her so desperately.

"No!" she cries as I turn away. Behind me, she struggles with Father and stumbles into the hallway. I turn at the front door when she screams my name. Father's behind her, holding tightly, keeping the two of us apart.

"Please," she says, hands out, beckoning, face soaked with tears. "Come back to us. Leave the AA. It's done enough to this family."

"It's too late for that," I say. The boy she watched leave for training and the man standing before her now are two radically different animals. The AA disciplined that boy, stripped him clean of everything—feelings, past, thoughts—and gave him a new identity.

"Aren't you unhappy?" she asks, whimpering the words through her tears.

I consider this. "No more than anyone else." Here's more feeling—regret, made sweet only because it's something.

I leave before she can respond. No one bursts out onto the porch after me. By the time I reach the sidewalk, all traces of emotion have drained away, leaving an empty, throbbing shell. I've made a mess of this along with everything else. My fingers, so adept at destruction, can't summon the delicacy necessary for touch. I resign myself to it, to everything. Mother, consumed by her own sadness. Father, burned alive by the strength of his rage. Josh, destroyed by his misguided sense of liberty. And me, an automaton that can neither feel nor touch.

THIRTY-FIVE

I keep myself busy, occupying my mind so it doesn't consider the trip outside the Capitol City. I lock myself away in the Complex for days at a time, working out at the gym, avoiding sleep, eating only what I must in order to stay conscious and alert because the empty pulling in my stomach is feeling.

When the leaves begin to turn, I take to wearing my winter uniform. My recent leanness makes me feel the cold more than I have during previous autumns. With no way to put on weight—I exercise too much and eat too little—I know I'll suffer when winter comes.

Intelligence hands down assignments with more regularity as the weather cools, keeping Third Shift busy with raids. The constant scheduling leaves me very little time to join my old pack on the streets. Sup3 never joins us at all, as the uptick in illegal activity increased his paperwork tenfold. I'm up to my neck in it as well, but it keeps me steady. As long as I'm battling disorder on the streets, I can keep it out of my head.

I take lunch in the courtyard when my schedule allows, preferring to eat my sandwich or salad while seated beneath a tree with the autumn wind on my face. I'm always alone out here, but it's a comfortable loneliness because no one's present. The uncomfortable loneliness comes when I'm in the company of others. It feels as though a thick pane of glass is separating me from everyone else. In a way, it has always been like this for me. But now the chasm's so broad, I don't hold out much hope of ever crossing it to meet those on the other side.

*

I leave the gym after running eight miles, lifting weights, and taking a blisteringly hot shower. When the elevator doors open on floor one ten, I see Deux waiting outside my office.

"Good morning, comrade," he says with more enthusiasm than an agent ought to possess this early.

I nod instead of returning the greeting. He's bursting with a youthful exuberance that exhausts me simply to watch. He places a report on my desk that I don't pick up. It's from the raid the night before, which I couldn't attend, though I plan to take part in the one slated for next week. I'll also join my former pack for double duty and neighborhood watch over the next couple of nights. I feel best when on the streets, keeping order. Enforcement agents all start this way—in the thick of it, doing dirty, necessary work. Such a shame that, as an agent moves up the AA ladder, he also moves farther away from the kind of work that originally attracted him to the agency in the first place.

"Anything of interest to report?" I ask.

"Site one wasn't a speakeasy at all, though we did encounter several citizens acting suspiciously in an alley well after voluntary curfew."

I lift an eyebrow, which should send a clear message—*Explain or continue.*

He clears his throat and continues. "Site two, however, was active. We destroyed it and took twenty-seven traitors into custody."

"Any useful information?"

He shakes his blonde head. "Mostly just begging and weak justifications. The usual." He sits back in the chair, a look of grim satisfaction on his face.

I lean over my desk, giving him the top of my head. I have my own reports to file. Three floors besides one ten conducted raids tonight. If I'm lucky, the paperwork will take me the better part of the night. A busy mind is a steady mind.

Deux's even breathing draws my eyes away from my writing and I realize I never heard him get up to leave. He's still sitting in front of me, hands twisting in his lap and expression expectant. Instead of excusing my subordinates from a meeting, I do one of two things. If it's not my office, I leave the room without a word. If it is my office, I move on to other things, leaving the person to figure out the best way to exit quietly.

"Something else?" I ask.

He shakes his head. "No." Thinking better of it, he nods. "I mean yes."

This display of ambivalence is odd. Either a man has something to say or he doesn't. He must decide this before interrupting his commanding officer.

Deux's in quite a state. I feel a small stab of worry at his sudden inability to follow subtle visual cues. It won't do for him to begin unloading any of his personal problems onto my shoulders. I have too many of my own.

Another tense silence forces me to speak.

"Get on with it or get out. I have work to do."

"Of course," he says quickly.

I'm mere seconds from ordering him to his packroom when he speaks again.

"I thought, I mean, I wanted to ask you—"he shakes his head firmly and starts again. "I wanted to know about the Loop."

I draw slightly back in my chair, as though threatened. "Why would you ask me?"

He swallows audibly. The thought of demerits, official reprimands that will never wipe cleanly from a permanent record, and the destruction of a working relationship with one's immediate superior would deter any other agent from pursuing this particular path, but Deux presses on as though oblivious.

"You're the only person in agency history to have been there so long and come out unscathed."

Here's feeling—a flash of anger at his complete lack of understanding—but it evaporates quickly. "No one leaves the Loop unscathed," I say.

Deux's light eyebrows crease. "But you—"

"No one."

We sit in silence before he finds the nerve to speak again.

"What was it like?" he asks, voice hushed like a little boy desperate for a story.

I sigh, unable to hold it back. "Worse than you can imagine."

The answer visibly shakes him. "Why did you volunteer?"

I give him a grim look that sets him further back in his chair. "I did what my government asked of me."

Keeping his eyes on me, he tilts his chin at a jaunty angle. "I'm going to volunteer."

Another flash of emotion—concern for my subordinate. Now I understand Sup3's position. But I don't have long to ponder it. The sensation leaves just as quickly as it comes.

"That would be an error," I say.

"I don't understand—"

"I don't expect you to." If I could erase those fifty-nine days from my life, I would, though it would also erase my guaranteed path up the AA ladder.

I watch him struggle with what he wants to say versus what he ought to do, which is keep his mind on his own affairs and allow others to do the same. The stricken expression suddenly seizing his face tells me he knows he went too far. He extended his hand, fingers stretching in hopes of touching mine. But my fingers don't know how to touch. They understand wrapping around a gun, folding into a fist and striking, hanging at my sides when I stand at attention. A prerequisite of reaching out is the giving of oneself to another, the touch only complete when one successfully trades a bit of oneself for a bit of that other person. My emptiness precludes giving. The shattered parts of me slip through my fingers, useless. When I take inventory of myself, I am less than zero.

"I shouldn't have spoken so," Deux whispers.

"No."

He darts for the exit without another word, never looking back. The door closes behind him, leaving me alone.

THIRTY-SIX

I work late into the night. The other three senior pack leaders come by at different points in the evening to drop off their raid reports, keeping their visits short and confined to agency business, none of them running wildly off at the mouth as Deux saw fit to do. I won't penalize him because I understand the need to sate one's curiosity. I see the way the other agents look at me in the halls. It seems every man in the Complex knows the details of my time in the Loop. They imagine brutal beatings, starvation, the most horrendous tortures known to man, all of them done to me as I smiled humorlessly and refused to break. But there was nothing heroic about it. The torture comes to me in disjointed images—my head underwater, a man in a black mask chuckling malevolently, a gun to my head as I asked for the end of my life—but the true torment only came afterwards. Those fifty-nine days stripped away everything, leaving me with the bleak realization that camaraderie doesn't exist, that touch is a childish dream. The torture is that we are, each of us, alone. And it's never-ending.

*

I tear the black bag off my head. The door opens a sliver, letting light in. I pull it open and stumble into the hallway.

No one.

I run down the hall, screaming for help, for anyone, voice echoing louder than my footfalls. The locked doors have names. This one reads *Josh*. That one, *Mom and Dad*. Another, *Lara*. I beat on them but receive no answer. A door's open at the end of the corridor, warm sunlight sparkling beyond it. I run fast and explode out into the clear blue of a silent day. I spin around, screaming, desperate.

No one.

I dash up the steps of the Complex. No one at the security desk. Nothing stops me from taking an elevator up to floor one ten. I burst into the hall. Empty. I call out. Nothing comes back to me but echoes. I go to the packroom. Empty. I go to my office and stand by the window, looking down at the city.

No one.

I turn to the poster of the Party Chairman. He's smiling. He knows.

I'm alone.

*

I sit up, gasping, heart racing, then drop my face in my hands and wait for my breathing to even out. My bearings return to me slowly. I'm in my office. At my desk. In the Complex. Not in a darkened cell.

I only fell asleep. I wipe the sweat from my brow. Exhale. Look at the poster of Chairman Goldstein, who's glaring, not smiling.

I stand, back stiff from crouching over the desk, and turn to the window. The streets are barren and the clouds so thick, I can't see a single star. It's late. The sun won't rise for hours.

Today's a Third Shift off-day. I've completed all my paperwork and put it in the hands of those who need it. I could find work to do, but I'm not in the mood. I don't think I'll be able to focus here after the nightmare. I need a good night's sleep, but don't expect one. I could also do with a decent meal and I have plenty of food back at my flat.

I ride the elevator down to the lobby and walk out into the early morning, taking note of the bored-looking agent at the security desk. I take the steps to the sidewalk, relishing the brisk weather. I look back at the Complex, admiring story upon story of luminescent glass stretching into the clouds.

The agency flag ripples in the night sky, a patch of solid black against clouds dark as bruises. I stood in this exact place once, beneath the shadow of the AA flag, with Lara in front of me, her face twisted by the truth of my loyalties—the same look my mother gave me when I came home wearing the armband. This flag stands for everything—selfless, unquestioning service, even to the detriment of all else.

I look down at my hands in the faint glow of moonlight, turning them to see every inch of pale, smooth skin. These hands have done horrible things and aren't finished doing them, but the ends justify the means. I'm sure of it. I must be, or this has all been for naught. When these ends come, perhaps we can bridge that chasm and find a way back to one another again. Touch will return and, with it, companionship, concern, altruism, even love.

It's difficult to put a finger on how I feel looking up at the Complex and the sky beyond it. I stand on the street, dwarfed by the building, miniscule in comparison to the regime and its ideals, which I share wholeheartedly, though my passion has waned along with everything else that once mattered. It isn't regret. I'm not sure what it is. Perhaps hope. Perhaps the yearning for something different, something better. I don't know. I know the emptiness within me, the throbbing places where things used to be that have gone missing. I know a lifetime of diligent service can't fill this absence, not on its own. I'm not sure what can fill it. I only know it aches.

I turn my back on the Complex. The wind kicks up, tossing my hair about my head and breathing some life back into me, as short-lived as the sensation's likely to be. I start down the vacant sidewalk in the direction of EQ, the streetlights carving a straight path out of the darkness in front of me, illuminating my way home. Without the whispering of the loudspeakers, the early morning's my only companion.

ABOUT THE AUTHOR

Tess R. Martin is a novelist living in South Carolina with her daughter and giant English Mastiff, Zoey.

Made in the USA
Thornton, CO
08/31/24 23:17:46